Praise for

JANE SHEMILT

"It's every mother's nightmare: the disappearance of a child. But in *The Daughter,* what appears to be a simple abduction soon turns into something far more complex and baffling. Jane Shemilt builds layer upon layer of tension in a thriller you won't be able to put down."
—Tess Gerritsen, bestselling author of *Last to Die*

"Shemilt injects a great deal of suspense into her narrative in both time frames, even as her fluid prose eloquently captures a mother's grief and painful journey to self-awareness." —*Booklist*

"Jenny is a strong and believable character.... [Her] journey is a memorable one." —*Publishers Weekly*

"A talented, fresh voice in literary suspense, she has crafted a nail-biting read about a mother's unrelenting plight to find her missing daughter. A story with multiple layers, your significant other might just find you hiding underneath the covers with a flashlight into the wee hours of the morning." —*MomTrends.com*

Also by Jane Shemilt

THE PLAYGROUND

the daughter

A Novel

JANE SHEMILT

wm

WILLIAM MORROW
An Imprint of HarperCollinsPublishers

THE DAUGHTER. Copyright © 2015 by Jane Shemilt. All rights reserved. Printed in the United States of America. No part of this book may be used or reproduced in any manner whatsoever without written permission except in the case of brief quotations embodied in critical articles and reviews. For information, address HarperCollins Publishers, 195 Broadway, New York, NY 10007.

Originally published in the United Kingdom in 2014 by Penguin Books.

First William Morrow mass market printing: November 2020
First William Morrow paperback printing: March 2015

Print Edition ISBN: 978-0-06-299343-4
Digital Edition ISBN: 978-0-06-232048-3

Cover design by Mumtaz Mustafa
Cover photograph © Martin Poole/Getty Images
Author photograph by Kate Shemilt

William Morrow and HarperCollins are registered trademarks of HarperCollins Publishers in the United States of America and other countries.

20 21 22 23 24 CPI 10 9 8 7 6 5 4 3 2 1

*To my husband, Steve, and our dearest children,
Martha, Mary, Henry, Tommy, and Johny*

the
daughter

Part One

Chapter 1

DORSET, 2010
ONE YEAR LATER

The days grow short. Apples litter the grass, their flesh pockmarked by crows. As I carry logs from the stack under the overhang today, I tread on a soft globe; it collapses into slime under my feet.

November.

I am cold all the time but she could be colder. Why should I be comfortable? How could I be?

By evening the dog is shivering. The room darkens; I light the fire and the flames pull me near as the regrets begin to flare, burning and hissing in my head.

If only. If only I'd been listening. If only I'd been watching. If only I could start again, exactly one year ago.

The leather-bound sketchbook Michael gave me is on the table, and in the pocket of the dressing gown there is a bitten red stub of pencil; he told me it would help to draw the past. The pictures are in my head already:

a scalpel balanced in trembling fingers, a plastic balle-rina twirling around and around, a pile of notes neatly stacked on a bedside table in the dark.

I write my daughter's name on the first unmarked page and underneath I sketch the outline of two black high-heeled shoes lying on their sides, long straps tan-gled together.

Naomi.

BRISTOL, 2009
ONE DAY BEFORE

She was swaying to music on her iPod, so she didn't notice me at first. Her orange scarf was looped around her throat, schoolbooks scattered everywhere. I closed the back door quietly behind me and slid my bag to the floor; it was heavy with notes, my stethoscope, syringes, vials, and boxes. It had been a long day: two surger-ies, home visits, and paperwork. Leaning against the kitchen door, I watched my daughter, but another girl was in my mind's eye. Jade, lying in a bed with bruises flowering on her arms.

That was the chili in my eye. They squirt chili juice into an elephant's eye to distract him while they mend his wounded leg. Theo told me that once. At the time I didn't believe it could work, but I should have taken it as a warning. It's easier than you think to lose sight of what matters.

As I watched Naomi, I imagined painting the curve of her cheeks as she smiled to herself. I would outline them with a paler shade for the light trapped against her skin. With every step her blonde fringe jumped softly against her forehead. When it lifted, beads of sweat along the hairline glistened. She had pushed up the sleeves of her school sweater; the charm bracelet moved up and down, up and down the smooth skin of her arm, almost slipping off. I was glad to see her wearing it; I thought she had lost it years ago.

"Mum! I didn't see you there. What do you think?" She pulled out her earphones and looked at me.

"Wish I could dance like that . . ."

I stepped forward and quickly kissed the velvety bloom along her cheek, breathing her in. Lemon soap and sweat.

She jerked her head away, and bent to pick up her books in a swerving movement that had her quick, glancing grace. Her voice was impatient: "No, I mean my shoes. Look at them."

They must have been new. Black, very high heels, with straps of leather binding her feet and wrapping tightly around her slim legs; they looked wrong on her. She usually wore pumps in colored leather or Converses.

"The heels are incredibly high." Even I could hear the criticism in my voice, so I tried to laugh. "Not like your usual—"

"They're not, are they?" Her voice was triumphant. "Totally different."

"They must have cost the earth. I thought you'd spent your allowance?"

"They're so comfortable. Exactly the right size." As if she couldn't believe her luck.

"You can't wear them to go out, darling. They look far too tight on you."

"Admit you're jealous. You want them." She smiled a little half smile that I hadn't seen before.

"Naomi—"

"Well, you can't have them. I'm in love with them. I love them almost as much as I love Bertie." While she was speaking, she stretched down to stroke the dog's head. She turned then, and, yawning widely, went slowly upstairs, her shoes hitting each step with a harsh metallic noise, like little hammers.

She'd escaped. My question hung, unanswered, in the warm air of the kitchen.

I POURED MYSELF a glass of Ted's wine. Naomi didn't usually answer back or walk out while I was talking. I stashed the doctor's bag and notes in the corner of the coat closet, then, sipping my drink, started walking around the kitchen, straightening towels. She used to tell me everything. As I hung up her coat, the sharpness of the alcohol began to clear my mind; it was part of the bargain and I'd weighed it all up long ago. It was simple. I did the job I loved and earned good money but it meant I was home less than some mothers. The bonus was that it gave the children space. They were growing up independently, which was what we'd always wanted.

I pulled the potatoes out of the cupboard. They were covered in little lumps of soil so I rinsed them quickly under the tap. Thinking about it, though, I realized she hadn't wanted to talk properly for months now. Ted would tell me not to worry. She's a teenager, he would say, growing up. The cold water chilled my hands and I turned off the tap. Growing up or growing away? Preoccupied or withdrawn? The questions hummed in my mind as I hunted in the drawer for the potato peeler. Last summer in my medical practice I had seen an anxious adolescent; she had carefully sliced the delicate skin of her wrists into multiple red lines. I shook my head to drive the image away. Naomi wasn't depressed. There was that new smile to set against the impatience, her involvement in the play against the silences at home. If she seemed preoccupied it was because she was older now, more thoughtful. Acting had given her maturity. Last summer she'd worked with Ted in his lab and she'd become interested in medicine. As I began peeling potatoes, it occurred to me that her newfound confidence could be key to her success in interviews. Perhaps I should celebrate. The starring role in the school play would also increase her chances of getting into medical school. Interviewers liked students with outside interests; it was known to offset the stress of becoming a doctor. Painting worked like that for me, dissolving the stress of general practice. With the tap back on, the brown mud swirled around and around in the sink and then disappeared. I'd almost finished Naomi's portrait and I could feel the pull of it now. Whenever I painted I was in a different world; worries melted away. My easel was just upstairs in the attic, and I wished I could escape more often. I dumped the potato peelings in the garbage and took the sausages out of the fridge. Theo's favorite had been bangers and mash since he was a toddler. I could talk to Naomi tomorrow.

Later Ted phoned to say he was held up at the hospital. The twins came back home ravenously hungry. Ed lifted his hand in silent greeting as he took a plate heaped with toast upstairs. I could hear the bedroom door close behind him and pictured him turning on music, falling onto his bed, toast in hand, eyes closed. I remembered that about being seventeen: hoping no one would bang on your door or, worse, walk in and talk to you. Theo, freckles blazing in his pale face, shouted out the day's triumphs as he crunched biscuits, one after another, emptying the tin. Naomi came back through the kitchen, her wet hair lying in thick points on her neck. I hurriedly pushed sandwiches into her backpack as she walked past me on her way out, then stood at the open door for a few minutes listening to her footsteps going slowly down the road, gradually becoming fainter. The school theater was just a street away but she was always late. She'd stopped running everywhere now; the play was sapping her energy.

"Though just fifteen Naomi Malcolm's Maria is mature beyond her years . . ." "Naomi mixes innocence and sexuality in a bewitching performance as Maria; a star is born." Being tired and wound up was worth it for those reviews on the school website. Two more performances after this: Thursday, then Friday. Soon we would all get back to normal.

DORSET, 2010
ONE YEAR LATER

I know it's Friday today because the fish lady comes to the cottage. I crouch down under the stairs as her van draws up outside, the white shape smudged by the old glass of the door. The woman rings the bell and waits, a squat, hopeful figure, head bobbing as she searches the windows. If she sees me I will have to open the door, compose words, smile. None of these are possible today.

A small spider scrabbles over my hand. Bending my head further, I breathe dust from the carpet, and after a while the van rumbles away down the lane. It's a day for being on my own. I lie low and wait for the hours to pass. Fridays still hurt.

After a while, I get up and find the sketchbook I left on the hearth last night. I turn over the page with the picture of her shoes and, on the next one, draw the overlapping circles of a silver ring.

BRISTOL, 2009
THE NIGHT OF THE DISAPPEARANCE

I knelt on the kitchen floor, opening up my medical bag to check the drugs against a list to see what I needed. This job was easier away from the office; there were fewer interruptions if I picked my time. I was groping into the depths of the leather pockets so I didn't notice her come silently into the kitchen. She walked past me, and the shopping bag she was carrying knocked against my shoulder. I looked up, keeping a finger on my list; I was running low on acetaminophen and Demerol. Naomi glanced down at me, her blue eyes clouded with thought. Even through the thick makeup she'd already put on for the play there were dark lines under her eyes. She looked exhausted. This wasn't the moment to ask the questions I'd wanted to.

"You're almost done, sweetie. This is the second-to-last performance," I said brightly.

Clothes were spilling from her bag; the heels of her shoes had made little holes in the plastic.

"Dad and I will be there tomorrow." I sat back and

looked up, studying her face. The black eyeliner made her look much older than fifteen. "I'm longing to see if it's changed since the first night."

She looked at me blankly, and then gave me the new smile; only one side of her mouth lifted so it looked as if she was smiling to herself.

"What time will you be back?" I gave up and got to my feet reluctantly; I never managed to finish anything. "It's Thursday. Dad usually picks you up on Thursdays."

"I told him not to bother ages ago. Walking with friends is easier." She sounded bored. "The meal will finish around midnight. Shan will give me a lift."

"Midnight?" But she was tired already. Despite myself, my voice was rising. "You've got the play again tomorrow, the party straight after. It's only a meal. Ten-thirty."

"That's not nearly long enough. Why do I always have to be different from everyone else?" Her fingers started tapping the table; the ring that some boy at school had given her was glinting in the light.

"Eleven, then."

She stared at me. "I'm not a baby." The anger in her tone was surprising.

We couldn't argue all night. She would be onstage soon. She needed to calm down, I had to finish sorting the medicines before cooking supper.

"Half past eleven. Not a second later."

She shrugged and turned, bending over Bertie where he lay at full stretch, sleeping against the stove. She kissed him, pulling his soft ears gently; though he hardly stirred, his tail thumped the floor.

I touched her arm. "He's old, sweetheart. He needs his sleep."

She jerked her arm from my hand, her face tense.

"Relax, darling. You're a triumph, remember?" I gave her a quick hug, but she turned her face away. "Only one more day to go."

Her cell phone went off, and she stepped back, her hand resting on the draining board as she answered. Her fingers were long. She had freckles, tiny ones that went as far as the second knuckle, light gold, like grains of Demerara sugar. The nails were bitten like a child's, at odds with the pretty ring. I folded her hand in both of mine and kissed it quickly. She was talking to Nikita; I don't think she even noticed. She was still young enough for the knuckles to feel like little pits under my lips. The phone call finished and she turned to go, a little wave at the door, her way of making up for being irritable.

"Bye, Mum," she said.

LATER I FELL asleep by mistake. I put the kettle on for her hot-water bottle at about eleven, and lay down on the sofa to wait. I must have drifted off almost immediately. When I woke up, my neck ached and my mouth tasted stale. I got up and, pulling my sweater down, went to put the kettle on again.

The kettle was cold under my hand. I looked at the clock. Two in the morning. I hadn't heard her come in. I felt sick. She'd never been as late as this. What had happened? The blood thumped painfully in my ears for a second until common sense took over. Of course, she had let herself in by the front door and gone straight up to bed. Asleep in the basement kitchen a flight below, I wouldn't have heard the door shutting behind her. She must have dropped her shoes soundlessly in the front porch and then tiptoed upstairs, quietly, guiltily, past our room and on up to hers, on the second floor. I stretched as I waited for the kettle to boil; she could still have her hot-water bottle. I would wrap it up and tuck it in beside her; she might sleepily register the warmth.

I went upstairs slowly past the boys' rooms. Ed snored suddenly as I passed, making me jump. Up another flight to Naomi's room. The door was open a crack and I went in quietly. It was pitch dark and stuffy, smelling of strawberry shampoo and something else, bitter with citrus at the back of it. I felt my way to her chest of drawers, and, pulling out a shirt, slipped the hot-water bottle inside. I stepped carefully over to the bed, half tripping on strewn clothes. My hands moved to turn the cover back around her, but it was smooth and flat.

The bed was empty.

I snapped on the light. Tights spilled from open drawers; there were towels and shoes on the floor. A thong lay on top of a red lacy bra on her bedside table, a black half-cup bra on the chair. I didn't recognize any of these things; had her friends changed here too? Naomi was usually so tidy. A bottle of foundation had tipped over on the dressing table; a stick of lipstick lay in the small beige puddle. Her gray school sweater had been left on the floor, with the white shirt still inside it.

The cover of the bed was slightly dented where she had sat on it, but the pillow was quite smooth.

Fear curled in the pit of my stomach. I put my hand on the wall and its coldness seemed to travel up my arm to the inside of my chest. Then I heard the front door shut two floors down.

Thank God. Thank you, God.

I put the hot-water bottle under the duvet, far enough down to make a warm place for her feet. They would be cold by now in those thin shoes. Then I ran downstairs, careless of the noise. I wouldn't be cross, not tonight. I would kiss her, take her coat, and send her up. I could be cross tomorrow. My footsteps slowed as I rounded the corner of the stairs and Ted came into view. Ted, not Naomi. He stood looking up at me. He was wearing his coat, and his briefcase was by his feet.

"She's not back." I was out of breath; the words were difficult to push out. "I thought you were her coming in."

"What?" He looked exhausted. His shoulders were hunched; there were deep circles under his eyes.

"Naomi hasn't come home yet." I went close to him. A faint smell of burning clung about him; it must have been from the diathermy, spluttering heat, sealing cut blood vessels. He must have come straight from the operating room.

His eyes, the same sea-blue as Naomi's, looked puzzled. "Her play ended at nine-thirty, didn't it?" An expression of panic crossed his face. "Jesus, it's Thursday."

He'd forgotten that she had canceled Thursday pickups, but he never knew what was happening in the children's lives anyway. He never asked. I felt the slow swell of anger.

"She walks back with friends now. She told you."

"Of course she did. I'd forgotten. Oh well." He looked relieved.

"But tonight was different." How could he be so relaxed when my heart was pounding with anxiety? "She went out for a meal with the cast."

"I can't keep up." He shrugged. "So, she's out with

her mates. Perhaps they're having such a good time they stayed on."

"Ted, it's after two . . ." My face flushed hot with panic and fury. Surely he realized this was different, that it felt wrong.

"That late? Gosh, I'm sorry. The operation went on and on and on. I hoped you'd be asleep by now." He spread his hands in apology.

"Where the hell is she?" I stared at him, my voice rising. "She never does this, she lets me know even if she's five minutes late." As I said it, it occurred to me that she hadn't for a long time now, but then she had never been as late as this. "There's a rapist in Bristol, it said on the news—"

"Calm down, Jen. Who is she with, exactly?" He looked down at me and I could sense reluctance. He didn't want this to be happening; he wanted to go to bed.

"Her friends from the play. Nikita and everyone. It was just a meal, not a party."

"Perhaps they went to a club after."

"She'd never get in." Her cheeks were still rounded; she had a fifteen-year-old face, younger sometimes, especially when she was tired. "She's not old enough."

"It's what they all do." Ted's voice was slow with tiredness. He leaned his tall frame against the wall. "They have false IDs. Remember when Theo—"

"Not Naomi." Then I remembered the shoes, the smile. Was it possible? A club?

"Let's give it a bit longer." Ted's voice was calm. "I mean, it's kind of normal, still early if you're having fun. Let's wait until two-thirty."

"Then what?"

"She'll probably be back." He pushed himself away

from the wall, and rubbing his face with his hands, he began to walk toward the steps at the end of the hall that led down to the kitchen. "If not, we'll phone Shan. You've phoned Naomi obviously?"

I hadn't. God knows why. I hadn't even checked for a text. I felt for my cell phone but it wasn't in my pocket. "Where the bloody hell's my bloody phone?"

I pushed past Ted and ran downstairs. It must have fallen out and was half hidden under a squashed cushion on the sofa. I snatched it up. No text. I punched her number.

"Hiya, this is Naomi. Sorry, I'm busy doing something incredibly important right now. But—um—leave me a number and I'll get back to you. That's a promise. Byee."

I shook my head, unable to speak.

"I need a drink." Ted went slowly to the drinks cupboard. He poured two whiskeys and held one out to me. I felt the alcohol burn my throat, then travel down the length of my gullet.

Two-fifteen. Fifteen minutes to go before we would ring Shan.

I didn't want to wait. I wanted to leave the house, I would go down the road to the school theater, wrench open the doors, and shout her name into the dusty air. If she wasn't there, then I would run down the main street, past the university, storm into all the clubs, pushing past the bouncers, and yell into the crowds of dancers . . .

"Is there any food?"

"What?"

"Jenny, I've been operating all night. I missed supper in the canteen. Is there any food?"

I opened the fridge and looked in. I couldn't recognize anything. Squares and oblongs. My hands found cheese and butter. The cold lumps of butter tore the bread. Ted silently took it from me. He made a perfect sandwich and cut off the crusts.

While he was eating, I found Nikita's number on a pink Post-it note stuck to the corkboard on the cabinet. She didn't pick up either. The phone was in her bag. She had pushed it under the table so she could dance in the club they'd managed to get into. Everyone else wanted to go home, her friends were leaning against the wall, yawning, but Naomi and Nikita were dancing together, having fun. No one would be able to hear Nikita's phone ringing in the bag under the table. Shan must be awake too, waiting. It was only a year since her divorce from Neil; this would feel worse on her own.

Half past two.

I phoned Shan and, as I waited, I remembered her telling me a week ago how Nikita still shared everything with her and the stabbing moment of jealousy that I'd felt. Naomi didn't do that anymore. Now I was glad Nikita still confided in her mother. Shan would know exactly where we could pick them up.

A sleepy voice mumbled an answer. She had fallen asleep, like me.

"Hello, Shan." I tried to make my voice sound normal. "I'm so sorry to wake you. Do you have any idea where they are? We'll pick them up, but the trouble is . . ." I paused, and attempted to laugh. "Naomi forgot to tell me where they would be."

"Wait a moment." I could see her sitting up, running her hand through her hair, blinking at the alarm clock on her bedside table. "Say all that again?"

I took a breath and tried to speak slowly.

"Naomi's not back yet. They must have gone on somewhere after the meal. Did Nikita say where?"

"The meal's tomorrow, Jen."

"No, that's the party."

"Both tomorrow. Nikita's here. She's exhausted; she's been asleep since I picked her up hours ago."

I repeated stupidly: "Hours ago?"

"I collected her straight after the play." There was a little pause and then she said quietly, "There was no meal."

"But Naomi said." My mouth was dry. "She took her new shoes. She said . . ."

I sounded like children do when they want something they can't have. She had taken the shoes and the bag of clothes. How could there not have been a meal? Shan must be mistaken; perhaps Nikita hadn't been invited. There was a longer pause.

"I'll check with Nikita," she said. "Phone you back in a moment."

I was outside a gate, which had just shut with a little click. Behind it was a place where children slept safely, their limbs trustingly spread across the sheets; a place where you didn't phone a friend at two-thirty in the morning.

The kitchen chairs were cold and hard. Ted's face was white. He kept bending his knuckles till they cracked. I wanted to stop him but I couldn't open my mouth in case I started screaming. I picked the phone up quickly when it rang and at first I didn't say anything.

"There was no meal, Jenny." Shan's voice was slightly breathless. "Everyone went home. I'm sorry."

A faint buzzing noise started in my head, filling in the silence that stretched after her words. I felt giddy, as if I was tipping forward, or the world was tipping back. I held tightly to the edge of the table.

"Can I speak to Nikita?"

By the tiny space that followed my question, I could measure how far away I had traveled from the gate that had clicked behind me. Shan sounded hesitant.

"She's gone back to sleep."

Asleep? How could that matter? Nikita was there, safe. We had no idea where our daughter was. A wave of anger was breaking on top of my fear.

"If Nikita knows anything, anything at all that we don't, and Naomi might be in danger—" My throat constricted. Ted took the phone from me.

"Hi there, Shania." There was a pause. "I appreciate how difficult this will be for Nikita . . ." His voice was calm but with an edge of authority. It was exactly how he talked to the junior doctors on his team if they called him for advice about a neurosurgical problem. "If Naomi doesn't come home soon, we may need to call the police. The more information you give us . . ." Another pause. "Thanks. Yes. See you in a few minutes, then."

The boys were sleeping in their rooms. I leaned into the warm, breathing space around their heads. Theo had burrowed under the duvet; his hair, sticking up in a ruff above its edge, was stiff under my lips. Ed's black fringe was damp; even in sleep his eyebrows swooped down like the wings of a blackbird. As I straightened, I caught my reflection in his mirror. My face, lit by the streetlamp shining through the window, looked as if it belonged to someone much older. My hair was dark and shapeless. I dragged Ed's brush through it.

As we drove past the school theater, Ted stopped the car and we got out.

I don't know why. I still don't know why we had to check. Did we really think you would be there, curled up and sleeping on the stage? That we could wake you and that you would smile and stretch, sleepy and stiff, with some explanation about taking too long to change? That we would put our arms around you and take you home?

The glass doors were locked. They rocked slightly as I pulled at the handles. There was a night-light in the foyer and the bottles in the bar were shining in neat rows. A torn red and yellow program lay on the floor just inside the door; I could make out red letters spelling "West" and "Story" on different lines and part of a picture of a girl with a blue swirling skirt.

Ted drove carefully, though I knew he was tired. He had pressed the button on the dashboard that made the back of my seat warm up. It made me sweat, and nausea seemed to rise from the deep leather upholstery. I glanced at him. He was good at this. Good at looking serious, not desperate. When Naomi was in difficulty during her birth, his calmness had stopped me from panicking. He had organized the epidural for the Caesarean section, and he was there when they lifted out her small, bloodied body. I wouldn't think about that now. I looked out of the window quickly. The streets were shining and empty. A fine rain had started to mist the windows. What had she been wearing? I couldn't remember. Her raincoat? What about her scarf? I looked up into the roadside trees as if the orange cloth might be there, tangled in the wet black branches.

At Shania's house Ted knocked firmly. The night was silent and still around us, but if anyone had been passing in a car, they would have seen a couple like any other. We were wearing warm coats and clean shoes as we waited quietly, heads bowed in the rain. We probably looked normal.

Shania's face was prepared. She looked calm and serious as she hugged us. It was hot in her house, the gas fire flaming in her tidy living room. Nikita was hunched on the sofa, a cushion held tightly to her, her long legs in rabbit-patterned pajamas tucked beneath her. I smiled at her, but my mouth felt stiff and trembled at the corners. Shan sat close to her on the sofa; we sat opposite and Ted took my hand.

"Ted and Jenny want to ask you about Naomi now, babe." Shania put her arm around Nikita, who looked down as she twisted a thick lock of her dark hair in her fingers.

I moved to sit by her on the other side, but she shifted slightly away from me. I tried to make my voice gentle.

"Where is she, Nik?"

"I don't know." She bent and pushed her head into the cushion, her voice was muffled. "I don't know, I don't know, I don't know."

Shania's eyes met mine over her head.

"I'll start, then," Shan said. "I'll tell Jenny what you told me." Nikita nodded. Her mother continued: "Naomi told Nikita that she was going to meet someone, a bloke, after the play."

"A bloke?" Ted's voice cut across my intake of breath. "What bloke?" The word in his mouth sounded dangerous. Not a boy. Older. My heart started banging so loudly I was afraid Nikita would hear and refuse to tell us anything.

"She said . . . ," Nikita hesitatingly began, "she said she had met someone. He was hot."

I uncrossed my legs and turned around to face her properly. "Hot? Naomi said that?"

"That's all right, isn't it? You asked me." Nikita's forehead puckered, her eyes filled with tears.

"Of course," I told her.

But it wasn't all right. I'd never heard her use that word. We had talked about sex, but as I desperately scanned my memory for clues, I couldn't remember when. Relationships, sex, and contraception—Naomi didn't seem interested. Had she been? What had I missed?

"Was he . . . did she . . ." I groped in a forest of possibilities. "Was he from school?"

Nikita shook her head. Ted spoke then, lightly, casually, as though it wasn't important.

"This guy. She must have met him before?"

Nikita's shoulders dropped fractionally, she stopped twisting her hair. Ted's calmness was working but I felt a stab of anger that he could manage it so easily. I could hardly keep my voice from trembling.

"Yeah. I think he was around in the theater sometimes." She glanced down. "You know, at the back."

"At the back?" Again, barely inquisitive.

"Yeah. Where people waited. Maybe." She looked up and there was reluctance in her dark eyes. "I didn't really see."

"What did he look like?" I asked quickly.

"Don't know." Nikita didn't look at me. There was a pause. "Maybe dark hair?"

She moved nearer Shan on the sofa and closed her eyes. I didn't think she would tell us anything else, but Ted was asking another question.

"And tonight? What did she say to you about tonight?"

There was silence. Nikita was completely still. Then Shan stood up. "She's tired now." Her voice was firm. "She needs to go back to bed."

"Tell us, Nikita, please." I touched her on the arm lightly, carefully. "Please, please tell us what she said."

She looked back at me then, her brown eyes wide with surprise. Her best friend's mother was a busy figure in the distance; cheerful, running in and running out. In charge of her life and her family. She didn't plead.

"She said"—Nikita paused for a fraction—"she said, 'Wish me luck.'"

Chapter 2

DORSET, 2010
ONE YEAR LATER

Autumn deepens into winter. In the morning the silence presses coldly against my face.

I listen, though I'm not sure what I'm listening for. By now I should have learned the absence of the sounds that I took for granted: the muted steps of bare feet, the distant kettle, murmuring radio voices, and the porcelain clink of the coffee cups on the edge of the bath. The noises one person makes are quiet, careful, separated out. They ebb into silence. I open the window and the softly crashing breath of the sea comes into the room like something alive.

I touch her bedroom door as I pass to the bathroom. She chose this room when she was small. It was never really her bedroom, because until the past few months it had just been our holiday home, but we all thought of that room as hers. As a child she liked to pretend the little round window under the thatch was a porthole and that her bed was a boat.

The police took the mattress away, and all the bedding. The wood of the door is cold and damp under my fingertips. Ted washed the blood off the floor; I haven't been inside since I arrived.

The wavering reflection of the window frame fractures around my hands as I lie in the bath water. When the bell rings I get out quickly, a towel around me, then my dressing gown. At the top of the stairs my steps freeze. I can see a man in uniform through the glass of the front door. My heart goes so fast I feel faint and I hold the banisters. This could be the moment they have come to tell me they have found something in the mud of a field: the heel of a shoe perhaps, soft and rotten, the gleam of a silver charm, the white of a tooth. There is nothing they can tell me that I haven't thought of, but I stop as if I've been shot. Then I see red somewhere on his jacket, a bulky bag. Someone with a special delivery. When I open the door, he hands me the post: the order of small paintbrushes from the art shop in Bristol. On the mat already is a postcard of a Welsh mountain from Ted's vast collection. His way of keeping in touch. No message, as usual. I sit at the kitchen table and my heart slows. The sketchbook is in front of me and I pull it toward me, open it at the next page. When the police came to the door, and I saw the black and white, the padded jackets and the badges, her absence became official. It was still dark but it must have been early morning, maybe four or five A.M.

The pencil is rough in my fingers; I can feel the chips where it's been bitten as I draw a little hooded top, shading between the folds with short gray lines.

BRISTOL, 2009
THE NIGHT OF THE DISAPPEARANCE

The policeman at the door was in his mid-fifties, his colorless eyes sunk in soft pouches of flesh. Whatever natural expression he had was overlain by a veneer of professional calm, though his eyes, moving quickly over my face, betrayed his unease. Behind him was a small woman, brown hair in a tight French pleat, immaculate red lipstick. I thought I could see anger tamped down. Perhaps she'd had to get up specially, put on the crisp uniform and the thick makeup.

"Dr. Malcolm?" The man's voice was carefully neutral.

At home I didn't call myself doctor; I was the children's mother, my husband's wife, but if this policeman thought I was a fellow professional he might try even harder.

"Yes." I stood back to let them in.

"I'm Police Constable Steve Wareham and this is Police Constable Sue Dunning."

He took off his hat; there was a little ridge running around his thin gray hair. He shook my hand and spoke quietly. He was sorry for us but not the sort of sorry I was afraid of. I'd been afraid he would say sorry for your loss. The woman was brisker. She nodded but put her hands behind her back as if she didn't want to touch me; I was the kind of woman whose child doesn't come back home.

I took them to the kitchen. We had just returned from Shan's house and I needed to watch the clock. It was ten hours since Naomi had walked out of the back door, and I wanted to tell them immediately about the man whose shadow seemed thrown against the bright walls of the kitchen. In my mind I was screaming at them to hurry. Leave now. You might catch them. He is driving with her down a long street in the rain, he is going into a house, he is locking the door, he is turning around to face her, she is crying. No, of course not, she never cries. Hurry.

Ted began talking; he started from the beginning, which was what they wanted. They wanted everything and it took an hour. They asked for her laptop, then her birth certificate and passport. They tried the cell phone again, but there wasn't an answering message, or even a ringtone this time. Out of charge. Naomi's phone was often dead, it didn't mean anything. When Steve Wareham told me they could have traced the location of the phone if it had been charged, I fought back a surge of helpless anger and fear.

I gave them her school photo from last term. I stared at it for a few seconds. It had been taken a few months ago, but still, she looked so young. It was as though I was looking at another person with a wide smile, her bright hair pulled back in a ponytail, her face shining. I thought of the foundation pooling around the little bottle. She hadn't looked like that child in the photo before the play. Did she have hobbies? Maybe. I didn't know. I was at work all day, I couldn't know everything. The constable raised an eyebrow briefly. What school, what doctor, what dentist? (Dentist? What, dental records? The brief spasm of pain on Ted's face showed he had got there too.) School friends? Names? Boyfriends? Not a boyfriend, no. Someone who waited at the back of the theater. He had dark hair and she thought he was hot. He's got her. He could be hurting her at this very moment; his hands tight around her neck. Perhaps he's forcing her down on the ground, pulling off her clothes, pushing her under him, the side of a hand in her mouth to stifle her. I pushed my fingers hard into my own mouth, biting them to stop myself screaming.

They wrote everything down.

Police constable Sue Dunning gave me a missing person form to fill in. She said it was too soon to call it an abduction, no evidence as such. My hands were shaking, so I wrote slowly. They kept talking to me, asking questions. Height, about five foot five. Weight? One hundred ten pounds. Yes, she was slim. No, not anorexic, just one of those people always on the go; she ate plenty.

Are you hungry? You didn't have supper, did you? I didn't mind about that then, because I thought you were going out for a meal. You should have told me, I could have made you something.

What was she wearing when I last saw her? She was coming downstairs with her bag and I think she was wearing a raincoat, or was it her school coat? Perhaps her little gray hoodie. Let me think. I can check in her closet and let you know.

I hope it was a raincoat; it's raining, you'll get wet.

She was going to change into a dress for the . . . for after . . . and new shoes. They were black with straps, high heels. Different. They may have been a present, do you think? A trick, a bribe. She was wearing a charm bracelet. That might be important. The bag she was carrying had little holes in it. I don't know, Tesco's? Waitrose?

Don't try to run in those shoes, you'll break your ankles. Take them off, and then run.

Were there problems at home? Had she gone missing

before? Had she ever tried to harm herself? The questions were relentless. I was exhausted. They hadn't understood anything. She was in the play. She was tired, of course, tetchy sometimes, but underneath she was fine. And all the time, I was listening for her footsteps; she might walk in at any moment, an excuse ready-made, amazed at the fuss. All this would fade into a nightmare.

Steve Wareham was still speaking. "Before we go any further, we need to search the premises."

I stared at him. Didn't he believe anything we had said?

"What?" Ted's voice was incredulous. "Now?"

"You'd be surprised." He didn't mean to sound patronizing. "You wouldn't believe the number of missing children we find still at home; kids hiding in the closet. Making a point."

They looked upstairs, Ted showing the way. They went into the loft, the cabinets, and the closets. They were methodical and quiet, so thankfully the boys slept on. They looked in the garden shed and the garbage bins. I waited in the kitchen, my hand resting on the phone. When they had finished, they looked tired.

"Someone from the force will come back later." Sue Dunning was faintly embarrassed. "You will have to be eliminated from the inquiry. Routine measures."

She didn't need to be embarrassed. They were being thorough; that meant they would find her.

Ted asked what would happen next and she reeled off a list: file the report, contact the school and the theater, visit Nikita for a witness statement, look at Facebook, examine her laptop, and the cell phones of friends for texts, interview the teachers, go to clubs, pubs, restaurants, garages, railway stations, seaports, airports. Interpol. And, if she's not back in twenty-four hours, get the media involved.

Airports? Media? Ted put his arm around me.

"One final thing. We'll need her toothbrush," Steve Wareham said quietly. "In case."

The pink toothbrush looked oddly childish in the yellow plastic mug in her bathroom. Sue Dunning slipped it into a little plastic envelope and it wasn't Naomi's anymore. It was DNA from a missing person. In case.

"Thank you for your cooperation." Steve Wareham stood up stiffly, hand in the small of his back. The lines on his face looked deeper. I wondered what it must feel like to face parents like us, and for a fleeting moment I felt sorry for him.

"We will fully inform the day shift, which starts at seven A.M. There will be a meeting with the senior manager of the Criminal Investigation Department, not, of course, that we know there is any criminal activity involved at the present time." He took a breath and continued: "In the meantime, it would help us if you searched for clues here in your house, in case there's anything you might have overlooked. Go through everything that's happened in the last few days and weeks. Anything that seemed different about your daughter. Write it down and tell us. I'll take the laptop away with us for now."

He smiled at us as he picked it up, and his face became gentler. "Michael Kopje will be in contact. He's the family liaison officer for this area. He'll be around in a couple of hours."

A couple of hours. What about the next five minutes, and the five minutes after that?

They have a picture. It'll help.

But it doesn't show the way her hair shines so brightly it looks like sheets of gold.

She has a tiny mole, just beneath her left eyebrow.

She smells very faintly of lemons.

She bites her nails.

She never cries.

Find her.

Part Two

Chapter 3

DORSET, 2010
ONE YEAR LATER

The faint morning bustle that washes up the lane from
the village has faded. The morning sinks into a dull afternoon and, unannounced, grief settles closely around
me. It will pass as long as I stand quite still. On home
visits in the past, I could tell from the door if patients
were sick by how still they lay. Appendicitis, a ruptured
abdominal aorta, meningitis—the muscles become rigid
to shield the disaster unfolding inside. In the summer I
lay motionless as the hours dissolved, watching the dust
dance in glittering columns as the sunlight slid through
each window in turn. I wanted to die, but I knew then as
I do now that one day I might look up and she could be
there, framed in the doorway. And, of course, I would
never abandon the boys; besides, her dog sleeps in my
kitchen.

On cue Bertie yawns, climbs out of his basket, and

wags his tail. His opaque eyes track me as I cross the kitchen. His neck is warm under my fingers when I clip on the lead; the deep fur has toughened with age. I shove the notebook and pencil into a pocket. The back door of the kitchen opens into the garden, which leads onto fields. Mother gave me the cottage before she died. It was lucky that she did; it gave me somewhere to hide.

Lucky. Good luck, this is my lucky day, wish me luck. A trivial word to describe the weight of those swings of fate that open or close against you, like great doors banging in the wind. Naomi never thought she would need luck. She thought she had been born lucky. I thought she had been too; I thought we all had been. Only a year ago, I thought we had everything.

It's hard to see exactly where it began to change. I go back, over and over again, to different points in time, to work out where I could have altered fate. I could pick almost any moment in my life and twist it to a different shape. If I hadn't decided to become a doctor, if Ted hadn't taken the books out of my arms in the library years ago, if I hadn't been rushing that afternoon in my office, if I'd had more time. Time was running out but I didn't know it then.

I climb the cliff path, waiting as Bertie jumps stiffly up the ledges of gray rock. At the top the wind blows spray against my mouth like rain. It seeps between my lips, salty, more like tears than rain.

My mind goes to the afternoon in my doctor life, when the clock started ticking down the hours of Naomi's last days with us. The afternoon I met Jade, the chili in my eye.

Sitting on a rock, the sea and sky stretching in front of me, I pull the sketchbook from my pocket and begin to draw a toy giraffe, smudging the coat and making the edge of one ear ragged. Bertie settles to wait, his head on my feet, whining softly from time to time.

On the second of November a year ago I had no way of knowing that we had only seventeen days left.

BRISTOL, 2009
SEVENTEEN DAYS BEFORE

It had been raining all day. Patients were coming in off the narrow street with dripping clothes and wet hair, letting in the swish and rumble of the main road at the end of our little cul-de-sac. Our practice was near the docks, set back a little between a pine furniture shop and a rubbish-strewn parking lot where the weeds grew high and thin through patches of broken tarmac. The streets nearby were dense with small Victorian terrace houses; when I drove to work, nudging the car through the narrowing streets, I would glimpse the dark water off the docks between old warehouses.

The practice was popular, or perhaps just convenient. The small waiting room was always crammed with patients, though the few minutes we had for each never seemed enough. In the allotted seven minutes it was almost impossible to give people what they wanted. All the same, I thought they knew we were on their side; at least I thought so until that afternoon. I remember quite a lot; in particular I remember the smell.

By late afternoon, my room smelled bad. Sweat, blood, and stale alcohol. Flesh took on a greenish color in the harsh overhead light. The blinds were drawn over the window to keep out the street, and in here it was as though that world didn't exist. It was hot. Toys were scattered over the floor. The basin in the corner was full of bloody metal, covered over with blue paper towels.

I was tired. Mrs. Bartlett's examination had been difficult—it had been hard to see the cervical polyp for the bleeding—and she would need referral to a clinic tomorrow. I glanced at the list on my screen, and as I cleared the basin, then washed my hands, I thought about the next patient. A temporary resident. Yoska Jones. Polish? I yawned into the little mirror above the sink; my hair had escaped the clasp and was wildly curling around my face. My mascara had smudged again. I narrowed my eyes at my reflection, hoping his problem would be straightforward so I could make up time. I called him in. Mid-twenties. High cheekbones, tanned skin. It took a second to see he wasn't ill. I could sort this quickly.

"How can I help?"

"Back pain, runs in the family." A Welsh accent. His hand, strong and weathered, lay close to mine on the table. I put my hands in my lap.

"What do you think brought this on?"

"Carrying my kid sister around." A defensive note crept into his voice. "She likes to sit on my shoulders, but she's getting heavy."

"Carrying children doesn't help." It's tempting, though. I used to carry Naomi everywhere, long after she could walk on her own. I liked the weight of her, her face against mine. "Best to let her walk on her own."

I caught a flicker of anger in his eyes, but in seven minutes advice was more important than sympathy and I had to look at his back. The long erector spinae muscles on either side of his spine were as smooth and thick as a pair of snakes, but when he lay on his back he winced as I raised his legs. Sciatica. His reflexes and sensation were normal. When I told him what exercises he needed to do and prescribed some analgesia, he smiled and shook my hand. The laying on of hands had worked its magic: his hostility evaporated completely. He left with a leaflet of advice and his script, his foot accidentally tipping a toy as he went. It spun across the room and crashed into the wall. I picked it up as the door closed. It was the little plastic duck with the faded orange beak that had been chewed so often it was frayed into soft spikes, and the wing had come cleanly off, leaving a sharp edge. There was a muffled clang as it hit the bottom of the metal garbage can. I called the next patient in.

I knew Jade was ten, though she looked much younger. She stood motionless as her mother took off her parka, her school sweater, her skirt. There were bruises on her face, her arms, and her legs. She seemed perfect apart from the bruises, but her pretty face was blank. She watched me closely as she clutched a tattered velvet giraffe. I had seen her at least four times this year; there had been tiredness, ill-defined abdominal pain, poor appetite, and now coughing. Nothing had jumped out at me before, though I had noticed her dirty clothes and the matted hair that hung in silvery ropes. I had simply given advice, and tried to reassure her anxious mother. This time it was different. The bruises were new. I smiled at Jade, but the room seemed to turn darker around her.

Her mother, in bulging fake fur, talked quickly and loudly, leaving no gaps between her words. Gaps held clues, but her words fell out in a tight line.

"Still keeping us awake with the bloody coughing."

The woman's hard green eyes tracked mine.

"Something else as well."

The caked face pushed in close and little blobs of hardened mascara trembled when she blinked. Her fingers with long pointed nails gripped her daughter's shoulders tightly.

"She comes home covered in bruises. She says she trips over a lot. We think it's the other kids. Picking on her."

"Why are they doing that?"

"I don't know, do I?"

I uncurled Jade's fingers and put the steel disk of my stethoscope into the small palm so its coldness on her chest wouldn't shock her.

"Can I listen to your tummy?"

The bright head made a small movement up and down.

I put my stethoscope on top of her undershirt first to gain her confidence; her hair fell over my hand and I saw something black scuttle up a strand toward her scalp. When she stopped holding her breath, I lifted the undershirt to listen and saw that the bumpy little rib cage was bruised; there were more bruises on her backbone. I could hear the mother's voice become louder and faster as she watched me, but I stopped listening to the words. I kept my face under control as I felt the tender lumps on a rib. There were small crackling noises in her chest. I examined her everywhere. By the time I saw bruises high on her inner thighs, wings of worry were beating in my head.

I typed a script for antibiotics as her mother pulled her clothes back on over her head. If I mentioned the lice as well, she might never come back.

"This should help her chest; she needs a spoonful three times a day. I'll need to check her again, so could you bring her back in two days?"

She nodded, staring at the script in her hand, and turned to go, pulling Jade after her quickly.

I went to see Lynn, our practice nurse. She was in her room, humming quietly as she refilled her tray with bottles and syringes. When I told her about Jade, her brown eyes narrowed in concern.

"Jade's never been brought in for immunizations. She saw the substitute nurse last summer, bad fall, grazes to her arms." Her neat hands flew over the keyboard. "The father was here a few weeks ago as well, stitches in his hand. Off his head with alcohol that afternoon." She glanced at me with a worried frown. "I had the feeling he would lash out at any moment."

I had encountered drunken men with open head wounds on Saturday nights in the emergency room while training. I remembered the obscene threats, the wildly aimed punches while I sewed skin edges together with trembling fingers.

So Jade's father was that kind of man.

"What do you make of the mother, then, Lynn?"

"Don't really know." Lynn leaned toward the screen. "Doesn't come in for her smears. It's on here that she saw Frank for depression last year and was prescribed citalopram, but she didn't come back for follow-up."

As she spoke, the pieces of the jigsaw began to slot together neatly.

"Thanks, Lynn. Any chance that you could, say, contact the mother about the immunizations . . . ?"

"And use it as a chance to go visit? 'Course I will."

I phoned the social worker, left a message. Tracking

down the school nurse took longer. It wasn't the day for her drop-in clinic, but the school gave me her work cell number. She picked up on the second try.

"Jade Price? Yeah, I know Jade. Quiet little thing. Not a happy child."

"Why's that?"

"She gets left out. The other kids treat her like a leper."

The raspy voice wanted to gossip. I kept it brief.

"Does she get into fights? Her mother said—"

"Like I said, the kids don't go near her, too quiet. The nits don't help. Her dad fetches her from school sometimes, drunk as a lord, full of temper."

Another piece of the jigsaw clicked into place. The community pediatrician was out; I'd try later. As the senior partner, Frank would need to be told, but it would have to wait until tomorrow now, as I was running late. The patients would be waiting with pursed lips, checking their watches. The beating wings of worry had gone, leaving a feather edge of panic. When my cell phone vibrated in my pocket, I picked it out and gave it a fleeting glance. Ed. I'd have to remind the children not to phone me here; there was never time to talk to them. I called the next patient in.

Nigel Mancey pushed his insurer's medical report across the desk at me. "They're on about how I've got blood pressure." He grinned.

As I wrapped the cuff around his curdy white upper arm, his thick fingers tapped the table; they looked like shiny pink sausages, the cheap kind with thin skins that split open with one touch of the knife. His blood pressure was high but not dangerously so. He took the lifestyle booklet and blood test forms, then left to make a follow-up appointment, muttering to himself.

The air in my little room seemed used up. I was grateful when Jo, our receptionist, brought me a cup of tea between patients. She wore her fair hair piled high on her head, but by this time of day little strands were straggling loose. She set the white china cup gently down in a space on the desk between notes. As I took the first sips, I looked at the framed photographs on the wall. They were out of date now. There was one of Naomi at five, smiling so broadly her eyes had disappeared, tightly holding Bertie, then a new puppy. The boys were leaning in, half hidden, grinning down at her. There was another from a party the previous New Year's Eve. Ted's arms were around us all; he must have said something funny because we were all laughing except Naomi; she was staring at the camera so intently she seemed to scowl. I pulled my attention back and called the next patient in.

The dark afternoon eased into evening. Patient followed patient in a steady rhythm and for a while I felt I was winning. Then Jo put her head around the door, her eyes wide with worry: little Tom had just been brought in with an asthma attack. His mother, a pretty teenager with dreadlocks, was silent with fear. Tom was sweating, his skin tugged in between his ribs, the wheeze was ominously quiet. I switched into automatic mode: soon he was breathing in Ventolin bubbled with oxygen through a pediatric mask, too tired to resist. His head began to loll, and he slept deeply. The ambulance arrived soon afterward to take them both to the hospital so he could be stabilized overnight.

The room was quiet after they had left. My stethoscope lay on top of tattered envelopes with notes spilling out. Blood forms were jumbled together and a wooden tongue depressor was on the floor. The beige surface of the tea was ringed with a milky white circle. I did all the end-of-office things, tidied notes, and recorded letters on the dictaphone to the pediatrician and social workers. No visits. Jo left for home, her good-byes echoing in the empty waiting room. I made a list of things to do in the morning and stuck it on the black face of the computer.

The street was empty. Orange lights shimmered in the oily puddles. The pine furniture shop was shuttered, and faint noises and shouting laughter came from the pub. My old Peugeot was alone in the parking lot; with my back to the dark space behind me, I fumbled for the keys, fear briefly prickling in my mouth. Once inside, my other life was instantly present in the smell of dog, mud, and wet suits; it reminded me of the fullness of our lives. What we had was hard won, but most of the time I knew we were lucky. There was a tattered sheet of math homework on the floor and a pair of sneakers stuffed under the front seat. I found a jelly candy in a crumpled cellophane bag jammed into the side pocket. It tasted sugary and sharp. I turned on the ignition and eased the car forward.

Chapter 4

DORSET, 2010
ONE YEAR LATER

In the fields near the cottage the dense scent of earth, sharply cut with grass, brings the memory of children playing late in a darkening garden, or is it the smell of funerals? Naomi's face floats in the gray space in front of me, her cheeks shadowy as if in a box. Quick, think of the sea, whose sound is following us. But the distant suck and splash become a heartbeat. At six weeks she was all heart. I'd sneaked an early scan but the translucent throbbing muscle on the screen had made me tense even then. How could it not get exhausted? Later, checking some childhood cough, my ear pressed against her perfect skin, I had heard that fast bird-beat. Was it conceivable that she realized at the end, if there had been an end, that her heart was slowing? Is there enough blood in a dying brain to register that the heart has stopped? My feet catch against the jutting root of a tree and my head hits hard against the roughened trunk. I'd forgotten the shock of physical pain; chili in the elephant's eye.

I used to keep a supply of bandages in the linen closet. The dusty shelves are full of old blankets but at the back my fingers close over the little cloth bag. Once she fell off the garden wall, tearing her scalp. When I brushed her silky hair at five, I could see the tiny scar.

Was she hit on the head? Scalp wounds can be fatal so quickly. I thought I was done with this torture, but this is a bad day when thoughts slide along memories, sharpening them like knives.

I quickly clean the cut, pat it dry, and pull the edges together with Steri-Strips. As I finish, Bertie noses into my leg, whining softly. I've forgotten to feed him, and the steadying little ritual of opening the tin, spooning dog food into his bowl, mixing in biscuits, restores the evening's normality. It was the same back then.

BRISTOL, 2009
SEVENTEEN DAYS BEFORE

The pile of ironing on the stove was warm under my hand, and the fat orange heads of a bunch of chrysanthemums glowed against the black outside the windows. A peppery smell of meat scented the kitchen from the casserole I had left to cook slowly while I was at work.

Bertie pushed his head against my leg and the day began to lose its grip. I fed him and took him out. As he scuffed in the blown leaves and drank from puddles, lights glowed from the windows of the houses we passed; I caught the gleaming edge of a bookcase in one, in another a table set with shining glasses. It was hard to imagine that these perfect houses had closets somewhere like the one we had at home stuffed with bits of alarm clocks, old keys, computer leads, and mugs with broken handles. As I passed the last house, someone inside closed the tall wooden shutters.

The Downs at the end of our road led to a grassy stretch above the Clifton Suspension Bridge. The steel girders had vanished in the dark and the fragile light-beaded strands looked as if they were floating. A memory glittered like the river far below; the bright sea in Corfu had shone with a million broken points of sun last summer. Swimming, I had glimpsed darkness beneath me shelving down into the depths, and terror had crawled at the edges of my scalp. If I forgot how to make the automatic movements that kept me afloat, I would sink, drifting unseen and helpless into darkness, hands grasping at emptiness. I had turned onto my back and swum to the rocks; as I sat on the rough gray surface surrounded by the rasp of cicadas and the scent of thyme, the heat had seared away the fear. Pulling Bertie after me, I began to hurry home, my feet echoing on the pavement; it wasn't possible to forget automatic movements, that was the point. Your body remembered.

THE TWINS WERE playing their guitars, sprawled on the window seat. Ed nodded briefly, his shoulders hunched, his long fingers flicking over the strings. He had grown this year, thinned out so the bones of his face were angular under the skin, his cheeks hollowed, but as I stared at him, absorbing the changes that still surprised me, his eyes looked quickly away from mine and I remembered that he had tried to call me.

"Sorry I missed your call, darling. I wanted to phone back but there was an emergency. Maybe leave a message at reception another time, or wait till I get home?"

Ed shrugged. I couldn't tell what he was thinking, but then I hadn't for a while now. I couldn't even remember when we'd last had a conversation. Naomi had been quieter too. I paused as I took my coat off. Was that what happened as children grew? A process so gradual that in the future I would never be able to pinpoint the exact moment when I became just a figure in their hinterland, watching from a distance. My eyes went to Theo; head back and eyes closed, he was strumming and singing loudly, tie half off, his art books scattered over the floor amid toast crumbs. He looked up suddenly and grinned, his wide mouth splitting his freckled face. I wanted to hug him. Theo at least was still Theo, jokey, uncomplicated, and happy. Ed was watching, so I smiled at both of them. They had always been different, though they'd had exactly the same love and attention. Perhaps it proved the point that character is predetermined. I liked that explanation; it let me off the hook.

Four ounces of butter and four ounces of sugar, soft drift of flour, brilliant yellow egg yolks. Sharp white apple flesh cut into the baking pan, batter poured on top, into the oven. Another kind of automatic; colored in and scented.

The back door crashed open.

"Hey, doggie." Naomi in a belted black coat bent over Bertie. "Did you miss me, then?" Her fair hair fell forward in a shining sheet onto his nose, and he sneezed noisily. She looked up, but her smile faded when she saw me by the stove and she didn't return mine. Her voice was sharp.

"I know what you're going to say, but don't bother. I'll do homework backstage. I can't miss rehearsals. Going to change."

"I wasn't going to say anything about homework." I was stung. "But if you've got lots . . ."

She turned silently and then she was climbing upstairs with dragging footsteps. A distant door slammed. She used to race up those stairs. She was tired. I sliced the tops off beans; they were still her favorite, tossed in butter with a sprinkling of roasted almonds. Tired and edgy. The play rehearsals were relentless on top of the standardized tests. The boys gathered books, drifted to the stairs, talking. Theo quietly mocking Ed, something about girls, low-voiced so I wouldn't hear.

Peace then. The safe feeling of children home and doors shut against the night. I drained the potatoes and beat them into soft clouds, made Naomi sandwiches to keep her going, and prepared a thermos of hot chocolate. I'd save her some supper. Jade Price's image hovered in the warm kitchen for a moment; she'd looked so thin this afternoon. I wondered whether anyone would be giving her supper.

The back doorbell rang: Naomi's friends collecting her on the way to rehearsal. She came back through the kitchen, and then disappeared amid a welter of young voices.

Upstairs, the front door opened. Car keys rattled onto a table, quick footsteps came down the stairs into the kitchen.

"You smell of hospitals," I murmured, my cheek against Ted's rough cold one. The sharp tang of disinfectant always clung to him when he first came home, layered under the faintest scent of lavender from the operating room scrub. I wanted to stay close, but he drew back and smiled, looking over my shoulder.

"Hey, that looks good."

He leaned past me to break off a fragment of warm cake, and then bent to pull a wine bottle off the rack. He poured two glasses and held one out.

"How was your day?" he asked.

There was a shine of excitement on him, so I didn't tell him about the bruised child, Naomi's irritation, or that I had remembered how it felt to be in the sea, out of my depth.

"Fine," I said. "What about yours?"

"Fantastic. The child's completely better. Lots of international interest, the press has been phoning the hospital all day."

He started pacing, unable to keep still, running his fingers through his hair so it stuck up in blond clumps. As I watched him, the thermos on the table caught my eye, left behind with the neat little packet of sandwiches.

"She's stopped screaming. No more hallucinations." He looked at me, blue eyes shining. "An operation to cure psychotic symptoms—it's a groundbreaker."

At supper Theo's freckled face and Ed's darker one lifted, dipped and lifted, eating, looking up at Ted. He took us through the tense moments of delicate probing to destroy disordered cells deep in the brain. The child had presented classic symptoms of psychosis with paranoid delusions. On the ward she had thrown scalding water on other children and bitten nurses. Today, after the operation, she was drawing flowers.

The phone rang, the *Daily Mail* wanted to know about this new miracle cure. Ted took the phone upstairs to talk.

Theo pretended to drill Ed's head with the blunt end of a fork. "I'm going to cure you, once and for all."

Before Ed could escape, Theo had pushed him off the chair and wrestled him to the ground, shouting, "The voices in my head are telling me to kill you."

"If you go away now and do your homework, I'll let you off the washing-up." That kind of deal usually worked. "Theo, have you shown Dad your art project yet?"

"Which one?"

" 'Man's Place in Nature.' He's bound to see it in the exhibition."

"I can't, he'll kill me."

"Darling, just get it over with."

Once they had gone, the kitchen felt drained of noise. I began to gather the smeared plates. Ed had left most of his supper. Too much toast. I was still there when Naomi came slowly through the door, an hour later than I thought she would.

"How did it go?" I asked, looking at the dark shadows under her eyes.

"Fine." A smile hovered. I waited for a little story about someone joking around; maybe the director was pleased with her singing or the way she said her lines. I watched her pull off her coat, pour herself a glass of milk, and lean against the stove to drink it.

She seemed to be somewhere very far away; she looked sideways at me, not fully meeting my gaze.

As she headed toward the stairs, I couldn't help myself: "So what happened?"

"Stuff. I'm tired."

Once she would have followed me around, a flow of talk, questions, doubts, jokes. I would have had to tell her I needed space to sort e-mails, but she would have followed me to my desk, sat on the arm of the sofa, carried on talking. That seemed a long time ago.

Now, as she brushed past me, there was the faintest scent of something acrid. Tobacco.

"Naomi?"

She turned impatiently.

"You haven't been smoking, have you?"

Her blue gaze seemed clearer than usual. She shook her head. "Izzy was smoking in the changing room afterward. She was upset because Mrs. Mears kept going on at her about her lines, so . . ." Naomi shrugged. "Where's Dad?"

I stared at her for a moment. I didn't believe her, but I would know if she was habitually smoking: her clothes would smell of tobacco. She would be coughing. One cigarette really wasn't a big deal. I let it pass.

"The great neurosurgeon is in his study, fielding the world's press," I replied.

She started going up the stairs.

"Aren't you hungry, sweetie? You forgot—"

But she'd disappeared into the shadows at the top of the stairs.

Chapter 5

DORSET, 2010
ONE YEAR LATER

I forget when I last touched anyone or was touched. I kissed Naomi's hand in the kitchen a year ago. The warmth of Theo's rough hug last Christmas has long faded. I see Ed every month but he avoids the slightest brush against me. Ted and I shared a bed till I left, but we lay apart, facing away from each other. In the nursing homes I used to visit on my rounds, the residents sat beached at the rim of a room, old hands reaching for mine, greedy for contact; now I've turned it around. Not touching has become a scrupulous act. I take care to avoid the accidental touch of fingers in the shop as the man gives me my change. If someone comes to the door, I step back. So when I see the old lady lying across the steps of her bungalow as I come back up the lane one afternoon, I am surprised how automatic it is to reach out to her. Her skin is pale but her pulse is full and regular, my hand on her chest lifts and falls. Beneath her eyelids the pupils are equal in size. She looks so peaceful that I hesitate, wondering how to rouse her without startling her. I know that jolt into reality, though sometimes I was glad of it.

BRISTOL, 2009
SIXTEEN DAYS BEFORE

I woke with a sudden start. In my dreams I had been tumbling through space full of harsh voices, and the relentless fall of water. There had been tapping, coming closer; Jade was crying somewhere. The relief of morning seeped into me gradually. The crying became the call of gulls, blown inland by the wind. There was a magpie outside our window, chattering as he swayed in the empty lime tree branches; the twiggy ends were tapping against the window. Somewhere in the house above me, Naomi must have been having her morning shower. The water would be falling around her in a shining column.

I curled my feet around Ted's and watched him as he drifted lighter in sleep. His cheeks were looser than they used to be; the light picked out gray flecks in the blond where the hair feathered into his neck. I moved closer, shaping myself around him. Our bodies felt warm and safe together. The frightening dream melted away.

We'd planted two lime trees close together eighteen years ago, when we knew I was pregnant with twins. We had a competition to see whose grew the fastest, but in the end they had twisted together into one huge trunk. Even the branches were entwined. In the summer the morning light in our room was stained green, but at this time of year twigs filled the space with black crossing lines.

Ted made a content waking sound. He always woke happy. His hand felt hot on my shoulder and moved slowly down my arm, then to my back, pulling me close in. Our faces touched, his mouth on my cheek.

The radio switched itself on, cued to start at seven. Tuesday, the third of November, the voice told me. I had to get up now. I needed to catch the pediatrician, and I was on call. Regret and guilt slipped around me like a familiar coat.

"Sorry." I kicked back the duvet. "Sorry. Sorry."

"I'll put the kettle on." His footsteps went slowly down the stairs; his voice came back up sounding distant.

The bright hot water around me in the bath was soothing. No harm done, I thought, as I watched Ted's calm face while he cleaned his teeth. I sipped the dark coffee he had brought me. It doesn't matter.

We talked through our day to come: my visit to Jade Price, Ted's clinic, and the lecture he would give after that for the students. He paced onto the landing and back as he dried after his shower, thinking, talking. Suddenly he caught sight of the posters for Theo's art project stacked outside his bedroom door ready for laminating at school. He stopped abruptly, and crouching down began to leaf through. So Theo hadn't shown them to him last night; he was keeping his head down. They were a series of Naomi in the autumn woods in the Brecon Beacons, taken on different Sundays in October. Each time the trees lost more leaves, Naomi had taken more clothes off. At first just her gloves, then her shoes, her coat, and her sweater. Ted whistled in admiration at

the way Theo had captured the shapes and colors of au-
tumn, and Naomi's pale face glowing against the trees.
He grew quieter as he worked his way down the series.
In the end, Naomi was naked; caught within twigs. Her
eyes stared out, darkly challenging the viewer. I sensed
Ted's dismay in his silence.

"Sweetheart"—I stood behind him, wrapped in a
towel, my feet puddling the wood—"I know what you're
thinking . . ."

"You don't know what I'm thinking," he said quietly.

"It's a metaphor. If we open ourselves to the natural
world, shed our sophisticated layers, it will protect us in
turn. I know Theo—"

"Stop saying you know everyone. You don't." His
voice got louder. "It's got bugger all to do with the natural world. He's exploiting her, making a series of risqué
photos to get attention. She's too young to see that, but
surely you can."

"Ted, it's art."

"I can't believe you'd use that clichéd excuse for pornography."

"It's not pornography." My voice was rising too. "She
was wearing underpants, for God's sake; she kept her
coat on until she was hidden. Nikita was there. Naomi
threw her clothes out to her as she undressed." I paused
for breath. How could he think Theo would exploit her?
He and Naomi had always been the closest of the three
children, even when they were little.

"You're missing the point again," he said curtly.

I stepped back from the fight. There was no time.

"Let's talk about it tonight, with Theo."

"Nothing more to say." He shrugged.

Time had run out. Arguments were often left unfinished and seemed to disappear, untended bonfires burning out, leaving only a pile of ashes behind. Ted, with clothes on, was harder, surer, walked quicker. He gave me a kiss that missed my mouth, his eyes somewhere else. The door shut behind him.

Naomi appeared as I was gathering my bags. She still looked tired, despite the night's sleep, and moved around the kitchen slowly, finding folders, scarf, and hockey boots. She seemed absorbed in the day to come and didn't look at me when I suggested breakfast.

"Not hungry," she said briefly, knotting her scarf as she watched herself in the little mirror on the wall by the phone.

"Have something, darling. Toast? An egg?"

She wrinkled her nose in disgust without replying, and then bent to the dog.

"Love you, Bertie."

She kissed the air above his head and left; the door slammed. She came back for her cell phone and left again.

The boys appeared, sleepy and silent. Ed looked disheveled, with unknotted tie and half-combed hair. He poured muesli and ate it slowly, reading the side of the packet with concentration. Theo leaned against the fridge door eating the rest of the apple cake, his eyes closed. Then they left, bumping shoulders as they went out the door together, both carrying Theo's art folder, shoulders hunched.

It was time for me to leave. I followed them but turned at the door, sucked back by the warm disorder. Teeth marks in the buttered rind of toast, a glittery pool of spilled sugar, bent packets, open jars. I wanted to stay, shut the mess into cupboards, and restore order to the surfaces. My mother, as her younger self, seemed to be watching from the shadows behind the hanging coats in the hallway, so close I could feel her breath behind my neck, her chin on my shoulder. She was telling me to stay, tidy up, and keep watch as she had done. I quickly pulled the stacks of shoes apart until I found the new red ones with heels. I put them on, becoming the professional, the doctor, and I slammed the door shut behind me.

Outside I met Anya being dropped off by her husband. Under her coat was the patterned apron she wore to clean our house. She always worked calmly, her gentle hands honoring each task. No matter how hard I tried, I ended up pushing at things angrily, running from one unfinished job to the next. She and her husband came from Poland. Whenever I saw him, he scowled at me. I wanted to tell him that Anya made my life possible, but that would have made him angrier, as if my life was more valuable than hers. His hostile glance flickered over my warm coat, the leather bag, the tall house behind me.

As I unlocked the car, I waved to Mrs. Moore opposite; she was putting out her small items for recycling. Ted had left ours on the sidewalk last night: the rinsed bottles of Shiraz, the exotic cardboard sleeves from ready meals, copies of *The Telegraph* folded neatly edge to edge. Mrs. Moore straightened up, her hand in the small of her back. She looked toward me and her old mouth cracked open briefly. I could just see the soft shape of her son, Harold, as he bobbed uncertainly at the bay window. He was about thirty, with Down's syndrome. Her husband had left years before. I wondered, as I did whenever I saw her, what kept her going day after day. She was still staring at me as I started the engine and pushed the knob of the radio, and it came to me unexpectedly that it could be the other way around. Perhaps I needn't feel guilty about how much more I seemed to have than she did; she watched me rush in and out, she would know how late Ted came home from work every day. She might even feel sorry for me.

THE MORNING SLID away quickly. Three women, one after the other, derailed by the mess of ordinary biology: periods, pregnancy, menopause. As I listened and examined, I wanted to tell them that this was normal life, not illness. In other cultures there might be celebrations; perhaps I was the celebrant here, providing recognition of these rites of passage. The last patient, though, Mr. Potter, was really ill. Aged ninety, he had polished his shoes, walked down the hill, and waited his turn to tell me he had left-sided central crushing chest pain. I looked at his sweaty face, at the smile he was attempting that trembled on his lips. There wasn't much time.

"Sorry, Doctor, I didn't know. I thought it was indigestion. I didn't want to bother you." He spoke with difficulty. Gasping for breath. "Who will feed my cat?"

He used the phone to speak to his neighbors while I organized his admission to coronary care. He was changing worlds: Behind him was his tiny clean council flat, the faded wedding photos on the brick mantelpiece, the flare of the gas fire with the empty chair opposite his, and the warm presence of a little cat. Ahead of him was a world of high bright lights, tubes, and bleeping monitors; the staff around the desk would be too far away, or too close, breathing into his face, or talking to him as if he were a deaf child. I wanted to tell him to wear his war medals.

FRANK SAT BEHIND a leather-topped antique desk, making phone calls. He lifted his eyebrows, smiled, and nodded at the chair. There were two mugs of coffee on the desk in front of him, the fragrance filling the room. I sat down.

He put the phone down and sighed, wrapping large hands around one of the mugs. His glasses were askew; no bit of desk was visible beneath the rubble of instruments, pens, and forms.

There had been a bureaucratic screwup by the Primary Care Trust; appraisals were changing again. The coffee warmed me and I began to relax. We talked about the morning.

"I've referred Jade Price to the community pediatrician. Possible child abuse. I didn't tell the mother I would at the time, so I'm going round to the house later today."

Frank listened to the story, eyes wary.

"I know the Prices. Be careful, Jenny, and look from all angles. They don't strike me as abusive."

"There aren't that many angles," I said, remembering the bruises and Jade's exhausted stillness. "The family profile fits. Her father's an alcoholic bully. Her mother's depressed."

"Why go round? You could simply phone."

"It will be difficult to tell her I suspect the family of child abuse. I can pick my moment better face-to-face."

I paused as another thought occurred to me. "There might be more clues at the house as well."

"Do you want me to come with you?"

"What? Why?"

"They could run rings round you, or get nasty. You seem a bit . . . preoccupied. I mean, not just about this. Something's ruffling the feathers."

Frank hadn't been a family doctor for thirty years for nothing.

"Oh, you know. Family stuff."

"Ted okay?"

"Fine, mostly. In fact, his star is in the ascendant," I said, remembering the glimmer last night, the excitement that had shone from him.

"Kids? My favorite godchild?"

"Naomi's changed. Quieter, I think. Can't quite put my finger on it." As I said this, a pulse of worry thumped in my head. What was I missing?

"Up to something, I expect." He grinned. "Fifteen-year-old girls spend their lives up to something."

"She usually tells me." Not lately, though, not for weeks. Months, even.

"Knowing Naomi, she will, in her own time. What does Ted say?"

"Hasn't. Well, I didn't run it by him—too much happening." I smiled ruefully. "We always run out of time. One of us goes to sleep."

"God knows how you do it all. I've only got one and Cathy's at home all the time."

I didn't like it when people said that. As if I must be cheating. There was no magic. It wasn't even difficult. I just had to keep going, and I knew exactly how to do that. Sometimes it felt as though I was escaping from one life to another and back again. I wasn't sure exactly what I was escaping from each time, but it seemed to work; I told my friends it gave me a built-in excuse if something went wrong. Over time I'd realized that if it meant I had to leave the children to sort themselves out, they usually did. Now I had only myself to blame if Naomi was learning to be independent. I'd wait until her guard was down and she was ready to talk. I'd overlook the cigarette, then once she'd told me what the matter was, I would help.

If I was asked, I would say she was happy, that Ted and I were as well. I would say we were all perfectly happy.

THE PRICES' HOUSE was on a road near the docks, a mile or so from the practice. The area near the river had been reconstructed; the old warehouses were now brick-and-glass offices and a gym. But the glamorous architecture didn't go deep. The Prices lived a couple of streets back. I parked the car and walked, looking for number 14. One or two windows had broken glass patched up with cardboard; in a front garden there was a television set leaning into the mud. None of the doors seemed to have numbers. I stopped near a group of boys who were standing around a motorbike, the sleek machine at odds with the street. The boys were thin, shoulders up against the bitter wind. One of them sucked at a can, tilting it high, carelessly, so the fluid fell on his face. A yellowing sheet of newspaper blew against my legs. I pulled it off and let it go, watching as it flapped against the lamppost. I went closer to the group.

"Hi. I'm looking for number 14?"

The tallest boy jerked his head up.

"Jeff Price? What for?"

A smaller boy stepped forward, shifting his weight from side to side, a hand-rolled cigarette gripped in his teeth, bare white arms tightly folded. He jerked his head silently at a house with a yellow door.

"Thanks for your help." I smiled quickly at them all.

"Up herself, isn't she?" someone said as I turned away, and one of them threw his can into the road.

There were rows of bottles outside the yellow door, some had fallen over. My feet tapped a pile on the step sending them crashing to the path and a small wave of laughter hit against my back.

The door was slightly ajar, and the smell of urine and beer reached outside. The bell didn't work, so I knocked; there was no answer. I pushed the door wider, stepped inside the narrow, dark hall and called, "Hello? Mrs. Price? It's the doctor, from yesterday."

"Who's this, then?"

A huge man emerged from the darkness down the narrow hall. His stained dressing gown fell open, revealing a mat of graying chest hair. As he came barreling down the corridor toward me, my hands tightened on my bag.

"The doctor. I'm . . . the doctor."

"Oh yeah? What might you be after?"

"Your wife brought Jade to see me yesterday."

The change was sudden and complete. His mouth opened in a wide smile and his eyes widened.

"Bless you, love. I'm dead worried about her and all. Come in, meet Mother."

I would tell him soon. After I had met his mother I would warn him I was worried about his daughter being abused, though I might not use that word. I would tell him that I had referred her, for safety's sake. He gestured me down the hall and through a narrow door at the end. "Say hello to the doctor, Ma. She's come about our Jadie."

The smell of ammonia made my eyes water. An old lady sat close to the fire where a thin bar of red glowed. An ancient parrot of a woman, with eyes sunk in folds of dry skin and thin claws gripping the arms of the chair. Her limbs writhed and her cheeks bulged rhythmically in constant chewing. Under her seat the carpet looked dark and wet.

"She can't help it. I'll make us a nice cup of tea. Make yourself comfy, love."

I looked for somewhere to sit but every surface was crowded: blister packs of medication, balls of tissues rolled up together with dark green deposits gummed in the creases. Plastic toys littered the floor and were shoved under the television. There was a child's painting of a house stuck to the wall. The heat and the smell were intense. I went into the hall and listened. I could hear the kettle whistling, rattling crockery, the sound of something smashing and curses from Mr. Price. I looked up the narrow stairs that twisted into darkness. I was listening for a child, but I didn't have time to hear anything.

"Looking for me, love?" Mr. Price appeared, steaming mugs in each hand. He followed me back into the sitting room, his hard stomach pushing me ahead. "Here we are, Ma."

He balanced a mug for me on a pile of newspapers, blew noisily into another, then tilted his mother's chin and spooned tea into her mouth; brown dribbles ran down her chin and onto her pink nylon nightdress. Next to her chair there was a family photo; from where I was sitting, I could make out the small shape of a child dwarfed by her parents on either side.

"About Jade . . ."

"Yeah?"

"I'm worried about . . . her bruises."

"Tracey told me. This cough. She feels hot sometimes. You know, properly sweaty. And she's off her food, getting thinner. All the bruises."

"I wondered how she got them." I watched him intently as I said this.

"That's just it. We haven't got a clue. Not a dicky bird."

"That's part of the reason I want to send her to the hospital for a checkup—the bruises."

"Hospital. Fuck me. You think it's serious, then?" His forehead wrinkled, he sounded genuinely worried, and I saw what Frank meant. This man could run rings around me.

"Anything we don't understand is important." I kept my voice level. "I want her checked out by a pediatrician."

"Oh yeah? And who's that when he's at home?"

"A children's doctor. Someone to look into the problems that happen when children have injuries we don't understand. Like Jade. To be honest, we are worried in case she's been hurt by someone."

"Those bloody little blighters at school."

I'd tried. I'd tried hard enough. If I forced a confrontation, he might take her and vanish.

"They'll send her an appointment or they may call if they see a space coming up in the next day or two. Could even be this afternoon."

"Thanks, Doc." His face creased in a smile that looked convincing. "I'll tell the wife."

I stood up, ignoring the tea. His mother jerked and writhed silently in her seat.

"It's okay, she's going." Mr. Price leaned toward his mother, shouting in her ear. "Say good-bye to the doctor."

The parrot eyes flicked in my direction. She knew. You couldn't live in a house with a child who was being hurt and not know. She probably guessed exactly why I was here.

The gang of boys was still there. One of them held a bag to his face; another was lolling against the lamppost, swaying slightly, eyes closed. Two were squatting, heads low, hands dangling. They didn't see me pass. The narrow street was darker, the strip of sky looked gray green, and it had begun to rain lightly. I checked my watch as I hurried: four P.M. Theo would be in the art studio, arranging his photos for the exhibition. Ed would be rowing for school team practice, serious-eyed, muscles straining. They were about the same age as this group of boys. But I didn't feel lucky, I felt afraid.

It was cold in the car, and I turned the heater and the radio on. The local news was being read. Rapist attacks inner Bristol. Flooding. Chocolate factory closing down.

Suddenly I wanted to speak to Ted; I wanted to hear his voice. I turned the radio off, pulled out my cell, and tapped his number. His voice told me he was unavailable, to leave a message after the tone. This was different from the last answering message, one he had recorded at home when there had been a faint backwash of music, a pan crashing, and children's voices. This was just his voice, clear and confident. He sounded very sure of himself and very far away.

Chapter 6

DORSET, 2010
ONE YEAR LATER

I enclose the old lady's thin wrist with my fingers. Hers is an image I have gathered in without knowing, like a tree by the road that I often drive past. She has until now been no more than a bent shape in a bulky coat. I'd known she was old by her stiff, dipping gait. Sometimes, in the long slow hours of night, I'd look out of my window and see a comforting point of light from her bedroom window. Now she is lying at an awkward angle: her neck is wedged against the doorpost, her arms have fallen across her body, hands bunched.

"Hello? Can you hear me?"

No answer.

"Does it hurt anywhere?"

Nothing.

"I'm going to lift you up, hold on."

I slide one arm under her shoulders and the other

under her splayed knees. Close up, her white skin is finely wrinkled; there are brown blotches on her cheeks. Her thin lips are pale and her white hair drawn back so tightly the bones of her forehead are outlined. She has the look of a sleeping cat and she weighs no more than a little girl. As I push her door wider open with my shoulders, I am back to doing what I used to do every day, when looking after people was a routine part of life.

BRISTOL, 2009
FIFTEEN TO TEN DAYS BEFORE

The days passed quickly. Ordinary days.

Were they ordinary? It seemed so at the time. In my memory they remain just that: gray-blue days of routine and little dramas. Ordinary, even though they were the last days of family life, ordinary, though it turned out that almost everyone was lying.

I worked in the practice, routine prenatal clinics and daily office patients. At home Ted and I talked, argued, made love when we weren't too exhausted. Ed had a couple of days off with a bad cold, and I left him undisturbed and sleeping on those mornings, drinks and acetaminophen on his bedside table. Theo got a commendation for his woodland photo series, and Naomi's rehearsals were more frequent and lasted longer. Ted spent more time at work. His paper was accepted by the *Lancet*. We celebrated late at night with a bottle of wine.

If the days felt ungraspable, as one slid into the next, at least life was running smoothly onward. The trick was simply to balance it all. Family. Marriage. Career. Painting. If the balance tipped in one direction and work took up more time, no one complained. It sometimes felt as if I was rehearsing for real life, so if it went wrong it didn't matter. One day I would have it all organized. I would be the perfect mother, wife, doctor, artist. It was just a question of practice. If I made mistakes, I could simply try again.

At work there was always a fresh sense of starting over. Every morning the basin was clean, new blue paper lay on the examination table, the toys tidied away into the box underneath it.

Jade was admitted to hospital on Thursday, November 5. In her letter, the pediatrician's secretary had mentioned Mr. Price. He'd thrown chairs in the waiting room and broken a window. The police were called and he'd been arrested. I had handed the load on, so I tried to put it from my mind, but I couldn't shake off the image of his face when I had told him I had come about Jade's referral. He had seemed so pleased. I decided it was simply that he knew he had been out of control and was relieved that someone was going to stop him.

The following Monday I got to the office early for the quiet space before the patients arrived. I checked the results while I was sipping my first mug of coffee, and Mrs. Blacking's liver-function tests were still on the screen when the phone rang.

"Dr. Malcolm?"

"Yes?"

I wedged the phone under my chin as I scrolled down. There were red dots by all the liver enzymes on the screen. My hunch had been right. The thin hair, red palms, and the spidery veins on her cheeks had given her away; the forgetfulness wasn't just the menopause. She hadn't told me about the bottle of sherry at the back of the cupboard, the one she probably bought with the milk from Tesco's every day. I sent an e-mail to Jo to ask her to make Mrs. Blacking an appointment.

". . . from the Children's Hospital."

"I'm sorry, I didn't quite catch—"

"Dr. Chisholm. Pediatric consultant from the Children's Hospital. You referred Jade Price."

I put the mug down and held the phone properly.

"Yes, I did. Thank you for—"

"I would like to talk about the case with you, Dr. Malcolm."

I was glad he was taking this seriously but there wasn't time now. "Perhaps I could phone you back later this morning? My office hours begin in three minutes."

"I'd prefer to talk to you in person. I'm free at one—I've canceled a meeting."

I told myself I needed him, so I had to be polite. "One today? I'll have to see if that's possible."

"Please. It would be helpful. My office is on the fifth floor of the Children's Hospital."

"I'll ask Frank, Dr. Draycott, my partner. Perhaps he can—"

"Good. See you later."

I could see this consultant very clearly. He had wings of gray hair, perfectly brushed. He'd be holding the X-rays in a large, freckled hand, looking at them through silver-rimmed glasses, nodding at the old spiral fractures, the footprint of child abuse. He wouldn't be thinking about my day, the phone calls, and the visits to hidden flats down roads where parking was impossible. He wouldn't know about the referrals, the scripts to sign, the feeling of lateness, and the struggle to fit it all in before the end of the day. He wanted to talk to me about Jade, and I knew I had to go.

AT ONE PRECISELY, I tapped the door with "Dr. Chisholm" spelled out in neat gold lettering in a little black frame. He stood up as I went in. He was thin and dark, with intense brown eyes that watched mine closely so that he caught the flicker of surprise.

"It's okay. Everyone is fooled. Sadly, I lost my Ghanaian accent at Oxford." His handshake was tight and brief. "Thank you for coming. Sit, please."

I sat down on a gray plastic chair and he took his place behind the desk. It felt like an interview somehow. I spoke quickly: "Thank you for asking me to meet you. It's a difficult situation . . ."

"Jade is ill, Dr. Malcolm."

"Yes. Her father didn't give anything away, but I think it's been going on for a while. She's obviously very depressed."

"Very ill." He looked at me without expression.

"The social workers—"

"She has leukemia." His voice cut smoothly across mine.

"Leukemia?" I was confused, or perhaps he was. He must be talking about another child.

His voice was continuing: ". . . so we are certain no one abused her. Unwashed maybe, lice and so on. Unwitting neglect from inadequate parents, though I suspect she is loved. No, she has acute lymphoblastic leukemia."

Jesus.

"Blood tests show atypical lymphocytes, blast cells. No clotting capacity. She is dangerously anemic."

How the hell had I missed that? Everything was suddenly, shatteringly, obvious. She had been passive with exhaustion, not because she was depressed but because she was anemic. The chest infection was secondary to nonfunctioning white cells. The bruises were due to poor clotting, not abuse. She had come back four times and I hadn't listened, hadn't believed her mother. A hot wave of guilt was breaking over me.

Dr. Chisholm kept pace with my thoughts and outstripped them.

"We have her on intravenous antibiotics. The MRI scan is booked for tomorrow and then we start the chemotherapy."

"Do her parents know?"

"Not yet. That's why I wanted to see you. It's a delicate situation. In the clinic I told them we needed to admit her to investigate the possibility of nonaccidental injury. They asked if that's what you had thought."

"I went to their house specially to inform them." But that was a mistake, I knew that now. I had judged them partly by their house, by the street it was on. "I tried to tell her father."

"People choose to hear what they want to." His eyes flashed before he looked away. "I have no doubt you tried your best, Dr. Malcolm, but I'm afraid they had no idea at all. Mr. Price felt accused; he was angry."

Angry? He would want to kill. He had blamed "those

bloody little blighters at school," but the suspicion had fallen on him because of me. I could see that bull-like figure hurling the chair through the window in helpless rage.

"The tests came back this morning. From here on we take over. I knew this would be a surprise, so I thought I would tell you myself. I also wondered if you wanted to inform her parents. It might be best in the long run for you to discuss the diagnosis with them at this point. Build trust."

Discuss? What was there to say? That I had made a terrible mistake because I hadn't believed what they were saying? That I had stereotyped them in the worst possible way?

His eyes looked hard into mine. I couldn't tell if he was sympathetic or contemptuous.

"What's the prognosis?"

"Between twenty percent and seventy-five percent five-year survival. We have to wait for the scan results. Jade has an unusually large number of abnormal white cells in her bloodstream, which worsens her prognosis, as you know." He was still watching me closely. "So, as her first point of contact, what do you want to do?"

I wanted to run away from the guilt that could drown me. I had referred Jade in the end but for the wrong reasons, and too late, months too late.

"I'll go and see her parents, of course." I thought for a moment and added, "I'd like to see Jade. At least I can tell them how she is."

"Follow me."

He moved smoothly from his desk, through the door, and out into the corridor. I almost had to run to keep up. She looked all right, I'd say to her parents later.

She looked better. It wouldn't be long, I'd tell them. It's lucky she's in hospital now. She was laughing—no, perhaps not laughing. She was smiling. I said . . . then she said . . . then she laughed . . .

I wasn't sure at first why we had stopped at the second bed. There was a little boy in it. Very thin, with closed eyes and spiky fair hair. He looked about six. There was a drip in the arm that lay outside the sheet. Then I saw the giraffe, dirty against the crisp white linen. Some of the bruises were green now, but there were new red and mauve ones too.

"We cut her hair to make it easier to get rid of the lice." He spoke very quietly. "But it will also help her adjust to the hair loss. We had her permission and the permission of her parents, though, as I say, they don't know the diagnosis."

I wondered how long before she would go completely bald with the chemotherapy.

Dr. Chisholm was talking softly; it was as if he'd read my thoughts. "We don't yet know what combination of drugs we will use. That will depend on the scan."

"Jade?" I whispered. "Hello, there. It's the doctor."

Dr. Chisholm looked at me. His eyes said: Doctor? The doctor?

"Jade has met lots of doctors now." He sounded dismissive. "She's asleep."

I ignored him. "Jade? I'm going to see your mum and dad now. I'll tell them—I mean, I'll give them . . ." What? What would I tell them? Was there anything to give them?

Her eyelids flickered open.

Maybe it was because she had heard my voice before or maybe it was because she heard me say Mum and

Dad, but for a second, less than a second, she looked at me and she smiled.

It was only as I turned the car on the oily concrete of the hospital underground parking garage that it came to me. Of course, she couldn't have known it was my fault or that she could have been helped so much earlier if only I had listened.

Chapter 7

I am immediately in a warm kitchen, tidy and teeming with color. I take in orange-patterned linoleum, a dark red table, yellow cabinet units with white handles, a bright blue stove, and a red sofa by the wall. A fire is glowing, a television screen flickers from the corner, several large embroidered cats crowd on a chintz-covered armchair. Bertie has followed us in; before I can stop him, he eats the small squashed pile of cat food in a bowl and then settles by the fire with a little grunting sigh. I put the old lady down on the sofa, slide off her shoes, then sit next to her. With my hand on her pulse, I scan the room quickly. There are photos on all the surfaces: an elderly man wearing a cap, digging in a garden, a dark-haired young woman with a baby, a small boy at the edge of the sea, holding another child's hand. Family everywhere. I am taken back to our kitchen at home, so steeped in family that I used to think if I pressed my ear against the wall I would hear the children's voices, stored inside. When everything began to go wrong, going home was all I could think about.

BRISTOL, 2009
TEN DAYS BEFORE

I drove away from the hospital as fast as I could, overtaking a student driver and then jumping forward at a crossroads before the lights changed. As I accelerated down Park Road, little groups of words slid and twisted away in my mind.

I thought the bruises . . . there was never long enough . . . I know you told me . . . I'm sorry.

The sun was streaming through the windows at home, lying in unfamiliar lines on the floor. I rarely returned this early. Anya left the kitchen door bolted; no one would be at home now to let me in, so I used the front door. There was a pair of sneakers on their sides, just inside. I picked them up. Ed must be here. He didn't really need to take his shoes off because we'd taken the carpets out years ago. No curtains either. The rooms were empty spaces, shiny dark wooden floors, a piano, walls of books stacked and sorted. A refectory table so Ted could spread out his papers easily.

Now my footsteps sounded hollow as I walked through the echoing rooms. Despite their ordered perfection, we hardly used them. Ted always worked in his study, the children lived in their bedrooms or the kitchen. I went down the wooden stairs to the basement kitchen and the warmth rose to meet me. I held the sneakers closely against me, too closely because later I saw they had left an uneven muddy smear across my shirt.

Ed was sitting in front of the computer in the living space that opened off the kitchen. As I walked over to see him a screen folded down into the corner and another came up, full of numbers. I was so pleased to see him I felt slightly dizzy. I sat down near him on the arm of the sofa. I wanted to kiss his cheek, which always smelled of warm toast, and rest my hand on his springy dark hair. He winced away as I approached. I had to learn new rules all the time.

"Hi, darling." I spoke to his back. "You're home early."

"Math coursework." He didn't look at me.

"Ed, I'm only saying . . ."

"Lessons canceled. There's a talk about that rapist."

"Yes?"

He kept his eyes on the screen.

"I gave it a miss. It's for the girls. How to not walk home on your own, how not to talk to strangers. Tedious."

"What did they say about the rapist? Why today?" Something else to worry about. "He's on the other side of Bristol, isn't he?"

"Christ, questions." His fist was clenched on the table. "Some teacher thought they saw a random guy lurking about the girls' boardinghouse." He looked at me quickly, eyes screwed up, hiding something. "I need to get this done. I'm way past the deadline."

"Hot chocolate?"

"Yeah, okay."

I made it quickly; as I put it in front of him, I let

my hand rest on his shoulder for a second. Close up, I was surprised that he smelled stale. I hesitated, and he glanced up, frowning.

"Thought you were normally at work," he muttered.

"Well, I am. Normally."

"Cutting?" The dark eyebrows lifted, his attention was snagged.

I was startled. " 'Course not. Are you?"

"Told you, it's just a talk for the girls. Once I've done this, I'm back on track."

"Okay. Good."

I wanted to tell him then that you can spin off track so easily, one mistake and you've lost your way.

I let myself sit close to him for a few minutes, absorbing his aura, his tall frame slouched in the chair, large feet with crumpled socks, and the smooth back of his neck. He turned to look at me again. Checking, not used to my stillness.

I started to explain. "Work things are a bit . . . I'm a bit stuck on something."

"Yeah?" Shoulders hunched, eyes wary.

"It's all right, though. I'm sorting it."

The broad shoulders relaxed. "Only, I need to finish . . ."

"Fine." I picked up the sneakers again. "These are yours, darling, they'll need a wash. And, Ed . . . don't forget to chuck your clothes in the wash sometimes as well . . ."

He took the shoes, gave a little grunt. His face moved close to the screen again. I patted his shoulder briefly and moved away.

In the kitchen I made a cup of tea and looked at the garden through the curling steam. The trunks were fused in the darkening light. I phoned Ted and this time got through. He listened.

"God. That's hard for you," he said when I paused. "Sorry, Jen."

"Don't be sorry for me, be sorry for Jade."

"I've done the same—worse. Remember what happened with that young girl's spine? Paralyzed. Terrible."

"Yes, of course. That was terrible," I agreed. That mistake had almost led to a court case; Ted's guilt had deepened into depression. For a second I felt ashamed, I hadn't thought then to give him the comfort I needed now.

"But everyone knows the risks of neurosurgery. They sign consent forms. You explain things. The Prices didn't realize there was a risk in trusting me, and I never thought about leukemia. I didn't manage to hear anything that they said . . ." I stopped, remembering how I had ignored what they had told me, allowing my thoughts to spin in a different direction.

"I'm in the middle of something, Jenny," he said quickly. "I can't talk now. I'll try to get home early. I'll get some wine."

AFTER OFFICE HOURS that evening I phoned the Prices. No one answered. Frank and I had arranged to visit them the following morning, but I decided to go now anyway. The street was empty. The windows of number 14 were dark. I knocked, waited, knocked again. I pictured Ma inside, listening, writhing in her seat in the dark. After a while I went home.

That night the boys were at a careers talk and Naomi at her play rehearsal. It was just Ted and me. We shared the bottle of wine and sat for a long time over the empty plates. Ted held my hand, and the warmth crept into my wrist.

"What shall I say to them, Ted?"

"Tell them the truth. You went on the evidence in front of you; it's all we can ever do."

"She said she didn't know about the bruises. So did he. But I didn't believe them. They both told me about the cough. That was the evidence, but I'd made up my mind already."

"We're not lawyers, Jenny. There isn't always time to weigh things up, not on a first meeting."

"It wasn't the first meeting; anyway we do behave like lawyers. We make judgments all the time."

"Judgments?"

"The Prices were guilty of being poor. Of not being able to tell me clearly, or at least in language I understood or believed. Guilty of having a bruised child. Now they're being punished."

"You have to go by instinct sometimes."

He leaned over and kissed me deeply. I tried to turn away, but his lips held me, his tongue pushing, nudging in.

He wasn't listening either. Going by instinct wasn't enough. I pulled my head away. Because of my preconceptions I hadn't referred her early enough, and then, when I eventually did, it was on the basis of the wrong diagnosis. Instinct had failed me completely.

The boys and Naomi came back. The boys ate quickly and went upstairs, catching up with work. Naomi shrugged off my questions about the rapist; the girls went about in groups, she said, and were checked in everywhere. She leaned against the table, eating spoonfuls of leftover gratin dauphinois that were stuck to the edges of the dish in front of us. She answered us between mouthfuls. The rehearsals were going brilliantly. The teachers were talking about drama school. Her expression was inward, secret. Possibilities were obviously beginning to unfurl. I watched her guarding her thoughts and decided not to push her with more questions. I was too tired anyway to focus on her answers. After a while she went upstairs.

Ted and I silently did the dishes, tidied up, and put food away. I loaded the last of the laundry. We walked upstairs, side by side, hands touching. My legs moved slowly, heavy with exhaustion. Halfway up, Ted put his arm around me, pulling me in. By the time I reached the landing my breath was coming quickly. The children had gone to sleep so we talked in whispers.

I forced myself to strip, shower, put on a new nightdress, comforted by its softness and lace. Ted came up beside me as I stood at the mirror. They say you marry someone who looks like you, but I've never seen it. Ted was tall and broad with a blue stare. I came up to his shoulders, and my Irish grandmother looked back at me with the face from the photos in our family album: dark curly hair, light eyes, freckles. Ted looked at me in the mirror and the hand on my neck tightened. His fingertips felt hot, widely splayed under the edge of my hair.

In bed we turned to each other wordlessly. I was ready for his mouth now, and I let his kiss open me further and further. His mouth tasted of wine. I knew his smell, the way his muscles felt, his shoulders, his flat belly with the hair thickening at its base, the weight of him. I knew him by heart. But tonight it was different. Tonight it was rougher and faster. Ted pushed me down hard, then the nightdress was around my neck, and he was quickly deep inside and moving and I was moving back, as if the stress of the day and the exhaustion had tipped us into a different place from where we usually were, giving us space to plunder. No preamble. Not gentle. This was biting and held wrists, open mouths and eyes wide open, straining and pushing against each other like animals. Then suddenly, shockingly, pleasure.

Then falling apart so we lay with limbs sprawled, tangled. Unmoving. Not speaking. Ted bent over me, licking tears off my face I didn't know were there. He fell asleep almost immediately afterward, breathing deeply with his face turned away on the pillow. I lay awake for a while, letting my hand rest on the dip of his back.

Sleep, when it came, was like a blanket being thrown over me. Complete. No dreams at all.

Chapter 8

DORSET, 2010
ONE YEAR LATER

She has probably fainted, but it could be anything: a heart attack, a diabetic coma, a stroke. Maybe she's had a fit or an abdominal crisis of some kind, though her face is symmetrical and her abdomen feels soft. There could be clues—medication on a table or a blood-sugar-testing kit somewhere—but the house doesn't have the neglected air of chronic illness. She stirs, her lips move, then her eyes open, puzzled rather than frightened. She looks directly at me as I explain how I found her, and I notice her eyes have the milky rings of cholesterol around the iris. I hold her hand as she slowly gathers her words. The swollen joints and fragile skin are familiar; they feel just as my mother's old hands used to. I feel a tug of guilt that I am sitting with a stranger now, but I never had time for my mother the year before she died.

BRISTOL, 2009
NINE DAYS BEFORE

I was pushing notes into my bag when the phone went.

"Hello, darling."

I was caught. Damn. "I can't be long, Mum."

"Are you working today, then?"

"Yes, you know I work every day, except for Fridays."

"It's just that dizzy thing again. Silly, isn't it? Last night I felt really poorly, so I thought—"

"Poorly? What do you mean, Mum?"

"Just poorly. I can't explain, Jennifer." The tone was accusatory, returning me to twelve years old. "Let's talk about something else." Her voice picked up: "How's Jack?"

"Jack?"

"Your husband, darling."

"Mum, Jack is Kate's ex-husband."

"Of course. Silly me. Who's your husband, then, darling?"

I can see her as clearly as if I am in the same room. She will be looking out at the empty paths around her sheltered accommodation; she sighs and touches her pearls, looking back at the television set with its bloom of dust and the neat piles of magazines. There's a smell of mothballs and Pledge. Her memory is bleeding away. I mustn't lose my temper.

"Ted. Look, Mum—"

"I don't know what to do about the cottage. Kate doesn't want it."

Not the cottage now. "I'll come and see you. We'll talk about it then."

"Tomorrow?"

"Friday. My day off."

"How lovely, darling. It's only that I feel poorly."

FRANK WAS WAITING in the parking lot at the medical office. I got in his car and was surrounded by taped chords of a violin concerto. He looked grim.

"Let's get this over with." He eased the car out of the lot.

"Sorry you have to do this, Frank." His patients had been canceled for the first part of the morning; we hadn't even had time to go through the day's results properly.

"Not like I've never made mistakes. It's you I'm worried about."

"What mistakes have you ever made?" I looked at him; his eyes were focused on the road.

"Missing the case of hyperthyroidism, so that chap went off his head."

"He was all right after he had treatment," I reminded him.

"What about the ankle fracture I thought was a twisted ankle?" He shot a quick glance at me.

"You'll have to do lots better than that."

"I'm not telling you the really bad ones. Look at the Medical Protection Society magazines. That'll make you feel better."

I did look at them, often, picking them off the top of the lurching piles in our bedroom. They made difficult reading. Children with pyrexia left unvisited, then the midnight dash to the hospital with meningitis; the altered bowel habit that was cancer, not irritable bowel;

the headache that was a brain tumor, not stress. I read them with a sinking heart.

"Makes me feel much worse."

Jeff Price opened the door and stood aside, stony-faced.

We crowded awkwardly into the narrow hall. His face was so near mine I could feel the heat from his skin. He jerked his head in the direction of the kitchen.

"Come down here. Don't want Ma to have to hear this." He led the way to the kitchen, where he stood with folded arms, waiting.

"I made a mistake," I said, my face felt hot. I had the sudden sensation that I might start crying.

"That's great, that is." It was obvious Mr. Price was not going to forgive me. "My child is taken into the hospital on suspicion of abuse, I get arrested and cautioned before they let me go, and you're telling me you made a mistake?"

I'd been taught to own up to mistakes in medical school, but now I wondered if that was the right advice. It seemed to be making everything worse. The vein that ran down one side of his forehead began to throb visibly as he spoke.

"Mr. Price," said Frank evenly, "Dr. Malcolm has come round with important things to tell you."

"I asked a hospital doctor to see her because of her bruises." I tried to keep my voice from trembling. "We didn't know—"

"I told you that I didn't know about them bruises. I told you when you came snooping around here before, when I thought you was trying to help."

"I'm sorry." The words sounded small in his kitchen.

"So? It's not going to go away just because you decide to feel guilty all of a sudden. She's still in there, isn't she? They cut her hair and all. Just for flipping lice. When can we get her?"

"Not yet. They told me yesterday when I went to the hospital . . ." I paused; this should be told gently, bit by little bit, but it was too late for that. "This is not good news, Mr. Price."

"What are you on about now? Hang on." He raised his voice. "Trace. Tracey, get down here, will you?" He stared blackly at us, and pulling a cigarette from a crumpled packet on the table, he lit it and inhaled deeply.

I sensed Frank watching closely and I fought the impulse to step behind him.

Mrs. Price came into the room in a dressing gown. She was smoking and had been crying; the mascara had run down her cheeks in black lines.

"Hello, Mrs. Price."

She looked at me with no expression.

"I'm sorry but I have some difficult news for you both."

"Difficult for who, Doctor?" Mr. Price's voice got louder. "Out with it, then, for Christ's sake."

His wife put her hand on his arm. Her fingernails looked different today, bitten to the quick.

"I'm afraid she has a disease in her blood." I paused, looking at their faces, which had suddenly become blank with disbelief. "It's called leukemia."

"That's cancer, isn't it?" Mr. Price's voice had dropped.

"Yes, it is; a kind of cancer, one that we can treat." I was nodding as I spoke, trying to project a confidence I didn't feel.

"Bleeding Christ," he whispered.

Mrs. Price sat down heavily, her eyes fixed on me.

"How do they know? Could be wrong, couldn't it? Hospitals get things wrong all the bloody time." Her voice was defiant.

"From the blood tests. They've done them twice. I'm afraid there is no doubt."

They stayed silent for a minute; I watched Mr. Price's head sink between his shoulders.

"What now?" Mrs. Price was twisting her hands, her eyes fixed on mine.

"She needs to stay in the hospital for the moment."

"Then what?" her husband asked.

"She will have some powerful drugs, which have been shown to be helpful."

"No." He spoke slowly. "I mean, will she die?"

By now I should have been able to answer questions like that, but there was never an answer, or at least not an easy one. "It's a serious diagnosis. Many children survive and go on to have normal lives. I can show you statistics—"

"Let's go to the hospital." Mrs. Price got up. "Now. I can't listen to her anymore, not with my child going to die."

"She has a good chance. We can't know yet—"

"If she dies that will be your fault." She turned her head away as she said it, as if she couldn't bear to look at me anymore.

"Dr. Malcolm made sure Jade got to the hospital." Frank spoke carefully. "She knew the bruises were serious. The tests were done immediately. That wouldn't have happened without her intervention."

I don't think the Prices even heard him.

Mr. Price looked at me. "The wife brought her to see

you four times. Four times. You could have done something and you never bothered. I'll bloody have you for this."

Although, afterward, I could never remember if that was what he actually said or if that's what I thought he said. In any case, his eyes told me exactly what he was thinking. They had looked at me with loathing.

Chapter 9

DORSET, 2010
ONE YEAR LATER

The old lady stares at me, confusion in her eyes, and then frowns as she looks around the room. "I was weeding the step . . ."

I slip my hand from under hers. I've been careful to avoid tangling with other lives, but it's beginning to feel too late: I can't leave her yet.

"I think you fainted." Her eyes turn to me as I continue. "I live opposite—I've seen you . . ."

She nods and smiles. She's seen me too, of course; she must have noticed that I've kept myself apart in the village. She probably knows about Naomi too. "I'm Mary," she says.

"I'm Jenny. Can I phone anyone?" I glance at the photos. "Your family?"

"I'll be right as rain in two minutes." She looks unhappily around her kitchen. "It's so untidy." To me it seems vibrant with life.

"Sorry I've caused you this trouble." She continues, "I'd offer you a cup of tea . . ." Her voice is uncertain.

"I'll make it."

The metal kettle sits neatly on the stove. In the fridge there are bowls covered in plastic wrap, bagged lettuce leaves, brown eggs in an enamel dish. A china milk jug with a yellow cow painted on the front. On the shelf next to the sugar is a stack of cardboard boxes: furosemide and perindopril. Medication to lower her blood pressure may have lowered it so much she fainted. I find a little brown teapot on the shelf above the tablets and two china mugs.

Drawing a stool near the sofa for the mugs, I pick up a cushion from the chair and slide it under her neck. Her skin is cool.

"Can I get you a blanket?"

She sips her tea and color edges into her pale cheeks. She nods toward a door.

"Through there, if you can be bothered, dear."

As I go through into her bedroom, I am invading deeper into her territory. She has held on to it; luckier than my mother, who had to relinquish hers. Her hovering dementia took hold after Naomi disappeared and she died without knowing who I was, though she had been all right when she gave me the cottage. Everything had still been all right then.

BRISTOL, 2009
SIX DAYS BEFORE

It was dark early morning when I drove into the front entrance court of my mother's housing complex. Little globes of light picked out identical pathways that spread like fingers to shining front doors. A lifetime that had been spent marking out and burnishing her territory had shrunk to a path and a door that were the same as everyone else's.

Her fragility surprised me each time. The blotched skin of her hands stretched thinly over deep blue veins, crêpey lids drooped over her pale eyes. Moving slowly with her walker, she led the way into the soulless little sitting room. As I massaged her lumpy feet, her talk turned quickly to the Dorset cottage. She wanted me to have it. I thought of the early family holidays there with our children, the salty swimsuits flung to dry over the stone garden walls, the sound of seagulls, the sloping bedroom walls, the ammonites my father had built into the outside walls. It was tempting, but I hesitated.

"Please, Jenny. Take it. Have it now. Kate doesn't want it. One less worry for me. I've seen my lawyer."

One more worry for me though. The children had long grown out of the cottage. They liked windsurfing in Lefkada and the little cafés in Corfu. Ted loved fishing in Wales with his friends.

WHEN I ARRIVED home, Naomi was on her way out. "Got to go now, Mum." Her face was flushed; she pushed past me in a hurry. Her dress beneath the open coat was red, low cut with glinting mother-of-pearl buttons on the bodice. It looked silky, unfamiliar.

"What's that you're wearing? Isn't it a bit low? What about food?"

"Nikita lent it to me. I'm trying it out for the play." She turned to look at me accusingly: "The fridge is empty. I'll grab something backstage." Then she was at the door, pulling it open.

"There must be something in the freezer," I said quickly. "I'll heat it up."

"Why did you go to Gran's, then, Mum?" Theo called out loudly. He was sitting at the table leafing through his portfolio and didn't look up.

"Wait a moment. Naomi, when—"

The door closed behind her.

"Cut her some slack, Ma," said Theo in a bored voice. "Dress rehearsal tonight, play in a couple of days—she's all over the place."

I put my bag down on the floor and switched the kettle on. "All over the place?"

"Yeah." He looked thoughtful. "Cross, then singing, then grumpy again. Just nerves."

Of course he was right. I made tea for both of us, then dug around in the freezer under loaves of bread and spilling packets of peas until I found some plaice fillets I'd bought months ago and a half-full bag of fried potatoes.

"So, Mum," persisted Theo. "Gran. Is she okay?"

I put the fillets on a plate and into the microwave to defrost. "She wants to give us the cottage."

"Wicked!" His face lit with pleasure; he slid off the kitchen stool. "I'll tell Ed."

"He's back?"

"Asleep. I'll get him."

The last time we had gone to the cottage, just over a year ago, they had mostly lounged inside. They went to Bridport for a film. I couldn't remember if they had even gone into the garden, and certainly not as far as the beach.

Ed came down to the kitchen, clothes rumpled, rubbing his eyes, Theo smiling beside him.

"I thought you'd outgrown the cottage," I said, puzzled.

"If it's ours we can have parties down there." Ed's voice sounded different, happier. "It would be cool. After finals—"

"Ed, it's for the family, not parties."

"I bet Gran wouldn't mind."

"I would." They were pushing too far. "It would get into a mess."

"Don't do that." Ed frowned.

"What?"

"Pretend to give something and take it away a moment later. I'm going upstairs. I've eaten already." He walked out of the room.

Theo shrugged. "Yeah, we had some pizza. Got homework."

"IT'S NORMAL THEY should want to take a few friends," Ted said much later, as we sat over supper. "Let them go. It wouldn't kill anyone to let them borrow the cottage."

At that moment Naomi walked in slowly, her eyes black with tiredness. As she passed me to stand near Ted, I smelled alcohol.

"Darling, have you been drinking?" I asked, surprised. She had never liked the taste when she'd tried it at Christmas and family parties.

She was leaning against the table, taking fried potatoes from Ted's plate, and she stared at me for a moment.

"Makeup remover. Stinks of alcohol, doesn't it?" she said, smiling, her mouth full. Her face was rounder than normal. Thank God she wasn't dieting like her friends, but I didn't like the thought that she might have been drinking, even less that she might be lying. She was shutting me out again. I didn't believe the story about makeup remover. A glass of alcohol didn't matter, but secrets might. I looked at her. She'd changed back into her uniform, her face was clean and shining; she looked like a schoolgirl again. Schoolgirl secrets were harmless I'd had lots, I couldn't even remember them now.

"What happened to that dress Nikita lent you?" I smiled at her. She needed to know she could share her secrets if she wanted to. I was on her side.

"Mrs. Mears didn't think it was right for Maria." She shrugged. "She's in charge. What's that about the cottage?"

I explained and she straightened up quickly.

"That's so what we wanted. Unbelievable."

"Who wanted?"

"We've got the weekend off before the play begins. We could go to the cottage. Just for a day. Tomorrow. Please, Mum."

"We?"

"The lot from the play, James and everyone." She paused; she was watching for my reaction. "And Nikita, of course."

"How would you get there?"

"James drives. If he borrowed his dad's car, we could all fit in."

"James?"

"He's repeating the year, one above me. He plays Chino."

"James," I repeated. I vaguely remembered a red-headed boy who had helped when Naomi was struggling with math a year ago. "Didn't he come round to help you with homework a while back?"

"He helped Nikita too." She frowned and began to bite her nails.

This was the moment. Her guard was down, and she might be ready to tell me what had been on her mind.

"You all right, darling? Any worries I can help with?" Keep it light.

Her eyes looked strained. "A break would be great. Please, Mum." She sounded close to tears.

She'd been doing too much. I knew it. Emotional; a little down. Of course she could have the cottage. It would cheer her up. They wouldn't damage anything in a day.

Chapter 10

DORSET, 2010
ONE YEAR LATER

The colors in Mary's bedroom are warm: terra-cotta walls, pink circles on the carpet, and a bright blue mohair blanket neatly folded at the bottom of her bed. I pick it up and hold it against my face. A tabby kitten is sleeping on the quilt in a small patch of sun; its delicately patterned sides rise and fall minutely. Through the window there are two dug vegetable patches and brown hens are pecking the ground in a chicken-wire enclosure. As I look, the sun vanishes. A gray cloud has pulled itself across the sky and the edge hiding the sun is thickly outlined with glowing orange. The blanket feels very soft. As I stand there for a moment, the peace in this room is so palpable that I want to lie on the bed next to the kitten and close my eyes. I haven't sensed peace like this for as long as I can remember. Way back last year maybe, one Saturday in Bristol. Probably the last time Ted and I were together and happy.

BRISTOL, 2009
FIVE DAYS BEFORE

Saturday felt like a holiday. Ted was home. I phoned the hospital in the morning. Jade was stable following her first episode of chemotherapy. I said I would visit after the weekend. I didn't know what I would do or say, but it was a start. Ted and I went to the City Art Gallery, then we had lunch in a pub, reading newspapers side by side. We hadn't done anything like that for a long time; even simple things got edited out by Ted's work. He often, more often lately, spent Saturdays catching up at the hospital. But he seemed absorbed by the pictures in the gallery and though the hospital called him a couple of times, and though we were in the midst of jostling crowds, it felt as if we had escaped.

The house was quiet when we came home. On a whim, I borrowed a 3B pencil of Theo's and some of his paper. I began to sketch a picture of Ted as he sat reading through an article that he was writing for the *British Journal of Neurosurgery*. He had his finger to his right eyebrow and was stroking it back and forth as he read. I drew that too. The pencil ran over the white grainy paper, the gravelly friction leaving a thick trail of gray. He looked at me from time to time and smiled. A deep sense of peace unfolded around us. It occurred to me then that this was how it could be one day, when we had done with work and the children had their own lives.

When the door opened quietly, I thought it was the wind and I got up slowly to shut it, unwilling to break the spell. I was surprised to see Naomi was just inside, standing completely still. There was a look on her face that was new. She was intensely preoccupied, looking downward, and her lips were moving. I couldn't tell if she was smiling; I thought for a moment she was counting or perhaps trying to remember something.

"Naomi! You gave me a fright, sweetheart. You're home early."

"James had to get the car back."

She didn't look at me, but took her coat off and hung it up.

"How was it?"

"Great."

"So what did it look like?"

"You know, just the cottage."

She sounded tired.

"What about the garden?"

"The garden?"

"Was it covered in weeds?"

I hated to think how neglected the garden must look. When she was little, Naomi had loved digging and planting, then discovering what had happened while she had been away between holidays. We hadn't tended to it properly for years now.

"Didn't notice." She shrugged.

I felt a flash of disappointment. "Did it smell okay in the kitchen?"

"Smell? How is it supposed to smell?" She looked blank.

As a child, she used to run in first and inhale deeply. She said that even the cupboards smelled of the cottage:

a grassy, salty smell mixed with the faint scent of polish. "What about upstairs?"

She looked over my head, to where Ted had come to stand behind me.

"Hello, lovely girl. Hungry?" He looked at her, smiling fondly.

She shook her head. "I'm meeting Nikita. I'll go and—"

"She didn't go with you, then?" I felt confused.

"Yes, she did," Naomi said quickly. "We didn't get much chance to talk, though . . ." She began to bite her nails.

Ted gave her a hug. "You had a good time and your friends enjoyed it, right?"

She nodded and pulled away quickly. "I need a shower."

Her voice shook. She was tired, so tired as to be tearful, and I moved toward her. She turned abruptly and as she leaned to pat Bertie, who was pushing against her legs, the light caught a gleam of silver on the index finger of her right hand. I tried again.

"New ring?"

"James gave it to me. It's a friendship ring," she replied swiftly.

"Pretty. So does that mean . . . ?" I reached to touch the ring.

She snatched her hand away. "He gave one to all the girls in the play; he found them in a box with the costumes."

"Aha. He stole them, then?"

I had meant it as a joke, but she rolled her eyes impatiently. Before she could answer, the door banged open. The boys almost fell in. They were out of breath, their faces red and sweaty. They were wearing shorts and muddy running shoes, which they kicked off at the door.

"God, you're filthy." Ted sounded amused.

Theo looked triumphant. His fringe was sticking to his forehead; there were beads of sweat on his cheeks and a smear of mud across his chin. "I won."

Ed was white-faced. He bent over, struggling for breath. "You cheated," he gasped.

Naomi ran for the stairs. "I'm having a shower before you both use all the hot water."

"What's the matter with her?" Theo asked. "She looks perfectly clean."

"Compared to you." Ted looked at Ed's legs, streaked with separate lines of dried mud.

"Hey, not bad." Theo was bending over the table where I had left the sketch of Ted.

"Get off. You're dropping muddy sweat all over it." I pushed him away.

Ted put his arm around Ed, oblivious of the mud.

"The nurses on the neurosurgical ward asked me yesterday when you were coming back for more work experience. Think they liked you. I wondered . . ."

Ed looked away. "Thanks, but my university application form is in now."

The boys went upstairs slowly, not talking.

"What's happened to Ed? He's very grumpy and he usually comes in first by a long way," Ted said.

"God, Ted." It struck me with force that if he left work earlier sometimes he might understand how busy the boys' lives were. "Science exams. Coursework. Rowing. He's exhausted."

"Naomi sounded pretty fed up as well." He nodded toward the stairs where she had disappeared.

"She's tired too," I said lightly. Ted always told me I was too neurotic about Naomi. "A bit emotional, maybe. The play's taking it out of her. Plus she's growing up, so naturally she's more"—I searched for the word that would encompass the little changes I'd noticed—" 'preoccupied.' " I picked up the unfinished sketch, smiling to show I wasn't worried. "Hormones kicking in. Exams in sight. Underneath, she's the same as she always was."

Ted laughed. "That's lucky, because for a moment there I thought she minded all the questions."

I stared at him. "What do you mean, all the questions? I'm interested in what she's been doing. How else am I supposed to find out?"

Ted put his arm around me. "Face it. You're a control freak, sweetheart." He gave me a kiss and continued: "Perhaps if you were around more—"

"Don't be patronizing. She would hate it if I was around more." I pulled away and looked at him, my voice sounding loud in the quiet kitchen. "How can you possibly criticize me? Since when have you been around to find out how anyone was? I'm going upstairs to finish the painting of Naomi. Don't let anyone disturb me."

As I walked up the last, narrow flight of stairs, I could hear Ed calling out a question. Ted could deal with it. How dare he suggest I should be here more often, he who was never at home? My heart was thumping with fury. In the attic my easel with the unfinished portrait of Naomi stood in the middle of the little whitewashed room. As I stared at it my heart slowed, the irritation of the last hour began to fade away. Her blue eyes seemed to glitter with life; I found my brush and began to tone them down.

BRISTOL, 2009
THREE DAYS BEFORE

On Monday, the long rush of the day drew itself down to the evening. We had tickets to see *West Side Story* that night, the first performance, and again for Friday, the last night. The house was clean and tidy when I got back after work. Anya had laid the table for supper before she left, putting napkins by each plate with a little flower. Shan and Nikita were coming as well as my sister. I started to cook the meal for later. The chopping and stirring were soothing after the busy office; I watched the white onions deepening to brown, the stiff curry paste loosening in the heat, becoming orange. The blending colors reminded me of painting, mixing pigments on a palette, and I wished I had time to slip upstairs and carry on with the portrait of Naomi.

Kate arrived early, wearing a simply cut tweed dress with ankle boots. She set the champagne glasses out on a tray. My sister's hands around the long-stemmed glasses were smooth, the nails shining red and perfectly oval. Her streaked bob swung and shone.

"How's life?" I asked carefully; she had been divorced for only a few months.

"Since Jack left, you mean? Totally wonderful." Kate shot me a glance. "I get up when I want. No disgusting socks to pick up. No cooking, ever. Best of all, I don't have to wait up, wondering who he's screwing."

"Kate—"

"Don't be sorry for me. Divorce is great. Try it sometime. You look exhausted." She smiled mischievously. "Is your husband still coming in at all hours of the night?"

I glanced at her for a second. "I'd have a hard time

if I didn't trust Ted completely. He's always worked ridiculous hours. I just go to sleep when he's on call." I didn't mention the argument we'd had recently; after all, it wasn't really his fault that he wasn't home much.

"So why are you so tired? Is it Naomi?" she persisted. I shook my head, but she continued: "Don't you remember what we got up to at her age? Mum didn't have a clue."

"That was different. We were different. Mum never noticed anything anyway." I was irritated now. "Naomi works really hard; she doesn't have time to get up to anything."

Kate lifted an eyebrow. "Ah, the perfect daughter. What about the boys?"

I poured some white wine into a glass and gave it to her. "It's not the kids. I've been trying to get Naomi's portrait finished."

"Don't you ever stop?" Kate took a sip. "I think you're on a treadmill and you're frightened of what could happen if you stop."

The curry bubbled on the stove and I tasted it, adding a fraction more coconut. I didn't reply, and Kate gave a little shrug. She always tried to provoke me, but this time I let it go. Opalescent stones glowed at her ears and her makeup was perfect. I had changed from my work suit into a dark skirt with a black sweater; my tangled hair had been quickly twisted into a claw grip, and I'd found some eye shadow that I put on with a finger. These days I often cut my nails with the kitchen scissors before leaving for work. She wouldn't believe me if I told her I kept going because I wanted to. I wanted everything, despite the tiredness and the shortcuts.

As we left to walk to the theater, I saw Harold Moore watching from the window opposite. I wondered if his mother ever took him to see a play. I'd never seen him outside; perhaps she didn't want people staring. I waved to him and he moved out of sight. Kate turned to me as we waited for Ted in the foyer. "Don't take any notice of me. We get what we choose," she said. "You chose a lot more than me. It's just that it seems too much sometimes."

Later, in the theater, we sat together in one long line, Ted and me, Kate, Ed and Theo. I noticed how the light from the stage gilded all their profiles. The moment felt perfect. I was reassured. I hadn't chosen too much; it worked. Just. I felt lucky again.

As the curtain went up, my heart started to thud so loudly I thought everyone would hear. I wasn't prepared to feel so terrified for Naomi. But when she came on stage I stopped being frightened. I could hardly recognize her. Her Maria wasn't an innocent girl, she was a young seductress; there was something cruel as well as sensual about her in the scenes with Tony as she wielded her power. The audience was mesmerized. She made it seem so natural. She'd worked really hard to be this person—rehearsals had been relentless, night after night she'd come back late with dark rings under her eyes—but she had succeeded: she was Maria. Her own inspired version of Maria. No wonder she was exhausted.

At the intermission we were surrounded.

"Where did that come from?"

"What a star."

"Lovely voice."

The boys looked surprised. They fended off congratulations sheepishly. Ed was drinking wine quickly. Theo looked stunned. Ted was smiling with pride.

At the end of the second half, Naomi's Maria was lit with anger and determination. No weeping Juliet, no victim walking with bent head. To me she seemed set on vengeance.

EVERYONE APPLAUDED AS she walked into the crowded kitchen later, and she let me hug her. As I laid my cheek against hers, an unmistakable aromatic scent rose from her hot skin. Alcohol. She'd been drinking again.

I pulled back and stared at her, but her eyes were already searching the room and didn't meet mine. Just then, Theo pushed forward and gave her a hug, swinging her off the ground. Her mouth trembled, but Nikita wrapped a long silky orange scarf around her, and whispered something that made her laugh. Kate would tell me we drank like fish as teenagers. It was normal for teenagers to experiment, I told myself. But, a voice whispered in my mind, that's something else to add to the tiredness, the distance, the silences, and the scent of tobacco. As I watched her hug Nikita, I resolved that I would speak to her properly, soon, at a time when she was less tired. Meanwhile this was her night. I had to loosen up.

At supper, I walked around the table, delivering naan bread to each plate. Naomi was sitting at one end, close to Nikita, their heads touching. Bright blonde and shining dark. I paused for a moment, pleased to see them together.

"When?"

It was the awed note in Nikita's voice that caught my attention.

"Thursday. Hey, what do you want?" Naomi swung around and looked at me accusingly. "You're not allowed to listen in."

"Here's your naan, darling." I'd let it go. I had to, tonight. "Here is yours, Nik. I just caught something about Thursday."

Naomi's face became smooth. "We're all going out after the play on Thursday, to celebrate."

"Thursday? But Friday is the last night."

"Exactly. There's a party then, but some of us wanted to hang out and talk, so we thought we'd go for a meal on the second-to-last night." She looked at me questioningly.

"Sounds good to me, sweetheart. Just don't overdo it."

She was busy with performances after that and hardly at home. In the end I didn't have time to talk to her, as I had promised myself I would. Three days later she came into the kitchen with her plastic bag and her different smile. Then she vanished.

Chapter 11

DORSET, 2010
ONE YEAR LATER

Mary's hand, a little twisted claw, holds the edge of the blanket as I tuck it around her on the sofa. There is a pause. Her cheeks flush, she seems embarrassed.

I blurt out quickly: "Don't worry. I used to work as a GP so I'm used to people fainting. I saw the pills for blood pressure. Perhaps you should have a checkup?"

"Those wretched pills. More trouble than they're worth. You've been very kind, my dear."

There is another little pause. I sense the questions about me collecting, unasked.

"You're welcome." I get up and Bertie follows me to the door. "Sorry he ate all the cat food."

"That kitten is getting too fat." Her pale blue eyes sparkle. "Come back soon. I'll make the tea next time."

I say good-bye and shut her door carefully. Without meaning to, I have made a friend. And I realize that during the last hour the fear that has been shadowing me for a year moved back a little.

BRISTOL, 2009
THE NIGHT OF THE DISAPPEARANCE

After the police left we heard their car move away, the sound of the tires on the wet tarmac becoming fainter. Outside, pale gray light was edging the dark air out of the garden, and as I pushed the window open, my elbow knocked over a little stack of books on the sill. I picked up a red notebook and read "Naomi Malcolm. Chemistry," written in careful italics. Red hearts had been drawn all over it with a pen; several had been too heavily inked and were slightly smudged. I let my hand rest on the soft paper for a moment.

Ted went upstairs to sleep for an hour.

I stood in the kitchen alone and it came at me. Raw fear, fierce and sudden. I bent my head to catch my breath, as if I was battling against a wind. My hands felt as if they would burst with terror, my face hurt, my scalp crawled painfully. Tight pulses of dread traveled from the back of my mouth to my sternum; when I put my hand over that hard dagger of bone, it seemed to be throbbing. My thighs were weak. It was difficult to walk.

As the bile rose up my throat and through my nose, it came to me suddenly that this could be the moment she was dying and that was why I felt like dying.

I retched again and again, and it took all my strength to wipe the tears and vomit off my chin with toilet paper. Afterward, I closed the lavatory seat and, kneeling beside it, laid my head on my arm across the lid. In the corner, where the linoleum met the wall, I saw a triangular stain of old urine and a fragment of yellow paper from a tampon cover.

I went back into the kitchen. It was getting light. Half past seven. The boys would be up soon for school. That yellow paper could have been there for weeks, but my thoughts spiraled downward: What happens to normal cycles if the body dies? Blood would continue to leak for a while, cooling as the body temperature dropped. I checked the clock again. Eight hours had passed since she should have been home. She wasn't dead. No, she was in a highway café, her mouth around the rim of a cup of hot chocolate, or she was on the wide wet sand of an early morning beach, playing Frisbee. A cold slice of bare skin would be visible where her pants slid down each time she stretched her arms. She had decided not to phone, but I wasn't angry. I'd never be angry again. I would understand everything. I promised. I promised God I would go to church every bloody day for the rest of my life if she could be safe.

I climbed the stairs slowly. It would feel like this to be old. Every movement slow and difficult. Ted was lying asleep on the top of the bed. He had kicked his shoes off, and his jacket was over a chair. His mouth was open and he was snoring quietly. The soft rattle that often kept me awake was comforting now. It seemed so innocent. I lay down next to him. Not touching but close enough to let his warmth seep into me. Mad fragments of words hit against the lining of my skull. The insides of my eyelids were red.

Outside, birds began to sing.

Chapter 12

DORSET, 2010
ONE YEAR LATER

The wind has got up while I've been with Mary; a storm is brewing. Between the thatched roofs, the cliffs in the distance bloom emerald against a sky that has darkened to a glowing gray. I am caught, wondering how to match that intensity in paint. Even as I watch, the light drains and the sky becomes ashy, then a flash of lightning cuts the gray. As I reach my door there is a crack of thunder. Bertie whines. The rain starts, soaking us in a moment as I struggle with the lock, my wet hands slippery. I notice that the rain has made my skin look tanned and unfamiliar. Inside there is a dull thudding sound; upstairs a window has blown open and is banging against the outside wall. The crashing of the waves on shingle comes through the window. As I reach for the window's handle the wind whips my hair and blows icy rain into my face so it's hard to breathe. The raw power of the storm is terrifying but exhilarating; a different kind of fear from the cold dread that has waited for me each morning for a year.

BRISTOL, 2009
ONE DAY AFTER

I woke, immediate terror wrapping tightly around me. Next to our room I could hear Theo stumbling out of bed, walking to his shower, turning it on, singing. I knew his eyes would be almost closed. The sound of the water woke Ed in the next room, and I could hear the noisy yawns that dwindled to quiet mutterings and sighs. I looked at my watch: 8:30 A.M. I'd been asleep for less than an hour. I wished I could stretch out this time of their not knowing.

Downstairs the lights were still on. The smell of coffee made me nauseous again.

I put cereal and bowls on the table. Milk, juice, spoons. The boys came down. I waited, searching for the right tone.

"Naomi's not here."

I thought my voice sounded normal, but the boys halted in their tracks. Theo, leaning against the table and drinking orange juice from the carton, jerked it away from his mouth. Ed, pouring cereal, scooped the box up, catching the stream of oats. They waited.

"She . . . didn't come home last night. She wasn't doing what she said she would be . . ."

"So?" They both said it together.

Ed shrugged. "What's the fuss about?"

I caught at that gratefully; was that what it seemed to be, then? A fuss? A chink of hope opened.

"She had told us she was going out for a meal with the cast, but we think she met someone else instead—we don't know who yet."

"So?" said Ed, again.

Theo looked blank. "How do you know?"

"We asked Nikita."

"You made Nikita tell you Naomi's secrets?" Ed sounded incredulous.

"Ed, we waited till half past two in the morning . . ."

"Christ, so you spoke to Nikita in the middle of the night?" Ed's tone was furious. He pulled out the cutlery drawer so fiercely that knives and forks clattered out onto the floor. "Fuck." He bent to pick them up, dumping them down loudly on the counter.

"The police may come to your school today to ask questions," I told them both. "They may even talk to you."

"The police as well? She's probably sleeping it off with a friend." He looked at me angrily. "Sometimes I can't believe you."

"Did she mention anything to either of you?"

Ed shook his head briefly and walked out then, not waiting for Theo. I was shaken by his anger. I didn't understand where it came from, but it had offered me something. We were just making a fuss.

"She didn't say anything to me either." Theo's fair eyebrows were drawn together in a tight V, the tender skin in narrow parallel ridges above them. "But she hasn't been talking to me as much as she used to." His words came slowly, as though he was realizing this for the first time. "I s'pose she hasn't been here as much, the play . . ." His voice trailed off uncertainly. Then he looked at me, his voice thin with worry. "Where's Dad? Does he know?"

"What do you think, Theo? 'Course he knows." I put my arm around him. "We were up most of the night. He's still asleep."

"What's going to happen?" He sounded lost.

"Sweetheart, we're going to find her. The police are helping." I tried to sound as if I believed what I was saying, as if my head wasn't filled with screaming questions.

"The police. God. Okay." He hovered. "I'll ask people. I expect she'll just, you know, phone or text."

"Yes. Thanks, darling."

He leaned over, the soft stubble of his cheek briefly grazing my face before he left.

I DON'T KNOW how long I sat at the table. The room began to swim, the hot rims of my eyelids slowly touched together. My head must have been dipping toward the table because, when the phone rang, the noise wrenched me upright.

"Detective Constable John Harrison."

"Yes?"

"From the Criminal Investigation Department. So, Mrs. Malcolm—sorry, Dr. Malcolm."

"Yes?"

"No news at the moment. We've checked all the hospitals. Naomi hasn't been admitted, which of course is a good thing. We phoned the school and I'm going there soon to interview some of the teachers and the girls."

His voice was serious. The chink of hope closed again. He knew we weren't making a fuss.

"I'd better let them know."

"No need. We've done that. One of the team will come and see you again around midday. They will need to interview your other children as soon as possible."

"Theo and Ed?"

So they were suspects? Why the hell weren't the police scouring the countryside for a man and a frightened girl in a car? A bloke, that's what she had said to Nikita. That told us nothing; he could be tall and striking with powerful shoulders strong enough to overwhelm her. He could be the opposite, younger, smaller, ordinary-looking, maybe a kind face, so she was tricked into liking him. Could she really have gone with him on purpose, having arranged it in secret? There was hope in that thought, but I knew it was false; she wouldn't have left without telling us. Not after a lifetime of warnings about strangers and cars.

"Well, Dr. . . . Mrs. . . ." Perhaps I wasn't a fellow professional after all, perhaps I was just a mother with a missing child; he was confused.

"Jenny."

"Okay. Jenny. Just routine procedure. Pays dividends in the end."

"Routine procedure for a routine disappearance?"

Somewhere she might be whispering my name.

"I didn't mean that, Jenny. You would be surprised how many young people disappear for a while, then turn up, right as rain. In the meantime, we leave no stone unturned. Play it by the book, as it were."

There must be lists of clichés in his notebook; I wondered if they were alphabetically ordered. Perhaps he had separate entries for each occasion . . . disappearance, abduction, rape, murder.

"The thing is, Constable . . ." I stopped and breathed in slowly, like you're taught to do in prenatal classes, when the contractions come. Breathe in and count. Let it out slowly. "The thing is, I don't know how to do this waiting."

His voice changed and became more real.

"You hang on, Jenny, you hang on tight."

My eyes stung.

I went back upstairs. Ted was in exactly the same position; the creases across his shirt hadn't altered. I ran a hot bath and lay in it for a few moments, then, towel around me, phone in my hand, still wet, I crawled in under the duvet beside Ted. Blackness came instantly, as though I had been hit.

WHEN THE DOORBELL rang I fell out of bed, pulled on jeans and Ted's sweater, and I was downstairs by the time it sounded again. The man on the doorstep was standing completely still. There was an unsmiling moment of appraisal. He was stocky, gray hair against a weather-beaten face, tight lines fanning from the gray eyes. Sad mouth. At some time his nose must have been broken. His face wasn't quite symmetrical; perhaps the left eye was bigger than the right or else a slightly different shape. He looked carefully at my unmade-up face, tangled hair, large sweater, old jeans, bare feet and saw, I supposed, another victim.

"Michael Kopje. Family liaison officer."

His South African accent was immediately familiar, taking me back in a brief flash to my gap year in a mission center in that country and to the tough farmers in battered pickups, coping with drought and cattle disease. Capable in a crisis.

His handshake was brief and firm.

"Like the hill?" Did I say that? In spite of everything?

The lines around his eyes deepened, and for an instant his lips smiled but then they turned down again quickly. He didn't ask me how I knew, and I was glad. I didn't want the exchange about Africa, if he knew my Africa or if I knew his.

"I'm Jenny. Come in."

I took him to the kitchen, switched on the kettle, and went upstairs to wake Ted. He got up instantly and came down with me. I followed his eyes to the clock. Midday.

"It's been over twelve hours since our daughter should have returned. The only support we need is information," Ted said. He sat down opposite Michael Kopje, staring at him across the table.

"That's why I'm here."

"So, what can you tell us?"

"Sue Dunning has spoken to the drama teacher, Mrs. Mears, and to the whole cast of the play. A girl called"—he quickly pulled a notebook from his jacket pocket—"Nikita gave us some information about Naomi."

I didn't like the way he said her name, calmly, as if he knew her. I sat next to Ted and took his hand. I felt a sudden flash of anger. We would never have met this Michael Kopje if Naomi was here, but by malevolent fate he, a stranger, was assuming possession of her name. I glared into his gray eyes and he looked down;

in that second I saw he recognized how I felt and some of the clenching fury began to fade. He left a little pause and then began talking again, quietly.

"The girls were left to change after the end of the play but they weren't alone in the building. Mrs. Mears said an older boy was waiting in the lobby so she left them, also knowing the caretaker would be along later to lock up."

"What boy?"

He hesitated a moment. "Edward. Your son."

"Ed?"

"He told Mrs. Mears he was going to walk Naomi home."

I sat there stunned. So Ed had been there, and he hadn't told us. Nor had Nikita.

"Please carry on, Mr. Kopje." Ted was sitting stiffly, his mouth set.

"Call me Michael. Nikita told us that Naomi was due to meet a man. She wanted to wait with her but Naomi told her not to bother; Ed was there, you see. When Nikita's mother picked her daughter up, the theater was apparently empty. What time did Ed come home last night?"

"I don't know. I fell asleep."

Michael's eyes seemed to widen at this. Did I seem like a careless mother, whose children were allowed to wander in at any time of night, unchecked? I hadn't meant to fall asleep. I was sometimes so tired that sleep overtook me as soon as I sat down. It was pointless to explain any of this; how could it matter now?

"It seems as though Ed left almost immediately after Nikita," Michael said.

"He should have bloody well stayed," Ted whispered.

I punched Ed's number on my phone but it went straight through to voice mail.

Michael Kopje continued, as if he hadn't heard Ted. "Nikita told me she knows almost nothing about this man. Naomi first mentioned him about two weeks ago. Nikita thought he might have been there in the back of the theater on one occasion, but she never saw him close up."

"Someone would have seen a stranger, surely?" I shifted in my seat, leaning forward. "If you ask the teachers—"

"I was coming to that. Mrs. Mears told us she once saw a man in a seat at the back of the theater during a rehearsal. She thinks she saw Naomi getting up from the seat next to him. Apparently she told Naomi that friends and parents weren't allowed to come to rehearsals. Naomi told her that she hadn't invited him, he'd just turned up anyway."

As Michael paused, I wondered if the man had been at the performance we saw. I searched in my mind for a stranger hovering at the edge of the room somewhere during the intermission. Had there been someone by a pillar, a tall figure half hidden or a turned head at the bar, someone looking sideways toward our group? Perhaps. But I could just as easily be imagining it.

"Did Mrs. Mears notice his appearance?"

"It was unlit at the back of the theater. He was sitting down. She thought he might be a parent." Then he looked at both of us. "Did Naomi say anything to you about a new relationship? Or did anything else happen that struck you as unusual?"

Ted said no at exactly the same time that I said yes. Michael turned to me.

"She didn't say anything, but something was different," I said slowly.

"How different?"

"She was quieter. I only realized it after a play rehearsal. She came back late and seemed very distant."

"Distant?" He waited, pen poised over a page in his notebook.

I glanced at the stove, next to which Bertie was now sleeping. She had been standing right there when she had glanced sideways at me.

"She used to talk to me a lot," I said. "About everything. That night it occurred to me that she had stopped doing that; I thought it was tiredness with all the play rehearsals and homework, but . . ."

I stopped as a new thought unfurled.

"But . . . ?" Michael repeated.

I remembered the quick hostility over homework, the silence that followed. "Thinking back, it was as if she deliberately wanted to shut me out."

There was a pause; I could hear the faint scratching of his pen, then Ted looked up quickly, his voice cutting across my memory.

"The cottage," he said.

Chapter 13

Locking the window so it can't blow open again, I strip off my sodden clothes and leave them on the floor in a heap, putting on pajamas, thick socks, an old sweater. Downstairs the cottage feels cold and empty after Mary's warm bungalow. I pace backward and forward; my body feels horribly alive. What has escaped or what have I allowed in? Something has pulled at the corner of my mind and let in flickering colors where I had made calm black space. An image is forming that demands to be captured. Behind the desk is the old portfolio of paintings. I pull it out quickly to find a blank canvas, then scatter paint tubes on the table. I want to paint the color and sound of the storm.

Some of the other pictures have escaped; one falls to the floor. Before Bertie can walk on it I pick it up; it's the portrait of Naomi that I never finished. Her eyes still glow, her mouth is smiling. She looks faintly triumphant. They say the youngest gets away with things the older children are forbidden. I had told Ed that he couldn't have parties in the cottage, but I let Naomi. She got her way over almost everything; that was her undoing.

BRISTOL, 2009
ONE DAY AFTER

"She went to the cottage last week," Ted said. He stared at Michael, who had stopped writing and was looking at him questioningly.

"The cottage?"

"Sorry," Ted said quickly. "Jenny's parents were going to retire to a holiday cottage in Dorset they'd had all their married lives, but her father died. Her mother made Jenny a gift of the cottage very recently." He sighed impatiently. "Anyway, we let Naomi go there last weekend, before the play started. She said she needed a break; she wanted to go with some of the cast to relax. It seemed reasonable enough at the time."

I remembered how she had stood inside the door quite silently. "She was very . . . preoccupied when she came back. She didn't tell us much about the day."

Ted and I looked at each other.

"Who did she go with?" asked Michael.

"Friends from school. From the play," said Ted. "At least that's what she told us. A boy she has known for ages. Other cast members. Nikita."

"Did they pick her up?" Michael was writing again now.

"No, she went to meet them," I told him, feeling sick. Had that been true?

Ted and I got to our feet at the same time.

"I'll need the address." Michael glanced up at us. "A key."

"No need," Ted replied. "I'm going now."

Michael pushed his notebook inside his jacket and stood. He pulled out his cell phone and spoke into it. We heard him request a driver and two officers to accompany Ted to the cottage.

"I'll be fine on my own. I'd rather," Ted said abruptly. "If she's there, she might be frightened if a whole load of policemen roll up."

Michael paused on the phone. He said quietly to Ted: "If she is there, and someone is with her, you may panic him."

We stared at him wordlessly; unforeseen possibilities seemed to swell in the air of the kitchen. Panic him into doing what?

As Michael moved away, speaking again into his phone, I turned to Ted.

"I'm coming with you," I told him.

"You haven't had enough sleep." His eyes scanned my face.

"It's just a couple of hours, for God's sake. I can sleep on the way."

"Stay," he said. "In case."

In case I heard her footsteps running toward the back door? Her voice calling to Bertie that she was home and he could stop pining now? Those familiar things had already taken on the sheen of an impossible luxury.

———

WHEN THE DOORBELL sounded, Ted and Michael went upstairs to open the front door to the policeman who was driving Ted to Dorset. I heard voices, the door slammed, and then Michael's footsteps came down again into the kitchen.

I put the kettle on and looked at the clock: 1:30 P.M. Fourteen hours. It would be more by the time they got to the cottage. I wondered if they would drive the way we used to, the M5 to Taunton, then across country to Chard, Axminster, and Bridport. The final three miles to Burton Bradstock, with the sea between the hills on the right. The children getting impatient by then, wanting to stretch their legs.

"I'm sorry, Jenny," Michael said simply as he walked into the room.

"How are you going to find her?" My voice rose uncontrollably. "What about the rapist? Every second—"

"It's not the rapist," Michael interrupted. "He was picked up ten days ago; he's in custody. We are doing all we can at the moment. We have taken prints from the dressing room, the theater, the seats, and the changing rooms. Her friends are being interviewed." He looked at me carefully, checking I was following. "We are asking residents and the school about cars in the area at that time and checking the CCTV cameras in all the local garages and on roads going out of Bristol." I watched him as he went through the list; his gray eyes were serious. "We are also putting together a photofit from Mrs. Mears's description and it will go out on television on the six o'clock news this evening. We are taking this very seriously."

It made it better but it made it worse. I was sliding

down somewhere I had never been before, hands out, trying to hold on.

He stood by the kettle, found the jar, then milk, made two cups of coffee. He gave me one of them and sat down again, facing me across the kitchen table, which was still littered with packets of cereal and the carton of juice, dirty bowls and mugs of cold tea.

"We are making some assumptions here," he said. "We have to look at other possibilities, however unlikely."

"Other possibilities?"

"There are several. First, there are good possibilities."

I looked up quickly. "How do you mean, good?"

"She is with a friend; she is sleeping or she has simply taken time out."

"Naomi would never do that; besides, she had one more performance to do."

"Perhaps the pressure . . . ?"

"No." I shook my head. I wished I could believe that, but however she might have changed, whatever we had missed, I knew she wouldn't have just left the play like that.

"Then there are other options. She met the unknown man for a brief while, or maybe not at all." He was telling me she could have been abducted from the theater by someone completely different, or on the way home perhaps, randomly, by some brutal stranger.

I stared at him in silence. Which would be worse? Someone who had befriended her, planning to do her harm, or a stranger hiding in the shadows outside the theater door, or farther away, down the street? I stood up but my legs felt too weak and I sat down again.

"Does anything else unusual cross your mind? Something you may not have noticed or have gotten used to? Enemies?"

He passed me a notebook and a pencil. Holding the pencil in my hand steadied me.

I looked at him; he knew how to help, but the downturned edges of his sad mouth told me he didn't like this part of his job.

"You're used to this," I said. "You know what to do."

It sounded like an accusation; I could see he was considering his reply carefully.

"Yes. But every time it's different. Like your job. You must see lots of people with the same sort of illness, but no one is ever the same; there is no set routine." He was right, of course. I nodded and he opened his own notebook. "Who lives next door?"

"Flats, people come and go. Mostly young couples. We don't know them really."

"Opposite?"

"Mrs. Moore and her son. He has Down's syndrome."

Michael wrote that down as well.

"Anyone else at all?"

Enemies, he had said. I thought of Anya's husband scowling at me when he dropped Anya off. Mr. Price's eyes last time I had seen him. Friends were easier. Nikita. Naomi had lots of other friends at school, but the only other one I could think of now was the boy who had helped her with math, James. The one she said she had gone to the cottage with, the one who had given her the ring.

I began to write my list slowly; it took a long time to marshal my thoughts. When the phone rang, I started up, heart thumping, but Michael moved swiftly to answer it.

"No comment," he said tersely after a small pause, then repeated, "No comment." As he hung up, he turned to me.

"The media will be intrusive." He had dealt with this before as well. "I'll prepare a statement for you for now, asking them to respect your privacy."

I stared at him. All I cared about was Naomi, seeing, hearing, touching, holding her. Privacy seemed completely irrelevant.

I finished the list and gave it to him, and he stood up to go. I didn't want him to; it felt less desperate with him there. He said he would be back in two to three hours.

AFTER HE LEFT I sat still for a long time, incoherent thoughts racing through my mind. Eventually I stood stiffly, glancing at the clock. Sixteen hours now since we had expected her back, twenty-two since she had walked out of the door. Just then, I remembered her voice as she said good-bye, but, strangely, I couldn't remember if I had said good-bye to her.

Chapter 14

DORSET, 2010
ONE YEAR LATER

I lay green wash on the paper, then mix sap green and crimson for a grayish green, but the color is too cool, it needs to glow, darker, thicker. I layer on viridian green and raw umber. The purple and deep brown of the sea lifts up to the edge of the sky as if it would swallow it. I stipple white spume along the crest of a wave but mostly I want the dark heaving shapes of water. Even as the painting takes shape, I feel the rope it is offering me. I imagine it is rough with salt and wet under my hands. I stop from time to time to put wood on the fire, swallow wine, a sandwich, pacing as I eat.

Sometime after midnight the picture lets me go. The fire is flickering low, and the room feels warm and safe, though outside the storm is still raging. Last year our lives were destroyed in a raging, pitiless storm. I'd clung on then because I thought we would find her and because of the boys. Theo and Ed kept me going.

BRISTOL, 2009
ONE DAY AFTER

Theo came home from school in the late afternoon. He had bought fish and chips in a white paper bag translucent with grease, and the smell of vinegar made me feel sick again. When the phone call came, I used the nausea as an excuse to go upstairs, so that Theo wouldn't hear the conversation.

Ted's voice sounded strained. "The cottage is empty. No one's here. No one's been here in the last twenty-four hours."

So she hadn't been taken there. I waited.

"She was here, though. Last week, like she said. Only . . ."

"Yes?"

"She . . . they . . ."

"What?" My head was tingling with impatience.

"The bed's been slept in. There's a stain, through to the mattress."

"Slept in? But she didn't stay the night." Then his other words caught up with me. "What d'you mean, stain?" I asked, my voice trembling. "What sort of stain?"

"Blood."

"Jesus." I can't speak for a second. "How much?"

"Difficult to tell. They say it's several days old. And it's smeared on the floor as well." He was speaking quietly. Someone must be near, perhaps listening to what he was saying. "You can tell how old it is by the color—that's what this officer says. He's in forensics. And the wine in the glasses has dried. Definitely there for longer than a day and a night."

"Wine? What wine?" I didn't know what he meant.

"There's a bottle next to the bed, two glasses."

Glasses of wine next to the bed? She never drank alcohol. She had smelled of wine after the rehearsal and at the dinner after the first performance, but I thought that was probably because everyone was drinking. I thought she hated alcohol.

"It must have been the friends she went with, some of the kids she knows are much more . . . grown up . . ." Even as I said it I thought of the little girls who came to the practice, pregnant at thirteen. But Naomi wasn't like that. She'd never had a boyfriend. I'd told that to the police. It wasn't possible she'd been in bed with someone.

"She didn't go with friends." Ted's voice came back harshly. "That was another lie. There are only two sets of footprints. It was just her and that fucking guy. You thought she didn't tell us much when she came back the other day? Hardly surprising—she was traumatized." There was a rasping intake of breath. "He got her drunk first . . ."

Even as I flinched from the words I tried to think beyond them. "If that's true, that's all right," I heard myself saying. "Drinking together, that's a good sign."

"What? Good she was drunk when he raped her?"

I flinched at his cold incredulity. "No." She had been standing so quietly inside the door. "We saw her when she came back from the cottage. I would have known if something bad had happened. She was so calm." I spoke more quickly, feeling more certain. "Think about it for a moment. If you have wine with someone in bed it means you are relaxed and talking. Enjoying—"

Ted cut in. "A local team arrived about an hour ago. They are taking samples—fingerprints, photos, DNA."

I kept the wineglasses in my mind. He would have poured her a glass, put his arm around her; she would have sipped it, smiling at him, pretending she liked it.

"The wine means he liked her." I spoke carefully. "The blood is because it was . . . her first time. So if she is with the same person now, he won't hurt her. Not if they . . . they made love." The words sounded ridiculously out of place. But love was better than rape, better than murder.

"Wake up. Of course it must be same person, but it doesn't make it any less dangerous. It will all be part of a plan That was just the start." His voice shook.

There was a silence and then he told me they were getting another team down. There would be house-to-house questioning in the village. It was all going to take longer than he thought. I wished then we had known more people in the village, but we had never stayed long enough to make friends; we'd always been absorbed in family, making the most of Ted's time off with us. Now I wished I had reached out. I would have had someone to ask if they'd noticed anything different, or if there had been strangers lurking in the village.

I went back to the kitchen. When the phone started ringing, I lifted the receiver, but when I heard the bright voice of a journalist rapidly introducing herself, I quickly cut the call. The phone rang again immediately and I ignored it.

Ed came in. He stood still when he saw me and for a moment he looked frightened. I put my arms around him. His eyes were bloodshot. Had he been crying? He stayed quite still, his muscles tense.

"It's all right, Ed. It's going to be all right."

"Nothing's all right."

He shrugged me off, walked into the little sitting room next to the kitchen, and sat down on the sofa. I sat next to him; he got up and sat in the chair. I heard Theo open the fridge door.

"Whatever happened, I'm on your side," I said quietly.

"What d'you mean?"

"Michael Kopje from the police force came to see us. Apparently you told Mrs. Mears—"

"Fuck."

"You don't have to tell me now."

"Oh, yeah?"

"They might need to check with you. Obviously I want to know about Naomi—"

"See? You never mean what you say. Ever."

I waited, watching the anger burn in his face.

He looked down. "I told Mrs. Mears I would walk Nik and Naomi home. While I was in the loo, Shan turned up and took Nik."

"Yes, I know she did."

"After that, while Naomi was changing, she yelled through the door for me to go. She told me a friend was coming to walk her home. She made me go."

I knelt in front of him, held his arms. "It's not your fault, Ed—or it's everyone's, mine and Dad's as well. Naomi always makes people do what she wants." As I said it I knew it was true and it gave me hope. It meant she could make whoever had taken her let her go. Ed turned his face away.

Theo leaned against the wall wearily. "Mrs. Mears resigned," he said.

I stood up and turned toward him. "Why?"

Behind me, Ed got up and walked out.

"A member of staff is supposed to be in the theater with the kids at all times. She must feel awful . . ." Theo's voice trailed away.

I felt sick again. So Mrs. Mears knew that if she had acted differently Naomi might still be here, but whatever guilt this teacher felt couldn't compare to the terror Naomi might be going through. The agony we were enduring. Blazing anger surged inside, but I knew it wouldn't help because then I would have to feel angry with Ed as well, and the useless rage would swell and block out everything else. I had to stay sane.

"No one's saying anything to me," Theo said. "No one wants to talk to me at all. It's weird."

I tried to explain: "They think they should say something, but they don't know how to, so it makes them feel awkward. It doesn't mean they don't care. Perhaps you'll have to take the first step."

"I tried, but two guys just walked away. It's as though I've got some disease they're frightened of catching."

I hugged him quickly. We had to talk to each other properly soon, but I couldn't tell him what they had found in the cottage yet. How could I worry him when it didn't make sense? At six we watched the news. Even though I watched and listened, I took in only fragments. "Naomi Malcolm . . . Last seen by friends immediately following her performance in a school play yesterday . . . The police are looking for a dark-haired man in his twenties or early thirties to eliminate him from their investigation . . ." Then her picture, another school one I hadn't seen. She looked even younger. Her smile was wide; not the new half smile. Her eyes were open and trusting. They wouldn't be trusting now. To everyone else in the world she was somebody else's child. I switched off the television.

There was nothing much in the kitchen cabinets but no one was hungry anyway. I made Ed a sandwich, which he ate in silence. After the boys had gone upstairs, I walked around and around the kitchen, winding myself tighter and tighter, until I felt about to snap, like a weighted fishing line that has been reeled in to the breaking point.

"Help me . . . help me . . ." I whispered over and over again, clenching and unclenching my hands, sweating, drenched in despair.

I WAS STILL in the kitchen when Ted came back much later. He went straight to the liquor cabinet and found an old bottle of whiskey at the back. He drank quickly, tipping the glass rapidly upward.

"They got the stuff they needed; they're analyzing it. He must be stupid. He left fingerprints all over the place. You could see them on the wine bottle." He drank again, put the glass down and looked at me for the first time. His eyes were narrowed. "We'll get the bastard. He could have gone anywhere with her, but we'll be able to get him now."

"What about the blood? What did the police say?"

"They didn't say anything to me. It was mostly smears on the sheet and in the footprints."

Not that much blood, then. She hadn't been hurt. I

would have known. Just a week ago her silence had been intense. She had been guarding a secret, not an injury. What had she been thinking about? Her lips had been moving—had she been saying his name?

Ted's voice was angry. "I've been thinking about who would do this. Someone normally powerless, showing the world that he could take what he wanted, sex with a little girl in her parents' territory. She might have been flattered, not realizing that all the time he is saying to himself: this is easy. The first part of the plan."

"Slow down." I took his hand; it was trembling, like mine. "What plan?"

"Don't they call it grooming? He'd obviously worked it all out." He was whispering now, his breath came in little gasps. "Sleeping with her in the cottage was the first part of it. He must have done that to gain power over her, so she would go out with him after the play, unsuspecting."

Ted must have thought this all through on the long journey home; now his words tumbled out as if he couldn't contain them anymore.

"By the time she realized it was a mistake, it would be too late. He would have taken her miles away. She could be a prisoner anywhere. He is free to hurt her however he wants. Rape her. Kill her."

At least Ted's voice was quiet as he said those words. I walked to the bottom of the stairs and listened. It was quiet. The boys were asleep. I thought of how the empty cottage must have smelled. Perhaps the curtains had been drawn so the mess in the room was suddenly revealed when Ted had pulled them back; there might have been flies buzzing at the windowsills or dead in the dregs at the bottom of a glass. The journey back would have seemed endless; it would have been difficult to wait in the line by the suspension bridge over the Avon. His eyes looked tortured; I put my arms around him.

"Perhaps it was different," I whispered. "Perhaps it wasn't like that at all. What if he loves her? If he loves her, he won't hurt her."

Ted didn't reply, and the hopeful words disappeared into the silence as completely as if I had never spoken them.

Chapter 15

DORSET, 2010
ONE YEAR LATER

The wind gets up again later. I wake suddenly as the window rattles, catching as I do the edge of a dream. Harsh knocking. The sound of water. I'm dreaming the memory of another dream. Then a blast, shocking the night. Shaking everything, it has the quality of splintering. I listen, frozen still. Something has been broken out there. Despite the noise and my fear, I float and drift on the surface of sleep, aware that my hands are open and moving on the sheet, searching.

There is a difference to the morning: the absence of sound, the unusually brilliant light. I look through the window and the garden has disappeared. Unseasonably bright sunshine lies over wreckage. There are shards of bark and broken pieces of tree trunk everywhere. The apple tree has gone, carved up and scattered by the storm. Large wooden splinters have fallen on the garden walls and blackcurrant bushes. The gate has been crushed.

There is an old saw in the garage. Oiled and still sharp, immaculate as my father kept all his things, it hangs on a nail next to the chopping ax. A robin is pecking around the torn disk of turf at the base of the tree, whose rough twisted roots now point toward the sky. Bertie noses the glistening boughs of wood, cocks his leg by the wall, and settles by the broken gate. Sawing into the great sections of trunk, I throw off the coat, and then my sweater. My hand slips with sweat as I work the saw back and forth. The peaty smell of the fresh wet wood reminds me of bonfires before they are lit, and of hiding in the bushes as a child before bed. The dark curved branches of the crown stir another memory, which I can't quite reach. I work on through the changing light of the morning. At my feet is the little hopping, whirring bird, looking and pecking. At midday I drink water and keep going until my fingers can't bend around the handle anymore and the skin on the palms is bleeding.

I kick off my mud-clogged boots outside the open back door, and walk into the cottage. The rooms feel washed with fresh air after the storm. A smudge of yellow shows through the glass of the front door. There is a small bunch of yellow chrysanthemums on the step, with four eggs in a plastic ice-cream container. Mary must have left them. As I put the flowers in a milk bottle; my hands are so tired they tremble. I hold one of the eggs; the very shape feels kind. I can't remember when I last ate an egg—a year ago? It is freckled; there is a tiny soft feather stuck to its smoothness, a faint brushstroke of mud. I boil it quickly and eat it, then boil another, then another. I have no butter and no egg cups, so I peel the eggs and fold them into slices of bread, into which I have pushed a knifeful of Marmite stiffened with age. I found the pot at the back of the cupboard. I scrape the egg shell and bread crumbs into the bin, a sudden burning image as I do of Naomi's freckled baby face at two, of Marmite soldiers.

Mary is better or she wouldn't have been able to leave presents here. I walk out quickly before I can change my mind. Her cottage door is open and voices come from inside. I back away, but Mary has heard me.

"Don't go running away," she calls.

There are bunches of bright flowers in cellophane wrappers on the table, heaped packets of cake. Villagers have heard she wasn't well. Mary is sitting by the table in an apron; her cheeks are pink-brown, unlike the papery white of yesterday. A bird-thin man stands in the middle of the room, eating cake and dropping crumbs. A dark-haired boy is smoking a hand-rolled cigarette at the table, texting rapidly with both thumbs. He is introduced as Mary's grandson, Dan. He nods at me, looking up with eyes half shut against the smoke. The bird man steps forward, eagerly offering his hand.

"Derek Woolley. Neighbor. Retired solicitor and chief bell ringer." He laughs self-consciously.

"Jenny."

His handshake is flabby; his eyes on mine move quickly from side to side as if to catch escaping secrets. I know his questions will be intrusive. I am tired of the ugliness of curiosity.

"So, Jenny, how long have you been here? Of course, I've seen you and the family in the past, weekending as it were . . ."

I don't remember this man from then; since I've been here, I've turned my head away when anyone passes me in the street.

"Since the summer." I glance at the door. How soon can I escape?

"Jenny was the one who helped me yesterday, Derek. She picked me up." Mary speaks quickly into the silence.

"Aha. So you're our Good Samaritan. I've always wanted to ask—"

"That's the bell. They've started already. You'll need to hurry now." Mary holds the door open. "Perhaps you could tell them I'll be along for choir practice on Tuesday as usual—they'll be wondering."

Derek Woolley shrugs, empties his cup, and picks up another piece of cake as he leaves, nodding briefly at me.

"Sit down, dear," Mary says to me, shutting the door behind him.

Dan, on the way home from Sixth Form College in Bridport, has come by to help in her garden. Mary asks me if I want help too. She heard the tree fall last night. When I get up to go, Dan, still texting, holds the door for me. Something in his face, unformed and restless, reminds me of Ed.

Back in my cottage, the play of light and shadow is different; looking outside again I notice that the curving bars of the crown of branches make a pattern. Then I see that, for a second, Naomi's face has slipped among them. Of course, that's what the curved and fallen branches reminded me of; Naomi's naked body within twigs. Theo's pictures.

BRISTOL, 2009
TWO DAYS AFTER

Michael Kopje and two colleagues stood in the kitchen early on Saturday, November 21. Ted was sitting down, still tired from his trip to the cottage the day before. His skin was pale and his eyes bloodshot. Neither of us had slept more than an hour. I had made breakfast, cleared up, brushed my hair. My mind was empty, which was good; I needed an empty slate on which to write a plan, uncontaminated by fear. There was a drill for medical emergencies, simple letters to remember Don't waste time on emotion, we had been told as students, just follow the drill: A for airways, B for breathing, C for circulation. Think, don't feel. I reached for the cups and made tea. Think in a list.

Michael watched us closely. He spoke slowly; he might have thought we wouldn't understand. They were following all the clues in the cottage, and collecting information from neighbors. The old lady opposite thought there might have been a car parked outside the cottage for a while, though she wasn't sure. No one so far had seen Naomi or anyone else. DNA samples from the sheets and towels and CCTV evidence from local garages had been collected. Michael was here today because they needed to go through Naomi's room, then all the rooms in the house again. He wanted to speak to Theo and Ed separately, at the station, in the presence of a support worker. This part was routine. He introduced two colleagues, Ian, a heavy man in his mid-thirties, and Pete, a young Jamaican. They would be helping with the search, which could take all day.

Ted said he had to go to the hospital. There was a little silence after his words. They sounded normal to me, he had said them so often, but Michael nodded respectfully. Pete looked impressed.

I followed him outside, shutting the door behind us.

"Do you have to go now?"

He looked down at me, but his mind was already at the hospital. I realized this would be his way of coping.

"Of course I do," he replied. "I'm on call."

"Christ, Ted. Hand it on." My grip tightened on the door handle.

His gaze didn't flicker. "If I go now, it will only take an hour. I don't want to use up too many favors of my colleagues at this stage."

I understood what he meant. But I had always understood. It didn't make it right.

I woke Theo and Ed and explained what was happening. Ed turned back into sleep; Theo was awake quickly and sat up, worry crumpling his forehead.

I took Michael to Naomi's room. I had left it untouched, as he had asked me to, but I wouldn't have put away anything anyway. I couldn't bear to change how she had left it. Now, seeing it through Michael's eyes, I wanted to hide the clutter of unfamiliar underwear and clear away the scattered makeup. I could feel his eyes taking it in, red lipstick protruding in a domed stalk, lying on its side in the small pool of foundation, the lacy bras, the thong, the unmade bed. But that wasn't the real Naomi. Naomi was here, I wanted to say, in the cello against the wall, the photos of Christmas and Corfu in the shell frames that she made, in the friendship bracelets in the bowl. The dried autumn leaves behind her mirror. She loves autumn, I wanted to tell him. She collects leaves, like a child does. She is just a child. That bra must belong to a friend, the thong as well. They can't be hers. I've never seen them before. But then, I hadn't seen the shoes before either, the high-heeled ones with straps. There was that smell of alcohol and cigarettes, the way she had turned away when I spoke to her. What have I missed? What clues do I need to understand now, quickly, before it's too late?

Michael reached up and was looking through her books, glancing at me. I nodded. He picked out every book and shook the pages. On the second shelf down, a third of the way along, he pulled out a slim book which I hadn't noticed. The shiny cover was patterned with flowers. Inside, as he flicked the pages, I could see her rounded handwriting. It looked like a diary. I wanted to snatch it back. Naomi's thoughts, if that was what she had written there, didn't belong to Michael. They were hers, mine to look after for her. I put out my hand.

"I need to go through this," he said quietly.

"So do I."

"I'm sorry. But . . ."

"Please can I have it?" My hand was stretched out, the fingers trembling.

"I know how you feel—" he said.

"No, you don't." Don't say that, I continued silently. You've never lost a child of your own. I looked at him. Perhaps he hadn't had a child; he had the unscathed look of a childless man.

"You're right." He sounded contrite. "Of course I don't know exactly what you are feeling. But there could be vital clues in here."

Perhaps Naomi's things didn't belong to her anymore; perhaps it was right to let strangers plunder her secrets, if it helped to find her. In her absence she had forfeited her right for privacy. Think. Don't feel. ABC.

"Please look through it first." He handed the little book to me then. "But I will need to take it away afterward. It's evidence. I'm sorry."

Did he think I would alter things, or tear out pages? Would I have done?

I sat on the bed to read Naomi's words. I flicked through the pages. Her writing was smaller and tighter than I remembered. My eyes skimmed the lines. The first entry was dated nearly two years ago. January 2008. Something about Christmas presents. I opened it at another place. August 2009. Three months ago. I saw the words Dad and hospital. I turned to the last page for a name, a place, anything to go on. The last words:

Cottage tomorrow. J. 10 weeks.

She must have written this just a week ago. J? Ten weeks until what?

Back a page. A scatter of penciled hearts overlying three letters. XYZ. The X and Z had been written in black, the middle letter in red, a little heart just touching the forked top. No names anywhere. No dates.

Hockey first away. Cut science, bring cigs.

Naomi cutting science? She loved science. Smoking? I put the diary down for a second, feeling giddy. These notes could have been written by a stranger. I looked rapidly around the room, my glance stopping at the little mirror. She had looked at her face in the glass just two days ago. Who was she becoming as she put on her makeup?

Further back:

Theo got commendation. Thanks to me.

His photos of her in the tree. That bit made sense.

XYZ. After school. Tell N.

Those letters again. After school . . . the play? Words or scenes to learn for the play, maybe? N for Nikita? Nikita had been so silent, so awkward when we saw her that night. What else did she know?

Michael was looking in the closet now, pushing the hanging clothes apart and picking up her shoes, turning them over. He went across to the chest of drawers, opened them one by one, felt under the clothes. I had to be quick. I jumped further back in the diary, seeing just a list of dates and times that started back in August, the school holidays. The same initials. And a new one, K.

XYZ. K nearly finished.

If it was in August it couldn't have been the play. She'd done some coursework over the holidays, was that what she meant?

Michael sat beside me on the bed.

"I can't find anything I understand, though N could stand for Nikita," I told him. "The only thing that's clear is she was smoking and missed science." Michael looked at me, then away. He was sorry for me but didn't want to show it. I pointed to the page. "There are groups of letters that keep reappearing, XYZ. Some sort of a code? Letters at the end of the alphabet might have a special significance. 'K nearly finished'—schoolwork nearly finished?"

Michael looked carefully at the words. "Initials of friends or a place?"

I shook my head. I didn't know. He took the book gently from me and put it in a plastic folder.

"I'll photocopy this and give it back to you. In the meantime, see if you can think of anything."

At that moment there was a knock at the door; Ian came in. He looked excited.

"Something you should see," he said breathlessly. We followed him downstairs.

Ian had found Theo's photos of Naomi's naked body hidden within branches. Michael looked at them, frowning slightly.

At that moment Theo walked out of the bathroom. His face, wet from the shower and disarmed by sleep, darkened with incredulity as he realized his pictures had pushed him into the nightmare. He explained the theme of his project and how Naomi had wanted to take part. Ian, eyes narrowed, asked Theo to repeat what he'd just said. I could tell he didn't believe him.

"You can ask Nikita," I said quickly, moving closer to Theo. "She was there; she'll tell you."

Michael went to phone Shan. He arranged for us all to meet at the police station. He said it was a useful place to get some questions out of the way. All I felt was burning impatience that this would hold up the search.

In my head was a moving image of a car with Naomi inside, her face pressed against a window, driving past me. I could have stopped it at the moment it passed me, but I was just too late. No, if I ran I could still stop it, but that moment passed too. It became endlessly just too late, too late, too late . . . The desperate feeling replayed itself in a loop as I drove to the station, and the little car in my head that was taking Naomi away drove farther and farther until it became a speck in the distance and vanished.

In the police station Shan and I sat side by side outside the rooms where the children were being separately questioned in the obligatory presence of a voluntary support worker.

Shan stared straight ahead at the closed door and her voice was quiet. "I know you're going through hell, Jenny, but don't drag Nikita in. She's already told you everything she knows."

"I'm not dragging her in." I was breathless with surprise, with anger. "It's a police investigation."

Shan didn't reply.

"Naomi had a diary." My voice was trembling. "Nikita's initial is in there; Naomi might have told her something secret and Nik is frightened to tell us in case—"

"What secrets?" Shan's voice was harder now. "Naomi hasn't been round much lately. They haven't got secrets. They're not little kids."

"You can't know that for certain."

"I know my daughter, Jen. Leave her. She's upset enough."

I know my daughter. The words seemed to echo along the narrow corridor with its green shining floor, hitting against the high walls that were marked with black scuff marks. At the far end I could see a policewoman at the desk, her expression calmly severe. She probably told herself she had to be professional, which in her world meant tough.

After a long time one of the doors opened and Nikita came out, followed by Michael. She looked upset and went quickly over to Shan, who put her arm around her. Nikita rested her head on her mother's shoulder, while I looked away. Michael opened the adjacent doors and the boys came out. Theo squatted down, hands hanging between his knees; Ed leaned against the wall, his eyes closed. He looked exhausted.

"Thanks." Michael included us all in his gaze. "Great help. Sorry to have to drag you all here. No one's in any trouble. I understand about the photos now and I apologize for having to ask all these questions." He looked at me. "Sorry," he said.

I took the boys home. They were silent. There was nothing to say.

Chapter 16

The unseasonable November weather holds after the storm, a late Indian summer scented with bonfires, the smoke twisting through sunlit branches still hung with the last shriveled leaves. Smashed tiles lie in the road, a window frame rests on glinting shards of glass. The man who owns the shop bends awkwardly over his paunch, his stocky legs spread wide, to pick up scattered milk crates and an overturned metal bin. Wisps of ginger hair fall forward and he wipes them carefully back into place with thick fingers, all the while talking with relish of the storm's wreckage in the village.

Then he says, "Mary told me young Dan will be cutting up what's left of your apple tree today. I'll take whatever you don't need. Cash."

I go inside the shop and turn toward the shelves, feeling breathless. Is this what happens when you step outside your space? People start to close in around you. I should have known. I put apples in my basket, coffee, and a little pot of Marmite. My hands are stiff from yesterday's sawing and I almost drop the jar of coffee. Dan will stumble awkwardly into my quietness. I'll have to get something for him to eat. Biscuits, baked beans. Not enough. There are frozen hamburgers in the small freezer. I reach for milk, juice, beer. A bag of onions in a dusty cardboard box—I can manage this, he's just a boy. I remember that I'll need to pay him and ask for cash-back at the register, turning my head from the man's curious stare. I hear the whine of a saw as I approach the cottage. Over the low wall I can see into my garden, where Dan's bent back and thin arms are weighted with the machine in his hands, chunks of wood already piled around his feet. Bertie pulls free of his lead and bounds up to him as soon as I open the garden gate. I freeze, thinking Dan might drop the machine in fright, or spin around, hurting himself, but I needn't have worried. He straightens, turns it off, leans down to pat Bertie. He pulls off the scarf he had tied around his nose and mouth to keep out the wood dust. Close up, his face is flushed and sweaty. Dark hair sticks in clumped strands to his forehead; his eyes are uncertain, his smile lopsided. Again I am reminded of Ed, who had that same shyness before it hardened into blankness. Dan ducks his head and glances away; I've been staring at him, looking for Ed. He gestures to where he has put the crown to one side, near the wall. The larger branches, still attached, hold their clawlike shape.

"Can I take those?" he asks.

Theo's photos of Naomi hidden among branches.

My face must have changed because Dan's voice falters in the silence.

"Only I make sculptures, out of wood. I sort of use shapes that are there already. I like those." Then he says, "They're a bit like hands."

Hands made of curving wood. I make them kind hands, holding her carefully.

"'Course, Dan. Sorry. Help yourself." I pull myself together and smile at him.

Theo's photos fade and I go back to enter by the front door in case the mail has arrived. There are three cards on the mat. My heart lifts.

One is a sepia picture of Bristol docks as they used to be. Anya's tidy writing on the back. It's her third card to me:

All is fine.

Anya

She stayed, as she promised, even after I left, and for a second I see her picking up Ted's scattered socks, washing the hardened food from his nighttime plates, gently wiping the dust from the photos next to our bed. I usually send her a card of the beach in reply, though there is nothing much to tell her except that I miss her.

There is another card from Ted, a river scene this time. As usual he hasn't written anything. He may not even be in Bristol; he probably goes to more conferences now that there is nothing to keep him at home.

A thick blue stripe and white spray. Hockney. It's from Theo, and for a second I think my memories have surely conjured this up.

In California for a w/e, making a
"Splash"! My pictures in SF City Gallery!
Trip paid for by year prize (wood/
nature series). Coming home for Xmas.
(With Sam?)

x Theo

Christmas with Theo. The past four months in New York must have flashed by for him, crowded with study and all the new experiences the scholarship has bought him, but I long to see him; the fair eyebrows, the sheer length of him, the smattering of freckles. His laugh. How suddenly, briefly, he will still put his head on my shoulder as he did when he was little. The way he lingers late in the kitchen, leaning his frame against the wall, eating cereal, wanting to talk. His fierce, occasional hugs.

I don't yet know much about Sam, apart from the fact that he's an architecture Ph.D. student. Theo sent me a photo once, his arm around this man—long studious face, heavy glasses, smiling. Something I hadn't seen coming. Or had I? Ed had never teased him about girls; it was always the other way around. I'd thought art was his main focus and that was why he'd never had a girlfriend. I never went beyond that; I'd been blind to the subtext, unwilling to encompass complications. Blind to Naomi's secrets too, though hers had led to disaster, not love. I put the postcard down as that thought flares. Out of the window I see Dan moving by the tree, and from here it looks easy, the wood falls as if effortlessly, the low screeching muted by glass. I close my eyes, and into my mind comes the image of the tree crashing over in the dark, changing the landscape of the garden forever.

Ted might not be welcoming to Sam. I want to welcome him. Theo has found someone to love; he has so much love to give. At the same time I'm frightened. Unknown territory. How will Ed feel? How do I feel? I run water into the kettle, sort out the shopping. I know that I mind that he will never have children. I mind that the world may make it hard for him. The man in the shop would whisper to his customers if he knew; in the tiny world of the village they might be curious, gossiping.

I make Dan a mug of tea, and take it into the garden with the packet of biscuits; as I put them on the step for him, he sees, giving a thumbs-up sign. The garden feels warm, and fetching my sketch pad, I try to catch the lines of the branches, their curves gleaming in the bright November air, like dark arms swimming, cutting space instead of water. The sun shines brilliantly on the paper, highlighting sooty grains in the harsh lines of charcoal. All the while the robin makes sudden flutters around the stumps of wood, pecking at the dust, flying to perch on the fallen branches. Walking around the twigs searching for other angles, I sense Dan's presence lightly behind me. Lying down, the wet seeping into my sweater, I have the perspective I've been looking for. Lines curving upward and away above me, coming together at their tips, enclosing a globe of air. Complete.

When the church bells from the clock tower ring out twice, I go inside to cook the hamburgers; as they fry in the pan the unfamiliar, rich smell makes my mouth water. I've been living off apples, toast, and coffee for as long as I can remember. Suddenly craving meat, I cook them all, adding onions, then pile them together between slices of bread, and take them outside with two cans of beer. We sit together, on the stone step of the back door in the sun. Dan devours one hot sandwich after the other. I eat more slowly, with the warm light on my face, enjoying the taste of the food. The moment feels good.

"Thanks." Dan's smile is gap-toothed.

I shake my head. "Thank you. You've done lots here already."

"Yeah, well. Gets me out."

"Out of what?" Looking sideways at him, I sense he doesn't mind this thrown-out question.

"School, home. Other stuff."

"You like making things?"

"Yeah."

"Wood?"

He nods. "I like finding shapes in the pieces, jigsawing them together."

The sleepy unsure look has vanished. He is looking at the twigs, moving his hands, his voice louder than before.

"You're lucky to know what you want to do," I tell him.

"Yeah?"

"Lots of people don't."

He looks at me.

"My dad doesn't want me to make arty stuff for a living. Calls it a waste of space. Wants me to go into the police, like him."

"Will you?"

"Dunno. I s'pose."

His eyes are clouded with struggle.

I stand up and take the plates. "Not easy, choosing."

"Bloody right." He gets up, slides the scarf back on his face.

I come out again to finish the charcoal drawing but it's colder already, the brightness has gone, the twigs look dull. It all changed in that brief time. Dan starts to gather up the logs into a pile against the wall. Bertie tracks him back and forth, sitting against his legs when he stops. Perhaps Dan reminds him of the boys; they have fallen out of his world completely.

Dan stops for tea, hunkering down on his heels. Bertie pushes into him and he falls back, surprised into a laugh. Later we carry more logs together, and stack them beneath the overhang of the garage. Dan says he will come back to split them.

As he swings his backpack up, he notices the smashed gate. He picks up the pieces of wood tenderly and lays them out carefully, like bones. He looks at the gaping wall. "I could make a new one. Using these bits and some new as well. If you want."

"Could you?"

I take all the cash I had got earlier and I put it in his hand. A hundred pounds. I had felt reckless when I got it out. Usually I hardly spend anything. The thick wad feels glamorous, unreal, so many sheets of paper. We both stare at it.

"I don't want all that."

"Well, so I can ask you back."

"Okay."

I watch him go down the road, toward Mary's cottage, bending forward with the effort of pushing the wheelbarrow we have filled with logs for her. He is at that time when the future has no shape. One day it will come close up against him, and in boredom or panic, maybe because something pulls at his sleeve, distracting him, he will make his choice.

That night I don't paint or draw anything in my sketchbook. I think about Dan's choice, which will lead him to everything else waiting in the future. The choices I made led me to Ted, to Naomi, to here. How could I have known? If I go back far enough, it didn't feel like I was choosing so much as taking. In my gap year, teaching in Africa, a child had walked past me on her way to the classroom. She was limping. When she showed me her foot, there had been an ulcer on the underside, as big as a clementine, packed with stones and grit. At its base I saw pink strands of muscle. After that it seemed obvious. I knew what I wanted. Back then I was completely sure. When you're young, you think you know everything. When I look at Naomi's portrait, I see determination, I see certainty. Sometimes, especially late at night, I think about the terrible moment when that certainty deserted her and she realized, as she must have done, that she'd made the wrong choice.

Chapter 17

DORSET, 2010
ONE YEAR LATER

Hello, darling."

"Hi, Mum."

Ed's voice is faint; I strain to catch at how he is through the crackling sounds on the line. I sometimes wonder if people listen in.

"How are you?"

"All right."

He lost his cell phone a week ago, so I imagine him in a corridor, leaning against the wall by the phone. The white paint would be smudged with little black marks where fingertips have been pressed hard against the paint. He will be staring out through the plate-glass window. People pass and look—he is tall and good-looking, people have always looked—but his face will be as guarded as his voice. The pale hand holding the phone is thinner than a year ago, when it was strong and brown from rowing. I noticed on my last visit that his nails were lined with dirt.

"Sorry, darling. I know I'm phoning ahead of schedule, but I couldn't wait. I've been thinking about Christmas."

"Already?"

A little flat word. Barely a question. I carry on quickly, my voice sounding irritatingly bright, even to me.

"Well, it's December. I know we didn't do Christmas last year, but I thought . . ." That it's time for you to come home. You've been away too long and I miss you. ". . . you might want some home cooking?"

"They may want extra help, they're short-staffed."

That could be true, I can't tell. He volunteered to stay on at the end of his program, helping in the kitchen in return for a bed. Mrs. Chibanda said giving back was part of the process. I was glad when she told me he could remain at the unit. What would he have done here, with me?

"Dad's coming. He's going to Johannesburg for a meeting soon, but he'll be back by Christmas Day. I asked him to join us for lunch." I pause, remembering Ted's few terse words on the phone last week. "He sent his love to you."

There is silence. He probably doesn't believe me. He never asks about Ted or the separation. I know he sees him sometimes, but he keeps it to himself.

"What's been happening with you, darling?" I glance through the window while I wait for an answer. The sky is pale gray; behind the church is a banked mass of darker clouds. A few sea gulls wheeling high up flash white as they turn and fall. The garden has been swept bare of wood; Dan took all the branches. There is a ragged patch of bare soil where the tree used to be. Brown stumps of some forgotten vegetable and leafless black currant bushes stand in the patch my father used to tend. The new gate is in place, with its two colors of wood, the old bars and the raw new ones patched in. A sparrow balances on the top bar, and then, as a magpie swoops to take possession of the space, he flutters to the wall.

Ed's words come quicker as he tells me he goes running with Jake now.

I remembered the boy who let us into the center and his sweet smile. "Jake's still there?"

"Thought I told you. We share a room. His sister brings in cakes and stuff."

"That's great, Ed."

"She plays the accordion and lives on this boat."

Friends. A girl. I won't ask questions, but my heart lifts.

"Can I bring anything next week?"

"Pens, maybe a notebook." He pauses, and then continues, speaking slowly: "I've been writing this . . . diary. Dr. Hagan suggested it months ago. I've read a bit to Jake and Soph."

"Be careful. Only tell those things you want to."

"Well, obviously. But it has to be real. Naomi kept that diary, didn't she?"

Jesus. "Yes."

"I think it might've helped her. It helped you, didn't it?"

After we say good-bye I sit next to Bertie on the floor. He pushes his wet nose into my face and I stroke his warm ears. I have no idea if it helped her to write that diary. They weren't really her thoughts. She kept those to herself. I suppose it helped; it led us to James. I get up to take the sketchbook and pencil from the dresser, and find myself studying the pictures as though they have been drawn by someone else and there may be something there that will surprise me.

The warm kitchen is home now, with the chipped Formica table, faded brick floor, and the tiny, noisy fridge in the corner. It feels safe. The Bristol kitchen had begun to feel alien by the third day; I was pacing around it when Michael phoned to tell me what he had learned from rereading Naomi's diary. I can hear his words as I take the sketch pad to the windowsill and begin to sketch the magpie now strutting on the gate, one for sorrow.

BRISTOL, 2009
FOUR DAYS AFTER

". . . so I made a lucky guess that J might stand for her friend James."

"What? Sorry, Michael. Could you say all that again, slowly?"

I was pressing the phone so tightly to my ear that it hurt. It was getting more difficult all the time. I saw everything through a shifting kaleidoscope of her: she was smiling and laughing at first, then the picture would change, her mouth would open, screaming my name. I walked about the house, my hand pushing so hard over my own mouth I could taste blood. Nowhere in the familiar spaces felt like home.

Ted and I had spent Sunday listening and waiting, watching the clock, pacing, silently praying for news. Hour after empty hour passed by relentlessly; no one seemed to be doing anything to find Naomi and bring her back. In intervals of exhausted calm we had talked over what the boys should do. We all agreed it would be easier for them to cope if they had the normal structure of a day around them. I wanted to escape from the torture of waiting and go back to work, but Ted said I would be caught out if I did and break down. Frank agreed. When he came around in the evening he told me he had found a temporary doctor for the duration.

At least the boys slept; they went to school as usual. Ted had gone to work; he said he didn't have a choice. As I'd watched him from the upstairs window, I'd seen him straighten once he left the house and become his work self, his face changing as he thought of his day ahead. It would have been hard for people to have known that anything was wrong; he'd walked in his usual way to the car, his dark suit fitting smoothly over his shoulders, blond hair brushed. I'd looked through the glass, knowing my hair hung in strands, my feet were bare, and my face was haggard. There'd been two white vans parked beyond Ted's car, with satellite dishes on top. Seeing two men leaning against the side of one, paper cups in hand, cameras strung around their necks, I had moved quickly out of sight.

Michael's voice grew louder, bringing me back to the moment. "James was J in Naomi's diary. I've interviewed him and Nikita again. I'm coming over."

I heard the phone click and a few seconds later the doorbell rang.

My sense of time had stretched or shrunk, and I wouldn't have been surprised to see Michael standing there, but it was a tall flame-haired boy in a school uniform. His tie was knotted low, his shirt was untucked, and there were the grainy tracks of tears on his freckled cheeks. His eyes were so swollen it took a few moments to recognize him.

"James?"

"Hi, Dr. Malcolm."

I stared at him for a moment. "She's not here, James. We haven't seen her since Thursday evening."

Four days. Even though I had suffered every minute of that time, the facts still struck afresh as I said them.

"I know. 'Course I know." He looked angry. "I've been at the police station all night."

I took in his red eyes, the dark stains under them, and the faint stubble.

"Why?"

"I needed to tell someone. It's my fault."

His fault? What was his fault? What had he done? He read my face.

"No, I . . . Look, I don't know where she is, I mean, I wish . . . I just wanted to see you, to explain—"

He swayed on his feet and I grabbed his arm and pulled him in. He half sat, half collapsed on a chair in the kitchen and put his head in his hands. I made a cup of sweet tea and put it in front of him. The bell rang again. Michael this time. He looked serious, but his mouth relaxed into a smile when he saw me. As I stood back to let him in, I realized I knew his smell already, a calm male scent of clean ironed shirts and toothpaste. He felt close but that was an illusion; he was in a completely different place from me. Normal life was running on for him like it was for everyone. I could see it and smell it but I wasn't part of it anymore. The transparent skin of disaster separated me from his world. I couldn't touch that world; I couldn't even remember how it felt now.

James looked up with surprise at Michael, who smiled and touched him briefly on the shoulder.

"James has come to tell me . . . something," I said, sitting down, so I didn't loom over him.

"Good. We talked a lot last night."

Michael pulled out a chair and sat next to James. His movements were slow and I realized he probably hadn't slept either. The boy's face was very pale.

"I love her." James's words spilled out suddenly. "She loves me. I think she does anyway . . . She . . . we . . . We've been together for months."

Together? They'd both been in the play. Together for the rehearsals? I glanced quickly at Michael.

He said quietly, "They had been sleeping together for the last six months."

The room felt cold. I should turn up the radiator. Ted's economies were ridiculous in November. It wasn't possible. I would have known if she'd been sleeping with this boy. Naomi would have told me. Even if she hadn't, I would have known. I was her mother.

Perhaps James read my thoughts because he carried on: "She was going to tell you. Well, she knew you'd find out anyway."

"How was it possible? Naomi was here, or at school. I knew what she was doing . . ."

"After school. On weekends."

He spoke almost in a whisper; I leaned closer to catch his words. He went on quietly, "She told you she was with Nikita, but we actually went home. My home."

"Did your parents know?"

I remembered his mother. I used to meet her at medical events, a startlingly pretty redheaded nurse. His father was a pediatrician, a lot older.

"Dad works late. Mum left a year ago. Anyway the real thing is—"

So he hadn't told me the real thing yet.

"She'd started being sick sometimes."

Had she? I hadn't noticed.

"In the mornings."

I wouldn't have heard her vomiting upstairs in her bathroom, not from the kitchen, but I remember she'd stopped having breakfast. She had looked disgusted when I'd mentioned it, but she always ate supper so I didn't worry.

"She fell asleep in class."

The rehearsals were exhausting. I'd noticed she'd stopped running everywhere.

"So she did a test . . ."

There was a silence. How had I never put it all together? Not eating in the morning, the tiredness, the emotional ups and downs. It was so obvious. Michael was watching me with concern; I got up and walked to the window. Naomi, pregnant. I couldn't make it feel remotely real. I turned to James.

"Do you know for certain?" My voice sounded hard.

"She did three tests altogether."

"How many weeks?"

"We didn't know." His white face turned away from my stare. "She thought she'd missed two periods, but she wasn't sure. Ten maybe?"

Cottage tomorrow. J. 10 weeks.

"Wait. What about the blood on the mattress?" I looked at Michael, then back at James. "In the cottage, the weekend before the play began. When she went there with . . . the man. We thought she'd bled because it was her first time, but it can't have been her first time, she was already pregnant."

"What man?" James looked puzzled. "It was me. Us. I thought Naomi told you that we went to the cottage. After we . . . afterward . . . she bled, but she did another pregnancy test three days later, last Tuesday actually, and she was still pregnant. Bleeding a bit but pregnant."

So it wasn't the man who had made her bleed after all, the man from the theater, the bastard who had taken her. This made it worse. The man who had taken her now hadn't been the one to buy the wine; they hadn't shared anything. Not love, of course not that. He didn't care. And suppose she was still bleeding, miscarrying and bleeding, or . . . an ectopic.

I looked at the tear-stained boy sitting at the table and felt a blazing fury.

"What about you, James? What thoughts did you have about the pregnancy? What exactly was your plan?"

"I wanted whatever she wanted. I love her. I didn't really know what to do about the pregnancy."

I wanted to hit him; I wanted to kill him for making it more dangerous for Naomi.

"If you didn't know what to do about a pregnancy, why the fuck didn't you use a condom?"

He winced. Michael turned to me.

"She was on the pill," he said quietly. "But she sometimes forgot."

More secrets. How the hell was she on the pill? Did one of my friends prescribe it for her?

"You should bloody well have used a condom anyway," I shouted. "You should have understood what you were doing. You've made it far worse." I took a deep shuddering breath. "What about the man she was see-ing, then? Did you know anything about him?"

James lowered his head. There were tears in his voice. "I knew something had changed. It was soon after rehearsals began. I always used to walk her back home, but sometimes she didn't want me to; she said she wanted to practice on her own in the theater. Stuff like that. She wasn't the same. She stopped telling me everything."

"Go on." I hardly recognized my voice, it was so ex-pressionless. I imagined it was like the voice that the blank-faced policewoman in the corridor must use when she talked to criminals.

"I saw a man once. I was walking out of the changing room at the theater and I saw her talking to someone. I only saw him from behind. He was leaning against the wall, bending toward her; he had long dark hair, messy. I took it in because she was so kind of focused on him. She didn't see me, though I called out that I would wait outside. I waited for ages. Everyone left and she still didn't come out. So I gave up."

He started crying, deep, heaving sobs. "I should've gone back in. I should've looked at his face."

Michael got up. "It's all right, James. You must be exhausted. I'll drive you home."

"Wait." I felt a pang of remorse and put my hand on the boy's arm to stop him getting up. "She had stopped telling me everything as well. Look, James. You were careless. Stupidly careless, but you loved her. I realize that. I saw the ring you gave her and—"

"You gave her that ring." He looked at me blankly. "She said it had belonged to her granny. It was a family heirloom."

I stared at him. So she had lied to both of us. That man must have given it to her; perhaps even when he was leaning up against the wall that time. He might have chosen that very moment to slip the ring on her finger and that was why she was focused; she would have thought she meant something to him, and all the time it was a trick.

James got to his feet. He was going to say sorry. I didn't want to hear that; I didn't want to feel pity for this boy, this child, who may have tipped the balance of Naomi's life. Wherever she was, pregnant, perhaps still bleeding, she was in even more danger than I had thought.

"Tell me . . ." It was hard to ask what Naomi thought about being pregnant when I should have known. It's the kind of thing a daughter whispers to her mother, keeping it secret from everyone else. "What were her plans about the baby?"

He looked at me. Though his eyes were puffy, it was obvious that the question puzzled him. "She didn't want a baby." His laugh was strained. "That's why she wanted us to do it again, in the cottage. She wanted a miscarriage and she read somewhere that if we . . . if we made love, that might make it happen. She was really pleased when she started bleeding."

After he left with Michael, I sat down, my legs trembling. It was strange he should use those words. *Make love*. They hadn't been making anything; it had been the opposite. And the torn piece of yellow paper from a tampon I saw on the floor the night she went missing? She must have still been bleeding from the threatened miscarriage, not menstruating. Had she been in pain?

By the time Michael returned, my mind was spinning with possibilities. He sat close to me at the table. My thoughts rushed into words: "How do we know if anything James says is true? Perhaps he did give her the ring, as she said. How do we know if Naomi was pregnant, or even if she slept with him? Perhaps he never went to the cottage. He could be making this whole thing up." My hands were clenched on the table in front of us. I couldn't stop: "Perhaps the other guy took her to the cottage, but James might be the one who's got her now. Think about it. He was jealous about Naomi talking to this man, so he's hurt her or hidden her somewhere . . ."

Michael briefly put his hand on mine; his fingers were blunt-ended and warm. "He was at the police station all night, Jenny. He's telling the truth." His voice was very certain. "James and Naomi did go to the cottage that Saturday. A man walking by with his dog saw a red Volvo outside. It turns out they borrowed the car from James's father."

I closed my eyes. Michael's voice continued, listing all the evidence. I made myself listen.

"James said they stopped at the highway service station outside Taunton, so we are going through the CCTV tapes. We fingerprinted him last night so they can see if the prints match ones on the bottle and glasses." He paused; I opened my eyes and looked at him as he continued quietly: "I've also spoken to Nikita. She knew Naomi was pregnant."

They haven't got secrets. They're not little kids . . . Shan's voice had sounded angrily certain, but did she really believe what she had told me?

"What else?" I got up and walked around the kitchen again. "What else does she know? Did Nikita say if she knew Naomi had planned to leave?" The questions tumbled out randomly. "What was she going to do about the pregnancy?"

"She knew Naomi had met someone else she liked, and that she was due to meet him the night she disappeared, but Naomi hadn't told her anything about him. Nikita doesn't think she planned to go for good. She thinks she would have said something to her, some kind of good-bye." Michael looked at me briefly. "She knew Naomi wanted to end the pregnancy, that she was worried. Of course there was the diary; and the reference at the end to ten weeks."

She would have told herself a ten-week pregnancy wasn't far enough advanced to matter. She wouldn't know that tiny nails were forming on the fingers and toes; that's the kind of information no one wants if they have to do what Naomi was planning.

"All right." I put my hands to my head, as if to hold the racing thoughts still. "Let's say it happened exactly as James said, and they went to the cottage. How do we know he didn't take her himself that night? Perhaps he waited secretly for everyone to leave after the play, and then took her somewhere."

"His father was there that night to watch him in the play. James was Chino, remember? They went out for a meal at Hôtel du Vin afterward. We checked there last night and the staff remembered them. They showed me the copy of the bill."

Michael had been thorough. I was silent. I had wanted it to be James, hiding Naomi because he was jealous, because he loved her and he wanted to keep her safely his.

"Will it make a difference to how he treats her, whoever he is? Will he treat her better if he knows she's pregnant?"

Michael didn't answer, but I knew anyway. She would be a nuisance with the vomiting and the bleeding. In time, if he gave her time and if she didn't miscarry, she would become conspicuous.

"Let's deal with what we have." Michael's calm voice stops my train of thought. "We have a better photofit for the prime suspect from what Mrs. Mears, Nikita, and James have said, and that's going on all the lampposts in the area, along with a photo of Naomi's face. We are continuing to watch ports and airports, and we are starting a house-to-house inquiry today."

"Why? He probably doesn't live anywhere near here."

It seemed so random, so useless. She could be miles away. A tiny hut in Scotland, a garage in Wales. We didn't even know what he looked like, though my mind played with the new information. He was older, he had long messy hair, he was different from the boys she knew—was he attractive just because he was so different?

"Remember, we have to look at all possibilities at the same time." He had said that before.

"What sort of possibilities?"

He stood and dug his hands in his pockets. This must be difficult; his gray eyes were strained with effort. In the seconds he took to answer, some detached part of my mind wondered what he would look like if he smiled, really smiled. For a moment I wondered how his wife felt about the times his job stole him away. Did she mind? Would she worry? She might have gotten used to it, as I had with Ted. She would tell herself he was deeply committed to his job.

"Well, it seems likely she did arrange to meet this man, but it is possible he might not have turned up. In that case she might have begun walking home . . ."

I'd imagined this already. The theater was a few minutes away, and although we'd always asked her to call if it was dark, she might not have wanted to bother us. Her spiky shoes tapping the pavement would have been loud in the silent street, so she wouldn't have noticed the quiet thud of following footsteps until they were very near . . .

"We are going to interview the father of the little girl you told us about. You thought he might want revenge—"

"It can't be him. He's a father." For some reason my eyes filled with tears. "He loves his daughter too much to hurt somebody else's child." But perhaps it doesn't work like that. Perhaps there are no rules. I walked to the window and looked up into the street. The white vans were closed up now; the men with cameras must have been inside or perhaps somewhere else, watching the house out of sight. Other people were coming and going along the sidewalks, cars were driving up and down.

The man who had taken our daughter could be someone I knew or a man on the periphery of our lives whom I had never noticed. It could be anyone, anyone in the world. Perhaps that man over there, I thought, the one who is smiling to himself as he crosses the road. Perhaps he has Naomi somewhere, locked up and helpless. Why is he smiling? I wanted to run out, shout questions in his face, see if he looked guilty. I looked at Michael.

"How am I supposed to do this?"

His hand reached out again, and he grasped my wrist tightly.

"Tell me what to do, Michael." I kept still. I needed the strength I could feel in his hand.

"Step by step is how you do it." His eyes traveled over my face. "You have to look after yourself, that's the first step. Eat something. Wash your hair." He smiled at me. "I didn't tell you before, because I didn't want you to worry about it, but the appeal on television is scheduled for tomorrow morning. We'll need to prepare a statement. Can you let Ted know?"

By the time Ted came home, I had had a bath. I had even tried on a suit for tomorrow's appeal, though I'd had to roll the skirt top over to make it stay on my waist. My hair was wrapped in a towel; I was trying to eat a sandwich. I told him James and Michael had been here, and then, sitting close to him, holding his hand, I told him that Naomi was pregnant. He shook me off, got to his feet, outraged and unbelieving. He thought at first James must be lying. I told him everything James had said, and what Michael had told me as well, and the way in which fragments of her diary now made sense. Ted began to pace around the kitchen, I thought he was going to break something. Underneath his seething anger, I felt a bitter backwash of feeling break against me. He must be thinking that as her mother I should have known she was pregnant, even though she kept it secret. Perhaps he was right. When he was sitting down again, his face was white and closed. I put my hand on his clenched fist.

"Don't let this destroy us, Ted."

He looked at me blankly. I don't think he heard what I was saying.

Chapter 18

DORSET, 2010
ONE YEAR LATER

Mid-December. The year has deepened; every day the light becomes quieter. From high up on Eggardon Hill the little fields below us tilt to the coast; the slivers of sea in the distance are white as frost. The only noises in the silent countryside are my footsteps and Bertie's, crunching through the icy turf.

Bridport sits in a valley near the sea; its wide streets are busy at this time of year. The old stone buildings stand plainly to the road and, despite the garish lights strung about them, they look as they always do, as they must have looked two hundred years ago.

The bookshop door jangles open, but instead of the usual book-scented peace, the narrow spaces are jammed with people; there is a smell of wet hair and banana bubble gum. A broad woman with a disgruntled face steps on my toes and glances angrily at me, while a child nearby pulls books from a shelf and throws them on the floor. Naomi's books were easy to choose; she loved so many different authors: Lawrence, Kerouac, Mark Haddon, Stieg Larsson. Faced with the crowd in the bookshop, I collect an armful of novels for the boys and put them in a basket. My fingers linger on the spines of other books as I try to remember what Ted had on his bedside table a year ago. The novels I had chosen for him had always remained pristine under a thin layer of dust, so perhaps I never knew what he liked. I buy the books I have collected and leave, crossing the road under the clock tower as it strikes eleven.

In Boots I choose Ted a leather bag and collect toothbrush, toothpaste, washcloth, and soap, then wait in a jostling line to pay. A smear of pink glitters peripherally; turning my head, I see those little pots and tubes of makeup and shampoo that I used to put in her stocking, along with spotted panties, bracelets, tangerines, plastic cookies. It had been fun. I'd forgotten that. That world where fun was an end in itself had vanished with her. The games and silly jokes she played on the boys, the fuss at birthdays and Christmas, which they scorned but joined in—all that went when she did. No, of course it went before that. I stop in the line as that thought catches me again, and two girls behind bump into me, mutter, and laugh. The fun had stopped long before. I hadn't noticed exactly when; it had been gradual. I'd been busy. Even during the summer holiday before the autumn term began, she'd been quieter.

At the cash register, I snap back to myself, pay, and then awkwardly gather the bags that are around my feet. At least this year I have bought presents. Last year I tried, but I couldn't. Naomi had been gone just over a month. There were teenage girls and their mothers everywhere, choosing decorations, picking out little gifts, calling to each other for approval. I remember I had to leave my full basket on the floor in a shop and walk out in tears through the pushing crowds. Now, going toward the parking lot, I can just about bear to see the families inside these crowds. I see this mother, that child. Now I can watch them, though I couldn't before.

Once the shopping is loaded in the car, I drive home along the narrow lanes, past the golf course glimpsed through the tattered winter hedge, and the empty donkey field. The field beyond this has rows of empty trailers and a boarded up shop, dismal in the dull light, then the first little brick bungalows of the village. I know them so well I hardly see them. That was what happened with Naomi too. I stopped seeing her because I knew her by heart. I drive slowly past the church and up my lane.

As I bring the shopping in from the car and dump everything on the floor, Bertie noses at the unfamiliar mass of plastic bags. In the kitchen, the light suddenly darkens: someone has followed me to the doorway. I swing around, catching my head on the corner of the open cabinet, tearing the scar that had formed after my fall into the tree. It throbs immediately and the blood wells.

I recognize his shoulders against the light before I see his face.

"Michael!"

I am surprised by how glad I feel, but as I move toward him my hands feel weak with sudden dread. What has he come to tell me? The tomatoes drop and the foil-wrapped Christmas pudding rolls under the table. Bertie runs to investigate and pats it farther away with his paw.

"What's happened, Michael? Say quickly."

"Nothing. Nothing's happened." He spreads his arms wide, opens his hands to show they are empty, no secrets. "I was passing—"

"Passing?" No one ever passes Burton Bradstock.

"I'm on my way to Devon to see my folks. Christmas, remember?" Then his face changes, his eyebrows draw together.

"You're bleeding. You cut your head."

He pulls a white handkerchief from his pocket, and his hands are careful as he presses the wound through the soft linen. Close up, I catch that familiar, freshly laundered scent mixed with toothpaste. His mouth, inches from my eyes, is unguarded. My skin tingles with the surprise of touch and I am completely still. I feel him registering that. As his hands drop lightly to my shoulders he looks down at me.

"It's stopped bleeding now." He pauses. "You look well." His eyes are warm as he takes in my face. "I've wondered . . ." and he reaches for the right words.

I step back. "It's good to see you again. Sorry to greet you like a death's-head."

We stare at each other; he is taken aback by my words. He looks down and I can see how the brightness in my tone has jarred. What had he imagined would happen when we met? That brief kiss months ago in the kitchen in Bristol had come from a moment of exhaustion. My guard had been down; a mistake, nothing more.

"Coffee?" I turn, hands hovering over the mugs, waiting for the moment to pass.

"Yes. No. I thought we might go for a walk . . . I'll buy you lunch. When I was driving into the village, I saw signs to a restaurant on the beach."

I pick up the dropped food and push it into the fridge, then put Bertie on his lead. I check quickly in the mirror. He said I looked well. How is that possible? My hair is a wild black tangle and I never wear makeup now, but my eyes are blue against skin turned brown from walking by the sea. The fresh air and simple food have made my face recover. The mirror gives me back my curious glance, as though I am looking at someone whose face I recognize but can't quite place.

We go out together through the garden gate into the field.

"I've thought of you down here so often," he says, turning to me, smiling slightly. "It looks completely different from how I imagined it."

Did he think there would still be blood on the floor and dirty wineglasses? Desiccated flies on the windowsill?

"Are you all right, mostly?" His voice is careful; he wants to know but isn't sure how to ask.

Am I all right? As we walk through the field, then cross the road to the beach path, I think of the evenings in front of the fire, sketching memories. The stack of paintings behind the chair getting thicker. Dan calls after school sometimes to help with odd jobs. He's painted a room for me. We've become friends, though we don't talk much. I look forward to his company; he reminds me of my boys. There are cups of tea with Mary, and I've been to the library with her twice now. Theo phones from time to time and I visit Ed. Ted sends the occasional postcard or text when he leaves the country for meetings. But there is never a moment without pain at the back of it: her face is everywhere. Sometimes the need to know what happened is stronger than I can bear.

When I first came to the cottage, I would stand on the pebbles, with the icy water frothing around my legs, holding Bertie to stop me from walking into the sea.

" 'All right' doesn't quite . . . it's less than that, but—"

"Tell me."

And then we are talking, at least I am. He is listening. I am talking and crying; it feels dangerous to let the words flow unchecked but I can't seem to stop. The despair and loneliness of these last four months flood through me and he puts his arm around me. He lets me tell him everything until I feel emptied out and the tears have stopped. We walk up and down the beach while the wind catches the edges of the pounding waves, tears off bits of foam, and blows them at us.

The Beach Hut café is open. I haven't been inside for years, not since the children were small, when we would come in for fish and chips. In the summer there are noisy crowds eating out under a new awning, but today it's quiet. A few of the tables are occupied by old men reading the *Dorchester Chronicle*, dogs by their feet. The place smells of tea and wet dog. Michael orders fish and chips for us and within minutes we are given fresh slices of flaky haddock and piles of hot salty chips on thick white plates. We take them to a table by the window. I rub a clear patch on the steamy glass and watch the breaking waves crash on the empty beach.

My eyes feel sore with crying but I've let something go and I feel better. It's good to be here with Michael. With the sea outside it reminds me of being on a boat. No one can reach us, different rules could apply.

Michael says quietly that he's been promoted at work and then, looking outside, tells me that his wife left him six months ago.

I feel guilty; he has listened to me for so long. "You never said. I'm sorry."

"Should I have? Should I have let you know?" He looks at me and I look away quickly.

A year ago we had reached for each other one night in the kitchen in Bristol. Ted had gone to bed without a word; Michael had come by on the way home. I was tired and tearful, angry with Ted for being able to retreat into sleep. Michael's kindness had been something to hold on to.

Michael is looking out of the window again; the clouds are reflected in the gray of his eyes. The words come slowly.

"We married young." He stops, shrugs. "I don't want to bore you with my stuff."

"Tell me what happened."

"I don't talk about it much. It's over now."

"Tell me."

He hesitates a moment longer. "We got married at eighteen in Cape Town; she was pregnant. She miscarried after a few weeks . . ."

I should be able to hear these words, *pregnant* and *miscarried*, by now without an answering sharp stab of pain. Naomi's child would be nearly six months old. I count the months as they go by. If the pregnancy had continued and the baby survived. If she had. I clench my teeth together, and the sharpness fades a little. Michael hasn't noticed; he has carried on.

". . . thought England might be different, with less pressure from our families, better medical advice—but she didn't get pregnant again." He looks at his hands, then back at me. "I had to make a career, but the hours were long. It was hard for her. She was so alone."

I know how it would have been. By ten at night she would scrape his waiting supper into the garbage can. Another night she might arrange something, a movie outing or a play, and sit ready, waiting with her coat on at home until after the performance had begun, then she would sit on, simply holding the white envelope with the tickets inside. Days on her own, though the nights would be worse. Every month she would cry when her period came.

Michael continues. "She started volunteering for the Citizens Advice Bureau, then she got pregnant and this time she didn't lose it."

"So you do have a child . . ." His eyes are so serious that I falter. "Was it a boy or—"

"A boy. Not mine. The father is a lawyer she met in the bureau. Married, but he's left his wife." He pauses. "We should never have gotten married in the first place."

How could he have known, though? How could I? When you are young you have no idea what you will need as time passes or how strong you might have to be.

"Don't look so worried." He smiles. "It's history now. I'm sorry I took advantage . . ."

He's sorry he let himself say anything? Or maybe he's thinking back to the evening in the kitchen a year ago, and so I think myself back there too. His hand had been warm on my back, his mouth had held mine. After all, it had had the rough edge of something real, when nothing else had.

Outside, the air has darkened. The white surf glows through the rain; the waves farther back have merged with the mauve of early evening and have become invisible. It's colder than before, but the food and talking have warmed me. We walk back over the fields, hands bumping. Inside the cottage I feed Bertie, Michael makes the fire. It pulls at my heart to see him here now, quietly making my fire, bending seriously to the task. The kindling catches and flares. Then he turns to me.

I walk into his arms and we begin kissing as though we had never stopped. It is like the heat of sun when it's been cold and dark for a long time. He leads me to the fire, and takes off my coat, takes his off. We undress by firelight. He pulls the thick blanket from its place on the sofa, and covers us both. We lie together, touching along the length of our bodies; his skin feels familiar and new at the same time. Safe and dangerous. He has sensed my unease, and pulling slightly away he strokes my face in the dark.

"What is it?" he asks softly. "Tell me."

"How will this work? Are you allowed to do this? I mean—"

"Don't worry." I can hear the smile in his voice. "It's our secret."

Our secret? Should we have one? His arms are close around me, comforting, and my unease dissolves. His hands move slowly over me, and as my skin begins to heat I turn into him, pulled in by the warmth, wanting this now. Into my mind comes the thought that Naomi did this too; she must have been pulled into something secret before it changed into something dangerous. Then his mouth covers mine and we begin to move together as though we have been waiting for this for a long time.

BRISTOL, 2009
FIVE DAYS AFTER

"I'm sorry."

Michael looked stricken. His hand dropped to his side.

"It's okay." I felt too tired for this; I could hear the impatience edging my voice. "Don't look so guilty. It doesn't matter." I didn't want this to make any difference, because we still had to work together.

We were in the kitchen, Ted was upstairs.

After the television appeal in the morning he had gone straight to work. He had been there; he said it grounded him to carry on. It worked for him, but for me there was no ground, it had ceased to exist. I lived in a black space across which I saw him distantly. I felt sorry and angry from far away. I couldn't understand how he could go out, greet patients and colleagues. When he came back he ate quickly, standing up, then went to bed, gray with exhaustion.

Michael had come by late. The boys had gone to bed.

I was telling Michael how worried I was for the boys when I had started crying. He had put his arm around me. We had moved closer, he had bent his head to mine, and then, for a second, our mouths had met. I'd pulled back; it had instantly felt wrong. I was exhausted and he must have been too. A momentary reflex, that's all, created out of despair and loneliness. No one was to blame. We needed to get back to where we had been, so I told Michael about Jade. It seemed to work: as I talked I could see him settling into himself again, taking charge.

"I went to see Jade again today. I'd promised I would. I thought people would stare at me because my eyelids were so puffed up, but no one took any notice."

I realized as I spoke that when I had worked in the hospital, I had ignored them too, the army of the grief-stricken sleepless who sat invisibly in the wards, watching and waiting. "Her father was with her. He stood up when I got there. He's big. I'd forgotten."

"Why didn't you call me?" Michael asked. I heard annoyance in his voice. "I could have come with you. It might have helped. I'm supposed to be supporting you; it's my job, remember?"

"I wouldn't have expected you to come along; it was my mistake," I told him. "I'd got the diagnosis wrong. I had to sort it out."

"How did it go?"

"I took her some old books of Naomi's and she thanked me. She seemed glad to see me. She was fatter. The chemotherapy contains steroids, so it's an artificial sort of fatness, but she looked better all the same." I could feel the tears spilling out again. "But the most difficult thing was what happened with Jeff Price."

"What did he do?" Michael sounded angry.

"Nothing. He said sorry."

"What?"

I thought back to the moment Jade had taken the books and opened one.

"Whose writing is that?" She had turned to her father, showing him the pencil marks scrawled across the sky on the first page.

" 'Naomi Malcolm,' " he read. " 'My bed. My bedroom. Number One, Clifton Road, Bristol. England.

The World. The Universe. Outer Space.'" He paused, then added, "That's the doctor's little girl, Jadie."

"Won't she mind?" Jade turned her face toward me.

"No," I said. I had forgotten about the writing. "She's . . . bigger now." I tried to smile.

Perhaps Jade read my expression. "I'll give it back when I've finished," she said.

I nodded, unable to speak. Jeff Price walked down the aisle of beds with me. Children were lying in hot little heaps, faces flushed and stupefied with boredom. They were as silent as ill animals, swamped by layers of relatives who sat around them, watching television.

He stopped in the corridor outside the plastic doors of the ward.

"I saw you on the telly earlier. I'm sorry about what's happened. Not right. I know we had words but that's not right."

"Thanks." I paused. "The police are interviewing everyone. Even my patients . . ."

"Fine by me. Bring it on. Anything I can do to help. I've been here twenty-four seven, the nurses will tell them that."

He touched me on the shoulder and walked back, seeming to fill the corridor as he walked, lurching slightly from side to side, his feet in their huge white sneakers sucking noisily at the shiny blue floor.

The plastic doors had slapped shut behind him.

Michael was waiting patiently for my response.

"Jeff Price was sorry about Naomi," I told him again. "Perhaps you don't need to interview him after all."

"Well, it shouldn't take long."

It didn't seem as if I could stop what I'd started, even if I was sure Jeff Price wasn't involved.

"You were great on television." Michael smiled, changing the subject.

The lights had been hot and bright. They had made my eyes water but I didn't want people to think I was crying. I didn't want Naomi's abductor to know what he was doing to us. We were warned that if you show your distress it can make it worse. Parents become victims to be manipulated. At the same time, we had to do it. We had to reach out to the woman who might have glimpsed her blurred face in a car window in an unknown city and seen her open mouth calling for help. We had to grab the attention of the man serving in a corner shop, who might have noticed that the quiet man who normally just bought cigarettes was now buying extra things: food, tape, sanitary napkins for the bleeding. We had to tell the child on a bike ride to pick up the gray hoodie that was caught at the bottom of a hedge down a country lane, the one she had thrown out so someone would find it. I wanted the woman by the lights, the shopkeeper, and the child on the bike to be on my side.

"You were really great," Michael said again, when I didn't reply. "So was Ted. We'll need to see him again, by the way."

"I think he's asleep now. It's funny—he can hardly seem to keep awake but I can't sleep at all."

"Just a few questions; tomorrow would be better."

"I can probably answer them now."

"No. We need to ask him the questions."

He sounded serious, almost regretful. I didn't understand.

"What questions?"

"Not everything is adding up. We need to straighten a few things out."

I felt sick. Did we have to go over it all again, separately? Did this mean the police had decided not to believe what we were saying?

"Michael, please. Time is going by and every second—"

"That's why we've got to get this straight. Could you tell him he needs to be at the station in the morning? We'll collect him."

It sounded so ridiculous, like some television police drama, where the husband is needed for questioning and the wife becomes hysterical.

"If I can answer for him, it will save a lot of time."

Michael sighed quickly. "All right. Do you happen to know where Ted was the night Naomi went missing?"

I got up and started walking around the kitchen, picking up the glasses and cups that seemed to litter every surface. They knew the answer to that already. I was tired; I wanted to go to bed now.

"I know exactly where he was. At the hospital. His operation was running late. He had a difficult case—it happens all the time. If anyone doesn't believe that, it's easy enough to check with the staff at the hospital."

Michael stood up as well. His face was expressionless and it was as though he hadn't heard me.

"I'll let myself out," he said, and his voice sounded oddly formal. "Please tell him he'll be collected in the morning."

Once he'd left, I sat at the table, my eyes closed. Michael's words seemed to echo on in the silence. After a while I went to the phone and rang the hospital. I asked to be put through to the neuro operating room. Though it was late, a male assistant answered immediately. He sounded very young. I told him who I was and that Ted had asked me to check on the time he'd started in the operating room the previous Thursday evening. He had forgotten to record the length of the operation and needed it for a GP letter. The words came so smoothly it was as if I'd been rehearsing them rather than plucking them from the tumult in my mind. He left for a moment, then returned.

"Sorry to keep you waiting, Dr. Malcolm. Had to double-check. Sure you didn't mean Monday?"

"I am certain he said Thursday," I replied, my heart thudding.

The young voice sounded apologetic. "It's just that it was only Mr. Patel in neurotheater on Thursday. Mr. Malcolm's case was canceled. I can find out how long the operation took on the Monday if you want to phone me back?"

"Thanks. He'll be in touch if he needs to." I replaced the receiver and then I went upstairs and sat on a chair next to my sleeping husband. I stared at him for so long that his face changed and seemed to dissolve, in the way that your own identity does if you say your name over and over to yourself. In the end he looked like any man lying there, a stranger who I happened to have met, by accident.

Chapter 19

DORSET, 2010
THIRTEEN MONTHS LATER

A group of small children sing Christmas carols at the entrance to Dorchester station, huddling around a gray-haired woman at their center. The children are restless in their downward-slipping Santa hats, two are stamping on each other's toes, and the smallest girl wipes her running nose with her sleeve. The woman resolutely conducts the singing, but her sharply moving hands look as if she is painting punishments in the air. "Away in a Manger" spirals thinly outward as I walk toward the barriers to Platform One. There is something familiar in the way this woman is driving herself to play her part; she stands so upright, her voice is too cheerful. She belongs to a world I used to be part of, and as I look at her I remember its weight. There are no duties now to push me through the day. Life is stripped down and my roles are simpler: mother, not wife. If I had to put my occupation on a form, I'd write painter.

Ed's train is due. Sophie is coming with him. They didn't need him to stay for Christmas in the unit after all.

It only occurs to me now, too late, that a train journey could be difficult for him, with all the noise and crowds, after the routine and order of his days in the unit. In a few minutes the train rushes in, doors slide open, and then there are streams of moving heads to scan, so it's a jolt when his arms come around from behind to encircle my waist tightly.

"Ed!"

He is laughing. Laughing! I haven't seen Ed even smile for months. I needn't have worried. His face is unshaven, his brown eyes deeply alive, his long black hair shining. He has a backpack and his guitar is slung across his body. He turns, puts his arm around a girl almost hiding behind him.

"Mum, this is Sophie. Soph, Mum."

Her colors light up the drab station. Short bright red hair, green eyes circled with gray kohl, a green knitted coat, stripy blue gloves, orange hat, yellow boots. There is a silver ring through one nostril. She is carrying an accordion strapped to her back. Her face is watchful, calm, and very pretty. I take one of her gloved hands in mine.

"Hello, Sophie."

She smiles. "Hi."

"So lucky she could come," Ed says, looking at her. "She nearly couldn't. Jake wanted her to be there for Christmas lunch on the boat, but in the end it was all right."

I smile at Sophie.

"Thanks for having me." Her chin tilts a little as she says this. There is a soft Irish lilt to her voice.

In the car on the way back, Sophie sits close to Ed, and he points out the cliffs and beaches as we pass. I tell him Theo is arriving later with Sam, the partner we haven't yet met. Then he wants to know what time Ted is expected.

"Tomorrow or the next day. He's flying back from Johannesburg today."

"I reckon he's really on holiday."

I thought he kept in touch with Ed. So nothing's changed. He's been busy all their lives—birthdays, parents' evenings, sometimes Christmas and holidays. The burden of responsibility settles down on me again; it feels as heavy as it did during all those years when I thought he was sharing it. Ironically it got lighter after he left, or perhaps I just knew to brace myself. Why then does the disappointment burn now?

"Not on holiday. I told you, he's been at a meeting."

"Typical."

I check in the rearview mirror, but he's smiling again; there is even a slight air of pride as he slips an arm around Sophie. My father, busy and important.

"Good for your dad. I've always wanted to work in Africa," she says.

"It's only a conference," I tell her. "For a couple of weeks. His real job is in Bristol."

"Sophie works for Amnesty International," Ed says.

"That's impressive." I look at her face in the mirror; she smiles and shrugs.

"I just translate stuff. French and German."

"She and Jake can talk to each other in any language,

especially if they want to say something about me they know I won't understand," Ed says matter-of-factly.

"You wouldn't understand about you whatever language we spoke in. Would-be medics don't get themselves. Too busy being heroes in their own drama." Her lilting voice is amused.

They both laugh as if it's an old joke.

In the weeks after his admission to the unit we had skated around what he might do when he left. He never mentioned doing medicine again after he'd had to leave school. He did his final exams in the unit, and when his spectacular results came through, they only added to the grief, the sense of what might have been. He told me he's happy to stay on helping out for now. This isn't the moment to talk about plans. He seems as if he is fresh from a holiday.

Bertie is standing in the hall when I open the door. Ed's face crumples; he kneels down, puts his arms around the dog, and starts to cry. Bertie stands still, blinking. He sneezes once and then sniffs Ed's hair, tail wagging. Sophie kneels next to Ed and hugs him, laying her cheek next to his. I make tea. I should have seen this coming and prepared him in some way for how the past melts into the present.

After a few minutes, Ed gets up, blows his nose, and laughs shakily.

"Sorry, Bert." He bends and puts his hand on Bertie's head again.

"Shall we go to the sea now, and take Bertie?" Sophie asks.

Ed nods and they drink their tea; then they all go out to the fields through the garden. I watch him pause at the gate, touch the post. I wonder for the hundredth time whether he has yet found a place to put everything that has happened, to keep it until he can think about it and try to make sense of it.

I watch them cross the field, then it's time to take the chicken out of the fridge, slide butter and herbs under the skin, and put lemon and garlic inside. When it's in the oven I pour a glass of wine and take it to the wooden shed outside that I cleared for a studio a week ago, knowing there wouldn't be room in the house. With the windows clean, the light had poured through; the old leaves and dust and mouse droppings were swept away. There was a trestle table in there already. I bought a new heater and hung some of my paintings from the nails in the wall.

My oil painting of Mary's hands is on the table. They look like claws, the fingers deformed by rheumatism, the skin shiny and puffed. She calls them her witch hands, but they make tea, hold eggs and garden tools, bake bread. I've painted them loosely open for her kindness. If Mary is a witch, she is a good witch. Dan's hands are holding a piece of wood. They look careful and careless at the same time—the wood tilts out of his fingers, but he's trapped it with his thumb so that the holding and letting go are balanced. And there is a very new pencil sketch of Michael's hand. Last weekend he was sitting in here in an old deck chair, near the window. He was reading, and resting his hand on his knee. The sketch has captured the power of his fingers and the width of his hand. It needs finishing. I find my pencil, and, as I work, a few flakes of snow fall outside the window. I shade the marked curve of the muscles of the ball of his thumb and it's as though he's touching me. I close my eyes remembering the feel of his hands on my body.

Naomi's eyes, as they are in the portrait, shine at me behind my eyelids. Secrets are dangerous; she should have been careful. Should I be, of Michael?

Ed and Sophie come back. Their clothes are flecked with snow.

"I've never seen the beach in winter," Ed says as he strips off his wet coat. "It was so empty."

Sophie's teeth are chattering. "The cliffs were amazing, all those layers."

They go to bathe and shower, and later, after the chicken, after wine and coffee and washing up, they sit near the fire and Sophie plays her accordion. Ed joins in with his guitar. They look comfortable; this must be something they do often. I join them at a little distance, half in the shadows, sitting in my father's blue chair near the door.

"Who are we going to dedicate this to, then?" Sophie asks.

"Dad."

"Tell me about him," Sophie says sleepily. She lets her arms rest and her fingers stop playing.

"I told you. He's a neurosurgeon," Ed replies. "He operates on people's heads. You know, fixes their brains?"

I feel sad at this pride in his voice. Does Ted have any idea? Would he care? Two years ago I would have thought I knew the answer. No, I wouldn't even have asked the question.

"Must have been hard on you, growing up. I mean, you can't have gotten to see him much."

"It wasn't really hard." Ed is cheerful. "He was kind of around. He used to be there on holidays and stuff. He always came home at night."

He didn't, though. Ed was wrong. He didn't always come home at night.

BRISTOL, 2009
SIX DAYS AFTER

The phone was ringing as I woke. It was on Ted's side of the bed. I turned over to stretch across him but my reaching hand hit the wall. Of course. Spare bed, spare room. I heard Ted answer on the floor beneath me; his quiet orderly cadences meant it was a call from the hospital. I heard him get up and go downstairs to make coffee. He had kept to the usual routine, though everything around him was different. He would be wondering why I hadn't slept next to him; he would think it was because I had come to bed too late and didn't want to disturb him.

He wouldn't know that I had hardly slept, that, when I did, unspeakable nightmares had filled my mind, nightmares that were still there when I woke, thoughts so monstrous that I felt my head would burst open with them. Ted had lied. He hadn't been in the hospital the night Naomi disappeared. It was Ted who had taken her. Ted had picked her up from the theater that night and had secretly taken her away. Why would he do that? The answer was there, ready-made. When he had seen her play Maria, he had realized she was someone different now, not his little Naomi but another girl completely, grown-up, sexy, challenging. Perhaps he didn't like that, so he had—what? Raped her? Killed her? He would know how to; he would know precisely how to block the carotid artery, or crush her trachea. I lay there letting my darkest thoughts torture me until I felt sick and giddy with them. I knew there couldn't be any truth in them, but wasn't that what people always said when it turned out that the murderer was someone they loved?

I walked down the flight of stairs from the spare room and sat on the edge of the empty double bed in our room. Ted's returning footsteps were slow on the stairs, and then he came in. He put my coffee on the bedside table.

"Was I snoring?" He leaned to give me a kiss on the head, and then went into the bathroom without waiting for a reply. A give-and-take moment that was not what it seemed.

There were probably clever ways of getting at the truth, some trick I could play to catch him out, pockets I could search or a diary hidden somewhere; but I was too tired, too heartsick. I had to know quickly.

"Michael came around last night." My voice sounded flat.

"Yes?" His voice was thick with toothpaste.

"He wants you at the station this morning."

"That's not possible, I'm afraid. Why, anyway?" His voice was faint. He shut the shower door, not waiting for the answer. I quickly put on what clothes came to hand.

He looked surprised to see me dressed when he came out of the shower, toweling himself dry. He wrapped the towel tightly around his waist. His body was good for mid-forties: strong, slim, and tightly muscled. I watched his face, still smooth from sleep. A face I've looked at for years, one that I thought I knew better than mine.

"They need you for questioning."

"Sorry, Jen. You'll have to go." He gave a little shrug as he reached into the closet for a shirt.

"No."

"I'm really busy today. Back-to-back clinics." He chose a red tie to go with the blue striped shirt. "I know it's bloody awful, but could you answer their questions for me?"

For a second I wondered whether to wait, but I couldn't bear the surging nightmare anymore.

"They want to know where you were on the night Naomi disappeared." I wasn't sure if it was anger or fear that made it sound as if I was spitting these words at him.

His face hardly altered. If anything it became even smoother. Perhaps his mouth pulled down slightly, as though he had a little tic at one corner.

"You know that already."

I didn't want to hear more lies and I didn't want to look at him as he made them up. I got up and faced the window, looking out at the great, entwined lime trees.

"Where were you?"

"I told you at the time. I had a late operation—"

I turned to face him. "Your operation was canceled. I checked."

There was silence. He went on dressing, taking his suit out of the closet, finding socks. I crossed the room and wrenched the suit out of his hands.

"Where the fuck were you that night?" My voice was loud now. "Your daughter goes missing and you're not where you said you were. What does that mean? What are the police going to think?"

Suddenly his face became suffused with rage as he caught the echoes of my meaning. "What are you saying?" he asked angrily. I heard the boys begin to get up, and the thought of them, unsuspecting and sleepy, made it worse. He'd lied to all of us.

"Shut up," I whispered. "Let the boys go to school. You have to go to the police station; they're coming to collect you."

He stared angrily at me, his mouth set in a line.

"They can arrest you if you refuse to go with them for questioning."

I didn't know if that was true, it could be.

He paused, reached for the phone, and took it out of the room. I heard him canceling his clinic. He had chosen to go to work two days after Naomi had disappeared, but now he had no choice.

Ed left after a silent breakfast, and then Theo gathered his art portfolio slowly. He didn't want to go; perhaps he saw through the pretense. When it was quiet, I faced Ted across the breakfast dishes.

"Okay," he muttered, as though he was talking to himself. "Okay." He looked up. "I planned to tell you the day after it happened, but it was the night Naomi disappeared and I couldn't."

In that second the sick nightmare vanished. I knew what he was going to say and I told myself it didn't matter at all. Compared to the torture of thinking he had hurt her, the fact that he was going to tell me he had been unfaithful seemed insignificant.

"Tell me now."

He looked around the kitchen quickly, as if seeing it for the first time.

"It was just once, that night. I made a stupid mistake. She's young. I mean, she's not married."

I didn't care. I really didn't care. As I waited for him to continue, I understood in a flash why he had been so muddled about picking Naomi up; everything about home had vanished from his mind that night.

"I was tired. I had missed lunch. My operation was canceled and Nitin took the slot for an emergency. I'd just finished a late round and Beth was coming out of the ward at the same time—"

"Beth?" Beth in *Little Women* was the sweet one, generous, feminine. Everyone loved her.

"The head nurse on the neurosurgical ward. She saw I was exhausted. She said there was a restaurant near the hospital that was better than the canteen, but when we got there it was closed, so I took her home."

I thought how Beth would have a peaceful home. There would be no muddy rugby boots by the door, no messy dog jumping up. Together they would go over the shared drama of the day's work. There wouldn't be family questions to tussle with, the kind that had no easy answers, like how much homework the children should be doing or how late they could stay out. Beth would give him a glass of wine, turn on music, and dim the lights. She would sit close and listen to everything he said. She wouldn't be too tired for sex.

"Why?" My voice didn't sound like mine.

There was a long pause, and then he shrugged. "I don't know whether it makes it better or worse, but there's no reason. She was there." He stopped, obviously wondering whether to continue in the face of my silence. Then, avoiding my eyes, he went on slowly, "You and I, there's never time . . ."

"Say it. Never time for sex?"

"We're tired. We go to sleep . . ."

"Why can't you say what you mean?" But I knew what he meant. He was saying it was my fault.

The phone rang. Ted answered it quickly.

"Hi. Yes, my wife told me. I'm ready now. Ring and

I'll come up." He replaced the phone and turned to me. "Michael's just parking; he's coming to collect me." He squared his shoulders. "I'm sorry, Jenny. I was going to tell you." He looked at me and I could see him thinking that something else was needed. "I love you, you know that."

The bell rang. I sensed the full weight of my anger and hurt holding off for the moment. There but not real yet, like the beating edge of a migraine before the pain starts. He stood staring at me for moments longer. His skin was still brown from his recent trip to California. When we met old friends from medical school, they said he was ridiculously unchanged. Sometimes I thought I did the aging for both of us; I had seen the little wrinkles around my eyes appear and deepen, the blue veins flare around my ankles, but I thought that was a fair exchange for what I had. I thought those kinds of changes didn't matter.

"I'm sorry," he repeated, as if saying it twice would make it better. "We'll talk when I get back."

Even then I decided there was no point in talking. Excuses didn't alter anything. I didn't want to hear them anymore. I even let him kiss me good-bye. When he'd gone, Naomi's face filled my mind again; there was no room for anything else.

Chapter 20

DORSET, 2010
THIRTEEN MONTHS LATER

Christmas Eve. In the morning there are footsteps, muffled laughter, then silence again. When Ted and I were young and newly together, love in the morning was warm and easy, no battles or bargains. How long ago was that? I hurry downstairs, not wanting to listen or remember. Bertie is curled and still in his basket. Suddenly afraid, my hands hover over him, checking if there is heat from his body but taking care not to startle him awake or he will struggle up quickly and look confused. In Bristol I would clip on his lead when he was asleep, wake him, and take him out. He faithfully kept up as I jogged through the streets. He couldn't do that now. I leave him to sleep.

More snow has fallen in the night; the twigs are outlined with a delicate ribboning of white. I lean my elbows on the windowsill to look at the new garden.

Naomi used to long and long for a white Christmas, but I must push that thought away quickly before it fills the day. I have family to look after.

There is a small wrapped parcel on the table. The paper is printed with trees and stars, and it has a brown label. I turn it over and it says: To Jenny, from Sophie. My fingers pause.

"No, Naomi, wait till Christmas Day, there's a good girl. Go to sleep."

I unwrap the little parcel, tugging at the tape. Inside is a bundle of charcoal sticks, thick and slightly bumpy, wrapped in tissue tied with red wool. Effort and thought went into this. The framed pictures of Dan's and Mary's hands are leaning against the wall. I pick them up and go out of the cottage quietly.

There is a new holly wreath pinned to Mary's door. She answers my knock quickly and looks relieved.

"Thought it was them lot already."

She puts the kettle on. Her family is coming later, and she will be cooking for everyone. Almost crossly taking the presents from me, she shoves them under the tree. Presents embarrass her; she doesn't know what to say. She likes giving instead. We have tea at the kitchen table. Her hands rest on the tabby coat of the little cat in her lap.

"Haven't seen any Christmas lights in your window. Where's your tree, then?"

"I didn't think to get a tree," I say. "I got as far as presents and food. That was enough."

Mary shakes her head. "Your kids will want a tree."

"Kids! Mary, they're grown-ups."

"Dan's coming by later. He'll find you a tree. He can drop it in."

I don't mind Mary winning. I don't agree with her, but that doesn't matter. As I leave, I give her a kiss and she scowls.

Ed and Sophie are in the kitchen eating breakfast.

"Wonderful charcoal, Sophie! Thank you."

She looks pleased. "My friend on the next-door boat uses an oil drum to make charcoal. He gets this slow fire burning and it takes about two days. There's special willow you can get, from Somerset."

"It's just the kind I like, really dark and smooth on the paper."

I run a basin of warm water to wash up, squirt in the dish liquid, and start to collect the plates from the table. Ed hands me his empty mug of coffee; his eyes are unsmiling.

"So art's still the most important thing in your life, Mum?"

"What?" I turn to him as I slip the plates full of crumbs into the soapy water, wondering if this is a joke.

He looks at Sophie as he speaks; there is no laughter in his face. "When Mum went up to paint, we knew not to disturb her, no matter what. Isn't that right, Mum?"

I feel winded with surprise. "You know that's not true."

"Come on." He leans against the table, arms tightly folded. He sounds different, angry, very sure of his ground. "It was the same when you went to work. You never answered your cell when I phoned. Never there when we got back from school. Used to drive us bonkers." He turns to Sophie again, gesturing, pretending to be amused. "No decent food of course."

Why is he doing this? "I know I used to paint, but it was mostly when you were at school—"

"Christ." Ed's voice gets louder. "Can't you even remember that you weren't around? Whenever I was ill, you left a box of pills by my bed and buggered off to work."

"I let you sleep—"

"Classic. What about the day you told us about the cottage? You said we could have it, then you changed your mind."

"It's only that I didn't want it used for parties—"

"You used to disappear to your 'studio' without warning," he interrupted. "No wonder we felt rejected."

When I went to upstairs to paint, I had been trying to find my own space, not rejecting the children. How could he even think that?

"Ed, art was never, ever the most important thing."

Sophie glances from Ed to me and back again. She tucks a stray lock of red hair behind her ear and looks down at her hands twisting the little Christmas card I had given her.

"'Course it was," Ed continues, still staring at me. "It was because you could make your pictures into what you wanted."

He wasn't like this last night. "What can you mean?"

"You painted the pictures, you were in charge. Nice, two-dimensional art. Not like us, though you tried your best. You thought you were in charge of us as well. You gave us rules. Millions of them." He is breathing hard and his eyes are bright with anger.

"I don't know where all this has come from, Ed. It's Christmas Eve—"

"It hasn't 'come from' anywhere. It's what I've thought all along; being here again has brought it all back."

"I didn't know . . ."

I put a hand out to touch his sleeve and he jerks his arm away.

"How could you possibly know? You never asked me. You were never there. You probably imagined I was the same as Theo." He laughs. "Well, perhaps not as perfect as perfect Theo, but basically twins think alike, don't they?"

"Of course not. I know you are completely different."

"You have no idea about me, any more than you had any idea about Naomi." His words are coming quickly, angrily. "No wonder she's not here now."

Ed stops, as if he knows he's gone too far. He makes a small movement toward me, and then abruptly turns toward Sophie. "Come on, Soph. Let's go for a walk." He takes her hand and pulls her to her feet. She lets him lead her out of the kitchen, but turns at the door to give me a brief unhappy glance.

My hands sting with drying dish liquid and I put them back into the bowl. The hot water covers them, and I stare down at the bubbles that cluster on my fingers by my rings; it occurs to me that I shouldn't still be wearing rings. Silence folds itself back around me, but his words are still inside it. My fingertips are wrinkled by the time I remember there is food to get from the farm shop in Modbury, the next-door village. I dry my hands, tugging at the rings, but my fingers have swollen in the water and I have to leave them.

I lift Bertie into the car and drive slowly, keeping my mind empty.

Snow has blown into the hedges, and the hills are dusted white. Not many people are in the shop. The heaps of vegetables and fruit in the old stone building look like a sixteenth-century Dutch still life. A brace of hanging pheasants drip blood from their beaks; their soft necks are twisted, and the jewel-bright colors of the male's head glow against the soft brown feathers of the female. Dark-green sprouts, creamy little potatoes, and shiny clementines spill out of wooden boxes, and there are dates in a sack by the wall. I buy bags of everything and pick up eggs, bacon, and a huge frosted Christmas cake and load them into the car. On the way home I stop at the sea, get out, and breathe in the bitterly cold salt air.

In the open, the silence in my head begins to throb with the words Ed had flung at me. Millions of rules, he said. Is that how it seemed? But surely he knows rules keep you safe. Bertie and I walk along the snowy turf behind the shingle. Our feet leave translucent prints in the thin layer of icy snow; the grass under mine is twisted and yellow.

A young girl is playing with a dog near where the surf is breaking on the beach. I can see her fair hair from here. A man stands nearby, hunched into a black coat. I wait until I can see her move before I carry on walking. She runs with her legs kicking out slightly. Naomi's run was arrowlike.

If there had been more rules or fewer, would she still be here? If there had been more, then she might have been safer. If there had been fewer, she might not have had to break them. But it wasn't just the rules. Ed was right: I hadn't been there enough. Naomi didn't talk to me in the weeks before she disappeared, but if I'd been there, ready for the moment, she just might have. If I had focused on all the little changes instead of pushing them to the back of my mind, I could have helped her.

I told Ted the children didn't want me around; had I lied to myself in order to construct the life I wanted?

Snow begins to fall again, thin cold flakes that lie separately on the ground. Alcohol hadn't fit with the schoolgirl who worked hard, so I'd pushed that to the back of my mind and believed her excuses. I even made them for her, so I didn't see the real Naomi, the girl who wore thick makeup and a thong, drank, smoked, and had sex. I pull my jacket tighter around myself as the snow drives into my face. I didn't see Ed either. I had been too busy to answer his calls to the office. I had told myself he was working hard, so the real Ed was left to drift into danger, unseen. Kate said our mother had never had a clue about us, but I was worse than that. I had seen the clues and ignored them.

The white sky has darkened. There are patches of snow on Bertie's coat but he stands still, without shaking them off. There is no one around; the young girl and the man have gone. It's time to go home.

When I go in with my heavy bags, there is a tree in the hall entwined with silver-sprayed ivy. Its base is buried in a bucket, wedged in with pebbles from the beach. There are lit candles on the windowsill nearby, in little glass holders. Sophie must have brought them.

Ed has left a note on the kitchen table.

> *Someone called Dan left the tree. Soph decorated it. Gone to pub.*
>
> *E and S*

The glow of candles on ivy is silvery soft. I'm still standing there, breathing in the green Christmas tree smell, when a low car glides quietly past the window on the snowy road, and turns into the driveway. The front door flings open and Theo is there, taller, broader, tanned. I want to weep with relief. As he bends to hug me hard, he smells different, something bitter and expensive. The warmth dissolves some of the hurt from the morning. He pulls back, turning aside.

"Mum, this is Sam."

Sam looks older than Theo, taller, more wiry. He looks different from his photo; perhaps it's the beard. The brown eyes behind his glasses are watchful.

"Hello, Sam."

We embrace, awkwardly. Two kisses, one on each check, which always catches me out. He gives me a bunch of flowers with a practiced little bow. Theo chats about the journey, his recent exhibition, what it feels like to be here at the cottage. He has acquired a trace of an American accent. I stand close to him, listening to his voice rather than his words, then I pull myself together.

"You must be starving."

There is the slightest pause.

"Not really." Theo gives me a quick hug. "Don't be cross. We stopped for lunch at the Beach Hut."

"But you were so near home."

"We didn't want to trouble you," Sam answers smoothly.

Did he need to get up courage before he met me? Does he want to show his power, that he can hold Theo back from us for as long as he wants? My mind touches these thoughts fleetingly.

"Well, you're here now, which is wonderful. You must be tired."

"I want to show Sam around. Which room?"

"Ed and Sophie are in his old room, but yours is tiny; you could have Dad's and mine?"

"Don't be silly. We'll manage with mine. I don't take up much space."

I sense Sam's eyes on mine, gauging my reaction.

"Fine by me."

"Thanks, Mum. Where is Ed?"

"Gone to the pub with Sophie."

"Sophie. Gosh, all these changes."

"Good changes," said Sam.

Bertie appears, disturbed from his sleep by our voices, and runs to Theo, his tail wagging furiously.

"Is this Bertie?" Sam sounds surprised. "He's older than I thought."

"Bertie!" Theo kneels to hug Bertie. He looks up at Sam. "How dare you, he's not old!"

He is old, though. Theo noticed it too.

"When's Dad home?"

I slip the cell phone out of my pocket, glance at it briefly. Still no text from Ted.

"Tomorrow."

They go to unpack and then take Bertie with them to look for Ed and Sophie. I put my old blue apron on; there are fish to slice and poach waiting in the fridge with the gleaming gray shells of prawns. I start to chop celery with onions and garlic, then turn on the radio for the carols. The familiar music fills my mind and the guilt and regret recede a little.

There's a knock at the door. I rinse my hands quickly, then walk to open it, my eyes streaming from the onions. It must be Ted, and he's lost his key. I feel slightly sick with anticipation, at the same time annoyed he will see me red-eyed, smelling of onions. I wipe my hands on the apron and open the door.

For a moment there is nothing to see in the dark, and then Dan steps forward into the semicircle of light. His face looks thinner than usual, sculptural in the shadow of his hood. There are deep hollows around his eyes. Without thinking I step forward and kiss him. He flushes darkly.

"Thank you for the tree. It's lovely." I try to cover his embarrassment with my words. "Sophie decorated it—she's Ed's friend. They arrived yesterday."

"Why are you crying?" he asks abruptly.

"I'm not crying. It's the onions—I'm cooking supper. Come in. Have it with us."

"No, I . . . Thanks for the drawing."

He looks at me intently, and then he turns and is gone. Shoulders hunched, sad and angry at the same time. He's escaping the family Christmas and has come looking for something. I feel I have failed him.

I stir the onions again, add the fish and stock, saffron, wine. The phone buzzes a message in my pocket. I wipe my hands and take it out.

Unable to make Xmas. Hope New Year. T

Not sorry. No love. No message for Ed or Theo. I had promised myself that I would never again allow him to surprise me with hurt. *Unable to make Xmas.* If his plane has been canceled, why not explain? I put my phone down without texting back. Over the last year I had worked it so that what Ted did wasn't important, and by now I thought I had made it true.

BRISTOL, 2009
SIX DAYS AFTER

Ted's infidelity wasn't the issue. We would deal with it afterward, when we had time. It wouldn't hurt then.

I told myself that I was good at this. I prioritize all the time.

Ted phoned from the police station later in the morning.

"I told them," he said briefly. "It wasn't too complicated after all."

Perhaps they had been complicit at the police station. It's a male thing, infidelity, they might have said to themselves; they probably thought that it didn't really matter.

When Ted reappeared in the kitchen, he looked better. There was even a glimmer of pleasedness about him, like a little boy who has done wrong but discovers he might get away with it. In another life I could have replayed back to him the practiced excuse of being at the hospital he had given me the night she disappeared, but I already felt we were very far from where I thought we had been then and there seemed no point. I was curious, though.

"How come they believed you?"

"They asked Beth to come in and . . ."

"And?"

"They phoned the restaurant where we tried to get a meal. They remembered telling us they were closed."

We. Us. I stood there, the words echoing in my mind as Ted watched me silently. I couldn't let this matter. I wouldn't allow it to get in the way.

"I've made a list of what we need to do," I said briefly.

Ted looked away. "It was unimportant, Jenny. I was tired and drunk. A stupid lapse. It couldn't matter less."

A lapse. Not a betrayal or a lie. After twenty years there were layers of how it mattered, but if I let go of where I was, I could get sucked into depths of minding.

"I don't want to talk about any of it now," I said.

"We can't just pretend it didn't happen." His eyes looked puzzled.

"That's exactly what I'm going to do for now. When we find Naomi, we'll deal with this."

"You don't care if I was unfaithful?" He sounded incredulous.

"What do you want, Ted? A scene?"

"Well, it would be a natural kind of . . ." He didn't know how to finish.

"I'm not doing it. There isn't time."

Something flickered at the back of his eyes. Disappointment? Triumph? Then he shrugged and spoke quickly. "You're right. We're losing time. What's on the agenda today?"

"Miss Wenham."

"Miss Wenham?"

"The headmistress. We have an appointment at midday."

"Damn. I delayed my clinic to start at noon because I had to go to the police station." He pulled his mouth down and spread his hands wide. Helpless.

Let it go. I can do it.

"It doesn't need both of us," I said. "I want to see if anyone at school has thought of anything since they saw the police. Then I've made five hundred copies of her school photo with information about when she was last seen."

"I thought the police had done that." He frowned as if he had missed something. "There's one on the lamppost outside; the school must have lots, of course."

"It's not for around here," I said. "I'm going everywhere in Bristol—clubs, pubs, railway station, bus station. Anywhere there's a space, I'm going to put them up." I was walking around the room as I spoke, collecting the file of pictures, Blu Tack, thumbtacks, hammer, nails.

"I could help this evening; perhaps I could get off later this afternoon."

I found it difficult to look at him.

"Michael will come with me."

"What do you think we should say to the boys?"

"Nothing."

He looked relieved. "Really?"

"They've got enough to deal with. You said it yourself; nothing important happened."

TED LEFT AND I had a bath. As I lay in the water, my body soothed by its warmth, unbearable images began to push themselves into my mind. Naomi dirty and longing for the comfort of a bath, her torn body crusted with dirt or, worse, covered with it. Soil in her ears and mouth. If she was dead, would her eyes be open? Would her mouth? I got quickly out of the bath, toweling myself dry fiercely. Think of something else, anything. Anything hopeful. The boys are coping. Jade is getting better. Survive, I told the white face in the mirror. Think of Naomi's smiling face as it was after the play, when Ted hugged her. It wasn't possible that I wouldn't see her again. "Survive till then," I whispered, but I wasn't sure whether I was talking to Naomi or myself.

I didn't bother with a coat, though it was a cold gray late November day. Outside the front door a weary-looking man in his forties pushed himself away from the garden wall, notebook in hand, a careful look of sympathy on his pudgy face. He started taking photos when it was obvious I wouldn't reply to his questions. I turned away and began to hurry down the road; for a while I could hear him puffing after me. The school was only five minutes' walk away. She had done this hundreds of times. Had she been watched in the last few weeks? Even as she was making a new relationship, was someone else tracking her, working out the times she came and went and when she was likely to be on her own?

Miss Wenham was in her study. A bulky woman in her fifties, she stood up to greet me. Her appearance never changed; speech day or sports day, the iron-gray hair was always neatly curled. She shook my hand.

"Dr. Malcolm, I'm so terribly sorry. Such an anxious time. We as a school are doing everything we can to cooperate with the investigation." As we sat down, her glance was searching. Not unkind, just curious.

"Thanks. I just wanted to see you in case something had occurred to any of the staff, or perhaps"—I could already see that she had nothing new to tell me, and I felt an overwhelming tiredness so that I could hardly finish my sentence—"perhaps one of the children might know something and have told you since the police came, or . . ." It was pointless.

She shook her head. "The police have been here three times now." She went on: "However, Mrs. Andrews is Naomi's homeroom teacher. She wanted to talk to you."

She gestured toward a chair. A pale young woman I

hadn't noticed until then stood up and walked forward to meet me.

"Hello, Dr. Malcolm. I'm Sally Andrews."

Her hair had slipped from a clasp at the side of her head and was falling into her eyes. She took my hand in a weak grip and smiled awkwardly. "I'm very sorry for what's happened." She flushed. "I've been trying to think, since the police came. They said to say if anything out of the ordinary struck us. Last night it came to me. There had been something different about Naomi." She sat down next to me on the sofa.

"What do you mean, different?" I asked her, more sharply than I meant to.

"For about two months she was a bit dreamy. I thought she was under the weather, actually. But she said she felt fine."

I was silent. Sally Andrews had noticed her pregnancy, though she hadn't realized it. I was no further forward.

She was carrying on: "I wasn't worried about the dreaminess really, but she asked me something about leaving school, which struck me as odd at the time." She swallowed. "She wanted to know if she could come back and finish her exams if she left early."

"Early?"

"I thought she must mean if she left after the standard tests. She might have wanted to take a breather then. Some girls do, and then they come back for final exams afterward. But last night I was in my bath when they were talking about Naomi on the radio again."

I imagined her slender body floating in the bath, hair in a bath cap, while her husband padded in and out.

"It came to me then that it was almost as if she'd known she would be leaving before the tests next summer. It's just one of those funny coincidences, I expect, but when I heard you were coming today, I thought I must tell you what she'd said. In case." She stopped talking; her cheeks looked pink.

After I had shaken her hand again and thanked both of them, I left. On the way home I felt like running. Perhaps Naomi had planned this, after all; she might have collected money over weeks, and worked out what to do about the exams she would be missing. If she had left on purpose, it changed everything. She would be all right. She would come back.

WHEN MICHAEL CAME to collect me, he looked surprised to see me ready in the kitchen, makeup on and the wad of photocopies in my hand.

"All set?" he asked.

I nodded and we left together. There was no trace of awkwardness as he opened the car door for me; he had obviously put that kiss aside easily. Could it be because he had done it before and he knew how to behave as if nothing had happened?

I told him what Sally Andrews had said. I could see him carefully judging the significance of her words.

"Naomi was pregnant," he said. "She was thinking ahead. The baby would have meant time off and possibly missing the standard tests. I expect she wanted to know if she could take the exams later."

The hope I had felt started to drain away.

"She doesn't sound like the sort of girl who would

cause her parents so much suffering. If this was planned, she would have let you know by now." He glanced over at me. "Sorry, Jenny."

Would she, though? The streets slid by the car windows, full of people who weren't Naomi. As I watched them walking along the sidewalks, alive and unhindered, I realized I hadn't just lost her; perhaps I had lost her long before she disappeared and I had no idea who she was anymore.

Chapter 21

> *Unto us a child is born.*
> *Unto us a son is given . . .*

The joyful morning voices escape through gray stone and stained glass, floating out over lichen-covered graves. Strange how everyone is so glad that Jesus was born when they know how the story ends. Surely they realize that if the girl in the stable had been told what would happen to her baby, she would have been heart-broken.

Naomi's birth by Caesarean had been so easy compared with the physical anguish of pushing out the boys; it had felt like cheating. She was lifted out and given to me to hold, blood-wet and burning against my skin. She had stared calmly into my face, her dark blue eyes serious, as if she recognized me. I didn't want to let her go, but they wrapped her up and Ted held her in the hot peace of the delivery room while I was being stitched. They had looked totally absorbed in each other.

Bertie sniffs at the church wall and cocks his leg. He trundles off down the bridle path with his head close to the ground. I follow, trying to keep up; waiting for the children to come back from the pub last night, I'd fallen asleep in the chair, so I woke feeling stiff and my pace is slow. The bridle path leads us down to the beach. The story in the village is that this little track is an ancient smugglers' way. At night, some in the village say, you can hear the crunch of booted feet on stone and horses whinnying, the echoes of oaths and the rumble of carts bearing caskets of rum. This morning there is only the delicate crack of ice below the snow under our feet. A male pheasant startles up from the hedge with his hollow rasping cry of alarm. Handel's music fades behind us as I follow Bertie farther down the bridle path.

We have come out onto the shingle; the sea churns with yellow foam. No one else is on the beach. As the sun rises, points of light shift and shine on the water; if I half close my eyes, I can almost make them like the city lights, which had seemed lit more brightly for Naomi's first night. The bereavement counselor had said to leave some memories as if wrapped in tissue paper, for when I felt strong enough. I feel strong enough now. I remember the city landscape had spread out like a shining canvas in front of me. From where I had stood in front of the window in the hospital, even at midnight it dazzled with light, magical and mysterious. I knew that the roads were thudding with traffic and there would be vomit on the pavement, pigeon shit, and blown rubbish. But, from the distance of the fourth-floor maternity unit, the streets had looked immaculate and celebratory. In the distance, Clifton Suspension Bridge blazed with lights, like birthday candles in a dark room. Her head was waxy under my lips, her hair like damp feathers. I had sat on a chair near the window, wincing as the catgut stitches dug into tender flesh. Naomi had stirred and whimpered. I had guided her head carefully, pushing in the nipple. As I fed her, I'd felt as connected to her as if she was still inside me. Ted had gone home to sleep. I imagined him facedown, head turned to my side of the bed, arm over my pillow. He would be peacefully snoring, and I remember smiling as I cradled her over my shoulder, her warmth reaching into my heart.

The snow has started again; time to go home. I look around, expecting Bertie to be just behind. He's not there. I know he came down onto the beach from the lane. The surf is high and fierce. In a few moments the waves have become sinister—where is he? I shout his name over and over, but my voice is whipped away by the wind. I run up the beach, half staggering on the shingle. He might have started up the path back home, and then I catch sight of him hidden behind a boat. He is lying down, shivering; a wave must have caught him. My arms strain to lift him. He is soaking and awkwardly struggles out of my clasp to stand with his tail wagging.

"Stupid, stupid dog." I lay my cheek against his silky wet head. "Don't ever do that again."

BACK IN THE cottage, everyone is up. The fire is blazing. I breathe in the scent of coffee and dough while I rub Bertie dry with a towel. Sam is wearing my apron and there is a shiny waffle-making machine on the table with a red bow on top.

"Your present," he says. "I wanted to give you a taste to go with it."

Golden crisp waffles are stacked on the plate. His smile is friendly. The edginess of our meeting yesterday has gone. I feel I am meeting him properly now.

Ed comes in from the sitting room; he avoids looking at me. He's probably glad I fell asleep so early; it meant there wasn't an awkward suppertime and at least I'd cooked them a good meal. He picks up a waffle and eats it whole. He is thinner than I had realized.

"When's Dad back, then?" he asks.

"He sent me a message yesterday. He's not coming after all . . . he says he's unable to make it. Flight problems, I expect."

"I knew it. I told you he was on holiday."

He sits down. Sam, stirring more waffle mixture, briefly touches Ed's shoulder.

"It's that woman's fault, isn't it?" Ed stares at me.

"What woman?" I look at him, puzzled. Is he blaming Ted's secretary for canceled flights?

"Oh for God's sake, Mum. You don't have to pretend for me. I know."

"Know what?"

"About Beth, of course. They came to see me to say good-bye just before they left for South Africa. I bet it's her decision. She probably wanted to stay on. Do a safari or something."

Her name sounds so casual in Ed's voice. Just once, Ted had said. He'd called it a lapse and I'd decided to believe him. The room is quiet. I sense Sam look at me quickly. I struggle to keep my face calm.

"He'd rather be with her. Obviously," Ed says briefly.

"It may not be that." I reach for the chair and sit down. "Perhaps he's held up somewhere."

"Stop protecting him." Ed shrugs. "I mean, who cares? Why does it matter, really?"

He's wrong. I'm not protecting Ted, I'm protecting myself. I look around the room. My mind reaches for its touchstones. The boys. Michael. Bertie. My paintings. The cottage. Mary and Dan. Theo comes in and gives me a kiss, then kisses Sam.

"Don't dare kiss me," Ed says to his brother, covering his head with both hands.

"Don't worry. I'm not going to touch your louse-ridden head." Theo reaches over for a waffle. "These look brilliant."

"Dad's not coming," Ed tells him.

"What?" Theo says indistinctly, his mouth full.

"Enjoying himself in Africa, with his girlfriend."

"Girlfriend?" Theo stops eating. "What girlfriend?" He turns to look at me.

"Mum's cool with it," Ed answers. "So who cares?"

"And it does mean"—Sam balances two more waffles on the pile—"all the more waffles for us." He laughs.

Thank God for Sam. I love him in that minute. Theo sees me smile and smiles uncertainly; in the moment of silence Sophie appears, in a red and orange sweater. She looks toward me, checking how I am.

"Happy Christmas," she says.

SAM LEADS THE way into the sitting room, where he stands in front of the roaring fire and opens one of the champagne bottles he brought; the cork hits the ceiling and frothing liquid spills over his sleeve as he tries to pour it into glasses. He gives the first glass to me.

"For courage," he says. His brown eyes are kind.

I smile back at him then and raise my glass. "Courage."

"Yeah, Mum. You have to be brave to have us lot for Christmas," Theo says.

Brave? They are rescuing me. I look outside quickly. In the garden someone—Theo? Sophie?—has scattered crumbs along the top of the far wall. The birds are little downward-tilted triangles feasting, fluttering up and down, jostling for places. A vivid image comes to mind. Our honeymoon. A tent in the Serengeti. Birds flying around us at mealtimes. Alighting on our table, fighting for crumbs. Ted holding me. We held each other all the time. Heat and sex and happiness. The smell of hot canvas. My skin prickles. They have been together for a year. Not a one-off lapse, after all. They are celebrating in Africa.

"Mum. We're waiting to open our presents."

He never stopped seeing her; he lied again and again.

"Ed, wait for Mum."

How stupidly trusting I'd been. The signs had been there but I had refused to see them, and, as I close my eyes briefly, it's as though I am breathing in the faintest scent of lavender.

"Look, Mum."

I open my eyes.

Theo and Sam have brought in a huge flat parcel from their car, propping it against the wall. Theo fetches the scissors from the kitchen drawer and hands them to me, but he keeps a hand on the parcel.

"On second thought, Mum, you may want to wait to open this."

"Wait? Not a chance." I have to focus on what's important right now. The lavender scent fades in the warm smell of the burning apple logs and the pine from the Christmas tree. This will be one of Theo's photos of New York perhaps, or of Sam. Theo and Sam against the New York skyline.

I start to cut the paper.

"It's Naomi, Mum." Theo sounds tense.

I pull the rest of the paper off.

All the photos are of Naomi. There is a large one in the middle, taken by the school for *West Side Story*. She must have been pregnant then. Her skin is luminous. There are at least a hundred other photos of her, different shapes and sizes. I take in three-year-old Naomi piggyback with Ted, five years old with an uneven fringe that she had cut herself, at ten with braces, waving from the branches of our tree, at twelve with a hockey stick and Nikita, laughing.

"Theo . . ." I can't continue.

"I'm sorry, Mum." He looks stricken.

Sam says in an undertone, "I warned you. Let's take it away."

He stoops to lift the heavy frame.

"Wait. It's wonderful. Don't take it away. Leave it here by the wall." I point to the space. "I'll hang it just by Grandpa's chair. That way I'll see it every day when I sit here. I'll be able to take it in, bit by bit."

"I found all these pictures when I went to clear out the loft with Dad." Theo looks happier now. "I've wanted to give them to you before but I thought it would

be better to wait. I probably shouldn't have given them
to you yet."

"It's a perfect present."

Ed puts more wood on the fire. Sam has insisted on
cooking Christmas dinner. He brought corn bread from
America and somewhere found cranberries and stuffing. Theo and Sophie vanish into the kitchen as well;
they don't allow me in.

"We want you to rest." Sophie smiles shyly and quietly shuts the door.

Ed is lying by the fire, his head propped on an elbow,
reading one of his new books. His body is relaxed, as
if he has said what he needed to yesterday. I watch his
eyes scanning back and forth. Maybe one day he will
see that it wasn't easy, and maybe that's as much as I
can hope for.

There is quiet knocking at the door. Ed gets up and
goes into the hall. There is a little pause, then: "Hey.
Your tree looks great. Want to see it?"

"No . . . I . . . just wanted to say my gran says the
wood has run out . . . could we borrow . . ."

The kitchen door opens; from where I sit I see Sam
come out and put a glass of champagne in Dan's hand.
His voice is welcoming: "You can't visit at Christmas
without coming in for a drink."

Dan comes in, slips his shoes off. He glances toward
me, questioning. I smile and raise my glass. He is wearing his hoodie again and his jeans have slipped down
on his hips. He looks cold, as if he's been outside for a
while.

Dan disappears with Sam into the kitchen. In a
while I see Theo in the garden loading the wheelbarrow with wood and then pushing it out through

the side gate to the lane, for Mary. She'll know Dan is escaping the family meal with his parents and she'll make his excuses.

There is almost no room in the kitchen. On the table holly and ivy strands weave between candles. Sophie has fed Bertie and he sits at her feet. Sam puts a steaming plate with crumbling slices of turkey, stuffing and gravy in front of Dan, who looks awkward.

"I didn't—"

Theo cuts in. "We've wanted to meet you. Mum told us how you used the branches of the old apple tree. I took some photos of my sister once, and the branches around her were like the ones Mum said you used for your wood sculptures."

Sister. My sister. I haven't heard those words in months. They make it sound as though she is still here. Ed looks at me. One arm is around Sophie and he raises his glass. He looks at me. His eyes are guarded, but not like they were before.

BRISTOL, 2009
EIGHT DAYS AFTER

Ed's eyes frightened me.

I had woken that morning into the realization that it had been a week and a day since Naomi had gone. Some momentum should have gathered. Instead everything seemed to have slowed down. I was simply waiting. Worse, I was pinned down, immobilized by fear.

"Enough." I said it out into the silence as I kicked the duvet off. "Enough." Today would be different.

Ted had gone to work already. Theo had left early

too. He'd put a note on the table to say he'd gone to as-semble the materials for his scholarship exam. He'd ap-plied for a photography course at the New York Film Academy the following year; the scholarship could be decisive, but I'd forgotten it was today. Normally I'd have sent him off with a good breakfast. We would have discussed timing and techniques, and I would have said good luck. Guilt reached deeply inside; I was letting ev-erything go. Ed came down as I was making coffee. He sat at the table and as I passed him I caught the stale smell again.

"So, Friday," I said as I tried to remember his routine. "Rowing practice?" Anya told me his sports clothes had been on his bathroom floor, soaking wet, for days.

He put two hands against the table and pushed his chair out so hard and quickly that I had to sidestep. He looked at me as he got up and that was when I noticed the fury in his eyes.

"I'm not a fucking child," he said just before he shut the door.

Anya came in quietly. She had brought a little pale pink cyclamen plant, put it in a pot on the table, and nodded to me. I knew it was supposed to cheer me up. For a moment my attention was caught by the creamy petals with their sharp-edged frill. Flowers went with illness and death and graves, but these were pink, like the ones I had carried at my wedding.

"Thank you, Anya, they're lovely."

She smiled as she began clearing the table. Anyone else's presence would have been an intrusion, but her careful movements were balm. Without her, the house would have descended into dirty chaos by now. Ed was suffering like we all were. It was worse for him; no matter how often we told him it wasn't his fault, I knew he felt guilty.

I found a white cardboard sheet wedged behind my desk; Theo had bought more than he needed for his woodland project. I wrote "Naomi" in the middle in blue felt-tip and then drew a series of concentric circles of increasing size around her name: the first for family, the second for school. I wrote Nikita's name here and ticked it because she had been seen by the police. James, another tick. Teachers, Sally Andrews, Miss Wenham. Tick. Tick. Tick. What about other teachers? Mrs. Mears, the drama teacher who had resigned? I needed to ask Michael.

I drew another larger circle around the circle for school, for people she saw often but not every day. Anya? Anya's husband? I looked at Anya quietly sweeping the floor. She sensed me watching her and smiled. I put a question mark next to Anya's husband, to remind me to check with Michael if he had been questioned by the police.

Neighbors belonged in this circle too. Mrs. Moore opposite, Harold her son, that shadowy figure at the window. Michael must have checked him too, but I put a question mark against his name in case.

What else? The play. Anyone who'd worked in the theater. Reception staff. Had Michael checked?

There was a sudden exclamation of pain. The broom clattered to the floor.

"You okay, Anya?"

"I stub my toe. Your doctor's bag. I don't see it there—new place."

"Sorry. Shove it back under the bench. Someone must've kicked it out by mistake."

Doctor's bag. Work. Another circle. Colleagues and patients. If I were to go back, something might jog my memory. Frank had said to be off for the duration, but it already felt too long. I wanted to do something. Even making this chart was doing something.

I showed the board to Michael when he called in, around midday. I wondered what it was like to come into this house and whether you could smell grief at the doorway. He took off his jacket and rolled up his sleeves; his arms looked strong. Something about his calm face and the focus of his gray eyes made me think of a soldier before battle.

He whistled in admiration. "That's like a professional inquiry layout. What about all the question marks?"

As I handed him a cup of coffee, I wanted to laugh. "The whole thing is a fucking question mark."

He bent closer over my chart. "Some questions have been answered, so we can cross them off right now. Like the school," he said.

"Mrs. Mears?"

"Yes. Her alibi checked out. She had exemplary references and records. Like all the teachers in the whole school."

"What about all the other staff?"

"Done. All the ancillary workers, gardeners, cleaners, cooks, and caretakers. The receptionist and bar staff at the school theater. They've all been questioned and their alibis checked."

He'd been busy. That was good, of course, but my heart sank; I had thought I was being useful, doing something that might get us closer to her. In reality I was trailing behind.

"Okay. Then there's my office," I said. "Should we look there?"

"We've interviewed your colleagues at work. They talked about Jeff Price as well, but he was in the hospital with Jade, like you said."

I lowered my voice. "Anya's husband?"

"Interviewed. Alibi checked. You gave us a lot of this information on the first night."

My optimism was leaking away. What had happened to my memory? All I could remember was asking the police to find her. Begging and crying.

I looked at my notes again. "What about the neighbors?"

"Finished yesterday, with Mrs. Moore," he said.

"What did Harold say?"

"He wasn't there." Michael sipped his coffee. "She told me not to bother going back. Apparently he can't communicate well."

"He never goes out and I'm sure he can communicate. She's protecting him." I pictured the small woman, her back to the closed door of the room where she had hidden her son. I leaned forward urgently: "He's always looking out of the window; he might have seen something."

"Then we need to see if he can tell us anything." Michael stood. "Do you want to come?" he asked. "It could be useful, but if I need to question him in depth, you may have to leave."

I took several copies of Naomi's photograph off the pile stacked next to my computer. As we crossed the road Michael paused and walked to the white van parked close to our house. Opening the door, he raised his voice, though I couldn't make out the words. He needn't have bothered. I didn't mind about the journalists; they hardly figured in the roaring terror that filled every moment. Ted hated them.

Mrs. Moore answered the door after a few minutes. She was wearing an apron tied tightly around her waist. Her face hardened when she saw both of us.

"Said my bit already." She nodded accusingly at Michael. "Told him yesterday."

"And Harold?" I tried to speak gently. "He could be helpful, Mrs. Moore. He watches out of the window, you can easily see the theater from here."

"He's having his dinner."

"If we could just have a word," Michael said quietly. "It needn't take long."

Inside the dark hall there was a mirror glinting in the gloom. Mrs. Moore led us into a large, immaculately tidy kitchen.

Harold wasn't eating, he was drawing. A plate with a half-eaten sandwich was pushed aside. He was wearing a striped short-sleeved shirt, tightly stretched over his curved back; his bare arms were plump and scattered with moles. He was breathing heavily, his tongue protruding as he worked. A box of crayons was tipped on the table, next to a stack of drawings. They were all smudged with blue wax. Michael picked up a drawing and Harold snatched it back.

I knelt by Harold's chair and showed him the photocopied picture.

"This is a picture of Naomi, Harold. You know Naomi."

Close up his face was completely smooth, no smile or frown lines.

"Gone," he said.

"Ah." Michael turned to Mrs. Moore.

"He knows that from the TV," she said grimly. "And he heard you talking yesterday. I didn't want him involved. I told him to stay quiet in the other room when you came last time. He doesn't know anything."

"Is that right, Harold?" Michael asked him lightly. "Or is there anything at all you can tell us?"

Harold stared at him blankly. He started scribbling hard with the blue crayons. We stood, looking down at him, reluctant to leave.

"Well, if you remember anything, please let us know," Michael said.

Outside, the white vans had gone. Michael smiled grimly. Back in my kitchen he made some notes while I phoned Frank, relieved to hear the answering machine; it meant not having to answer questions about how I was. Instead I left a brief message: they might need help; midwinter was always busy in the medical office. I was still by the phone when there was a loud knock. Michael, gathering his things to leave, went to answer.

Harold was standing outside, a wad of paper under his arm.

"Naomi," he said loudly. "Naomi."

Mrs. Moore appeared breathlessly at his shoulder.

"Harold wouldn't wait. It turns out he's got something to tell you, after all that."

Harold put his pictures on the table. There were about twenty in smeared blue wax. They all had a squarish shape with an oblong protruding from one side. He pointed to the shape.

"Truck," he said.

Michael sifted through the pile and drew out one where the blue shape was in front of an outlined square.

"That's the theater," said Mrs. Moore. "After you left he started on about your daughter."

A blue truck outside the theater? I thought back desperately. Had I seen a blue truck or even a blue car? Ever? Maybe there had been one, streaked with mud, a small dog with his nose to the sliver of open window at the back? Or had it been a big, dark blue Mercedes? Either could be true, or made up completely, conjured out of suggestion.

Harold had a screwed-up piece of paper in his hand. He was pushing it into the blue picture of the car. There was sweat along his upper lip. I saw where the razor had missed little clumps of hair by his right ear. He was getting angry.

"Thank you, Harold," Michael said quietly. "It's kind of you to help us find Naomi."

Harold stared at him. Michael eased the screwed-up paper from his grip and flattened it on the table. It was the photocopied picture of Naomi.

"Thank you," Michael said again. "That was very helpful. You have been more helpful than anyone else."

After they had gone, I glanced at Michael. "This could be important."

"Maybe," he replied. He inspected the picture again. "That rectangular shape joined to the square one makes it more like a pick-up van." As he turned to me, concern flitted over his face. I knew what he was seeing: my exhausted face, messy hair, red eyes. The new thinness.

"You look—"

"Don't tell me I look terrible. It doesn't matter a fuck." A shocked expression crossed his face, and I laughed, actually laughed. "If you knew how much I don't care about my appearance."

"The boys will," Michael said steadily. "Ted will. Your appearance is part of how you stay strong."

I knew that made sense, but it was almost impossible to think about my own appearance when my mind was full of Naomi, how she had looked when I last saw her, how she might be looking now.

I touched Michael's arm. "Do you think it will help, this blue van?"

"It might." He smiled down at me. "There are a lot of blue vans about, but it's one more tiny bit of information. One more thread. This is how it's done, you see. We untangle the threads, one at a time."

WHEN THEO CAME home he looked miserable. He thought he'd done badly in the art scholarship. Changing his mind too often, he had ended up rushing. We had supper together; Ed came in sometime afterward. He had been coming in later and later recently, often working in the library until it closed. He didn't want food; he had eaten at school.

After supper I caught sight of Theo lying on his bed, talking on his cell; he grinned at me more cheerfully. Ed had left his door open; he had fallen asleep on his bed with all his clothes on. I slipped his shoes off and covered him with a blanket. As I turned to go, the light from the landing caught a pile of bills on his bedside table. I looked closely. There were ten- and twenty-pound notes stacked in a neat pile, perhaps three hundred pounds in all. What was he doing with this money? Where did it come from? Ted transferred the boys' allowance from his account online, so it was unlikely that it was from him. Had Ed been working in secret somewhere? Perhaps all the evenings I thought he was studying at school he was working for money at a pub. Why hadn't he told us? Was he saving it to give to us, trying to make amends for not being there for Naomi in the theater? The thought caught at my heart. I wanted to wake him up and ask him, but even in sleep he looked exhausted. It would have to wait till morning. I tiptoed out and closed the door.

Chapter 22

The air in the shed smells stale after Christmas. Mouse droppings are scattered on the sheet of paper I left on the table, and the wax crayons have been etched with tiny teeth marks. My feet crunch on grit blown through the gap under the door. I shut the door again and go back into the house.

In the mornings when the light is still gray, I wander around the house in this nothing time between Christmas and New Year's. I can tell exactly where I am with my eyes closed. The air feels differently charged around the blue chair, the silky wood of the desk, the pile of books. Touching the familiar furniture is like touching my own skin. I look at the photos from Theo's montage one at a time. Today it's the baby in the carriage, her eyes serious, looking at the patterns the cherry tree blossoms make against the sky. The picture captures a starfish hand reaching to touch the shadow of the leaves on the inside of her carriage.

I miss the boys and Michael; he had tactfully arranged to cover at work when we thought Ted might be here at Christmas, though he knows we have separated. He calls every night, never in the day; our relationship is still secret from his colleagues. I don't know what would happen if they found out. I miss him, my body misses his. I find myself craving him unexpectedly. In my darker mistrustful moments I wonder if he knows this, if he wants to gain some kind of hold by his absence. Could he be playing a game? He has stepped across a boundary to make love—should that make me trust his motives more or less?

Ed has gone back to the rehab unit. He's planning to stay for a few more months, but he gave me no details. He didn't talk to me about his feelings again either, though Sophie gave me a hug as they left. His words echo on, and I turn them over and over; did I trade Naomi's life for mine? Now that I have all the space and time I ever wanted, I'd swap everything for a second of her.

Theo phones. "It's so good to be back home." Ridiculous to feel a pang. "Think I could live here forever." As he talks I hear the clink of bottles and Sam's voice singing *Carmen* in the background. Once Theo's relationship with Sam would have taken us time to encompass, causing a shift in the smooth track of our lives and the assumptions we made. Instead it has found its place easily.

After Theo's call, I try the shed again, shaking the little battered tin tubes of oil paints out of their box into a small heap on the trestle table: French ultramarine,

Indian red, Naples yellow, a whole geography of colors. Theo said forever; that's as far as you can see before you've been hurt, though of course he has been hurt. No, it's farther than that; it's as far as you can imagine, stretching to all the places and people that you think will always be there. But nothing lasts. Not places, not people, not love, nor the vanishing lives of children. Loss does, and I start to make thick straight lines with Sophie's charcoal. At the beginning I didn't see how I could ever manage the hours, then the days, the weeks, the months of forever, the dull metal of her absence never wearing any thinner. As I work, dark crumbs break from the sticks; and I blow them away. The boys don't talk much about Naomi. The space behind them is full of her, but their lives have gone beyond hers. Mine hasn't; I've endured, that's all.

I cross the vertical lines with horizontal bars to make a grid, thinking about the colors to put between the lines, luminescent, bordered by darkness but not stained by it; these spaces will represent the boys' lives. I walk in tight circles inside the shed, trying to think of a color for them, one that sounds a clear note but carries other darker ones within it. It's difficult to think of a pigment that holds light and shadow at the same time, perhaps a glowing cinnabar orange. I need more colors. I imagine some kind of rich desert dust that has been distilled by wind and heat. Then I remember the Byzantine paintings hidden in the caves of Göreme in Cappadocia. The frescoes on the walls looked backlit by sun even in the deepest caves. They had a rich, hopeful glow that was also somber. I experiment with strokes of oil paint on my easel. Cadmium yellow, cadmium pale? Something extra is missing. White? Red? Orange? I lay my brush aside to wait until I can catch it somewhere else. The sunset, or the yolk of an egg perhaps.

As I turn to go, my fingers knock a little bunch of kindling off the bench. I must have paused to look at a painting on the way to make up the fire, and left it by mistake. I pick it up, pull out a long twig, and twirl it in my fingers. The wood is gray brown, there are tiny bumps where next year's leaf buds would have formed, the bark is minutely pitted and delicately peeling in places, the stubbed end is split and frayed as if chewed, the ends open and spread like the thinnest fingers. I sketch the twig roughly, then again more carefully, larger, then larger still. Forms and shapes, waiting to change into something else; the idea for a large painting begins to form, a cycle of life. A triptych. An unfamiliar excitement starts to build, so light and distant I'm afraid I will spoil it by thinking about it. I focus on the minute buds, smooth, unformed.

After an hour my hands start shaking with cold and I have to stop drawing. Back inside the cottage, the excitement has gone. In the empty rooms the dark condenses around me, the familiar weight of sadness so heavy that I can't move. When the bell goes, I can barely walk to the door. Dan is on the doorstep, serious-eyed, hunched in his coat.

"Don't stand there"—I step outside, putting my hand on his sleeve—"come in. I was hoping someone would call, and here you are."

He walks in past me, looking downward, suddenly shy.

"It's good to see you," I tell him, taking his coat. "It's been too quiet since Christmas."

"You okay?" He looks hard at me, the green flecky eyes searching my face.

"Yes, 'course I am." My smile falters under his gaze. "Well, maybe not okay exactly . . ."

I expect he knows about Naomi from Mary, though I've never told her. As he stands there, he seems to be waiting for more, and some of my resolve breaks: "Maybe it's the time of year, but it's the second Christmas without my daughter, so it's like she's getting further away all the time. I'm wondering what it will be like on the third and then the fourth . . ."

He flushes. "I could stay if you like . . . Would you like me to stay?"

"Have you had supper?"

"Well, no, but—"

"Stay, then. Turkey curry? You can carve the meat off if you want to be helpful."

He comes in, sits at the table. I give him a glass of wine. He takes off his sweater and rolls up his sleeves as I get the huge carcass from the fridge. Even though it's winter, his arms are brown from working in Mary's garden.

"Nice tan." As I reach into the cupboard for spices and curry paste, I catch his slow blush; Ed used to be easily embarrassed like this. I should know better. "How's the deciding going?"

He carves carefully, the meat falling in curls on the board. "I'm thinking of going away for a bit." I glance at him, surprised. "Yeah." He looks down. "I saved some money. Theo told me about this art course in New York, cheaper than here, even. I've applied for the sculpture modules."

"That's great, Dan. Where will you stay?"

"Sam said I could stay on a mattress with them."

"That's fantastic. Do it." I fill up his glass again and clink mine against it. "How did you make up your mind in the end?"

The rice bubbles, I tip the turkey he has carved into the simmering sauce. The kitchen feels warm and like home again, as though Theo or Ed was here. Over food he talks about his family, how his mother is fine with his plans, and his father, uncertain at first, has now agreed to help him with the fees. He wants to know what I'm doing. His face lights up when I describe the grid painting.

"Sounds amazing, Jenny. Almost like sculpture." He hasn't used my name before; it sounds strange, though I don't know why. He could hardly call me Mrs. Malcolm. He leans forward. "I'd like to take some photos of your paintings, might give me inspiration."

I haven't shown them to anyone. "Maybe," I murmur noncommittally. His face falls, so I add quickly, "No one's seen them, some of them aren't even very good."

I'm tired suddenly. It's late. I let Bertie out into the garden and Dan stands up and stretches widely.

"I'll do the cleaning up."

"Thanks, but I always do it in the morning." I fetch his coat, relenting as I hand it to him: "Come back before you go away, Dan. I'll find something for you to photograph."

He turns at the door, looks down at me, says, "I want to take some pictures of you too. Your face."

My face? I feel confused with surprise. Then I laugh. "Not me, Dan. Mary's got a wonderful face. Take some of the young pretty girls in the village."

"I've taken loads of Mary already and I don't want

girls' faces." He looks at me almost angrily. "You're pretty anyway. Beautiful, actually."

"Rubbish, Dan." I try to laugh again.

Stretching behind him to open the door, I jolt when he reaches out and touches my face with his fingers; then he turns and is gone.

I shut the door and lean against it. I hadn't seen that coming, or had I? I start to clear supper, tipping away the leftover food, rinsing plates, scrubbing saucepans, annoyed with myself. How did I let that happen? Dan is even younger than my boys, yet tonight I had let myself be warmed by his attention—no, I enjoyed it. I've been careless; I won't see him for a while. I've traveled further than I had thought from my old life, the person that I had been, the good, happy, busy woman. I climb upstairs slowly. Michael's text comes through to say good night. I usually text back, but tonight I sit on the edge of my bed, my cell loosely in my fingers, while I stare into the darkness outside. If I go right back, to where Ted and I started, I've traveled much, much further.

Remembering back is like watching a film with actors playing our parts; I can see myself in the hot library. I remember the flowery minidress I was wearing and that my hair was piled anyhow out of the way; I was oblivious and absorbed in a dermatology book in the library. I'd come to the university from high school after a gap year in between, and took medicine very seriously, convinced that becoming a doctor was all I wanted. Edward Malcolm was in my year but moved in a different group. He had a car when no one else did; he played cricket for the university. Everything about him irritated me, especially his smooth good looks. I doubt if our paths would have crossed at all if we hadn't both been so ambitious, and if the library hadn't been so hot and crowded that afternoon. Summer 1985. I had been sketching out an essay that I planned to enter for a prize worth several thousand pounds. I was glad I had a head start on Ted Malcolm; he was after every prize as well, but he didn't need the money like I did. The library had been stifling. I scooped up an armful of books to take home, and then bumped into him on the way out. He casually took the top book off the pile I was carrying. I'd fought him for it, laughing but annoyed at the same time. He only gave it back when I promised to go out with him. It began then.

Pulling off my clothes, I get under the duvet. It wasn't a film, though; romantic films have happy endings. In real life only the beginnings are happy and nothing ends well. But then, nothing really ends.

Chapter 23

DORSET, 2010
THIRTEEN MONTHS LATER

On December 30, tired of missing Michael, I make a plan so as not to leave any gaps into which I might fall: a walk to Golden Cap. From this high point the Jurassic coast spreads wide on either side. In the summer there is the hot coconut smell of gorse, but at this time of year the air will be fresh and salty. I can look for colors, though I expect I will have to wait until the weather is warmer. I could always collect what I need to sketch for the larger work about change that's in my mind. I need leaves, twigs, tiny buds.

Bertie and I start out at seven. The village is still quiet, with a few lights on here and there, glowing from bedrooms where couples are waking up, curled around each other. Cups of tea are being passed carefully and set down on bedside tables. The scent of night is still thick in the misty shadows between the cottages. I walk quietly so as not to wake people still asleep. In the silence, distantly and then nearer, there are footsteps beyond the corner in the lane. They sound tired and uneven. Perhaps a farm worker coming back to his breakfast after milking, or one of the fishermen returning home to his bed after landing the first catch of the day.

A tall man comes around the corner, a thin, bent shape in the dark. It takes me several moments to recognize Ted. His walk is different, slow and slightly hesitant, not the old purposeful stride. He looks exhausted, as if coming to the end of a long journey.

I'd forgotten his text and feel sick with the unexpectedness of him here, now. If I stand by the side of the road he might walk past me. He would find the cottage dark and locked and perhaps go away again. I lean against a garden wall in the dim morning light; the stone is damp and gritty under my fingers. He won't see me unless he looks in the shadows, but he might hear my heartbeats, which seem to fill the space between us. He is level with me, he is passing. I hold my breath, but then Bertie runs toward him, tail wagging. Ted bends to him and I know he is thinking how like Bertie this dog is, then, realizing it is Bertie, he looks up quickly and sees me. He says my name and there is gladness in his voice. As he steps toward me, I move back, just slightly. I don't look fully at him yet; instead I look behind his head, where ivy is prizing apart the stones of an old wall. He tells me he has left his car in the pub parking lot; he didn't want to wake everyone with the engine rumbling under the windows of the narrow little streets. We walk back to the cottage; Bertie trots between us, looking up at him constantly.

In the kitchen he sits at the table with his coat on, like a visitor who isn't going to stay long. I make a cup of coffee and put it down in front of him, then step back.

"Why were you hiding just now?" he asks me, and even his voice is slow and tired. There are mauve marks under his eyes. His hair is grayer and thinner. His stubble is so long he must be growing a beard. "If I hadn't noticed you against the wall, you would have let me walk by."

"I wasn't hiding. I was waiting . . ." I make these words effortfully. I would prefer to stand here silently absorbing the strangeness of his presence.

"Waiting?"

My answer shapes itself, unsaid. Yes, waiting to see what would happen, hoping he would walk by, unknowing. All the weeks and months after Naomi went, I waited for him. He passed me by then, leaving me in the shadows on his way to someone else.

"It's all right, you don't have to answer." Ted shrugs and opens his hands with a little laugh; he has the red palms of a drinker. He sees me looking and closes his hands around the coffee cup. A few drops spill onto the tablecloth and spread into little circles.

"So, you're okay? Here, I mean. Of course I don't mean . . ." He stops.

"I'm okay."

"You look fine. Good, actually." He sounds surprised.

"Thanks."

"I mean you look pretty." His eyes narrow, appraising.

"Thanks." If I look pretty it's because of Michael, but I won't tell him, not yet.

"How were the boys?" He shifts in the chair, as if

trying to get comfortable. "When you saw them at Christmas?"

"They were fine." My heart is still racing fast; I can't make long sentences, but words spill out of Ted. After all, this isn't a surprise to him.

"I've missed them so much. I've seen Ed, of course." He is thinking of seeing Ed with Beth, all the times he took her to see him.

"What about Theo?" he carries on.

"He's fine."

"I should have been here for Christmas. I'm sorry."

His shirt is crumpled; perhaps he slept in it. His coat is too big for him. The smell of stale cigarettes fills the kitchen. What particular thing is he sorry about? Christmas? Beth? The lies?

"Do you think about Naomi much?" he asks abruptly into the silence.

I turn my face to the window, unable to look at him.

He goes on, his words coming faster. "I think about her all the time."

I glance at his face. Tears run into the gray stubble.

"At the moment it's the feel of her hands, when she was little. They were so soft. She used to put them against my cheeks and pretend that my stubble hurt and then we would pretend to bandage them." His nose is running; the tears are streaking the dust on his face.

I don't want this unfurling. I hand him a paper towel. He wipes his face. The bunched paper opens itself on the table, translucent with tears and mucous.

"I look for her everywhere I go." He is speaking so quietly I have to bend toward him to catch the words. "Once, in Cape Town, on my way from the hotel to the hospital, I thought I saw her. I followed this girl into a park. She walked the same way as Naomi." He smiles up at me. "Remember that little sort of bounce as she walked, as if she could keep going forever."

"Only she didn't."

"Didn't what?" He is still smiling, but puzzled.

"Keep going forever."

"Don't you think so?" He clenches his fist and bangs it softly on the table. "Don't give up. Don't ever give up. I still think we'll find her."

He stood up. "I've made so many mistakes."

"I don't want to hear this now, Ted. It's too late for all this."

He stands in front of me, swaying slightly on his feet, as though he is drunk but he doesn't smell of alcohol. His eyes are closing. His voice slurs.

"Sorry. Just need to sleep for a bit. Couldn't on the plane. Drove all night, must lie down . . ."

I run him a bath, and show him the tiny spare room. He stares at the ivory walls that Dan painted so carefully, the blue-and-gray-striped curtains, and the fire grate full of whitewashed fir cones. He takes in the rough pale blue cotton blanket, and his gaze rests on the little bowl of sea glass next to the bed. His shoulders relax. He takes off his coat and puts it on the wicker chair by the window. "Nice," he murmurs. "You've done something. Don't know what. It's nice." He sits on the bed, and then falls sideways with a sigh. His breathing alters almost immediately and becomes slow and deep. I undo his laces and heave his shoes off. He surfaces for a moment.

"Stay here? Sleep next to me?"

I shut the door and empty the bath water out. Then I go downstairs to the kitchen and take off the layers of outer clothes that I had put on earlier. The light is brighter now, but I hear rain starting. We wouldn't have been able to see much up on Golden Cap after all. I slowly unlace my walking boots and pull them off. Bertie rests his heavy head on my feet. He likes the rough feel of the wool under his soft mouth.

BRISTOL, 2009
EIGHT DAYS AFTER

Ted was late, as usual. Supper had long finished by the time he came home with lines under his eyes, and crumpled clothes pulled on after operating. I was glad to see him. He had promised me the episode with Beth was a mistake and I had to believe him. I needed him. I didn't have the energy for anger; in any case, what Ted had done began to fade next to the scouring anguish of Naomi's absence. He was silent as he went to the stove to get the meal, which had been keeping warm. The meat looked dried. The potatoes were shrunken, the greens stringy. I imagined his day and how he might have thought about hot food as he drove home.

"That looks disgusting, Ted. Shall I make you an omelette?"

"You don't have to." He took a bottle of wine from the cupboard, opened it, and poured out two glasses, and then he sat down heavily with a sigh.

"Sorry I didn't phone," he said as he sipped wine. "The operation went on all day. I'm later than I meant to be. Where are the boys?"

"Theo's around somewhere. Ed's gone to bed."

"This early?"

"He needs to catch up on sleep; he's tired all the time. Anya can't even get into his room to clean because he gets up so late. The worry is wearing him out." I started tapping eggs against a bowl. "Michael came by. Harold Moore told us—"

"Who the hell is Harold Moore?" He watched the egg mixture slide, frothing, into hot butter.

He listened as I reminded him; then I told him about the blue van.

Ted tilted his head. "I think I did see a blue car, maybe a van, parked outside the theater, actually. Once or twice, perhaps." He shrugged; he obviously didn't think it was important. "We'll probably find it belonged to the drama teacher or someone," he went on flatly. "I wouldn't have said that having Down's syndrome makes you very reliable."

"I think Harold would be a good witness. He watches everything. He was very focused on his drawing."

Ted didn't reply. I put the omelette in front of him and he began to eat it quickly.

"Michael is working on it." I sat down opposite Ted. "He is going to organize some kind of reconstruction. You know, a girl leaving the theater late, getting into a blue van."

"It was late and dark, so it may not help. What else?"

"Ted, couldn't you miss your Saturday schedule and stay at home tomorrow? If you think we are on the wrong tack with this, then what can you think of instead?" I paused, forcing myself to stay calm. "I made this kind of plan on a card. I want your input."

Ted pushed his empty plate away. "Show me."

We bent over the table, looking at the circles surrounding her name. Home. School. Neighbors. The theater.

"We need another circle," he said slowly. "Enemies. Grudge holders."

"You don't have those kinds of enemies at fifteen." I looked at him incredulously.

"Not her enemies. Ours." He spoke quietly.

"I thought that once, about Jade's father, even Anya's husband, but I was wrong. Do you really think anyone could hate us that much?"

Ted's eyes were thoughtful. "My registrar had his tires slashed once. He wondered if someone had a grudge. I mean, who knows what we do or don't do, by mistake. Doctors playing God."

"Christ." Something seemed to shift and loosen in my resolve. I began to cry.

Ted's arm came around me tightly. I smelled the familiar, slightly scented smell.

"Reminds me of summer," I murmured, my head against his shoulder.

"What?" He stepped back and looked at me.

"Lavender." I stood near him, unwilling to walk away. We hadn't touched for days. "Not criticizing. I like it." I took his hand.

He freed his hand and patted my back. "The nurses get to choose the operating room scrub, so it's scented, probably expensive as well." He bent closely over the cardboard.

"Speaking of cost"—I remembered the piles of banknotes in Ed's room—"have you been giving the boys cash instead of transferring their allowance online? Not sure it's a great idea to be so generous."

"Have I been generous?" He wasn't listening. He turned away, pulling out his cell phone.

"I saw that money, a pile of bills. You don't have to do that."

"Not sure what you mean, Jen. I haven't given the boys any cash for months. I set up a bank transfer to their accounts, remember? Let me just text my registrar. He needs to find the scans for tomorrow's list of patients."

I was so tired my feet throbbed and my eyes stung. Of course he couldn't miss the list, I shouldn't have bothered asking. Where the hell had all that money come from? I was too exhausted to think any more about the money tonight. I'd have to ask Ed in the morning. Ted went up to bed ahead of me and was asleep before I got in beside him. I tried to curl into him but he was lying on his front, head turned away. I rested my head on his shoulder. In spite of my tiredness, I stayed awake, trying to think what enemies I might have, hoping to block the images that swam toward me when I was tired and the waves of utter despair and dread that lay in wait for me everywhere.

BRISTOL, 2009
NINE DAYS AFTER

Ed was tipping cereal into his bowl at breakfast and some spilled over the edge onto the surface of the kitchen table.

"Why do you always have to come into my room?"

His voice was cold.

"Ed, you'd fallen asleep with all your clothes on. I just took off your shoes and covered you up."

"I'm not a child."

"So, the money?"

"None of your business, Mum, is it, really?" There was a pause. He shrugged. "If you must know, I'm doing a sponsored rowing event, a sort of gala. It's on Monday. I'm in charge of the money. That's why I've been late so much. I've been training."

It made sense. The tiredness, late nights at school.

Ted was still asleep upstairs; his operating schedule started late today, and I let him sleep on while I paced around restlessly. The fear was always worse in the morning, moving sharply under my skin. I could never be still or concentrate on anything for long.

I phoned Michael. He told me that they had checked all the regular and student actors who used the school theater. All had alibis.

"What next, Michael?"

"A possible reconstruction on Friday night. I'll let you know if that goes ahead."

So another girl would play the part of my daughter, another girl would get into a blue van outside the theater after 10:30 P.M., but then when the camera stopped rolling, she would get out again and go home. I wouldn't watch.

Frank phoned back in answer to the message I had left. He agreed to let me try a clinic if I was sure. Work was gathering pace. Run up to December. Usual seasonal coughs and colds. Could I start the day after tomorrow?

BRISTOL, 2009
ELEVEN DAYS AFTER

I hadn't been in my car for days, but my hands on the
wheel looked certain of what they were doing. In the
office, my room was immaculate. The desk had been
sorted. I put my bag down, pulled out my stethoscope
and auroscope, and put them next to the clean prescription pad.

Lynn came in and gave me a hard hug.

"I'm not going to be nice. You've got today to get
through. I'm next door if you need me." She left, brushing her eyes with her hand.

Jo brought me a cup of tea and kissed me as she said,
"We've booked you easy patients to get back into the
swing."

The first patient was a child. A silent little boy of six
with shiny bangs and huge brown eyes. His mother, in a
blue sari, sat silently on the chair. He told me what was
wrong in careful English. There were little yellow spots
at the back of his throat and his head was hot with fever.
The deep trustful eyes of the child and his mother were
soothing. When they had gone, I realized that for the
few minutes they had been here the torment had eased.
I took a mouthful of the hot sweet tea. Then a small thin
woman walked in, her shoulders bent. Life was a gray
blank. Speaking slowly, she told me how she could no
longer watch television, eat, or sleep. I asked her questions and organized blood tests, but then I just sat and
held her hand in silence as the tears rolled down her
cheeks until it was time for her to go. I saw fifteen patients in all; the very last one of the morning was a young
builder with a discharging ear. My auroscope light was

dim; I needed new batteries. I unzipped my bag. The small glass vials of morphine and Demerol were kept uppermost, safely stored in shaped foam-rubber compartments, along with liquid Nurofen and antiemetics. In the act of opening the bag I told myself I must check later to see if they were in date. But the vials had gone.

I stared at the empty sockets where they should have been. Had I got rid of them before and simply forgotten? Surely I would remember the feel of the smooth glass, the tiny crash they would have made as they went into the sharps disposal can. I opened the bag wider, my head singing with panic. There was less in the bag than I remembered. The little elastic straps at the side usually held the boxes of drugs that I used when called out on visits. Co-codamol. Temazepam. They were gone as well. Maybe I had forgotten to put them back. Had I left them in a patient's house? What if a child got hold of them?

This just took a few seconds to process. I found the batteries at last, fitted them, checked the young man's ear, and wrote a prescription, all in a daze. Perhaps the medicines were at home. Perhaps I had cleared out my bag and not put everything back, then Anya had put them in our medicine cupboard. I decided to wait until I got home. I wouldn't worry Frank yet.

Later, I went in through the back door at home. Eleven days ago I had returned from work to see my daughter dancing by herself in the kitchen, happy and unharmed. I leaned against the wall in the empty silence, wanting to lie down on the floor and cry like a child. Then I pushed myself away. She needed me to be strong. Today I had gone to the office. I had done it. No clues had sprung out, but sooner or later perhaps someone would come through the door and remind me of something I had forgotten. There had to be something I wasn't thinking of. Some veil I needed to push aside so I could see more clearly. Maybe it was just a matter of time.

I checked in our medicine cabinet, but there were no drugs from my bag there. I began to search in cabinets in the bathroom, next to my bed, in the kitchen. I left the doors swinging as I ran between the rooms. I looked in the utility room, by the dog food in the cupboard, under the sink. Nothing. I stood trembling, my hand on the ironing that Anya had left. The clothes were neatly piled beside a heap of paired socks. I picked them up and walked upstairs slowly. Everything that had happened must have affected my memory.

Frank would understand. I had probably thrown out the drugs and asked him for more, then simply forgotten. He might already have them waiting for me. I put fresh towels in the bathroom. Ed's rowing clothes were still on the floor. He must have forgotten too. His forgetfulness had spread into his life like mine had, but today was important, it was the charity rowing gala. I pulled out my phone and sat on his bed to call him, but only got through to his voice mail. He must be in a class. I called the school and asked to be put through to the sports center; eventually I was passed to a sports teacher, and I offered to bring the uniform in, knowing Ed wouldn't have time to come home.

"Rowing for charity?"

"This afternoon." I felt surprised the sports teacher didn't know. "I thought I could bring them in."

"Oh, I shouldn't bother, Mrs. Malcolm."

"Normally I wouldn't." I didn't like the amused voice.

"But he's had a lot to contend with. It's understandable if he is forgetful at the moment."

"Then he must have forgotten that we don't do rowing this term. It's cross-country running, Mrs. Malcolm. Rowing is next term." There was a little laugh, as though he had made a joke.

"It's Doctor, by the way," I said. "My name is Dr. Malcolm, not Mrs."

"I beg your pardon?"

I put the phone down.

I'd never done that before. It must have been because he kept using my name, like a reprimand.

My hands were still full of socks. I stood up and opened the top drawer of Ed's bureau to put them away. I had to hurry in case he came back. He would hate me being in his room. Why had he lied about the gala? What had he been doing the times he said he had been rowing? The drawer already bulged with socks. He must have been pushing the dirty ones back in, then. I pulled them out to make space. My hands met something small and hard. I pulled it out of the folds of a tie where it had been hidden. It was a little glass vial with tiny black writing on the side, and a yellow ring around the neck where it could be filed open to access the opiate inside.

Chapter 24

DORSET, 2011
THIRTEEN MONTHS LATER

On New Year's Eve, Ted's sleeping presence disturbs the morning. Bertie paces restlessly around my feet; let outside in the field, he pushes his nose into the wet hedge and sneezes. Briars attach to the curled hair of his thick spaniel ears and he stands patiently to be unhooked. Back in the cottage I make the first coffee of the day and he lies at the foot of the stairs with his nose on the bottom step, whining softly. Returning to the shed, I find the silver dollar plants that Mary gave me yesterday. I had seen them growing by her front door.

"Take the whole lot—glad to be rid of them. Here," she had said, handing me a bucket of corn, "while you're about it, feed the hens for me."

The dried seedcase of a silver dollar in my hand is veined and opalescent, sheathing the arrowlike seeds inside. My thoughts, planted a while back, grow quickly.

The triptych will have fluid boundaries, or perhaps be painted as if on the inside of a cut globe, showing seeds becoming flowers becoming fruit, then seeds again in a flowing circle. I sketch the outline of a plan.

It's noon before I stop and go back to the house. Ted is in the kitchen. He has found the dressing gown that Sam left; its soft black folds hang loosely. His face is greasy with sweat; his hair has fallen forward in separate wet strands.

"I feel awful." His voice judders as his teeth hit together. "Must have picked up a bug somewhere. Jesus. I'm going to be sick." He stumbles to the toilet and I hear him retch repeatedly. He climbs the stairs shakily and I follow him up, then he falls back into bed. I turn his pillow over and open the window, but he shivers and pulls the duvet around himself, so I close it again and pull the curtains together.

"Headache? Abdo pain?" His pulse is fast, his skin is burning.

"It's not meningitis. Or appendicitis." For a moment his lips are tugged into a smile, and then he closes his eyes. "Thirsty . . ."

The weight of his damp head is familiar. After a few sips he settles back with a sigh. The dark afternoon passes slowly. I take up more water, slices of apple, sweet tea. He wakes briefly; once he holds my hand and won't let it go for minutes at a stretch, mutters, then falls asleep again. I hear voices later, and assume he is better, talking on his cell. When I go into the bedroom, he is sitting naked in the chair, staring at the curtains. His eyes are unnaturally bright and his hands shake as he points to their stripes.

"She's in there," he says.

For a second I think he means he has seen Mary across the road through the lit window of her kitchen.

"She's behind those bars." He points to the stripy curtains and his voice gets louder. "She wants our help. She's in prison."

I feel his forehead: blazing hot. He grasps my hand with his sweaty one.

"Help her," he says and his voice shakes. "It's my fault."

He is ill. There is no need to feel frightened by his wild voice and hot hands. I give him acetaminophen and water. He holds my hand tightly, his eyes burn.

"It was my fault. I wasn't there. She's calling me, listen."

Part of me, the unreasonable part that believes in magic and ghosts, wants to ask him what she is saying and how her voice sounds. Instead I say as calmly as I can, "The temperature's making you hallucinate. She's not there, Ted."

"You don't understand. It was my fault." His voice gets quieter. He is whispering now. I have to bend close to hear. "She told me, but I didn't try hard enough."

"Told you what, Ted? Try hard enough to do what?"

He closes his eyes and his head dips low. He shrugs and mutters. I run a cool bath and help him in. His body is gaunt; his penis curled small in its nest of gray hair. His ribs jut out; his back is pale and sweat beads the vertebrae. The wings of his scapulae look like knives. I cup water against his skin and let it flow down his back. "With my body, I thee worship." Did we say that? Did we promise it would be forever? I can only remember the warmth of his hand holding mine. I thought promises were irrelevant.

Back in bed he murmurs words, and among them I catch "Naomi" and "stop" and "please." He rolls his head from side to side. Every half an hour I try to give him water, I sponge his forehead down. Later I change the soaking sheets. He sits in the chair, head drooping, jerking up, falling again.

"Sorry . . . sorry," he mumbles.

I help him back into bed and he lies down again with a little groan of relief, the kind he used to make when he came home and settled into his chair after a long day. But I don't live in his home anymore. I'm not his wife. The promises were more fragile than I thought. His eyelids drift down, and he sleeps.

In the kitchen I see Michael has sent me a message for New Year's; he is on his own, missing me. I text back that I miss him too, and tell him that Ted is here, ill.

The high-pitched voice of the broadcaster on the radio announces that it's midnight in Trafalgar Square. Big Ben tolls slowly against a background of explosions and screams. In the silence of the dark garden the champagne cork flies into the air with a hollow pop, then falls with a quiet rustle in the wet grass. I raise the bottle.

"Happy New Year, sweetheart."

The cold lip of the bottle bumps my teeth and the champagne tastes sour. She can't hear me. I tip the rest on the grass. Another year begins.

IN THE MORNING Ted's temperature is down. He eats toast and Marmite, drinks cup after cup of tea, and sleeps again. The painting evolves. The narrow seeds glow black in their silvery envelopes, their future forms hidden. What secret is Ted guarding? He said it was his fault, but what did he mean? There's a leathery rose hip lying with a pile of twigs on the bench. The cut I make with my penknife reveals the pyramidal seeds packed in rows, fur-tipped, unripe.

At night Ted sleeps on. I pull back the curtains in his room and open the window. It has stopped raining and the air feels fresh. I dream of black seeds falling, rose-buds cut before they have bloomed.

The next morning, as I come back into the kitchen from the shed, the air smells warmly of toast and coffee. On the table, Mary's plum jam spills down the side of the jar in swollen drops. Ted looks strangely large in the kitchen; his legs stretch to the other side of the table, hairy ankles and huge feet. For a second he is a stranger, and then he smiles.

"I feel great. My temperature's gone and I'm starving." He gestures toward the toast crumbs on the table and laughs. "I couldn't wait."

My face feels too stiff to smile. My space. My kitchen. My food. Then I feel ashamed. "I'm glad you're better."

"What have you been doing this morning?" he asks as he butters toast thickly and spreads jam. Does he really think we can go back a year in an instant?

"Working."

"Working again?" He speaks with his mouth full, sounding surprised. "In Bridport?"

"Painting, I mean."

"Ah. That kind of work. Sounds fun. Can I have a look?"

Fun? I can see the corner of the shed from the kitchen window. It contains almost everything that pulled me back into the world. I sense him realizing he has over-stepped a line.

"Okay. Maybe later," he says and stretches luxuriously. He has shaved and his face looks fuller. "Thanks for looking after me. I'll take you to lunch. Is that Beach Hut place still there?"

I cross my arms more tightly. "Two nights ago you said it was your fault," I tell him. "What did you mean?"

"Did I?" He looks wary and hunches forward to sip his coffee, watching me.

I carry on, although his closed face doesn't want me to. "You thought you could hear Naomi calling beyond the curtains."

"Christ. I must have been ill." His laugh sounds forced.

In that instant I know he is hiding something. I want to spring at him and claw out the truth. Though it will be old truth, too late coming, I have to know.

I sense him watching me closely. "I've tired you out already, Jenny. When I saw you the other morning, you looked so well. It's my fault."

What exactly had been his fault? My heart is beating hard.

"I'm fine." I will have to be careful. My glance encompasses him as I look out of the window. If I question him further now, he'll clam up. I'll wait, pick my moment.

"I'll have a bath and get dressed, then we'll go, okay?" He sounds cheerful again.

"Okay."

Later, we walk along the beach, our feet crunching on shingle. Ted stoops to pick up pebbles as we go. He looks at each closely, collecting the light-colored ones that shine like fat pearls veined with gold.

"When I was in South Africa I went to a stone market." He shakes the little pile in his cupped palm as he speaks, and the stones knock together. "At the back of some sheds were lumps of gray Kalahari picture stone. There were piles at each stage of being ground down; all the time the stones were getting better, brighter, losing the edges." He looks at me for a second, looks away. "Like us."

"I don't buy that." I take a flat white pebble from his hand and skim it hard across the water. "Suffering doesn't improve anything." The stone jumps three times, white against the gray, then disappears into a wave. "It makes you sad; it makes you bitter."

"You've changed, Jenny. What have you learned here on your own?"

"I've learned to survive." The gulls wheel above our heads, screaming into the wind.

It's crowded in the Beach Hut. A Christmas tree still stands in the corner. The lights and tinsel look tawdry in the clear gray light that comes off the sea through the windows. Ted leads the way to the same table where I had sat with Michael before, and I think about Michael's eyes and his hands as I watch Ted walk to the counter, organize food, and return with a bottle of wine. He pours for both of us and takes a long drink from his glass, in the way someone thirsty might swallow water. He breathes out heavily and looks at me.

"Well, I suppose we survived in different ways, didn't we?" Ted says. He begins to talk about South Africa, the hospital where he had initiated research, the drought, the wasted children, the rare brain tumors. He doesn't mention Beth.

I look at him, at the thin shoulders and the new lines between his nose and his mouth. It hasn't been easy for him either. I pour him another glass and he drinks again. When the food comes, blood from the thick steaks is seeping into the potatoes. I can't manage anything, but Ted eats as though he is starving; at the end he wipes his plate with bread, and leans back with a sigh. He smiles and raises his glass, nodding at me.

"I needed that. Cheers, Jenny."

"So," I speak slowly, "do you want to tell me what Naomi told you?"

"About?" He puts his glass down. His eyes narrow slightly.

I have to be careful. I think back to all those counseling courses and the language we were taught to use as trainee GPs.

"When you were delirious, you said Naomi had told you something; that you didn't try hard enough and that it was your fault." I make my voice unemotional. "It's obviously been on your mind. Do you want to tell me about it now?"

Ted stares at me a moment, then his face relaxes slightly.

"The thing is," he says and takes a quick sip of wine, "I did tell you. At least—"

"You told me?"

"Yes, you and the police."

He is defending himself already and that makes me frightened.

"What are you talking about?"

"Naomi taking drugs."

I want to laugh. After all that, he's got it wrong. "That was Ed." It must have been the illness, perhaps he is still ill. I say again more carefully, "Ed took drugs. That's why he went to rehab."

He replies, speaking more slowly, "That was later. Naomi tried drugs before that."

I stare at him and he continues. "Well, you remember I told you that Naomi took drugs once with friends? We were on our own; I think the boys were away. It was hot—"

"That? But that was nothing."

Summer. Eighteen months ago. The windows were open and the warm air had come in carrying the scent of barbecues and the faint tang of rubbish from the garbage cans outside. The boys were camping in Cornwall with the school. Naomi was playing tennis with friends. We had been drinking iced coffee after supper when he told me.

"Just once," he'd said. "At a party." He'd put his hand on mine, warm, reassuring. "All kids experiment with their friends. It's what they do. It's not a big deal. She's promised never again. Don't tell her that you know, or she won't trust me anymore; she doesn't want you to worry."

"You said it was just an experiment." I stare at Ted now.

He flushes and looks away while my mind races back to that moment. Experimenting wasn't the same as taking drugs, I'd decided. Naomi would be safe, because she was Naomi, my bright sensible daughter just doing one of those things kids do when they are growing up. Michael had asked me about drugs early on, one evening while we were waiting for Ted to come home from work, and it had seemed irrelevant then; I'd even worried he might think she really took drugs and would waste time looking in the wrong places.

"Jenny, did Naomi smoke?"

"No."

"Drink?"

"Not really."

"Drugs?"

"No. Well, actually she did, once."

"Yes?"

"A few months ago. Just that once, with friends at a party. She told Ted. It was just kids experimenting with weed. Not since. I'd know."

"I'll need the names."

I hadn't known the names. In the end Michael had asked her friends, and then all the kids in her school. No one owned up. It had all petered out.

The waiter appears and stretches strong brown arms over the table, collecting plates and cutlery; a few spots cluster at his hairline but otherwise his skin is smooth. About sixteen, seventeen, he looks as if he swims in his spare time, and wouldn't touch a cigarette. Ted asks him to bring coffee; he nods seriously and leaves.

"Why were you thinking about drugs when you were ill, if they were so unimportant?"

He smiles briefly. "I was ranting."

"Why, Ted?"

As he looks away from my gaze, his mouth becomes tighter. He starts to stroke his right eyebrow with his fingers, back and forth.

"I kept coming back to it in Africa. There were kids hanging around on the street corners in the township where the clinics were, or lying on the sidewalks, completely stoned. Children. It began to haunt me that I'd taken her word and not followed it up more."

"But just weed, only once, Ted . . ."

The color creeps into his cheeks again; he shifts in his seat and looks down.

"Weed was before, Jenny. It was ketamine."

I hear the clinking of glasses and the clatter of knives faintly. It was as though a blanket had fallen between us and the other people in the restaurant.

Ketamine. My face feels hot with shock.

"Fuck. How is it possible that you didn't tell me?" My voice is rising and the young couple at the table next to us cough quietly and stare straight ahead.

"I told the police." He glances at me quickly, then looks down again. "It was when I went to see them to tell them about . . . about Beth." He pours some more wine, tips it quickly into his mouth. "I told them about the ketamine then. They didn't think it was relevant, but they said they'd look into it."

"They?"

"Michael left me with a couple of policemen on duty. They took the details. I can't remember their names."

"And . . . ?"

"Nothing. No one got back, so I assumed it wasn't important."

"Anything could have happened to that information— they might have thought it wasn't relevant, they could have forgotten to file it or not filed it properly . . ." Inside my head it is hot and black; the blackness is swelling and filling my throat so it's difficult to speak.

"Policemen are professionals," he says.

"Professionals make mistakes." He looks away at that, tapping the table with his fingertips.

The boy comes back, bringing the coffee. He places the tray very carefully in front of me and unloads the little jugs of milk and coffee. He smiles and leaves. Pouring coffee, I remember Michael's advice: one step at a time, unravel each thread from the beginning.

"How did you find out in the first place?" I ask.

"It was when she did the internship with me in my lab. The summer holidays before her last term. Remember?"

Of course I did. I was the one who had encouraged her.

"Good for your CV, darling. It's a chance to find which it'll be, acting or medicine. You can go on ward rounds with Dad if you go in early with him. Ed did it."

She had jumped at the idea. She took pride in working at Ted's hospital. As the days of the internship wore on, she'd gotten up earlier and earlier, spending hours putting on makeup, getting ready, looking the part.

Ted's voice is continuing: "And she had the job of recording the drugs we used in the spinal cord injury trial; she was responsible for filling in the order sheet so we knew how many vials of ketamine to order to anesthetize the rats. She was neat and quick. I was proud of her."

He stops and puts his elbow on the table and leans into his hand. It makes his voice less distinct.

"No one ever knew. She was the one counting them, so when she took some vials, she simply ordered more to replace them. Once when I happened to notice that the order sheet didn't match what we had used, she said she had dropped a whole box." He looks down and speaks even more quietly. "She even showed me the smashed glass."

"Very clever," I whisper. "How did you find out?"

"She accidentally left her bag behind in the lab one day. I didn't know who it belonged to, so I looked inside.

I opened the wallet and found her bank card, but there were six vials of ketamine as well, carefully padded with paper."

There was a little pause. I imagined the sickness of that moment, how quiet the lab must have been, only the scampering of the rats in their cages and the sound of Ted's breathing.

"I took the ketamine out, and brought the bag home with me that night, then put it on the kitchen table for her to find the next morning. I left early; when she got to the hospital she came to find me and she started crying. She said she had taken it to give to friends."

I saw her explaining this to Ted: her hands over her eyes, and the fair hair spilling over her hands.

"She had smoked weed at that party with older kids, and when they found out later she had access to ketamine, they persuaded her to steal some. She promised she had never actually used any."

"Why didn't she come to me after that?" I am confused; I thought Naomi had told me everything back then, everything important.

"I suggested she should, but she said you wouldn't believe her at first and then you would have been disappointed, and how that would be worse than being angry."

He pauses, looks at me, worried about the effect of his words. I make my face blank.

"Go on."

"She said you expected perfection, not just from yourself but everyone else as well." He sips his wine and looks out of the window, his face unhappy. "You didn't allow people to be who they were. She felt you didn't know her."

"That's not true." I feel breathless. "I knew her better than anyone."

There was a little silence. I hadn't known her that well, though. I hadn't known about James or her pregnancy. She had shared much more with Ted. Was that because he didn't try to be perfect? He is looking down at the floor; I can see blotches on his scalp where the sun had struck through his thinning hair. The wine in the bottle is nearly finished. I pour the rest into his glass.

"I don't understand why you didn't tell me at the time."

He drinks the wine quickly. All the other customers have left. The waiter is wiping the tables, looking over at us.

"I'll pay for the coffee now. We need to go in a minute." He gets up, pulling his wallet from his jacket.

We've been sitting too long. I'm shivering, the dreary January afternoon seeps in from the outside. The Christmas tree lights blink pointlessly in the dull light.

BRISTOL, 2009
ELEVEN DAYS AFTER

The little glass vial was cold. I held it carefully in one hand. I went out of Ed's bedroom, down the stairs, and out of the back door into the garden, but the chill leafless space made no difference to the facts that were jostling in my head. I stood by the wall. Ed had been lying; I had no idea for how long. He had been taking drugs from my bag, maybe selling them, which would account for the money. Anya had stubbed her toe on the bag because it had been moved from its usual place, and not put back. Stealing drugs. It didn't seem possible.

But then, how was it also possible that Naomi had been gone for eleven days? I knew it was true because I had watched the clock hands crawl around the hours; I'd watched the phone as if watching would make it ring. I had taken her picture everywhere I'd said I would, and to more places besides—newsstands, post offices, the library, and the emergency room—and doing those things had helped blot up time. I had walked around the streets at night and sat by the docks staring into the black water. I had talked to Nikita and Shan and James. I'd ignored the journalists who still lined up outside to speak to me or phoned the house several times a day. And in between I'd simply stood, as I stood now, because sitting down was wrong, too comfortable. Today at work there were moments when I forgot, but I had been almost undone by the neat fingertips of a child holding tight to the desk edge.

If we could lose our child, any disaster was possible.

There was a little crack and I felt liquid in my hands and the sharpness of broken glass. The phone rang. I jammed it between my ear and my shoulder while I rinsed my hand in the sink, shards of glass and blood swirling down the drain. It was Michael to tell me that they had interviewed all the club owners in Bristol but nothing had come of it so far. He would come around tomorrow.

As I was wrapping my hand in a dish towel, I heard Ed come home. I stood at the bottom of the stairs, listening to him climb to his room and bang his door shut. It opened again, and I sat down on the bottom step and heard his feet come slowly down the stairs toward me until they were next to me. I stood up and saw that there were lines under his eyes that looked like red bars, his hair was dishevelled, and there were stains on his school tie. The shirt sleeves hung unbuttoned over his thin wrists. He had clearly lost weight, though I hadn't seen it before; how could I have missed something so obvious?

"You're back early."

He took no notice of that. "Have you been in my room, Mum?"

"But then it's not surprising, is it?" In spite of myself my voice was rising. "As there was no rowing after all."

"Yeah. Canceled. What about my room?"

It was the lie; if he hadn't lied, I might have been able to wait and see if he told me of his own accord.

"It wasn't canceled. There's no rowing this term. Why have you been lying to us?"

"Jesus." He flinched as if I had hit him. "Because it's such a big fucking thing with you. Joining in. If I pretended to go, at least you'd give me a bit of space."

"Space to do what, Ed?"

He looked down and shrugged.

"So you could steal drugs from my bag? What for?"

He stared at me without speaking and his face was paler than I'd ever seen it. His eyes darker and more desperate.

And then I knew. I moved quickly, and before he could twist away I had pushed up the loose sleeves of his shirt. On the inside of his left arm there was a mass of lumpy red scars. Old and fresh scars crisscrossing the antecubital fossa, made from needles inexpertly finding veins.

Chapter 25

DORSET, 2011
THIRTEEN MONTHS LATER

At the back of the beach the cliffs are unevenly hollowed out where the sea has sculpted the rock into little caves and crevices. In the summer these places are sour with the smell of old urine but winter storms have since sucked them clean. As we crouch down out of the wind between arms of rock, there is only the cold scent of salt water and fresh seaweed. Ted bends to light a cigarette, pulling one from a crumpled blue packet. He turns back to face the sea and sighs. The smoky fragrance of Gitanes instantly conjures forgotten images of twisted sheets, books under the bed, notes tossed on the floor. Making love after lectures. When did he start smoking again? Perhaps Beth smokes, though that doesn't fit my image of her. Perhaps they smoke after sex, as we used to. These thoughts skid alongside the worry for a few seconds and then drown in it.

"So, why didn't you tell me, Ted?" I ask him again.

He pulls on his cigarette, and there is a little pause. "She asked me not to," he replies simply. "She trusted me."

"Didn't it occur to you that I should know? You could have told me in secret . . ."

Ted shrugs. "You might have felt you had to take it up with her."

The cigarette smoke stings my eyes. I turn my face away.

He carries on, "Things are either right or wrong with you. Of course I know you would never have told the police—"

Before he can say words that will make it my fault, I stand up. The wind catches my hair, and blows it across my eyes. I snatch at the strands and hold them back roughly as the hot fury rises. I hate him at that moment, but I hate myself more. I want to pull out my hair in handfuls to throw away in the wind.

"She wouldn't have thought I'd tell the police. I've never punished her for anything." My voice is breathless. "I hardly remember Naomi doing anything wrong. She was always good, even when she was little."

"That's exactly it. How could she disappoint you? All that expectation made it easier simply to lie."

His words are like a net catching me at every move, cutting in. Everywhere I turn I was wrong. The sea has changed: crashing and hissing. My teeth hurt with the cold of the wind.

"I'm going home now." As I start to walk my legs feel stiff and move slowly. Ted follows me, cupping his fingers around his cigarette, stumbling a little on the shingle.

"Once she'd gone," I shout over my shoulder above the noise of the waves, "there was nothing left to lose. Why not tell me then?"

He catches up; leans close as he walks and puts his hand on my shoulder so his words are near my ear.

"You had too much to deal with." He is wheezing slightly. "Anyway, from then on, I watched the ketamine supply like a hawk. Not one vial ever went missing again." He stumbles once more, and tightens his hand on my shoulder. We have reached the top of the beach and he stops, holding me there with him.

He says more quietly, "I thought it was a one-off."

He stops talking. Three gulls fly swiftly past us, heading inland, taking refuge from a storm that is brewing out at sea where dark rain clouds reach down to the horizon. He clears his throat as we start walking up the little bridle path that leads to the back of the churchyard, our footsteps quieter on mud.

What would I have done if I'd known at that stage? I would have told the police instantly and anyone else who might have helped, but my feet stop as I remember back to the headlines in every tabloid newspaper: "Doctor's Teenage Daughter Missing" they had screamed. The school photo alongside had looked grainy in newsprint. Some of the papers used an old one of Naomi receiving a trophy after a swimming race. In her tight swimsuit she was all legs, her small breasts pushed together; she was fourteen at the time the photo had been taken, but pictures of a near-naked girl sold papers. If the media had got hold of the ketamine story, the headlines would have been more sensational: "Doctor's Druggie Teenage Daughter Missing." She would have felt betrayed; she wouldn't have come back even if she could. Then again, if the police had known about the ketamine, they might have found her by now.

I begin to walk quickly, as if by moving fast I can catch up with lost time. Ted's hand slides off my shoulder. We are now alongside the churchyard, where the path is dark and slippery with overhanging yew branches dipping low; in the autumn they drop their tear-shaped crimson berries and the ground is slimy with their broken flesh. Now the mud is swollen with rain and tiny needles of ice.

We are almost home by the time the rain starts. Mary is feeding her hens. She turns to us as we pass by her gate and we wave to each other, a brief wordless salute. She will understand how sometimes even pretending to smile is too difficult.

As we reach the door, Ted looks at me. His eyes are full of guilt and misery.

"Around the time I found the vials in Naomi's bag, there was a huge amount going on. I was being threatened with legal action for that girl's spinal operation, and I was back and forth to Sweden with the stem cell trials, which weren't going well either. I should have asked her more."

Inside the house, Bertie comes sleepily to greet us, his wet nose bumping our legs. I bend to him, my hands absorbing the warmth of his solid back, but I can't stand still. I pace around the kitchen, into the sitting room, back again. A window rattles in the freshening wind and the rain patters thinly against the glass. Ted takes off his coat and flicks the kettle on.

I turn to him as he opens the cupboard for mugs.

"What do you mean, you should have asked her

more, Ted? What more do you think you could have found out?"

"I could have asked her for more information. She told me it was for friends. I assumed she meant school friends, but it might have been someone else."

As I absorb that, a new thought strikes me. "What about Ed? Is there a link?"

"His problem was different. Naomi wasn't using drugs like him; she just . . . stole them."

"So did he."

Ted pushes a mug of tea across the table to me. "They both stole because they had access, but their reasons were completely different. Bad coincidence."

In the little pause that follows his words I tell myself that there is no such thing.

"I still think she was telling the truth," Ted continues, as he sips his tea. "It was just a one-off, for friends."

But she had lied so often. "Was Naomi ever with any of her friends in the hospital, or with anyone you didn't know from outside?" I ask. Someone encouraging her, taking the drugs, perhaps slipping her money.

"No. I always kept an eye on her, whether she was in the lab or on the ward. I would have seen."

"I didn't know she was on the ward as well."

"Yes, you did." He looks surprised. "It was your idea for her to do ward rounds with me. She liked the bustle. Sometimes I would find her chatting to patients while she waited for me. I think they took her for a medical student in her lab coat."

"Did she help with drug rounds?"

"For God's sake." He knows instantly what I am thinking. "Those drugs are locked away. You have to be a qualified nurse even to push the trolley around. She just used to sit with people, make friends."

"Did she meet her?" A sudden new suspicion flashes in front of me.

"Meet who?"

"Your girlfriend, Beth."

"She's not my girlfriend now. It's over." He gets up and stands with his back to me; he looks out of the kitchen window into the garden, where the rain is now falling in dark sheets. "And the answer to your question is no."

"How d'you know?"

He shrugs. "She was never round when I picked up Naomi. She often worked late shifts."

Beth would have seen Naomi, though. Curiosity would have compelled her. She might have wondered what it would be like to have a child of Ted's, might have played with the idea that Naomi was hers. The thought takes hold.

"Where's she now?"

"Who?" he asks again.

"For Christ's sake, Ted. Beth. Perhaps it's her all along. She's got Naomi, because she belongs to you and—"

"Stop." He raises himself on tiptoes and lowers again, hands deep in his pockets. He looks calm except for the fact that his hands are clenched so tightly the trousers are stretched over them; I can see the knuckles through the thick cotton.

"You know she was with me the night Naomi disappeared," he says quietly.

"I know that's what you told me."

"She was in her flat. She has an excellent alibi."

Is he talking about himself? He turns and catches my glance.

"Not me, the police." I can see he is still hiding something. "She called them because someone broke into her flat that night." He pauses for a fraction. "Then she called me."

"She called you?" My mind begins to jump down steps to a place I hadn't seen before. "So you weren't there for the first time, making a mistake because you were tired and drunk. You were already lovers. God, I've been even more stupid than I realized."

"I haven't had a chance to explain anything—"

How long does it take to tell someone you've lied? Minutes? Months? Years? I put down my mug of tea; it tastes unpleasantly flat. "I already know it carried on after you told me it had ended. I hadn't realized you were lying about when it started as well."

"How could I tell you with Naomi gone?" He has turned to face me.

I ignore his question, push away the past lies and the future ones. I need to keep focused.

"Beth called the police and then you because her flat had been burglarized." I speak slowly, working it out for myself. "The police should have made the connection later that Beth's lover was Naomi's father and her flat had been vandalized the night Naomi disappeared. This is important. Why didn't Michael tell me then?"

"He didn't know." Ted sits again, facing me across the table. "The police didn't find out I was . . . with Beth till later, when I went to tell them at the station. That night I waited, parked farther down the street from her flat, until the police had gone."

What had he been thinking as he hid there, in the

dark street? Was he ashamed? Perhaps he had been thinking about his research or the operation that had gone wrong? No, he must have been thinking about Beth. About sex with Beth later, once the police had left.

"Of course," I said. "Stupid me again. It had to be secret."

"I was going to end it . . ."

This isn't the point, I tell myself. None of this is. There's something I'm missing.

"What were you doing when she phoned you?" I start at the beginning again. One thread at a time.

"Getting into the car. I was bloody exhausted that evening." He shakes his head at the memory. "The court case had just crumbled, and I was wiped out. I was so relieved that the scheduled op wasn't going ahead; all I could think about was coming home. I'd even forgotten whether I had to pick Naomi up or not."

This has the ring of truth and I believe him.

"Then I got Beth's call. She was distraught and frightened. The flat had been trashed. They had even set fire to the kitchen."

A faint memory of the scent of burning floats past me, how Ted had stood in the hall thirteen months ago and I had smelled burning on him. I'd thought it was the diathermy he'd used in the operation, then I'd forgotten that instantly in the overarching fear of that night.

"They? More than one, then?"

"The police apparently thought it was a gang of some kind, maybe kids. Even when they knew about my connection with Beth they didn't think it was in any way related to Naomi's disappearance."

"What did they take?"

"Nothing seemed to have been taken." Ted shrugs; he has accepted the strangeness by now. "Her laptop, television, camera, jewelry—it was all there, jumbled up but there."

"Doesn't that strike you as odd, the night that Naomi disappeared?" I look at him, but he shakes his head.

"Break-ins happen all over Bristol every night." Ted sounds weary.

A thin child with bruises and tiredness. That combination hadn't been a coincidence either, or even child abuse. Jade had had leukemia.

"Did Naomi really never see you and Beth together?" It's getting difficult to sit still; I get up and rinse the cups, turning my hands in the water to warm them.

"No. I just told—" Then he stops as if a memory catches him. "Actually, now I think back, that's not strictly true. Beth came into my office once, but she saw Naomi and left again. Naomi didn't even register."

He was wrong. Naomi would have smelled Beth's lavender scent as she came in; she would have lifted her head and might have been puzzled at its familiarity, until she remembered she had smelled it on her father's skin. She would have looked out of Ted's window, the narrow one above the desk with the peacock-pattern curtains that I sewed years ago. At the same time she would be watching Beth out of the corner of her eye, so she would have caught the tiny glance between Beth and Ted. Naomi would have registered almost instantly.

"I'll need to phone Michael to let him know."

"Are you still in touch?"

I thought of his warm hands and serious eyes. Touching his mouth with my mouth.

"Yes." I look down, then away. Why should I tell him

about Michael? I owe Ted nothing now. "You'll need to stay and see him, if he agrees to come here."

"Of course. Look, Jenny . . ."

I do look at him then, and beyond the known shape of him, the new stubble and unfamiliar nicotine stains on his fingers, the longer hair and the reassuring smile, I see a middle-aged man grown older, tired, and bitter, as if he knows he has made mistakes and wishes he hadn't.

"I meant what I said. It's really over with Beth now."

"They do food in the pub," I say. "Come back when you need to sleep."

AFTER HE LEAVES I try to phone Michael but he doesn't pick up. I go to the shed. It feels cold and looks messy; usually I don't notice the mess. I haven't the heart to start painting, so I tidy jumbled seeds and rose hips. But I don't dream about them that night. Instead in my dreams I see Naomi throwing broken glass at the walls of Beth's burned kitchen and laughing. The laughter wakes me, and changes into the cry of a gull, calling in the night from its perch on the roof. I lie in the dark. The landscape of the past has changed. Ketamine. Beth's break-in. My mind goes round and round. How had I missed so much? But I know how easy it is to miss things. I hadn't seen what was happening to Ed. It could easily have been too late for him as well.

I give up the attempt to sleep again; I get up, go downstairs in the dark, and make tea. My sketchbook is on the side, but it's facedown, left open. Did Ted flick through it quickly, or study each picture in turn? Perhaps he was disappointed there are none of him. His wet coat is over the chair; the sleeves have dripped a little pool of water on the floor. I didn't hear him come in from the pub and go upstairs. I open the door to the garden and look into the black quietness. The storm that came in from the sea has already gone again. I shut the door and sit on the floor with my back to the wood burner, the mug of tea beside me. Scalpels are easy to draw; harder to capture the holding fingers, impossible to show how they were trembling.

BRISTOL, 2009
ELEVEN DAYS AFTER

Ed pulled his arm back and shook his sleeve down. He turned his head away and in the downward curve of his thin neck I saw how far away he had gone. I put my arms around him. I could feel him shivering.

"What's happened to you?"

He shrugged and moved away.

"I'm not angry." But I didn't think he heard. It was true, though. "I want to help."

He walked into the sitting room and sat down on the sofa, put his head back and stared at the ceiling. I sat beside him.

"Can you tell me what's been going on?"

His head lowered suddenly, brown eyes staring hotly into mine. "Don't you fucking dare tell Dad."

"Were you using drugs from my medical bag?"

No answer.

"There aren't enough in there to do this." I touched his inner elbow lightly as I spoke, but he gasped and wrenched his arm back. I had felt a swelling under my fingers, hot through the cotton of the shirt.

"I'm going to make a sandwich and a cup of coffee for both of us." Perhaps this was how you did it, by pretending to be calm and sensible, although when I saw his face drawn with pain I wanted to weep. "There might be an abscess there, Ed. I could take a look in a while."

We ate in silence, which didn't seem to bother him. He stared blankly out of the window as he chewed. Then, as we drank coffee, I began carefully.

"How are you feeling now?"

He glanced at me quickly, contemptuously. "Like shit, what do you think?"

"How long?"

"Dunno." He shrugged.

"How often?"

"Whenever."

But his shoulders went down as though talking was loosening something in him.

"What have you been taking?"

"Different stuff." A pause, then a low mutter that I had to lean in to catch. "Ketamine, mostly."

The danger he's been in makes me feel sick. "Where from?"

He looked sideways at me and then smiled scornfully: "Man in a club."

"Where are you going with this?"

"How the hell should I know?"

"Why drugs, Ed?"

He screwed up his eyes. "Because of all the other shit."

"What other shit?"

"Stuff."

"Like?"

"Theo," he said in a low voice. "Naomi."

"Theo?" The drugs might help with the guilt he felt about Naomi, although some scars looked old, so he must've have been taking drugs even before she disappeared. How did Theo fit in?

"Leave it, Mum." He started jigging his leg up and down.

I looked around the room as though the tools to unlock this were there somewhere, lying on the sideboard or just out of reach on a high shelf.

"It wasn't your fault she was taken. We told you that; even if you'd waited—"

"I said leave it."

"The money?"

He was silent.

"Ed, where did the money come from?"

The jigging got faster and faster, then he got up suddenly and went to the stairs.

"Where are you going?"

"The fucking North Pole."

I waited until his bedroom door shut, then I sat down and the room seemed to lower itself around me. There was a quiet ringing in the air like after an explosion, but it was inside my head. I looked at my hands on the table. The tendons shone through the skin in pale ridges; they were thinner hands now, but still strong. I had delivered babies, inserted catheters and drips, sewn torn skin, held the foreheads of my vomiting children. I clenched them tightly. I could grasp this. I had to.

HE WAS SITTING with his back against his headboard, earphones in. His bent knees supported a book, and as I came in he began turning the pages quickly.

I sat on his bed and he moved his legs sharply away.

"Some parents might involve the school. Some might involve the school and the police." The pages stopped turning but he didn't look up. "Lots of parents would insist on being told the details of what's been happening; I'm offering a deal."

He pulled out his earphones and waited.

"If you agree to go to a rehabilitation unit, then we won't involve the school or the police, and as long as you talk to someone and you stop, then you needn't tell us anything about where the drugs came from or the money I saw."

He stared at me silently. Then he looked down at the book on his lap, but his eyes weren't moving.

"Just leave school?"

"Yes, so you can go to a rehab unit."

He lay back and closed his eyes.

I gently took his arm, pushed up his sleeve and looked at the scars. Now I could see it clearly; there was a swelling the size of a small plum tensely stretching the skin.

"Ed, this needs draining. We need to go to the emergency room."

"You do it."

I didn't argue; it might make him retreat from the bargain I had held out. I got a sterile set from the locked box in my car. Lynn used to joke that I carried an operating unit around with me, but I'd found it useful over the years for patients who needed very minor procedures and who couldn't get to the hospital. It was often very satisfying, but this would be different. I found antibiotics in my bag. The thought of cutting my own son's skin made me feel weak as I walked back upstairs. I washed my hands in the bathroom in water as hot as I could stand. I knew I would hurt him. I had to find a way to deal with that so I could do this properly. I dried my hands on the paper sheet in the pack and slipped on surgical gloves; as I did so, I felt myself crossing that line, mother to doctor. This was just a problem to be solved. It was straightforward; I could do it. I cleaned his arm with an iodine swab, spread the paper above and below his elbow, positioned the cardboard receiving tray, and sprayed freezing anesthetic around and over the abscess.

"This will freeze it, but it will still hurt. You'd get a better anesthetic in the hospital. You sure, Ed?"

"Do it."

Doctor, not mother . . .

I took the scalpel and cut down sharply through the skin as it thinned over the bulging abscess.

Ed shouted as the skin split neatly apart and thick yellow pus spurted out from between the cut edges, streaming over his elbow into the tray.

"Jesus. Fuck." His forehead was beaded with sweat as he watched the lumpy mess curdled with blood rise in the tray. "Fucking hell. That hurts."

"Nearly done." I felt cold sweat trickle from my armpits, and with hands that I couldn't quite stop trembling, I carefully pressed the last pus out and syringed in antiseptic. Then I packed the wound with a soft yellow wick, bound it with a dressing, and watched while he swallowed a loading dose of antibiotics, penicillin and metronidazole. Acetaminophen. Tea.

Afterward I sat on the bed and pinned my trembling hands tightly between my knees. Ed was white-lipped.

"Don't tell Dad," he muttered between clenched teeth.

"Of course he needs to know. He'll have to know why you're leaving school, if nothing else. He won't like it, but he'll understand. He struggled to stop smoking himself, years ago."

"I didn't know Dad used to smoke."

"More than cigarettes, sometimes."

"Yeah?" Ed glanced up at me, his eyes briefly curious.

"Everyone's fallible. We all screw up sooner or later."

"Yeah? Even perfect Theo, the perfect son?"

Ah. He looked down at the bed cover, I couldn't quite see his face, but his words were bitter. I waited for more but he didn't talk about Theo again.

"I sold them," he muttered, his voice becoming indistinct. "For ketamine."

He'd been selling the drugs from my bag to buy the ones he wanted; there would probably always be someone willing to exchange Demerol and temazepam for ketamine. I leaned closer as he mumbled something else. I couldn't catch what he said and then his eyes closed and he slept.

I closed the door quietly and took the tray and gloves downstairs. My cell went off.

"It'll be on the news." The warning tone of Michael's voice put me on my guard. Ed's drugs. Someone must have found out, told a journalist. Thank God he's asleep or he'll think it was me. Michael was still speaking, and it took me a few seconds to understand that what he was telling me had nothing to do with drugs.

"They've found a blue pickup van, abandoned in the woods."

Chapter 26

DORSET, 2011
THIRTEEN MONTHS LATER

When the bath water empties it leaves behind a line of small stones that had worked their way into my shoes on the beach and pressed marks into my skin. I scoop them toward the drain; tiny residues of sea-sharpened rock, their wet edges glint black and brown.

After my bath I go outside to phone, my voice small in the white space of the icy garden. I keep the cell phone cradled close to my mouth. Ted's window is open; he might wake and hear. As I wait for Michael to answer, the black body of a spider, suspended by a thread from the coping, swings like a beady pendulum toward the stone of the garden wall. Michael's voice lifts with surprise when he hears me.

"Ted's still here." I push the spider with my fingertip toward the wall, and it clings to the rough surface.

"Ah."

"He was ill after he arrived, so . . ."

"So you're looking after him," Michael finishes.

"I've let him stay. He told me things about Naomi I didn't know. She had stolen drugs."

There is silence for a few seconds.

"Right," he says quietly.

"It was when she was doing an internship in Ted's animal lab. She left her bag behind one day and Ted found some vials in it." The words come out smoothly enough, but I feel breathless as I say them.

"Why didn't he tell anyone?"

"He told a policeman at the station, but it wasn't followed up."

The spider scuttles over the stone, searching for somewhere to hide.

"But he didn't tell you," he says factually.

"Apparently he didn't want to burden me with something that seemed irrelevant."

A pause, then his calm voice again: "Okay. What drugs?"

"Ketamine."

As if on cue the air fills with the ordered fall of pealing bells. Early morning bell-ringing practice spills innocently into the gaps and empty corners of the village, bringing with the sound a world of holidays, sunshine, striped lawns, and Sunday lunch.

"Ted used it to anesthetize experimental rats. Naomi was in the lab and had access to it. It's not a controlled drug and they trusted her."

The spider has vanished; I must have missed the moment when it dived into a gap between the stones.

"There's a big trade in ketamine," Michael says slowly.

"Naomi wouldn't have been involved in that. It was Ed who traded drugs, not Naomi."

Michael continues as if I haven't spoken: "I can get a list of users."

"A list of users? Ted says she just took a few vials for friends—"

"Users of ketamine are usually older than Naomi," he interrupts. "Less likely to be schoolchildren. She may have had other contacts."

That word opens a crack into the world that Ed had visited, where shadowy figures live in a network at the dark edges of life, organized and predatory. *Contacts.* The word for the partners of a patient who has chlamydia or gonorrhea; someone unknown, with the power to maim in secret.

"At least now we know what the K in her diary stands for," Michael says.

I'd thought it was shorthand for coursework. How naive I've been; Naomi must have thought so too, as she hugged her secrets to herself.

"I'll come to you." Michael's voice is decisive.

"Can you?" Tears sting my eyes.

"I'll be there in two hours. It would be helpful to talk to Ted too."

"Thank you." I want another word that says more, something bigger, but I can't find it. I remember to warn him: "He doesn't know about us."

"No, he mustn't know."

Perhaps he could be withdrawn from our case if it's known we are together, or he might be dismissed. This secrecy puts a weight on our relationship, flattening it somehow. Sometimes when I'm alone I think I have imagined it completely.

After our conversation finishes, I put my hand on the wall. The surface is rough and cold. The dark crevices must be full of spiders you never see, thick with webs and trapped things. My feet leave hardened patches in the stiff white grass as I walk back to the cottage. The air is clear and cold; it will be a day of sun and ice underfoot. I let Bertie out and he rolls in the frost. His body melts the ice when he stands and shakes himself, leaving a large uneven patch of green on the white lawn. The difference in the garden excites him; he seems to like the cold penetrating to his skin. He runs in circles like a puppy.

In the kitchen Ted is making a cup of coffee. He looks different from when he arrived, slightly fatter maybe, and he stands more upright. He is wearing his coat and a small case is by his feet. His eyes slide away from mine, then back again, like those of a guilty child.

"I'm sorry," he says.

He gives me the cup of coffee he has just made and spoons grains into another. He continues quickly, as if he thinks I might interrupt him before he can say what he has planned.

"She loved you."

I don't need him to tell me this. I curl my hands around the mug and lean against the draining board. The sun streams through the glass and lies in bright divided blocks on the floor, showing up the dust and stains at the edges.

"I did so many things wrong," he goes on, stumbling over his words in the silence.

"What, exactly?" I reach into the cupboard and then tip porridge into a pan. But I know there isn't an exactly. Everything I got wrong was somewhere in the shifting space between expecting too much and not seeing enough.

"Away, busy . . ."

How can he think it's that simple? That the reason Naomi went missing was because he was busy, as if all the other things he'd done and hadn't done didn't matter.

"What about the rules you broke?" I measure water into the oats, my hands shaking with anger. "So that she thought rules didn't matter . . ." I look at him, catching his small impatient shrug.

"If you mean Beth, I told you: Naomi didn't know. I was careful." He adds, as if it follows, "You know, it really isn't over between us." He moves closer, looks over my shoulder. "Why not put some milk with that? Makes it nicer."

"Michael's coming." I move a step away, adding a half cup more water.

"I've got an operating schedule tomorrow, so I've got to go back to see my patients. After that, I thought perhaps we—"

"I spoke to him this morning." I don't look at him as I stir. "He's coming to talk to us about the ketamine."

I scrape the porridge into a bowl, and put it on the table for him.

"I'll wait, then." He speaks slowly, watching me.

The air in the kitchen feels tight with words that aren't being said. "I'm going to work for a while," I tell him and shut the door behind me.

IT'S THE WRONG time of year for the flowers I need for my circle, but there may be something in the hedge in the field. My sleeve snags as I open the gate. A single frozen rosebud hangs by a blackened stem from the thorny branch that has hooked me. The outer layers must have died first, the tender inner ones later. I disentangle myself; the bud and its attached stem come off in my hand; the spider's web between the head and the stem stretches fractionally, then breaks.

Inside the shed, the rosebud defines itself on thick white paper. The petals are dark and stiff at their edges, which are folded back in tiny ragged collars; some of the petals are pink near the calyx but stained with spots and lines of mauve and deep brown. They are still tightly cupped in layers that meet at a point. If I start with pink for the petals and then overlay it with black I might get the glazed ash color. I don't want Blake's poem in my head, but as I work the words are there anyway, as if they have been waiting for me:

> Oh Rose thou art sick.
> The invisible worm,
> That flies in the night
> In the howling storm:

Thirteen months ago her world was safe. Home, school, friends. Now I know beyond that lit circle the world was full of hidden danger, waiting for someone to step outside into the dark shadows. It would take only one person, one contact. The rest of the poem unfurls in my head.

> Has found out thy bed
> Of crimson joy:
> And his dark secret love
> Does thy life destroy.

I try to paint, to focus so hard that all I see are dark colors and curved shapes. If someone loved her, surely they wouldn't destroy her. I shape the outline of the bud and my mind is so full that when the door creaks open, I spin around, surprised.

"I'm sorry, I've done it again." Michael is wearing a coat and scarf, his car keys are in his hand. He guessed I would be here and came straight across the lawn. His broad shoulders curve a little as if he is offering himself as a safe place.

I touch his face and the skin is warm under my fingers. "It's good to see you."

He turns his lips into my hand. "You look tired. I should have come sooner, but I thought you had the boys here."

"They left a few days ago. Come into the house or Ted will come and look for us."

Ted has laid out knives on the draining board like in an operating theater. There are neat heaps of chopped onions, little piles of spices, sliced parsnip. As we go into the kitchen he is holding the blade tip of the knife down with one hand and seesawing the handle rapidly with the other, mincing green strands of parsley. His coat and case are nowhere in sight.

"I want her to have a nourishing meal," he tells Michael after they have shaken hands. "She's been looking after me and now I need to look after her." As if he has sensed our closeness and is trying to reclaim me. He tips the onions into a pan.

Michael goes through to the sitting room. "Why don't you both come and sit down?"

Ted pulls the pan off the heat and follows us in, sits down next to me, a little too close, and puts his arm along the back of the sofa.

Michael takes the chair opposite and leans forward, intent and professional, looking at us. "When Jenny mentioned ketamine to me I ran a check. Our software enables us to access national lists of known users and dealers, and we can cross-correlate with other crimes committed as well."

Crimes like kidnapping, or crimes like rape and murder? I glance at Ted to see if he is thinking this too, but his head is down, absorbing the impact of Michael's words.

"I've brought some lists, starting with Bristol; when I typed *ketamine* in, about a hundred names appeared. I need you to look at them to see if any are familiar."

"Why would they be?" asks Ted.

"A name you might have heard Naomi mention in passing, for example, or a friend of a friend of the boys."

"I doubt she often came into contact with criminal drug users," Ted says drily.

"Naomi stole drugs. So did Ed." I turn to face Ted, my voice rising. How can he still believe so implicitly in his children's innocence? "Of course they could have come into contact with criminal drug users."

There is a silence. Ted pulls his arm back. As Michael looks down at his list, his cheeks are red. I feel a flash of disappointment; he is embarrassed because I lost my temper. I look away from both of them, out of the window to the grass and the sky and the trees.

Michael hands identical papers to each of us.

"Anything that jumps out at you, for whatever reason, would be useful to hear," he says.

Tom Abbot, Joseph Ackerman, Silas Ahmed, Jake Austin, Mike Baker . . . I read the names on the sheet. I've never seen any of them before. It's a relief and it isn't, it means we are no further forward. Ted shakes his head.

"Sorry. Nothing rings a bell."

"I've got an even bigger list that takes in the south-west." Michael is pulling more papers from his bag.

Ted starts reading down the new list; he reads quickly and turns the pages faster than I do. I want him to take longer, look more closely, but he's always read more quickly than me, cleanly taking what he needs from the text as though cutting it out. I read and reread, glancing at Michael, wanting to signal my gratitude, but he is reading the list as well, frowning slightly. He must be tired. I picture him going into his office earlier today, starting up the computer, printing the lists for us, driving for two hours to Dorset instead of what he normally does on Mondays. I don't know what that is, and it feels strange that I know so little about his life.

Ted has read through the new list before I finish. He puts it down.

"No luck," he says briefly. He walks into the kitchen and starts rummaging noisily through cupboards.

I carry on reading, trying and testing each name. Nothing is familiar. Michael walks over to me and puts his hand on my shoulder. A machine whizzes from the kitchen, stops and starts again. The heat from Michael's hand burns through to my skin. I close my eyes; after a few seconds he moves back to his briefcase, and pulls out two thicker sheaves.

"I've got a national list here."

"My God," says Ted, reappearing with a tray of steaming mugs. "You've cast the net wide."

Michael takes a mug of soup, and sips. "Thanks. I expect it's the same for you, when someone's sick and

you're not sure why. You'd work through all the possibilities. All those blood tests and scans. Detective
work."

Ted nods. "You've got a point. Sometimes it's just
finding that extra bit of information—a different pattern
to the headache symptoms, for example, the smallest
shift in electrolytes, or the most obscure shadow on the
scan—and there's your diagnosis."

The soup is warm and spicy. Ted has learned how
to cook. For a second I see Beth, my image of Beth,
flushed with heat from the stove, stirring a pan of soup.
Ted leaning over to look, kissing her neck. My eyes hurt
with reading the small type. I fetch the glasses I now
need for close painting, from the shed. When I come
back into the room, Michael, noticing my glasses, gets
up and switches on the light.

Ted smiles at me. "So my wife wears glasses nowa-
days. Suits you." I sit down opposite him, on the chair
next to Michael.

Michael hands us the sheaves of paper. "This is the
national list; where the drug users are linked with other
crimes there is an asterisk by their name. This one
covers Scotland, North England, the Midlands, East
Anglia, Wales, and back down to the south, including
London."

"There must be thousands here," Ted says.

I don't have to read thousands of names, though. It is
there, on the second page down, with an asterisk by it.
Yoska. Yoska Jones. That strange Christian name again;
suddenly I feel winded, as though I've been punched in
the chest.

"He had a Welsh accent," I say slowly. "That was odd."

"Who did?" Michael gets out of his chair and

crouches by mine. "What was odd?" His voice is urgent as he looks at me.

"It was odd because Yoska isn't a Welsh name."

Michael looks at the list of names I am holding, scanning down quickly.

"Yoska Jones, you mean? You remember him?"

"I remember a man called Yoska," I reply, looking down into Michael's face, and instead of his searching gray eyes I see brown ones, in a narrow face. Powerful hands, a slim, strong body, dark hair, high cheekbones. Then another picture replaces that and just for a second I see her handwriting: XYZ. The Y hidden between the X and the Z, drawn in red and touched by a heart. He would have warned her never to write his name in full.

"What was the matter with him?" Michael asks.

"That's the thing, I never found out."

"Why not? Didn't he say much? Was he difficult?" Michael's questions are fast, like bullets, hitting into me.

"The opposite. He was charming."

"Could you remember what he actually said?" Michael is looking at me hopefully. Ted, watching from the other side of the room, is shaking his head, and I can see he doesn't think I'll be able to reach that far back.

"Some bits, maybe," I tell Michael. "But it was over a year ago."

I remember that when he first walked in and sat down he didn't look like he needed anything, and that was strange in itself. People usually looked ill when they came to see me: in pain, or worried, or sad. Yoska's color was good, and I think he was actually smiling, or at least his mouth was. Perhaps there had been a scar, a small one under his left eye, which made the rest of his face look even smoother. The brown eyes in the slim dark face had watched me very closely. He hadn't looked ill at all, just curious.

"Write down what he said, if you can." Michael reached into his bag and gave me a blank piece of paper, already neatly attached to a clipboard. He felt in his pocket for the pen he always carried.

"It could be important. Write it down just as it happened."

"Word for word?"

"You'll be surprised what can come out of your memory when you do this. Try."

Then he smiled, as if it would be the easiest thing in the world to remember a seven-minute consultation that happened over a year ago. It was November the second. I know that for certain because he came in before Jade, so the date is imprinted in my memory.

I write the date at the top of my piece of paper, and underline it. Then I write what I think we said, and in between I try to remember how it was.

November 2, 2009

"How can I help?"

I must have said something like that; I think I kept it brief. I can remember being in a hurry because I had gotten behind early on. He had leaned toward me and put his hand on the table. I remember that clearly because patients didn't usually touch the table: it was my territory. Yoska's hand had been too close to mine and I had taken my hand away. It had felt like a power game, which he was winning. He'd been quick to answer.

"Back pain, runs in the family."

Back pain isn't usually genetic but I sensed he wanted a reaction from me, so I didn't argue.

"What do you think brought this on?"

Sometimes patients don't like that question, thinking the doctor should know; they don't realize it's useful to have their opinion. Yoska didn't mind. His answer came as quickly as if he'd prepared it.

"Carrying my kid sister around. She likes to sit on my shoulders, but she's getting heavy."

I could tell he didn't like it when I suggested he let his sister walk on her own. I had him down for the kind of man who didn't want to be told what to do, especially by a woman.

His straight-leg raising was limited on the left. I told him it was sciatica and gave him a script. I remember he smiled and shook my hand. I'd smiled back, relieved it had been simple after all.

Michael scans through the dialogue I've written, and Ted gets up and reads it over his shoulder.

"Will it help?" I look at Michael.

"Definitely." He nods emphatically. "If it's the same Yoska as on my list; though it's a bit of a long shot, of course—"

"It seems to have been a straightforward consultation," Ted says. "It's hard to see how this could connect to Naomi." He walks to the sofa and sits down again and begins to stroke his right eyebrow back and forth.

"I should be able to get a photograph from the database," Michael continues.

"Then what?" I stare at him, feeling the little hope of the moment fade away. "Even if the Yoska I saw in my office is the same man as Yoska the ketamine dealer on your list, what will that really prove?" The red Y in the diary seems to fade as I speak, the little hearts evaporating into nothing.

"I can't say precisely yet, but it could give us something to work with." Michael smiles at me then. "Step by little step. That's how it usually works, remember?"

Later that evening, after they had both left, I remember when Michael had said that to me before, about little steps and how they get you there in the end. It was eleven days after she had gone; a time when I had thought we were going nowhere at all.

BRISTOL, 2009
TWELVE DAYS AFTER

As we approached the bend in the road coming from Thornbury toward Oldbury on Severn, we saw the traffic cones and the yellow and blue of the parked police car shining brightly through the gloom of a winter afternoon. Already the light was going, and the rain was falling hard.

Michael stopped the Jeep tight against the hedge, got out, and walked over to where a policeman was waiting. Through the raindrops on the windshield, I watched them move toward each other and walk together through

the cones toward the open gate, then disappear from
sight up a puddled track.

I was glad Ted was on call and it was just Michael
who had brought me in the police Jeep. If Ted had been
here we would have been alone together now, waiting
for Michael to come back; the fear becoming larger as it
moved between us or surfacing in angry words. Instead
he was with Ed, who was still in bed with a bandaged
arm, and on hand for the hospital should he be called in
for emergencies. I was here because of a compulsion to
be where Naomi might have been since we last saw her.

After a few minutes Michael got back in the car,
bringing with him the wet freshness of outside. His
mouth had set in a grim line.

"The car's been left in a little copse to the side of the
field, farther up the slope." He nodded to the open gate
and the field beyond that. His fingers tightened their
grip on the wheel.

"What is it, Michael?" I asked him, but he was looking straight ahead. "What's happened?"

He took a hand from the steering wheel and put it
over both of mine as they twisted together on my lap.
"It's been partly burned out," he told me.

The warmth from his hands seeped into mine. For a
moment I wanted to cling to them, but Michael leaned
forward and started the car again. We edged slowly
toward the open gate, where the policeman pulled the
cones back and let us through.

My head was full of her name, like a prayer, as the
car lurched onto the rutted farm track, steadily climbing
up the sloped land of the field. I took in the ditch by the
hedge, the thick twiggy hedge, and the curving brown
fields. The ditch had been neatly cut and was full of

brown water. I thought of rats and the small dead things that might be under the surface. On a separate little rise, set back from the field, I could see a group of trees up ahead. From here it looked like any other brown clump of winter trees in south Gloucestershire, distanced by the misty air.

Michael halted the car below the rise and got out. I followed him. It had stopped raining; the air was dank and cold, smelling of mud and wet grass. It was quiet after the noise of the engine, but the silence slowly filled up with the sound of starlings in the trees and the sudden harsh calls of crows circling far above. I could hear cattle a long way off and the closer, quieter dripping of water as it came off the trees onto the ground. The gray sky was wide up here; we were higher than I had realized.

We climbed up the steep bank, our feet sinking in a mulch of withered beech leaves, and then we stepped over the blue and white tape that was threaded through the trees. Scratchy undergrowth pulled at my legs and I didn't see the van at first. It had been pushed under a lone conifer tree, and the charred lower branches were bare. The windows had gone and the metal of the roof was blackened. I stood next to it, imagining the flames that did this, the heat that destroyed the skin of the van, the noise, and the smell.

We walked around to the front, where the hood rested against a tree trunk. Fragments of blue paint were left, mostly peeling and stained black. The license plate had been wrenched off.

"This part was less burned," Michael explained. "The gas tank would have gone up first."

"I want to see inside, Michael."

"I thought you'd say that." He went back to his car, pulled something from the trunk, and returned with a pair of blue rubber gloves. I put them on, struggling the rubber over my wet fingers.

The passenger door had gone; I leaned inside and saw the wires and springs, all that was left of the seats. I put my hand into the empty socket where the radio had been. The glove compartment had been ripped out. I looked into the backseat. More wires and springs. The rain had come in so that under the front seat was a big puddle, the water black. I couldn't see what might be under it, though it didn't look deep enough to hide anything. I put my hand down between the springs and brushed my fingers along the metal at the bottom of the car; I felt the skin of the car as carefully as I felt the skin of my patients. Nothing.

"Why here?" I said to Michael. "It's so far away from anywhere. Not near a main road or a town or a railway station. There's no way to escape."

"Not obvious, is it?" Michael said. "Excuse me a second. I need to make a couple of calls."

He walked away from me through the trees, bending over his cell, and after a few moments I lost sight of him. I thought how in the spring this place would be quite different; there would be sun and shadows moving on the ground among the bluebells and wild garlic, the light would be green and gold as it came down through the beech leaves, and the little wood might feel like a cathedral.

I heard the noise of the rain starting again as it fell on the leaves, before I felt the drops on my head. It was darker now, and I wondered what noises there might be in the wood when the night came.

"We need to go." Michael had come back and was standing close to me. "There will be more of our men coming soon. The car has to go off for examination."

I stood there for a moment longer. What had been achieved after all? There was nothing in this burned car or in the woodland that brought me closer to Naomi, nothing even to tell us if this had been the car she had gotten into. Nothing apart from a few flakes of blue paint.

"Has this all been a waste of time, Michael? We are no further forward at all."

Michael gripped my hand for a second and let it go.

"You're wrong there, Jenny. We are moving forward all the time, but you have to be patient. It's easier for me; I've been trained to do this. Remember, it's steps like this, one after another, which will get us there in the end."

But the steps are too small, I thought. It will take too long. All the same, the weight of disappointment seemed to shift just a little.

"What will happen now?" I asked him.

"The car will be taken to the forensics garage at the police headquarters in Portishead and examined inch by inch; all the findings will be kept, in case further information comes to light that makes them useful. That's how it works, you see," he said.

Coming out of the trees I faced the view for the first time and saw how the green of the Severn estuary flattened out toward the broad river, some two miles from where we stood on the hill. The water looked brown between the high muddy banks where the bright hulls of sailing boats lay on their sides above the tide line. Away to the left the lights of the new Severn Bridge glowed through the dusk.

"Over there is Wales," Michael said, and he nodded at the hills that looked close enough to touch, just on the other side of the water.

Chapter 27

DORSET, 2011
THIRTEEN MONTHS LATER

Coming back from the shop on Tuesday, I notice Mary moving slowly through her garden carrying handfuls of feathers. She looks at me over the wall.

"Fox," she says. "Dug his way in." Rounded shapes spill awkwardly from her grasp, tubes twist through her gnarled fingers. Close up, these become the torn necks of two chickens. Behind her in the coop are piles of red-stained feathers. There are no soft background bird noises, no heads dipping and lifting.

In the tar-smelling darkness of her neat tool shed, I reach for two spades from the shining rows hanging against the wall; we dig a deep hole in the corner of her vegetable patch where the soil is softer. She tips in the six dead birds, their broken bodies bright against the walls of cold black soil. We trample the surface flat when we have filled in the hole. The images come, as I knew they would; they still flare and burn, though less often. Now it's her soft face that is under the soil, mud is matting her hair. I step away quickly. Mary nods at me as she takes my spade, and I wonder if she guesses.

"At least the leeks will be tasty next year," she says. "Blasted foxes."

Inside we sit together in silence on either side of her kitchen table. Sage and chives are bunched in a flowery teapot between us, and red, yellow, and blue squares of knitting spill from a paper bag, to be taken to neighbors for sewing into mission blankets. The stack of empty egg boxes sits next to them.

Her mouth purses around the lip of china and she pushes a tin of biscuits toward me. "Sandy brought these for Christmas. Don't like them myself." Mary's love for her daughter is buried deep. Sometimes I try to dig it out.

"She probably made them, Mary."

"If they look homemade that's because she bought them cheap at the school fair. She can't pull the wool over my eyes." Then she adds, as if inconsequentially, "Dan liked meeting your boys. He's planning on staying with them in New York."

"He told me." I reach out and rub a sage leaf between my fingers. "He popped in the other evening."

Mary's bright bird eyes half close against the steam from her cup. "The boy needs to get away."

Dan's face hovers between us.

"My old man left some cash for him." She nods at the photograph on top of the television. "For his education. Comes in handy now."

Deep-set eyes under thick eyebrows look sternly from the frame. He knew then that Dan might change.

He must have watched and listened to his grandson in the way that I didn't with my children. My regrets are just under the surface, waiting to emerge at any thought.

Mary gives a short laugh. "Dan's in a bit of a fix with his feelings." She looks at me sideways. "Thinks he's in love." She leans over, pats my hand. My cheeks feel hot, as though I am guilty of something.

"Mary, for God's sake, he's a child, like one of mine."

"You don't feel like a mother to him, that's all. Not your fault."

She stands, picks up the empty egg cartons, and drops them into her recycling bin.

LATER, AS I paint in the shed, Dan's shadowed face, uncertain and unhappy, gets between me and the paper. I haven't seen Dan since he came to supper. He would never admit to being in love, wouldn't want to talk about any of it. He would turn his face away, crushed. Or am I wrong there too? Does he want to talk about how he feels? I sit down on the bench, brushes in hand, and look out of the little window up to the gray unmarked sky. What do I know about how much space a person needs around them? I thought Naomi had needed space, but perhaps that was what I wanted her to need. It was easier that way. I can think that was true as easily as I can think that of course it wasn't. Everything has started wavering again. Time had taken me somewhere I could manage, but now I am sliding back to where I used to be. Since the drugs, since I saw the name Yoska again.

I stand up and look at the scatter of seeds on the paper; I make my eyes take in the tiny red oval fruits of the haws, the black dots at the top. Slowly they become all there is, these little waiting pips of life, shuttered, small, secret. The buzz of the cell phone breaks the silence.

"I've found a picture of Yoska Jones." Michael's voice sounds careful. "It's not his real surname. He has several aliases."

"What does he look like?" I hold the phone as tightly as if it were Michael's hand.

"Mid-twenties, medium build." Is it Michael's clipped policeman's description that makes me feel suddenly cold? "Olive complexion, brown eyes and hair."

I remember the slanting brown eyes that had watched my every move.

"I did some investigating," Michael carries on. "See you in a couple of hours." He ends the call.

My thoughts jump over each other, like Mary's chickens fluttering and scrambling in the dark to get away from the fox. What has he found out? If Yoska the patient turns out to be Yoska the drug dealer and he was involved, does that make it better than if it was someone I don't know? If he was the one who took her, is that good or bad? Bad, answers the voice in my head. Bad, bad.

Could I have said something else in the office? If it was him, and I had asked him to come back, or if I had referred him, he might have been placated. What if I had asked him about the sister he mentioned and offered to help?

In the house, I build a fire to welcome Michael. Theo's montage of photos catches the flickering light. The main photo in the center always holds me. Her face seems full of secrets. Today I look at her mouth, for the first time. I notice the lips have a little mocking twist. What about the photo before that one? In the corner there is a photo full of orange leaves—the first in Theo's woodland series—and she is laughing, her face taken up with mouth and teeth, her eyes too difficult to see. The one before that? Her profile on a holiday. Her eyes are trained on something out of the picture, slightly narrowed. What had she been thinking? She had been quieter than usual, texting, reading, or hunched over her diary. She hadn't fought with the boys so much; she hadn't come shopping with me. Ted had said she was moody. I look back further and see her at the New Year's Eve party the year before; Theo must have gone to collect the photos that were on my wall at work. I had noticed the intensity of her expression in this photo before, but now I see she looks even harder and more determined than I had realized. I sit down, trembling. Had she been waiting to escape for a long time? And when her chance came, had she been so focused on getting away at last that she forgot to be careful and took the first—dangerous—opportunity that came her way?

MICHAEL KNOCKS AT the door. He comes in and kisses me briefly, his eyes preoccupied, his lips cold against mine. He takes his coat off slowly, as I wait for this second to pass, then the next. Soon he will show me, soon I'll know.

We go into the sitting room; he opens his case, pulls out the photo. The face in the photograph has thick stubble, but I know him instantly. The slant to the eyes, high cheekbones, handsome even in a mug shot.

I don't want it to be this man; he was too cunning and his eyes had been so guarded. "That's him. My patient." Then I say quickly: "But even though this man came to see me and even though we know now he is a drug dealer in ketamine, that still makes it a long shot, surely?"

"Your office couldn't help because he was a temporary resident and he'd failed to fill in the address, but there's another connection," says Michael. "I know his face. I've seen him before."

"How come?" But, of course, a drug dealer. The police must meet them time and again.

"In the hospital."

"What hospital?"

"Frenchay."

Ted's hospital.

"He was part of a large family of gypos who kicked up in summer 2009." Michael's voice is curt. I look at him, surprised. Travelers are often irrationally feared and despised. Michael is different, surely?

He continues. "They created a fracas in the ward, started smashing up furniture, breaking computers. They took to breaking into local houses."

"Why?"

"They were angry. An operation on a young girl in the family went wrong." He stops, sits down on the sofa, takes my hand to pull me next to him. "A neurosurgical operation."

As he is saying it, even before, I know what he is talking about.

TED'S VOICE HAD been low, monotonous. Was it June or July 2009?

"Something bad happened at work. It was my fault."

He usually never said anything was his fault. I should have listened. I was stacking clothes for the boys' Duke of Edinburgh expedition on our bed. They were going to the Atlas Mountains with the school. I had checked off the list as I collected the clothes. It was hot; Ted had come home unusually early and had lain on the bed, his tie pulled off, shirt sleeves rolled up.

"What was your fault, darling?"

I glanced at him as I checked off thick socks, more comfortable inside climbing boots.

"An operation on this little girl. She had Hurler Syndrome . . . her spine was narrowed, she had a hunch-back."

His voice was so slow; I thought it was tiredness after a long day. He had been coming in later, working harder. I glanced at my list: sunscreen, sun hats, woolly hats as well because it gets cold in the mountains at night.

"Hurler Syndrome, that rings a bell." I turned to him for a moment. "Lysosomal storage disease? Lacking an enzyme so abnormal metabolites get stored everywhere, the spine, the liver?" I was surprised and faintly pleased I could remember from my exams years ago.

I think Ted stood up and paced then.

"I let Martin do the op. He wanted the experience. It went wrong."

I kept my finger on the place I had gotten to on my list.

"That's bad."

I added a fleece to each pile on the bed.

"It's my fault, you see. They think it is, anyway." He turned his head away and I couldn't see his expression. His voice was so quiet. "Happened on my watch." He sat down on the edge of the bed and put his face in his hands. "Might go to court."

"That's horrible, darling. Poor family. It wasn't your fault, though. You'll be all right, you'll see. They'll realize you weren't to blame." I sat next to him, resting the clothes on my lap. I couldn't see his face, so I took his hand.

"But I am to blame. Morally and legally." He moved his hand away after a while and I stood up, reluctant to leave the packing.

"I'm almost done here. Can you wait till supper? We'll talk about it then. Try not to worry."

But while I was still sorting clothes his cell rang; he had to go back to the hospital. I had supper on my own. I thought we would talk about it again; instead it quietly disappeared from view.

"IT WAS TED'S case, wasn't it?" I ask Michael fearfully.

"Yes."

"Shit. He was right, then." Grudge holders, he had said. Doctors playing God.

"What do you mean?"

"Way back, when I was making that chart of people we should question, Ted thought we ought to consider the possibility of revenge. He said you can easily make enemies; all it takes is one mistake." I can hardly breathe as I say these words. "I remember saying I didn't think anyone would hate us that much."

I get up to phone Ted and he answers almost immediately. "I've finished my list. I'm coming down now. I want to see the photograph."

"Yes."

"If it's him, then it's my fault." His words come fast before he hangs up.

I turn to Michael. "You thought of this too."

He frowns; I can see he is thinking back.

"A long time ago you asked me to make a list of enemies," I continue. "All I was able to come up with were Jade's father, Anya's husband."

He nods, remembering, and I feel the burn of regret. What if I'd known about Yoska then?

My teeth start to knock together, my body shivers. I must have caught Ted's virus. Michael puts a glass of whiskey in my hand, and then he runs a hot bath for me. The warm water stops the shivering, and afterward his arms are close around me. He kisses me and pulls me closer, but I feel too ill, too distressed to make love. He is next to me as I drift to sleep, but when I wake I'm alone; I can hear Ted's voice downstairs. I sit up confused, unbelieving that I could have slept, and then feel giddy when I stand up. My head is burning. Downstairs Ted takes a step toward me.

"Jesus, you look awful, Jen."

Michael puts his arm around me and pulls me toward a chair. The fire is burning steadily again, the room has been tidied. Ted stops and looks at me, then Michael, his eyes darkening with realization. His lips tighten. He is deciding not to say anything, not now.

"Where is it?" Ted turns abruptly to Michael. Michael picks up the photo from the table where I had left it and gives it to him carefully.

"It's one of them all right," Ted says. He is about to put it down, as if he can't bear to look, then glances at it again. "He was there the most."

I look at him, unable to speak. My head starts pounding and shiny little lines move at the edge of my vision.

"He was there all the time, actually." He turns to me and his voice sounds different, frightened. "Is that the guy in your office, the one you told us about?"

I nod. My voice comes out as a whisper. "What happened to that little girl? I never really knew."

"I tried to tell you." He stares at me. "You weren't interested."

I look at him to see if he really believes what he is saying. Is this some kind of excuse or was that how I really seemed to be? Is that how I really was?

Ted looks at Michael and his gaze is hard. "Shouldn't we be phoning someone? Shouldn't we be doing something this very minute, now that we know?"

"It's too soon to say that we know anything for sure." Michael's voice is quiet, steady. "I have a team working on this right now, tracing the family. The best way you could help is by telling us exactly what happened."

Ted pours a slug of whiskey into my empty glass on the table and he swallows it quickly. He sits down near the fire and looks into it as he speaks. His fingers are still tightly holding the photograph.

"It was almost two years ago. I saw the child for the first time in my clinic. The room was crowded with people standing against the wall, leaning on the desk, one huge family. They were Gypsies, that's what they told me, or was it Travelers?" He laughs briefly. "Anyway, I remember thinking the girl was lucky."

"Lucky?" Michael looks at Ted quickly, his gray eyes puzzled. "I thought she was ill."

"She was very disabled, yes, but they had all come in for her. Grandparents, parents, uncles, aunts." He pauses. "She sat in the middle on someone's lap, calm and smiling. She was obviously loved."

I stare at Ted. Why is he talking about family togetherness now? Is he punishing himself or punishing me?

"Where did Yoska fit in?" Michael asks.

Ted looks at the photo in his hand again and is silent for a while. "I was never sure of the family dynamics, but I think he was an older brother. Maybe an uncle." He stops and looks at Michael. "He was the quiet one with the power; the mother did the talking, but the group deferred to this guy."

Good power or bad? I remember back to those minutes in the office; the hands on the table, his smile, the way he had shaped the consultation.

"What did you tell them about the operation?" Michael has pulled his notebook out and his hands are moving quickly over the paper.

"In the clinic I went through what would happen if we left her as she was. She might have ended up paralyzed. I said the operation could be a cure, but there were risks," Ted explains.

"Did they really understand?" I ask. He nods.

"When they signed the consent, you must have gone through it again?" I probe him.

"Martin did the consent." Ted doesn't look at me as he replies. "The pediatric surgical registrar." He is looking at Michael. "The pediatric team shared the case, and Martin was interested. Unusual problem with the spine; we planned to write it up."

Why had the family become so angry if they had known the risks? Was it because no one had listened to them? If Ted had listened, he would have discovered the things they hadn't understood and he would have warned them properly. Ted continues.

"Because of the way the back was bent, it took longer than Martin had thought it would. The blood pressure dropped unpredictably during the operation, so the spine suffered ischemic damage."

"You've lost me now." Michael stops writing.

"Sorry." Ted smiles briefly. "The blood supply to the tissue of the spine was cut off, so that part of the spine died. That means messages couldn't get to the legs from the brain, or the other way round. She became instantly paralyzed."

A log shifts and falls. There is silence in the room.

It is difficult to stay still. I stand up, but my head is thumping and I still feel dizzy so I have to sit down again.

"What happened next?" Michael asks.

"I heard about the operation, but I had to leave early the next day. I had to go to Rome for a conference—"

"Why?" I interrupt. "Would it have been impossible to stay behind and talk to the family? Explain why you didn't do the operation, though you were the most senior surgeon?"

"We have an obligation to let juniors do complex cases." Ted's voice is sharp. "It's a training hospital."

"What happened then?" Michael has been listening quietly, now he glances at Ted quickly.

"When I came back after a week, the group had gotten bigger," Ted replies. "There was hostility. People around her night and day as though they were guarding her."

Of course they were. They would feel they had to stop anything else happening to her.

"I tried to talk to them but it was as though I was speaking in a foreign language."

Medical jargon is a foreign language, useful for keeping frightened people at bay.

"Did you say sorry?"

Ted shifts irritably in his seat. "Of course not. That would have been admitting guilt."

"It would have been acknowledging their grief."

But I was equally at fault. If I had really listened to Yoska, I might have understood why he was there. If I had asked why he needed to carry his sister around, he might have told me what had happened and I could have explained how operations can go wrong by chance, not negligence, and then he might not have needed revenge. Had he been offering me a chance to redeem Ted? Perhaps all Yoska had wanted from me was time. The nightmare regrets begin to circle me, closer and closer.

Michael looks at us both, then he stands up. "Coffee?" He goes into the kitchen.

Ted and I face each other. The room is dark now. I can only see his eyes, lit by the flames, staring at me.

I stare back. "Apart from it being a normal human thing to do, saying sorry means people have the chance to forgive you."

"What world do you live in, Jenny?" He gives a small bitter laugh. "Saying sorry gets you sued."

"But they tried that anyway, didn't they?"

Michael comes back with mugs of coffee. He brushes my hand with his fingers as he gives one of them to me, and it pulls me to myself. Blaming Ted will slow us up. Stay focused. Naomi's photographs glow in the firelight. I get up and walk across to touch the glass over her face.

We are trying to find you. We are getting closer. Wait for us.

I sip the coffee and sit down on the other side of the fire.

"Yes, they did." Ted sighs sharply. "Fortunately it came to nothing, no negligence could be proved, so it never actually went to court."

"When was the operation?" Michael asks; he has started writing in his notebook again and doesn't look up.

"In the summer," Ted says after a little pause. "I know that's right because I used to talk to Naomi about it when we drove to the hospital together. She was doing an internship. She seemed so interested in the case. It was helpful to talk to her."

"When was the internship?" Michael asks, looking at me.

"Early July," I answer immediately.

I know that for sure, because I still remember the disappointment. The boys were away on their expedition; Naomi's exams were over, and she had her internship to absorb her. I had looked forward to the beginning of July as a chance for Ted and me to do things together for once, the small things that other people do. Seeing a film, eating out. But that was when he started coming home really late almost every day. Huge amount of work, he had said. Colleagues on holiday. I had used the chance to catch up on adding to my appraisal documents, meet a few friends, but it wasn't what I had hoped for.

"Did Naomi's internship take her on the ward?" Michael asks Ted.

"It was lab work mostly, but she liked the wards," Ted answers. "She talked to the patients and their families."

"So she was there at the same time as the little girl," Michael says, looking at him. "And Yoska." Quietly, almost to himself, he murmurs, "Yoska could have worked out who she was and what she did; he would have got to know her in order to obtain ketamine. Lucrative revenge."

Naomi would have fallen for the charm and the power, the excitement of someone different from the boys at school. She would have been thrilled with her new secret; putting on the makeup every day that I had thought was for the job, so the exotic stranger wouldn't realize she was as young as she really was. Their developing relationship must have continued after she finished the internship, Yoska carefully gaining her trust; even while she was still with James, his hold on her must have been gradually increasing.

"Who was the head nurse at the time?" Michael looks at Ted.

"Beth," Ted says quietly. He looks away from me, out of the window, though it's too dark to see anything. "Beth Watson."

"Ah, yes, of course. Beth Watson." Michael looks at Ted. "There was a fire at her flat on the night of November the nineteenth." He pauses for a moment and glances at me; he knows that was the last time I saw Naomi, so the date is like a knife turning in a wound. Then his voice continues slowly, "I was telling Jenny earlier about the disturbance in the hospital. Traveler kids from Yoska's family." He glances at me again, then carries on. "We always thought the fire in Miss Watson's flat was a coincidence."

I watch Michael as he gets up from his chair and stands in front of the window. Behind him the glow of the firelight is reflected in the pane. From the outside it will look as if we are a warm and happy group, family and friends together.

"However, I now think that Yoska may have worked out the relationship between Ted and Miss Watson."

All he needed to do was to watch them together. Like I am sure Naomi did. Yoska would have picked it up quickly; Naomi might have told him anyway.

"I think it's possible the Travelers deliberately set fire to Miss Watson's flat, knowing she would call Ted," Michael says quietly.

Ted had stood in the hall that night and smelled of burning. I look at him briefly; his face is dark with guilt.

"It would have been in Yoska's interest to make sure Ted was later than usual going home, giving him more time to escape with Naomi. They would have hoped Ted's being late would delay the alarm being raised."

Michael looks at both of us in turn. "The real target that night was Naomi."

Target. Why did he have to use that word? It makes me think of bullets thudding into a circle on paper, a circle that represents a heart, her beating heart.

"There's something else . . ." A pause, then Michael says slowly, almost reluctantly: "We already know Ed exchanged the drugs he took from Jenny's bag for ketamine. It seems that as part of his revenge against Ted, it was Yoska who made it his business to give Ed the ketamine in exchange for those drugs."

We both stare at Michael in disbelief. Ed as well?

Ted gets to his feet. "That's not possible. He wouldn't have ever met Ed—"

"I went to see Ed yesterday," Michael interrupts, speaking quickly. "I hope you don't mind, but I felt there was no time to lose. I took the photo with me. He recognized Yoska as the man who supplied him with ketamine. He thought he was very generous; you see, Yoska had continued to supply him with ketamine long after Ed had run out of the drugs he stole from Jenny. Ed had nothing to exchange, but that didn't seem to bother Yoska."

Michael's words fall into silence. I see Ted struggling to take it in, pacing backward and forward in the room. Then he turns to face Michael.

"He couldn't have known who Ed was, how on earth could he have found him? Where?"

"It would have been simple for Yoska to have tracked Ed down from what Naomi might have told him about her family," Michael replies with quiet certainty. "His name would have been enough. Any dealer knows where to find potential clients: the school gates, the pub, clubs. Once the contact was made, he would have carefully manipulated Ed to obtain the drugs and, in return, supply ketamine to him. And continue to supply it."

A man in a club. Ed's words come back to me.

Ted continues to pace back and forth, hands balled in his pockets. "Why didn't Ed tell us? He must have known about Yoska and Naomi, so why the hell didn't he say something after she disappeared?"

"For the simple reason he didn't know." Michael's voice is very definite. "Ed had absolutely no idea because Naomi obviously would have kept her friendship with Yoska secret, and Yoska wouldn't have dreamed of telling Ed he was involved with his sister. Wouldn't serve his purpose at all."

His purpose, of course, being to strike at the heart of our family, inflicting all the damage he could in vengeance for his sister.

Michael tells us that the search will move forward quickly now, with the new information. He leaves later; he has work early the next day. He brushes my cheek with his lips as he goes out of the door. Ted is waiting at the foot of the stairs.

"How can you do this with so much at stake?"

I try to push past him. "I'm exhausted, Ted. And I need to sleep. We'll talk later."

"Have an affair, if you want. Who am I to criticize?" But his voice begins to rise. "He's a police officer. It's completely unethical."

"How can you even think about this now?" I take in his flushed skin, his eyes bright with fury. "Michael has helped more than you could know—"

Ted gives a contemptuous snort. "Of course he has. Men like that seek out women who are vulnerable; he's probably done this before."

He's jealous, even after Beth. I turn away without answering and climb the stairs slowly, sensing him watch me as I go. Now he knows what it feels like, but I'm too tired, too heartsick to feel any satisfaction.

Sleep doesn't come. Yoska set a trap for us. He caught both Ed and Naomi. Does Beth know that the night she called Ted was the night Naomi disappeared? I wonder if she feels guilty. If Ted had come home as he normally did, the dynamics of the evening might have been different. I would have woken sooner; we might have called the police earlier.

I had found Beth's scarf back then. Giving up on sleep, I go downstairs to find my sketchbook, open it up, and draw a strip of silk, as thin and twisted as the flames in the grate.

BRISTOL, 2009
THIRTEEN DAYS AFTER

The length of unfamiliar crimson curled itself loosely around the box of old CDs in the glove compartment. I had opened it looking for sweets for Ed to suck on because he felt car sick. As I bent closely over the open compartment, the scarf seemed to glow in the dark space: red for danger. A faint scent of lavender rose toward me.

"Any sweets?" Ted asked.

The lid shut with a metallic click. Everything in his warm, leather-scented car shut smoothly, edge to edge. The van I had seen in the wood the day before had no doors.

"No." I didn't turn to look at him as I replied. Someone had taken her away in that van. I needed Ted. We had more chance of finding her together. I had to put everything else out of my mind. What had happened with Beth was behind us. The scarf didn't matter now.

"We can stop at the next service station." Ted looked into his rearview mirror at Ed. "You managing, Ed?"

I twisted around to look at Ed. His face was gray, pressed into the angle between the back of the seat and the window. His eyes were closed and he didn't answer. He was pretending to sleep, perhaps he really was asleep. I edged the window down. Ted preferred air-conditioning, but Ed could do with fresh air.

I sat back and watched Ted's hands on the wheel. The fingernails were clean and close cut, even the fair hair on the backs of his hands looked neatly brushed. His face in profile was calm, even faintly content. How could that be? It took all my focus not to scream out loud and tear the skin off my face and arms.

When I'd gotten home the night before, I couldn't get that little wood out of my mind. The place had been sinister. Now my mind began to go down dark corridors, seeing Naomi being pulled out of the car, her terrified eyes, hands over her mouth muffling her calls for me, for Ted. The flames leaping, terrifying her. My own hands started to tremble. I pushed them under my thighs.

The quietness in Ted's face calmed me in spite of myself. He dealt in facts; he liked things that made sense. He was good at detail. I was glad of him yesterday after Michael had dropped me off. He had taken my sodden raincoat, washed my muddy boots, fed the dog. He told me that while Ed was sleeping he had made a next-day appointment for us to see around a rehabilitation center in Croydon that a colleague had recommended. He had taken the day off.

"We have to stop this now, Jenny. He needs help fast. The sooner, the better. Being at home now is terrible for him, you can see that."

Of course I knew Ed needed help. I was the one who had bargained with him for his cooperation, but it had all been organized so quickly. I had hardly had time to get used to it.

"What do you want us to do about school?" Ted asked, his eyes on the road.

I turned to the backseat again. Ed was watching

the road, his eyes flicking rhythmically backward as the telegraph pole's went by. He didn't answer, but his cheeks were tinged with pink, he looked better.

"Let's not worry about school," I said, still looking at Ed. "We'll sort it all out. It doesn't matter."

Ed's eyes went to mine and away again. He didn't believe me, but it was true. We had lost one child; we had to keep Ed safe. Nothing else was important.

The outposts of London began to appear. Bridges, a power station, a biscuit factory. Ted stopped at a service station, where we bought sandwiches and I checked Ed's temperature; it showed a small spike. The bandage around the crook of his arm had a wet yellow patch in the center. I gave him his midday antibiotics and more acetaminophen. As Ted filled the car with gas, I thought we probably looked like a normal family on an outing, taking our son back to the university after a break perhaps. No one would guess that this calm-looking, handsome man in fit middle age with fair hair and bright blue eyes had lost a daughter in the last two weeks, or that the thin dark-haired woman sitting in the front seat of his car was holding on to her sanity with both hands. If they had glimpsed Ed in the back of the car they might have thought he looked like any teenager.

THE CENTER WAS set back in its green space, on a quiet back street of Croydon, an old Victorian building with wide windows and a Gothic front door.

Ted parked on the gravel in front of the main house. A barefoot boy with a sweet smile answered the door. The tight knot inside my chest loosened just a little.

"Hi there." The voice had a soft Irish lilt, welcoming, gentle.

"Thanks, Jake. I'll take it from here." A small middle-aged man with light-colored eyes appeared behind Jake, and opened the door wider; he had gray hair in a long ponytail and a T-shirt stretched over freckled biceps. The boy called Jake smiled at Ed and walked off slowly, looking back over his shoulder.

"Come in. You must be Ed. I'm Finac."

We followed Ed into the hall and stood, uncertain, rumpled, and cold. Ed yawned repeatedly. Finac's glance took us in, rapid, dismissive. The parents, his eyes said: the problem.

He shook hands with us, unsmilingly. "Follow me."

He led us to a small room, where the thick smell of cigarettes hung above shabby furniture. Chairs with worn greasy patches were arranged in careful groups. Outside, large leafless trees stood around a lawn.

"Wait here. I'll get Mrs. Chibanda."

After a few moments a woman walked in wearing bright colors in softly draped clothes. Her dark skin was smoothly stretched over the bones of her face. She smiled as she shook hands; she smelled faintly of roses. Everything about her made me feel better.

"I'm Gertrude Chibanda, the manager. The buck stops with me." She leaned forward, smiling. Her teeth were perfect. "Finac here will be Ed's coworker if you all decide this is where Ed should be."

Finac glanced at us briefly and nodded.

"If you're okay with this, I'll talk to Ed on his own while Finac shows you round, and then we can talk while Ed sees where he might be staying if he agrees to come . . ."

We followed Finac down narrow passageways and into quiet rooms. There was a bleak canteen and a music room with peeling posters of Jimi Hendrix on the wall, a new drum kit, and guitars propped against the wall. We weren't allowed in the bedrooms.

Ed was finishing a large mug of coffee when we got back; he disappeared quickly with Finac. Gertrude looked at me, sorrow printed on her face.

"I'm sorry for what's been happening in your family. I lost a son to illness some years ago." There was a little pause. "I'm sorry," she said again simply.

I looked at her. "I'm sorry about your son. I can't imagine what that must feel like; but Naomi's not dead. She's just . . . just . . ." I couldn't continue. Conscious of Gertrude's stricken face and Ted's worried one, I turned to the window. The green blurred and swam as the tears poured down my face. Gertrude, still standing close, held out a folded linen hankie. It smelled of roses as well.

Two hours later, all the arrangements had been made. Finac had told us about the twelve-step program for recovering addicts and how it would work; Ed had decided to stay for a few days on a trial basis. I spoke to the nurse on site about his dressings. The doctor would be coming in that afternoon and he could get more antibiotics then. We would come up with his stuff in a few days and in the meantime I would speak to the school. Ed was silent before we left. He wouldn't look at us, and we left him sitting on his bed, staring into space.

"I like it," Ted said on the journey home. "I liked that woman, but not Finac. What is it about these people who want to make everything the parents' fault, as though we are the enemy?"

"That's because it is our fault." I felt almost too tired to speak. "We are the enemy. We didn't look carefully enough; we were too busy."

Ted put his arm around me awkwardly across the gap in the seats. "We couldn't have loved him more. We've given him everything."

I shook my head.

"We couldn't be there all the time," he said. "Kids have to grow up. Separate."

"Separate like Naomi did?"

"I'm on your side, Jen." Ted looked out of the window. "Right here, with you."

With me? How long had he been with me? Beth's scarf was coiled in the glove compartment in front of me; when had she last been in the car? And how could he possibly be with me when I had no idea at all where I was?

Chapter 28

I wake early; outside, the first layer of dark has lifted, leaving the garden as still and flat as a painting under the gray sky. In my dream she had been there, under the tree, shadowed by leafy branches, sun and shade playing on her upturned face. The school uniform she was wearing was tight on her. I had stood at this same window and tried to shout, but my voice came out as a whisper. I couldn't lift my feet, and as I tried to wrench them from the floor, sweating with effort, I woke.

Minutes pass. The stinging shock of the empty garden fades into the familiar ache that locates somewhere under my heart, settling down deeper into my bones, a weight to be carried. The windowsill is cool under my hands; the dream slips beyond my grasp.

My head is full; the facts that had lined up so neatly

yesterday start to whirl again. Yoska the ketamine dealer, Yoska the brother, Yoska the patient. Yesterday I was sure his name would lead us to her, but the clues that seemed so certain have dissolved into suspicions, loosely linked and sliding apart like snakes coiling and uncoiling around each other. There is no proof. Even if Yoska can be found, apart from that Y in her diary, there is nothing to definitely tie him to Naomi. He is on Michael's list of drug dealers, he had been on the ward with his sister, the children in his family had started the fire, he had supplied Ed with drugs, he had come to see me at my practice. A good defense lawyer might say it was nothing more than coincidence.

"We need something else," I whisper to myself. Outside, the branches stir the morning air and as the light brightens, the space beneath them is cleaned of shadows. "There must be something better."

The kitchen has been cleaned. I recognize Ted's way of folding the dishcloth: tightly, over and over. The sink and draining boards are clinically clean. I'd forgotten that about Ted, even his hands are immaculate. I imagine him scrubbing up before an operation, his blue eyes focused but remote above the line of his mask, intent on the operation ahead, and the sluice room around him as cold and shining as a morgue.

My office, ketamine, the ward, the fire. The little list runs through my head like ticker tape, pushing out the pictures of Ted. Yoska is the link between these worlds, but where is the proof we need?

Michael's cell is out of battery and switches to voice mail. I phone his office then and a woman answers. As I wait, I hear her voice telling him I am on the line.

Is there the faintest echo of amusement in her voice? A woman, again . . . it seems to say. You and your women . . . Then Michael comes on the line.

He listens carefully before replying. "It's enough as it is, Jenny. It's enough to make us want to find him and question him. We have started the search for the family." His voice is neutral. He is in an office, people must be walking in and out and maybe that secretary is standing close to him, looking through files in a metal cabinet.

"But you don't understand. He's clever. Really clever." Yoska's own family had turned to him when the little girl was in the hospital; Ted had said he was the one who knew what to do. He would know exactly what to say to any policeman who tried to arrest him, or to a lawyer trying to convict him.

"When we find him, we can take it from there." Michael's voice is confident, but I can tell he's not listening; he must be tired after his long drive the day before. He is probably signaling to the secretary to bring him coffee.

"He had that asterisk by his name," I say slowly. The light has darkened in the kitchen; clouds from the sea must be rolling in.

There is a breathing pause on the phone. I can hear the tapping of his fingers and the blip of the computer as he brings up the list.

"That was because he stole a car, years ago," Michael tells me.

I stare out of the window as I listen. The green smudges of North Hill through the raindrops on the window remind me of the wet copse and the beech trees by the Severn River, the burned van pushed under the branches. A plan is forming in my head.

"What records would have been kept from then?" I ask him.

"We would have his DNA." I sense he is looking at something as he speaks, signing papers maybe, the phone tucked under his chin.

"So if we can find recent DNA from him, linking him to Naomi, and it matches what you have, we will know for certain that the man who took Naomi is Yoska, a drug dealer with a revenge motive." My voice is fast, keeping up with my whirling thoughts.

"Jenny—"

"And then, when he's caught, that same recent DNA, matching what you will be able to take from him, will totally incriminate him." I pause for breath, my heart is beating fast and my hand clasping the phone is slick with sweat.

"There is no recent DNA." Michael's voice is patient. "Leave it, Jenny. The usual way we retrieve criminal DNA is from inside a body—" He stops. I can hear him swallow as if he wants to take back his words but it's too late. "I'm sorry, that was stupid."

There is a pause and I imagine him sipping coffee. Outside the window the rain has thickened; I can hear it on the thatch. Push those words away, blot them out.

"I'm going back to the wood where the van was." I start to scribble a list as I speak, focusing on the paper. Flashlight. Spade. Boots. Dog lead.

"The police raked it over, inch by inch." A note of exasperation creeps into his voice. It is strange how I can hear it on the telephone, quite clearly. I've never noticed it before.

"Things come to the surface, don't they?" I'm hurrying as I speak, so my voice is breathless. "Woods change."

The cottage feels warm. Ted had banked the wood-stove before he left. I look around before I leave in case there are things to put away, but it's tidy. It's always tidy. There is a spade in the shed, though it's not shining like Mary's was when I helped her dig the grave. Clumps of mud cling and I wash them off by the garden tap. Mary's birds had tumbled into the muddy pit; their feathers were all Naomi's favorite colors; but I'm not going to look for a grave. I'm going to look for something he touched.

THE JOURNEY BACK to the wood in Gloucestershire takes three hours. The traffic crawls through sheets of rain on the highway; the car shudders as trucks roar past us, splattering the windshield with dirty water. Bertie sleeps, his curled body on the seat next to me; my hand rests on his back as I drive.

I remember where the place is, between the market town of Thornbury and the little village of Oldbury-on-Severn. I find it easily; the familiarity is instant. I must have unknowingly stored away the bend in the road along with the gap in the hedge and the ditch. I put the car close into the hedge as Michael had. With Bertie beside me, I walk slowly along the side of the field toward the hill, the wet wind blowing in my face. As the field starts to slope upward, I suddenly want to turn and hurry back, the wind would be behind me, pushing me. I want to put Bertie into the car again, and drive away. It's midday. I could find a little café in Thornbury, sit with a sandwich in front of me, and watch everyone go about their normal busy lives and pretend my life is like theirs, and there is no need to go into the little wood ahead of us and search for something that might help find the man who took my daughter away a year ago.

My feet keep walking toward the trees, slipping now and then on the mud; a whole year but the countryside hasn't noticed. The copse is the same. The trees, no longer ringed by tape, look exactly the same. I hesitate before I enter the darkness under the branches, but I find where the van had been in a few moments because the trunk of the tree it was under is still blackened. Bertie runs around tree roots, nosing the ground. There is a change after all: two trees have fallen, one lies up against the burned tree, and the mud that clings to the torn-up roots looks new. It must have blown down in the winter storms. Bertie, excited by the smell of fresh earth, starts scrabbling and digging.

I dig near where I think the van was, shifting leaves with the spade, pushing them aside with my feet and my hands, then digging again. The spade hardly makes a dent in the ground. I'm looking for a gas can, a sodden glove. I push the spade into the soil again and again. After a while, I stop for breath. Rain slicks my hair into my eyes; I push it away from my face, and the mud from my gloves runs burning into my eyes.

My spade hits on roots. I dig up mud, stones, and bits of broken china. Nothing. Bertie whines and I ignore him. When I have done this circle, I will make it wider, then another around that, then another. Bertie starts to bark. I straighten and walk over to him; has he found something, anything? Beneath his furiously digging paws I see small white shapes. The wood swings about me and I fall to my knees. Bertie has hold of one of the shapes now, a curved, white, ridged bone in his mouth. He lets me take it. It's only the tiny rib of a sheep, perhaps a lamb or a little deer. Bertie is scrabbling now; he finds a skull, a long domed shape, with the molars of an herbivore intact.

Woods change. Things come up.

I sit back on my heels; Michael was right. There is nothing here. The clues must be somewhere else. I'm looking in the wrong place. I'm not being clever enough. I drop the little bone back into the mud. She would laugh if she saw me now or, worse, feel pity. I have no idea which.

BRISTOL, 2009
TWENTY DAYS AFTER

Ted and I had run out of things to say. Ed had gone. Theo spent hours in the studio at school and came back strained and silent. He watched me and I knew he wanted to say something but couldn't and I didn't try to make him; I couldn't say anything either. I was mired in silence. I hadn't the strength to speak.

In the office it was easier. I could pretend I was all right. I washed my hair and ironed my clothes so I looked normal. I saw the patients and dealt with their problems. I only went half time now. It worked. I didn't smile, I couldn't actually smile at anyone, but I did the job. I measured blood pressure, examined abdomens, looked at rashes, watched, listened, filled out forms, and wrote prescriptions. Naomi had never been much to my practice, so sometimes in my room, for a few minutes, it could feel like nothing had happened. I thought I would be able to go on doing this for a long time, but I was wrong.

Jade wasn't on my list for that afternoon, so Mrs. Price must have persuaded Jo to let them come in during a gap between patients. She came through the door shyly, holding a small bunch of flowers in front of her. Her mother was pushing her and she stumbled. She was thin but her bruises had gone and she was wearing a pink beanie pulled low, so no one would have seen she had no hair. It was only five weeks since she had been admitted.

I managed a half smile: "Hello, Jade."

Mrs. Price sat down, and Jade pushed herself up close to the large body, wedging herself tightly between her mother's knees.

Mrs. Price frowned. "Just thought we would come in."

I stared at her, my throat tightening.

"Well, I know what it's like." She pursed her lips. "I mean, when it's your own."

She stopped talking and stared back at me. I was on the other side now, the wrong side; I was the victim. It was difficult to know what to say to me.

She stood up and took Jade's hand. "What I mean is . . . Go on, then, Jade."

Jade pushed the flowers at me; she smiled quickly and then buried her face in her mother's fur coat.

When they were gone I shut the door behind them, stood against it for a moment, then slid down it, and knelt awkwardly on the floor. The flowers spilled from their cellophane beside me. My head bent forward over my knees and I could smell the dried bleach scent on the faded linoleum and see the little cracks that ran across it. Then my face twisted and deep sounds came up from my chest, like some animal might make if it was in pain. After a while I got up and ran the taps so no one would hear, and pulling the blue paper from the examination table I pressed it into my face. I had been mad to think I could come back to work so soon. I couldn't manage it. I couldn't manage anything. I wanted to go home and curl up in bed and lie in darkness. I wanted to stop breathing.

I slowly pulled out my chair and sat at my desk and took shuddering breaths. I managed to phone through to reception and Jo listened as I asked her to say I had been called out on an emergency. There was a back door; the waiting patients would think I had hurried away through that.

I sat on in my room. Jo quietly brought me a cup of tea and her arm came around me briefly. She had told Frank and he was seeing the patients on my list who couldn't wait. Then she left me to myself.

The room darkened around me. The world contracted to my hand on the desk. It was twenty days since Naomi had walked out of the kitchen. Every day, every moment of every day I had pushed away images of her in pain, tied up, torn, bloodied; her lifeless body in a plastic bag by a road or in a shallow grave somewhere. I closed my eyes, trying to reach a good memory, something bright and happy to block the images. The party on the first night to celebrate her performance. There had been so many happy voices in our kitchen that night; suddenly she came into my mind as vividly as if I was looking at a photograph. Naomi, standing by the stove, resting a stockinged foot on Bertie's back, had been on her own for a few brief moments. I had moved toward her but then I stopped; she was looking sideways so intently that

I followed her gaze to see what held it, but it was only black night outside the window. When I looked back at her again, I saw her mouth was curved, but it wasn't a smile for anyone else. It was inward, secret. She had looked quite different. It might have been the black costume she was wearing for Tony's death scene in *West Side Story,* but for a second she had become older, harder in a way I couldn't analyze. An edge of disquiet had crept into the noisy room. Theo went up to her a second later and said something and she laughed and became herself again. Someone touched my shoulder and I turned and the little scene went out of my mind. Until now. Here, on my own in the office, I realized that her smile had told me something. It was a clue.

WHEN I LEFT the practice it was dark and cold, but Naomi's room was warm. I had kept the radiator on and I sat there most evenings. Sometimes I thought that molecules from her skin or her hair might still be in the air and that, if they were, they might be touching my face or my hands. I imagined that if I kept perfectly still, I might feel them.

That evening I could hardly breathe for the hope that was gripping me tightly. I wanted her to have planned leaving. I wanted that to have been what she had smiled to herself about. I didn't care if she knew that it would hurt us, or even if she wanted to. It didn't matter, if it meant she was safe.

Her room had been searched by the police and by Michael. I would try again. If she'd had a plan, there might be a clue. Her thick coat was in the closet, with her school skirts. I felt in the coat pockets. Nothing. All her shoes, neatly lined up, the green pumps, the Converses, the flip-flops. I slipped my hand into one of the pumps, felt the smooth dips in the leather sole where her toes had been. I opened the drawers of her bureau, pushed my hands under the jumbled sweaters. Nothing. The ornaments on the mantelpiece had been shifted; expert searching hands had taken the photos out of the frames to feel behind them and had replaced them slightly crookedly. Everything else was in its place: the little china horse, the old autumn leaves, stones from the beach in Greece, a pot of blusher, her jewelry case.

Below me in the house I heard the front door open, and Ted's footsteps slowly cross the hall.

I sat on the bed and as I opened the white lid of the jewelry case, the little plastic ballerina in her pink net skirt pirouetted to faint broken music. I closed my eyes. When she had unwrapped the jewelry case on her sixth birthday, she'd found the curled coral necklace inside. Then my eyes snapped open. The necklace wasn't there. I searched the inside of the box. Where was it? She always kept the corals in her jewelry case. They must have been taken out, recently taken. They had left a spiky indentation on the soft bed of old satin. I checked on the mantelpiece, on the floor, under the rug. Then I ran downstairs.

"She knew. She planned it."

Ted was sitting in the chair, staring straight ahead, glass in hand. He turned to look at me blankly.

"Planned what?"

"Her necklace is gone, the corals that my mother gave her. They're gone. She must have taken them with her." I stopped for breath.

"How can you know that?" Ted's voice was low and flat. "She could have lost them years ago."

"They were taken out recently; you can still see the imprint."

"She lost them recently, then."

"No. She would never have lost them. She loved those corals. It means this was planned. She would have taken them with her. She knew she was leaving. That was why she smiled to herself."

"She smiled to herself?"

"Yes. At the party."

"What party?"

I ignored the question. My mind was spinning. I tried to remember back to the last time I saw her. Had she been wearing the corals then? Perhaps they had been in the bag with the shoes? The questions started to chase each other around and around.

"Jenny, you are completely exhausted." He stood and put an arm around my shoulder. "You look as though you've been crying."

His arm was heavy, his breath smelled sourly of alcohol. I moved back quickly.

"Don't . . ."

He looked at me then as if he hardly knew me. He shrugged and started toward the stairs.

I called after him, "It means she wasn't abducted, don't you see?"

He continued toward the stairs. "I'm too tired for this," he said. "Don't bother with supper for me. I ate something at the hospital. I'm going to lie down."

I watched as he went up the stairs, hauling himself by the banisters. It seemed to me then that he was slowly climbing out of my life. I didn't care. She had taken her corals. She had planned to go. She was safe.

Chapter 29

DORSET, 2011
THIRTEEN MONTHS LATER

Naomi is dancing. She is Maria dancing with Tony and you can see she is falling in love. It's different from the real *West Side Story*, but that doesn't matter in my dream. The tempo is slow to start with and they dance close together, mirroring each other's movements. Gradually the music quickens so they have to dance faster and faster, then it gets louder and louder until it stops being music and becomes ugly noise instead. There are stirrings in the audience. The lights begin to flicker so that the dance movements look jerky and strange. Something is wrong and mutterings spread. People are leaving the theater. The drums give a great crash, jolting me awake, leaving a fading echo in my head.

The beating of my heart slows in a few minutes. The dreams are happening every night now.

I haven't thought about that theater for months. I push

the hair out of my eyes so I can stare into the darkness at the images that are racing through my mind. He was a shape, a shadow, glimpsed at the back of the auditorium by the teacher and Nikita. James had seen him leaning against a wall inside.

Thoughts start to flicker in my mind like the lights in my dream. Had he left anything behind in the theater? A hat? Hairs from his dark coat brushing the seat? Anything that touched his skin could carry DNA. The police had looked in the theater, but they may have missed something. I'll phone Michael and ask him what they did. I can go myself and search. He'll think I've gone mad. Perhaps I have. Perhaps I'll have to look everywhere again—how else can I be sure there is nothing more? Somewhere in the world there will be something that will prove he took her. I only have to find it.

I lie awake for the rest of the night, questions turning and turning in my head. At seven I phone Michael.

His voice is guarded but gentle. "I've been trying to reach you, Jenny. I wanted to come and see you last night, but it got too late. I've been feeling terrible. I shouldn't have said that about finding DNA."

"You were right."

"No, I wasn't. There isn't a body, of course. There never has been. So of course there is no DNA."

He may be going to tell me again that the only place they find criminal DNA in the hunt for a missing girl is inside her body, but I already know this. I know they look in her vagina, her esophagus, on her clothes, in her hair. I don't want to hear any more words. If he doesn't say them, I won't have to see the pictures that go with them.

"I mean you were right that there was nothing in the wood," I explain, to stop him telling me anything else.

"So you went after all? Ah, Jenny." His mouth will be turning down at the corners. It was one of the first things I noticed about him; I remember thinking it was a good sign that things could still make him sad. "I told you the police had searched it all."

"Did they search the theater?"

"The theater." He repeats the words slowly.

"Yes. You see, I had this dream." But if he thinks I've gone mad he won't help me, so I begin again. "She was in *West Side Story*, remember?" A little pause follows my words.

"Of course I remember. We did a thorough search, starting with the changing room."

"What does that mean, exactly, a thorough search?"

A little sigh, an unzipping noise as he pulls his laptop from the case. "I'll phone you back with all the details in a moment."

They would have started with the changing room where she had become Maria, but, thinking about it now, she had used it only to change her clothes. Afterward, changing back into her own clothes, she used to keep the makeup on. She had always applied it at home before she left as well. Why was that? Perhaps she met him on the way there or the way back. She had looked eighteen with that eyeliner and foundation. What had that allowed him to do?

When the phone goes, I answer quickly.

"As I thought, they looked everywhere." Michael's voice is calmly certain. "I've got a list here."

"Yes?"

"They fingerprinted everything, door handles, taps, the seats at the back of the theater, toilets. They went through every cabinet, the costume baskets, wastebaskets, and the rolling garbage cans outside." There is a little pause. "They took up floorboards."

I didn't know that. So they thought she might be dead, even then.

"Jenny, this will have to stop." He clears his throat, speaks louder. "You'll drive yourself crazy." He pauses, and then carries on more quietly, "Leave things to us. You can let go."

"I can never let go." There is silence on the phone. I continue anyway. "Michael, when you catch him, he'll deny everything." Yoska will shake his head with a half-hidden smile in his eyes. "He will know that without proper evidence we won't have enough to convict him. We need something to prove he was with her."

"You can't look for it in the theater because of a dream." He gives a little laugh.

And I can't let the dream go; I can't let her go with it.

I REDIAL. THE headmistress of Naomi's school is in a staff meeting, but she phones me back after ten minutes.

Her tone is kindly. "How very good to hear from you again. I have so often wondered how you are getting on."

"Fine, thanks, Miss Wenham."

If she saw me, I'm sure that's what she would think anyway. The months by the sea have done their work. I look much better than when she last saw me. She wouldn't be able to tell that the wounds have been re-opened; the bleeding isn't visible from the outside.

"I was wondering about the theater," I say carefully. "There may have been things left behind, that the police missed." I hurry on, in case she interrupts and then I might lose my nerve. "I wanted to check. Something could still be there, even after all this time. I know it sounds stupid. Perhaps there's a hat or a jacket . . ."

My words are tumbling out too quickly, and in the listening silence they sound absurd.

Miss Wenham is hesitant. "You can look, of course you can, my dear. But it's unlikely you'll find anything. It's all very different now."

"Different?" They might have self-locking doors now. Keypads with passwords or a guard at the door. Lessons learned because of Naomi.

"Well, it's not finished yet," the measured voice continues, "but we are in the home stretch. A past pupil left us money in his will, to refurbish." There is a little pause, but I don't reply and she carries on. "There have been many changes, a new stage and so on . . ." Her voice trails away in the silence. She realizes she is being tactless.

"Perhaps I could come and have a look, just in case." I try to make my voice hopeful even as my heart is sinking. Too late, much too late.

"Once they've finished, one of the girls will take you round. Try again in a week or so. I'm so glad—"

I don't wait to find out what she is glad about. I put the phone down. It will be too late when they've finished; I'll go today. A jacket may still be hanging on a peg that they have all got used to walking by, a hat trodden underfoot, kicked into a corner somewhere. I can always look, even though I am almost fourteen months too late.

That's how it works in medicine sometimes; the thought strikes me as I back the car out of the garage. You look again, or someone else does, and get the diagnosis just when everyone has given up. It's sometimes the most obvious thing that no one has thought about. Jade's face seems to float in the mirror for a second. It's always worth looking again.

Bertie is in the front seat, nose on his paws, eyes closed, settled for the journey, but there is a knock on my window as I turn the car to face the road. Dan is standing there, taller in a new coat, collar up against the wind.

I lower the window. "Nice coat."

"Thanks. Gran's Christmas present. It's always snowing in New York in films."

"You're really going, then?" I hadn't realized time was passing in other lives as well.

"Leaving tomorrow. The course starts next week." His face is guarded but his voice lifts with excitement.

"Wait, I'll just park again."

"Don't worry, I'll come back later."

I know he won't, and if he does I won't be here. Switching off the engine, I get out quickly.

"Mary will miss you. I'll miss you."

He looks at his feet for a second and swallows.

"What's the plan?" I ask quickly.

"I'm staying with Theo and Sam till I find somewhere."

"Are you okay for money?" But it's a question too far. He steps back, his face closed.

"You sound like my mum."

"I am a mum, that's why."

"Not mine." He looks at me, his flecky green eyes staring directly into mine. He continues, "I'll let you know what happens." He pauses. "Theo will, anyway."

There is a second in which I might touch him, a second when he stands there, looking lost. As if he guesses my thoughts, he flushes and turns away. "See you later," he says.

Then he's walking away down the road and I haven't even thanked him. I draw level with him outside the shop and lower the car window, but just at that moment two girls come out of the doorway and greet him. He steps into the road; I see him in the mirror, leaning forward a little, looking after the car. A moment later one of the girls moves toward him and takes his arm. I turn the corner in the car and they disappear. He will go to New York; he will start a new life. It's all in front of him. A life to be lived, a whole uninterrupted life.

WE ARE IN Bristol by midday. When I was last here, it was summer. The chestnut trees on the Downs are bare and we missed the leaves falling. Naomi's favorite time of year. I remember how surprised the searching policeman was by the collection of shriveled leaves in her room and the little heap of shrunken horse chestnuts on the dressing table.

I park outside our house. Bertie whines at the gate, tail wagging. The gatepost is rough under my fingers, the paint is peeling. The windows look dirty, and the front garden is thick with weeds. Inside will be tidy; thanks to Anya. Ted will be at work now. I look up at the tall dark windows, remembering how in my last months here all the bright warmth had leaked away, and in the dark emptiness even my own footsteps had begun to take on the quality of a dream.

I had waited here from November through to August last year, our marriage unraveling in those nine months while hope faded and friends drifted away. Frank understood when I couldn't go back to work after the evening I had broken down. He found a temporary doctor again, but the thought of his waiting had added a sharp-edged layer of anxiety and I told him I wouldn't return. That loss drowned in the months of nothing that followed. I had lain on her bed, or the floor of her room, motionless, watching the daylight bloom and darken as the hours passed. I had wanted to die. Then one day I went to the cottage again. Ed had needed some books he had left behind on a previous visit. He had begun to work for his final exams by then and was staying on in rehab. The light in Dorset seemed different. It was clearer, the air felt warmer. I could hear the gulls from the garden. I came home again, but as the search for Naomi slowed down and as the weeks dragged by, I thought of the cottage more and more. By the summer I had made a plan, and by the end of August I had left. I've lived off my inheritance. Ted would have given me what I needed if I had asked, but I've lived simply and haven't needed his help.

For a moment I'm tempted to ring the bell. Anya might be here. But this house is Ted's territory now and I pull Bertie from the gate.

There is scaffolding outside the theater. Ladders are propped against the wall and cast-iron radiators lie in a Dumpster. A couple of vans in the street outside have their doors open; there are workmen inside on their tea break, hunched over steaming mugs. The doors of the theater are propped open. I hesitate, wondering if I can take Bertie with me. His presence gives me courage.

No one stops us as we go in, treading on the plywood sheets that protect shining new floorboards that have been laid in the entrance. Did they damage the old wooden ones when they took them up, looking for her body? The bar has been painted red; it's bigger now and there is a new mirror behind it. The air is cloudy with dust and smells of plaster. Bertie sneezes twice. I pull open the heavy wooden doors to the auditorium, the harsh scents of paint and wood dust greeting us immediately. It is larger and brighter than it used to be. There are no dream-dark shadows anywhere under the hard light that bounces off the newly smooth walls. The stage has vanished. Splintered planks lie in a heap, some broken in two, and there is a great stack of long shining ones for the new stage leaning against the wall. Bertie, pulling ahead of me, almost tumbles into the trap room, the dark pit that was under the stage and is now revealed. Below us, as we stand at the edge looking down, a gray-haired man in blue overalls is measuring the floor with a spirit level. There are a couple of wooden stools, a plastic fireplace, and a heap of dirty canvas sacks in one corner. He looks up, his forehead glinting with sweat. He nods briefly at me, then, noticing the dog, his face softens and he walks nearer, reaching up to pat him.

"You shouldn't have brought him in, though he's lovely. Got one a bit like him at home. Were you looking for someone?"

"My daughter was in a play last . . . before . . . She lost some things. They might have been put somewhere?"

"Lost property went out long ago." He shakes his head. "Thrown out, back in the summer."

My heart sinks. Stupid of me to come.

The man nods again, turning away, but in that instant Bertie jumps down into the pit, pulling the lead taut. I let go in case he is strangled. The man laughs, bends to the dog.

"Likes me, you see," he says triumphantly, stroking Bertie's ears.

"I'm sorry." I sit, swing my legs over the edge, and then jump down; it's farther than I thought and I land awkwardly, jarring my ankle. There is a stab of pain when I put my weight on that foot, and I can barely stand. "Sorry," I say again, conscious now that I'm being a nuisance and that I want to leave.

"Watch yourself there." The man comes close and helps me limp over to one of the bulging bags in the corner.

"Sit yourself down on one of those. Costumes. Can't hurt. Cup of tea?"

"Costumes?" I lower myself cautiously onto the canvas.

"The police left them here. Ready for the next time, like." He bends to fuss at Bertie, warming to gossip. "No call for plays since that young girl went missing. Terrible, that."

I need to get away from this man before he says anything else, but as I try to stand again he puts a hand on my shoulder.

"Don't you worry." He grins. "Sit yourself down. She's not in one of them bags."

I stare at him, feeling sick; no words come.

"You look a bit peaky." He looks into my face and then scratches his head. "Tell you what, you rest yourself right there and I'll get you a cuppa. Back in a tick."

He heaves himself up and disappears from view.

There are at least six bags. Something of Yoska's might have been found and bundled up in here by mistake. I slide off the bag I am sitting on and, kneeling, pull it open. It's a long shot and I've only got minutes before the man returns. Groping inside, I touch rough sacking and rope. I open another and drag out a thick black velvet jacket edged with gold binding and a felt hat with bent brim and bedraggled yellow feather. I stuff them back in. The third has army fatigues, neatly folded. What plays were they from? Naomi probably saw them. Did she tell me? Something else I missed if she did. The fourth bag has clothes that feel soft. I pull out a blue skirt and then, my heart banging, a police cap: Officer Krupke's. Quickly heaving the bag over I manhandle it all out through the narrow opening, red and blue skirts, flouncy tops, lacy dresses, silky wraps. As I tip the bag out completely, some purple netting, a pair of ankle boots, scarves and tights fall out onto the floor. No boys' costumes. They must have worn their own stuff for the stomping dances over the rooftops. I look at everything for a moment; I can see the dancing scenes where the skirts were swirling and Bernstein's music filled the auditorium. But now, like the trees and the mud, this bright heap of clothes and tumbled shoes tells me nothing. Just costumes, as the man said.

I grip the boots angrily to shove them back in the bag and my fingertips brush something silky that has been rolled up and pushed deep inside. Socks? A neckerchief? Unfurled, it's bigger than I thought, and spread on the floor it becomes a silky dress, a short red dress with a low front. Mother-of-pearl buttons. Nikita's dress. The one Naomi borrowed for the dress rehearsal, the one she didn't bring home again. Because it was hidden in the boot, the police must have missed it. I hold it to my face. Is there a faint scent of lemons? I mustn't cry. I spread it out again and register with the part of my brain that is coldly functioning that there is an uneven white-yellow stain on the bodice. Lifting the hem, I see it's inside the dress too. Footsteps approach, so I swiftly roll up the soft fabric and slip it into the pocket of my coat, bundling the rest back in the bag just as he appears. He swings himself heavily over the edge of the trap room and hands me the mug of tea.

"See you've been looking at the costumes." He looks at me, amused. "Any luck?"

I shake my head; the tea is dark and very sweet, restoring.

"Told you," he says equably. "All chucked out."

As I limp slowly back through the streets to the car, I want to wrap the dress around my neck under my clothes, next to my skin. But I leave it in my pocket. Michael will send it to forensics.

The windows of the tall house are still dark. I settle Bertie into the car, and pull away. My heart is knocking against my teeth with hope and dread.

BRISTOL, 2009
TWENTY-ONE DAYS AFTER

I couldn't wait to tell Ed about the missing corals. He would realize it was a good sign, and he needed to feel hope. Ed would understand that it meant she had planned to leave, and that she wanted something to connect her to home until she came back. He would be as excited as I was.

Ed's cell phone went straight to voice mail so I phoned the main office. Mrs. Chibanda answered. She went to get him and after what seemed like a long wait I heard his slow steps approach.

"Hi, Mum." He sounded tired, older.

"You okay, darling?"

"Why?"

"It's been two weeks."

Ed's sigh came lightly down the phone, but he didn't reply.

"I know they'd tell me if things weren't all right . . ." I heard myself blundering in the silence. "But it would be nice to hear from you."

"Leave it, Mum." He spoke loudly suddenly. "Leave me alone."

I closed my eyes. Since Naomi disappeared, everything was louder. Noises hurt, as though I was getting ill, as though I had lost a layer of skin. I'd forgotten how to talk to Ed. This conversation was already tipping the wrong way. I began to wish I hadn't phoned him.

"We think about you all the time." I didn't mean to say that; he wouldn't like that.

"Typical." He was whispering now.

"What do you mean?" I shouldn't have asked. It's not why I phoned.

"I mean, you would say that now." I had to listen hard to hear him; it was as if he was talking to himself. "Never talked to me before."

He's grieving for Naomi. Coming off drugs. He's alone. He doesn't mean any of this.

"I talked to you all the time, Ed."

"At me."

I left a little pause and began again. "Good news. Her coral necklace is missing."

"What necklace?" His voice is distant.

"The one with little orange sticks?"

"So?"

"She must have taken it with her. It meant she knew she was going away."

"Christ, Mum. She probably lost it or gave it away."

Does he want to destroy everything?

"Gran gave it to her years ago."

"All the more reason. You don't know her, Mum. You don't have a bloody clue."

After I had said good-bye and waited for him to hang up first, I walked to and fro in the kitchen. I wanted to get rid of his words. I didn't want to think about them now or the anger that seethed underneath them.

In the end I phoned Shan. I couldn't think of anyone else, though we hadn't been in touch since we sat side by side in the police station.

"Jen. I was going to call you today."

I didn't know how to answer that, but it didn't matter, because she carried on brightly, "It's been so busy." She gave a little laugh. "God knows why. Christmas, I guess."

Christmas? How was it Christmas? I looked out of the window, but the street was the same. I hadn't been to the shops for weeks. Presents would be beyond me.

"How are you?" Her voice altered in the silence and she sounded more like herself.

"Coping. Something good's happened, though. I thought I might come round." I wanted to see her smile; when I told her about the corals, she would hug me and say that she'd always known it would be all right.

"Unless you want me to come over there?"

"No, I need to get out." I had a shower and found clean jeans and a new shirt. I even put makeup on carefully.

The foundation felt dry and the lipstick looked garish against my pale skin, so I washed it all off again. As I drove, someone on the radio intoned the news, but it was background noise, until after a few moments I caught her name: ". . . missing now for twenty-one days." The complacent tone continued: "The search continues. All airports—" I turned it off, feeling sick. Michael had told me not to listen to the news.

Shan opened the door and immediately enfolded me.

"I'm sorry I was so awful at the police station that time. I've been a lousy friend."

She drew me into her sitting room and we sat down together.

"You look a bit thin, Jen." She sounded worried. Then she took my hand, and smiled warmly. "It's great to see you."

"Naomi had this necklace," I told her quickly. "I was looking in her bedroom yesterday, in her jewelry box—" Then I paused, hearing noises from the kitchen: a kettle being switched on, someone rummaging in a cupboard for mugs. Shan turned her head and called through the open door.

"If you're making coffee, Nik, Jenny would like a cup. So would I. A strong one, please."

"Coming up," Nikita called back.

Shan turned back to me. "She's struggling," she whispered.

"Struggling?" I repeated. An image of Naomi struggling in the grip of a man stopped me short. Nikita was in the next room, calmly making coffee. Her life was continuing. Naomi's had been hijacked. I shouldn't have felt angry; it wasn't Shan's fault.

"Yes," Shan whispered. "She feels it's her fault.

She should have told us sooner about Naomi fancying this guy."

I felt sick again. I shouldn't have come. Shan smiled quickly, guiltily.

"Sorry. Stupid me. Forget what I've said. You were telling me about the necklace in the jewelry box." She put her hand on my arm; the warmth went through my sleeve to the skin. She wasn't to blame if her words sounded wrong; there were no right ones anyway. I smiled back at her.

"It was made of coral. You know, tiny little strands of orange strung together? I can't find it anywhere."

The noises in the kitchen had stopped completely; I could hear Nikita's light footsteps quickly climbing the stairs that led up from their kitchen to the rooms above. I could hear the hope in my own voice.

"It was a present from my mother when Naomi was little. Naomi always kept it in a little musical box. But it's not there now. I've looked everywhere."

Shan was staring at me; I could see she was puzzled by my smile. As I leaned forward to explain, Nikita came in, a little out of breath, two cups of coffee carefully balanced on a tray. She bent over the table to clear a space and her hair fell forward in a dark sheet.

"Thanks, Nikita." I smiled at her. After all, she was Naomi's best friend.

"You're welcome." As she stood up, I saw her face was burning.

She held her hand out to me. In the center of her palm was a coiled strand of tiny orange strands, fragile and lovely.

"I heard what you said. They're not lost," she said hurriedly. "Naomi gave them to me, but don't worry, it's not like they were precious or anything. She told me she had never liked them. She was going to throw them away."

In a minute I would be able to get up and leave.

"God, Jen. You've gone pale. Have them back. You wouldn't mind, would you, Nik?" Shan looked worried.

"No. Keep them." If I spoke slowly, my voice wouldn't tremble. "When did she give them to you, Nikita?"

"Before her last performance. She threw them at me; she was laughing."

I stared at her. I was trying to remember when I had last heard Naomi laugh.

"I'll go now, I think." A few moments later I got up and left.

WHEN I GOT home it was cold and beginning to get dark. The day had gone by somehow and I hadn't realized.

"You don't know her, Mum."

I lay down and pulled the duvet over my head. From somewhere far away I heard Bertie barking for his supper, and then he stopped. I must have fallen asleep because I woke to find Ted was asleep beside me. The heat from him came in sweaty waves, and I rolled away as far as I could. I lay curled up, holding on to the edge of the bed, waiting for the hours to pass until morning.

"You don't have a bloody clue."

Chapter 30

DORSET, 2011
FOURTEEN MONTHS LATER

The newest snowdrop buds are sharp as teeth against the mud; others are flowers already, softer edged, their bent heads green-veined and vulnerable. As I lean close to absorb them, morning sounds filter through the silence: a robin scuffling in the hedge, gulls crying in the distance, the faintest sound of the sea breathing in and out. Thin-skinned peace stretches for a minute and another minute, and then I catch a flicker of movement behind me. Michael. His feet were silent on the wet grass. He looks small in the green space of the garden, unreal in his dark suit and shining shoes. His glance takes in Theo's shrunken pajamas, Ted's rubber boots. For a second we stare at each other like strangers.

"Why are you here?" I ask him quickly. "What have you found?" I stand quite still, waiting for his answer. The small noises fade around us.

"Are you all right? You look . . ." He stops.

Is he going to say weird? Mad? How could it matter what I look like?

"I saw the snowdrops from the window so . . . For God's sake, Michael. Tell me what's happened."

"Good news. We know almost for certain Yoska took Naomi and we think she went willingly."

I reach for him blindly, tears filling my eyes.

"How do you know that?"

"I'll explain inside." He takes my hand. "You're freezing, your lips are blue."

He is serious, almost angry. I probably frighten him.

"Are you sure it was him?"

"He's been seen. I'll tell you more when you've warmed up. You need some proper clothes on."

His tone jars, and his arm around me as we walk to the back door is irritating. I couldn't have got this far without him, but I must be careful; we're not there yet. I dress in the cold bedroom, fumbling buttons, ripping the wool of my tights. Michael meets me at the bottom of the stairs, a steaming mug of hot chocolate in each hand.

"I bought milk and the chocolate. I knew your fridge would be empty."

He's irritated too. She can't manage to look after herself, he is thinking, after all this time. He gestures with his head toward the sitting room.

"I've just lit the fire. Let's sit in there, it will be warmer."

He waits while I sit near the hearth, and carefully puts the mug on the table next to me, then pulls up a chair. His knees almost touch mine as he bends forward.

"We've got him now."

"Got him?" Is he in a police van, then? Or in a locked cell somewhere?

"Well, we haven't actually got him, but as good as, thanks to you. It was a perfect match with the DNA from his previous crime."

"What was?" What is he telling me? My heart starts to hammer in my mouth.

He looks at me and pauses, uncertainty narrowing his eyes; he is wondering how to tell me what he has found out. He says slowly, "His semen was on the dress you found."

I feel very sick. I move to get up, but he puts a hand on my arm.

"Wait." He clears his throat. "When they analyzed what was on the material, there was blood as well, Naomi's blood."

How naive I've been. I should have thought of this when I gave him the dress. I hoped it would help, but my thoughts stopped there. I've become good at blocking them. Blood and semen. Did he rape her, and then hide the dress in some boot? But as that thought begins to swell, another quickly follows. That night she came back in her uniform, having left the dress behind; she had been hungry, tired, smiling. She hadn't been raped, just as she hadn't been raped that time in the cottage with James. She must have made love with Yoska in the dress, then carefully rolled it up and hidden it where no one would find it: in a boot that she knew wasn't being used. She couldn't have acted so carefully, so deliberately after being raped. She must have wanted Yoska. Wanted sex with him.

I stand up at this thought. Michael's concerned eyes watch me above his mug as I walk around the room. It wouldn't have been her first time, of course. She was already pregnant. But she had known James for years. They were the same age; children playing at being grown up, innocent somehow. Sex with Yoska would be different. She would be really breaking the rules. I thought of that secret smile. That was Yoska. She must have been worried about the pregnancy, but he had made her happy.

I look out of the window, but instead of the garden and the sky my mind fills with a vivid picture of Naomi, with her back against the wall in the dark, stuffy trap room under the stage, her soft red dress rucked up high, panties around an ankle, one leg curled around his hip, holding him close. His dark head buried in her neck as his body pushes into hers. Her eyes are closed, the thick makeup on her cheeks smudged with sweat and saliva. I shake my head to drive the image away, but the thoughts race on. Afterward he would tell her she ought to go home so her parents wouldn't be suspicious. She would hold on to him, slip the dress off, and use it to wipe between her legs. She would put on the school uniform she had brought with her, and rolling up the dress, she would have shoved it quickly into the boot that she must have found in the canvas costume bag. She must then have buried the boot deep inside the bag, meaning perhaps to collect the dress another time, but she forgot.

The blood . . . "How much blood?" I sit down again, look at him, then away.

"Not much. Not more than usual."

My hands close tightly around the mug. I make myself ask: "Usual for a couple who've made love, or usual for rape?"

"After consensual sex there is often blood, small amounts, but it can be detected microscopically."

Is that why he said she went willingly? Michael has followed the same logic that I have; he has worked out that they made love and so afterward she would want to be with him.

"The cervix is more vascular in pregnancy." I'm talking mostly to myself. "She would bleed even more easily." The very next day, she had slept with James, trying to lose the pregnancy, but that hadn't worked.

Infections can make women bleed more easily too. Maybe there had been someone else as well; she could have picked up an infection before she got pregnant.

You must have been changing for a long time. Quietly becoming someone else quite different. How could I have known, when you hid so carefully behind the child we thought you were? How could I have kept you safe?

"It won't be long now before we get him." Michael's eyes, looking out of the window, are focused on the distance; they glitter as they reflect the white January sky. "We've traced the family to a Gypsy camp in Mid Wales." He lowers his voice instinctively, as though someone might be listening who would warn them off. "There's an illegal site in a field on a derelict farm."

As he tells me this, I remember the Welsh hills over the River Severn, close enough to touch from the copse where the van had been found. There had been boats lying on the bank. Once they had burned the van, it would have taken only a couple of hours to cross the river if the tide had been right. He would have known how to handle a boat. He had capable hands. I could see them steering a boat, pulling it above the tide line on the other side. I could imagine them reaching out for Naomi, carefully helping her out, keeping her safe.

"We are going into the camp at night," Michael continues.

"When? How do you know they are there?"

He looks down; he's not going to tell me when they are planning to go. Does he think that I would go ahead, run into the camp calling her name? Would I?

"We've been watching the site," he says after a little pause. "He's been seen, as I said." He looks at me briefly. "I don't want to raise your hopes, Jenny, but there was an adolescent girl with fair hair who briefly left a caravan yesterday and got into another. She was seen from a distance; nothing else identified her as Naomi. I shouldn't even be telling you this . . ."

I find myself standing, unable to breathe or move. These are the words I have waited fourteen months to hear. It might not be her, it isn't necessarily Naomi, but my heart is beating so loudly it is almost drowning out the words he is saying.

"There could be trouble." His lips tighten. "We'll take dogs. Firearms."

I look at his determined face and I begin to feel frightened.

"He might be hiding, but we'll search each trailer and horse trailer, every pile of rubbish." It's as though he is talking to himself.

They are together. Right now.

"We might have to arrest everyone."

"Everyone?"

In the dark children would start to cry, figures in nightclothes would emerge confused, blinking in the harsh light of powerful flashlights. Under the barking of police dogs, pulling at their tight leashes, might come, piercingly, the thin wail of a baby. These thoughts are spinning like black-and-white reels of film. The Gestapo rounding up their victims at night.

As Michael pulls his eyes back to mine, the pupils constrict rapidly. It makes him look angry.

"Yes." His voice sounds very hard. "The whole lot."

The sun coming through the windows picks out the gray in his hair. The frown lines between his eyebrows are sharp, as though the skin has been scored with a knife. I hadn't noticed that before. The morning light is unforgiving.

Naomi is there; she and the baby will be part of his family now. Travelers believe in family. She was pregnant; her relationship with Yoska would have offered her the chance to keep her child, with people who made time for children. They were there for the little girl in Ted's outpatient clinic; they stayed in the ward when other children would have been left on their own. Other children, whose mothers worked as much as their fathers did, as much as I used to. Children of parents who were so busy no one talked about the things that really mattered, or noticed that their children were changing.

"The women will have helped her when the baby was born." I try to speak calmly, but I want to shout and sing and dance. She's alive. Alive. He didn't kill her. They are lovers. He might have sought her out for revenge initially, and then something unexpected must have happened. He fell in love, despite his plan. She's beautiful, bright, exciting to be with. During the months of secret meetings he must have crossed some invisible line from using her for revenge to loving her; maybe even after his visit to me. He offered her a different world, he made

her smile; she would have loved him back. He didn't ab-
duct her; she went with him. He gave her a ring, he loves
her, and she's all right. My tears are streaming. I walk
quickly around the room, smiling, pushing my hands
into my mouth to stop myself laughing; I can be glad
later. Right now Michael must understand that Yoska is
important.

"Naomi, the baby, and Yoska. They could be a family
of three now."

It's Michael's turn to stand up. He puts his mug down.

"He's committed crimes. Sex with a minor, abduction,
imprisonment. Anyone who knew will be complicit."

"He may not have known her age. She looks so different with makeup on. She might have lied about how
old she was." I hold out my hand to him, make him sit
down again next to me. "If she's there, it could be because she wants to be."

He is silent, watching me.

"Don't . . . romanticize this, Jenny," he says after a
while. "He's a criminal. He belongs in prison."

I search for words that will make him understand.
"She met him in the hospital in July two summers ago.
She left in November. Four months. Long enough to
work out what she wanted. She left James in that time;
she chose a man, not a boy. She might have thought
leaving with him meant she could have her baby."

Michael gives a short impatient sigh. "She might well
have had her baby, but it wouldn't have been in the best
of circumstances. The kind of people who live like this,
well, they're not like us."

Is this what he thought when he was policing town-
ships in South Africa? I haven't heard him speak like
this before.

"Meaning?"

"They live in a different way."

I thought that was the point. I look around me at my books and paintings, the antique rugs my father loved. Echoes of life, not life. "She gave her necklace away. Perhaps she wanted something different." And all the while I am talking, my heart is beating faster and faster; I can let myself think of her face, I can let myself think of her child.

His voice gets louder and slower as if that might make me understand better. "They live in squalor, on land they don't own. They steal everything."

I look at his familiar face; perhaps after all I hardly know him.

In my heart I am speaking to her.

I feel sure you have a little girl. She will be six months by now; soon you will tell me her name.

"If she's there, it will be because she will be useful in some way. Remember that he deals in drugs. Naomi was stealing ketamine for him. There are drug gangs in Cardiff, and other rackets he's mixed up in." He doesn't say *prostitution* but the word is somewhere between us.

When Yoska had smiled at me in my office, he hadn't looked like a dangerous criminal. Perhaps the dangerous people are the ones you think you can trust, like Michael. Men who make judgments, men who need power. Could Ted have been right about him? That he has attached himself to me because I have been vulnerable? I don't care if he has exploited the situation, or if he wanted power over me. It only matters that he bring her back safely.

"I have to go." He drains his mug, stands up. "It goes without saying that it's all completely confidential, but even so it might find its way into the news. I wanted you to know before that happened."

He shrugs into his thick black coat and says quietly, "Ted should know, I'll phone him."

"Let me," I say quickly. "Better if I do."

His expression softens and he cups my face in his hands.

"Of course, Jenny. Tell him soon, though. As her father, he needs to know now."

"Thank you," I remember to say. "For coming to tell me. Be careful of . . . her."

"I'll let you know. Jenny, don't—"

"What?"

"Don't do anything."

I sit looking at my hands as the sound of his car gets fainter down the lane. I haven't done anything for a long time. I won't tell Ted yet. I'll wait till she's safely here. Michael will bring her back with him. I open the window to let the fresh air inside the hot room. She will run toward me. The tears start again, cold on my cheeks as the wind washes over me. I will hold her. My face will be against hers and her skin will smell the same. Her hair may be longer. She will be taller. She will bring me her little girl.

I have waited fourteen months; I can wait a few more days.

BUT IT ISN'T a few days. It's just a few hours.

I wake gradually to insistent knocking, confused by the cold and dark, my neck aching from where I have been lying awkwardly on the sofa. The flames have gone, the grate is ashy. The porch light has switched itself on outside and I see Michael through the glass. He must have left something behind and has had to come all the way back. I open the door. He looks down at me, and though I always thought I would know immediately, I don't. He looks exhausted. His mouth moves and I watch it closely because he is saying words that don't make sense. He is saying the same thing over and over, and the words come closer and closer until I understand.

"I'm sorry. I'm sorry."

He catches me as the room tilts and he puts me down carefully on the edge of the stairs.

". . . months ago," he is saying.

If I don't listen she might still be there in the dark beyond the open door. She might be standing outside, uncertain of her welcome, waiting with her baby in her arms. I stand up and try to push past him, but he stops me and holds me still.

"It was after the baby." He is dark against the light, and I can't see his face. "She had an infection."

"But you said she was there." I am screaming the words in his face. "A girl with fair hair, you said . . ."

"I shouldn't have told you that. It turned out to be a mother of two in her twenties. I spoke to her. I'm sorry, Jenny."

"Get him. He will have run away. You must find him." It was Yoska's fault. He let her die.

"Yoska's dead, Jenny. He was shot. He died just after midnight."

Michael holds me and he starts to talk. The words fly about my head like black crows.

"He came out of a van, shooting. We don't know why; he may have thought the camp was being attacked by a drug gang. There have been gunfights over drugs at the site before. He didn't give us a chance to negotiate. He kept firing at us; we gave him warnings." He shakes his head. "He just walked toward us, firing. It was as though he was asking to be shot. We had no choice." He pauses. "He was hit in the chest and died instantly."

Yoska killed. Naomi dead months before.

Michael lifts me as my legs weaken, and carries me through to the sofa in the sitting room. It's dark, but it doesn't matter.

"The baby, Michael." I grip his jacket. "Where's the baby?"

He holds me tightly so I am crushed into his chest. I feel his words through the bones of my face.

"The baby died with Naomi. They had the same infection."

The words have lost their power; they don't even make much sense. His voice reminds me of the way he used to talk to us in the kitchen in Bristol when we first met him. Slow and careful, he pauses often.

"Yoska's sister, Saskia, told us what happened. His parents are in police custody now."

The buttons on his jacket are hurting my cheek, but I stay completely still.

"The baby was born in the trailer. You were right; the women in the family helped."

Naomi would have gathered up the slimy little body in her slim child's hands and held her, the pain fading already, love sluicing through her. Would she have thought of me? Would she have understood in that moment how I must have felt about her?

"It was a girl, wasn't it?"

"Yes." He sounds surprised. "Yes. It was."

Naomi's world would have become the small sleeping face, the little sucking mouth, the tiny perfect toes curling and uncurling in her hands.

Michael is still talking. ". . . and after five days she felt unwell, restless and tearful. They thought it was emotional."

"She never cries." It sounds like an echo from a long time ago.

"The baby got hot," he carries on. "That's when they realized Naomi was also burning hot."

I always knew when she had a raised temperature, laying my lips on her forehead, I knew to within half a degree. It could have been postpuerperal fever. Streptococcal, deadly without rapid treatment.

Michael shifts on the sofa. "Do you want me to tell you all this now?"

Outside there are streaks of light already. I stand and hold the arm of the chair.

"Of course."

"When she began vomiting, Yoska called the doctor. They waited for three hours and in that time she became unconscious."

There must have been a lot of people in that trailer; it would have been stuffy. The fan they kept for summer nights would thump around and around like the beat of a nightmare. Naomi would be lying motionless in a sodden bed, the mottled baby sticking to her skin.

"Yoska was beside himself. He decided to take them to the hospital himself. When his uncle said someone would recognize her in the emergency room, Yoska smashed his nose. Just as he picked her up, Naomi stopped breathing. The baby died minutes afterward; they'd left it too late."

Too late. The words hang between us like the click of a door shutting.

Michael gets up to stand next to me, puts his arm around me. "Saskia said Yoska wrapped them in the sheet and very carefully laid them in the backseat of the car."

He pauses. "Then he took everything out of the trailer, all her stuff, all the baby's things, the bed, the table, everything. He piled it up outside, doused it in gasoline and left."

A funeral pyre. The roaring flames would have leaped high into the air. No one could have gone near. There would be nothing left. No hairbrush with long golden hairs tangled in it, no bracelets or scrunchies. There could have been a diary or the start of a letter to me. She might have gathered autumn leaves again, and put them behind a mirror. There will be no photos of the baby, no baby clothes.

"Where did he take them?" I ask Michael.

"It's a tradition among Travelers to bury their people secretly. No one admits to knowing where he took them."

Their people? Naomi was mine.

It's still quite dark in the room, but as I watch the streaks of light getting wider, a little flare of hope hisses into the silence in my head. "How do you know this is true? Why do you believe everything his sister said? Maybe she wasn't even there . . ."

He doesn't reply but reaches into his jacket and pulls something from a pocket; he puts it into my hand, cupping my fingers around its curved surface.

"Saskia said you should have this."

I feel the handles and though I can't see it in the dark,

I know there is a pattern of leaping frogs around the rim. At the very bottom, on the inside of the cup, there is a raised, painted, smiling frog.

"Drink up, sweetheart." Naomi's eyes were so blue as she watched me over the rim of the cup. *"The little frog is waiting . . ."*

Her baby cup for her own baby. I didn't even notice it was gone. I wonder what she did with all the buttons I kept in it.

Michael has his arm tight around me now; his breath moves my hair as he speaks.

"Even the children could tell us how she had died. Everyone said the same thing. They showed us the scorched grass and the empty trailer . . ."

His voice continues. I hear him more faintly, talking about fingerprints and swabs, keeping a high level of suspicion, digging at the site to start tomorrow. The trailers have been searched already. Some of the key Travelers are in custody; others can go, providing they stay in the locality. They will have to keep investigating.

"We need to find her body. Sooner or later someone will let slip the burial site."

I tune his words out.

So that was her home. Theirs. Just an empty box now. The moonlight will slant through the windows onto a bare floor. Perhaps it's shining on a little toy that has rolled away into a corner.

Michael's voice gets louder. "Yoska was away for two weeks and silent when he came back. He sat in his sister's trailer for hours every day staring into space—"

I interrupt him quickly. "I want to go to the camp, Michael."

Yoska's sister told the police she wasn't sure where he had buried them; but she might tell me.

"I'll take you over there soon, Jenny, when we've finished our investigation. I promise. We need to cross-examine all witnesses, dig up the site, and search every vehicle again."

Michael goes into the kitchen, pulling a flask from his pocket. I hear the kettle bubble, the clink and clash of cutlery. He comes back and watches me while I drink the coffee laced with whiskey. This morning, when he made me hot chocolate, she was still alive. Or was that yesterday? No, how stupid. She died months ago.

In the growing light, Michael's face is white with fatigue, and after a while he goes upstairs to sleep. I hear his shoes drop to the floor, the little noises of effort as he pulls off his clothes and then the bed creaking. After that there is quiet. The silence is so deep it's as though a faint tune that had been playing in the background has now stopped.

Ed said I didn't have a bloody clue.

But I did. I had a lot of clues. They had been all around me for a long time. I close my eyes and remember the last time I was in her room. It was the day Ted left me, the day I left the house. Even then I could have seen the clues.

BRISTOL, 2010
EIGHT MONTHS AFTER

Ted went for a long walk in the morning. He told me he didn't want to be there when I left for the final time. It was a Sunday. I remember that, because for years I had been used to him leaving every day of the week except for Sundays. When he had gone, I went upstairs to Naomi's room. The moving men were coming at noon. I had packed up what I needed to take to the cottage. The rest would stay in the house for Ted.

It was already hot. The sun was bright in a high cloudless sky, one of those perfect summer days children are supposed to remember all their lives. The room was empty apart from the bed and the curtains, which were closed. The air felt stifling. I opened the window and pulled the curtain back a little. Below me, the street was empty. The journalists had long gone, drifting away to other tragedies where the pickings were richer. As I watched, the air warm on my skin, a woman in a summer dress came around the corner, leaning forward with one hand on a stroller. She held a cell phone clamped against her ear and her head was moving. From here she looked like the little nodding doll that I'd loved when I was small but lost years ago. The stroller was deeply padded and I couldn't see the child at all. I watched until the woman disappeared from sight, her head still moving up and down.

The curtain beneath my hand felt edged with dust, heavy and soft. The material was striped gold and scarlet. Naomi and I had chosen it together, at John Lewis three or four years before. But we hadn't been together, not really. I had picked out a roll of leaf-patterned cotton in gray, white, and lemon yellow, imagining how the diffusing light would paint the room in fresh colors. There was another I liked with tiny flowers. I had turned to ask Naomi to decide, but she was already walking to the cashier carrying this exotic-looking cloth in a roll that was taller than she was. It was richly colored with shiny bands of yellow and red. It looked so gaudy with its big stripes. I told her it would stop the light coming in and how different her room would feel from the other rooms in our house. It would be dark and enclosed. Like a hidden cave, with no light, full of secrets. She had smiled. A forerunner of the little half smile. "That's exactly what I want," she had said.

Chapter 31

Into the silence of the kitchen at daybreak comes a sudden noise of tearing or burning; in a second the sound resolves itself as rain falling fast and hard on the thatch. The water against the window is the color of the gray sky. I must hurry with my letters. I want to start the journey and it will take longer in the rain. As I rip out the blank pages in my sketchbook for paper to write on, the flimsy binding comes apart in my hands and the pictures fall, fanning out as they hit the floor: the drawing of her shoes, a toy giraffe, the little hooded top, Michael's hands. Other pages flutter down on top of them and I leave them where they have fallen.

> *Ted,*
> *As I write this you are sleeping, but by the time you get it I will have spoken to you and*

*you will have told the boys. I thought if I sent
letters as well, it might help. I used to wonder
whether knowing would be better than
hoping. I can't tell. It doesn't feel real yet.*

*It wasn't your fault or, if it was, it was
mine as well. I should have been more
careful when Yoska came to see me. He
might have forgiven us. He must have been
unsure even then; he belonged to a family
so would have known how we would suffer.
In the end, I think he took her because they
were in love; we couldn't have changed that.*

*I'm leaving for Wales. I'm hoping
someone at the camp may tell me where he
buried them.*

Please tell Anya,

I'll come to Bristol as soon as I can.

Jenny

The scrape of my nib is tiny against the relentless rain. The kitchen feels warm and enclosed, but where will he be when he reads this? The boys will be with him; maybe Anya quietly moving in the background. I see her face, streaming with tears.

Darling Ed,

*By now Dad will have told you what
happened to our dearest Naomi.*

*At least she found what she wanted; lots
of people never do.*

*If she hadn't gotten ill, she would have
brought her baby to see us, sooner or later.*

I'm so glad you have Sophie.

> *I'll see you later today or tomorrow. I'm*
> *thinking about you all the time.*
>
> > Mum

I hope Sophie's arms are around him. I hope she is wearing her bright colors. She'll listen to him, make it easier for him.

I flick the kettle on. Bertie shifts a little at the noise, then sleeps. The coffee is black and scalding hot.

Theo's is difficult to write; it feels as though I am brushing his brightness with thick dark paint.

> *Theo darling,*
> *You will be on your way home so I will*
> *send this to Bristol. I hope Sam is there,*
> *sitting next to you.*
> *You said she didn't talk to you much*
> *before she left. It was the same for me. I*
> *think she was saying good-bye.*
> *She took the baby cup, the one with the*
> *frog at the bottom. I've got it now.*
> *When we find her and the baby, I'm*
> *going to bring them home. They will be*
> *buried here in the churchyard, so we'll*
> *know where she is.*
>
> > Mum

The rain is softer, the light stronger. Last two letters.

> *Nikita,*
> *I am going to phone your mum today,*
> *so she will have told you by now what has*
> *happened.*

> *Michael told me that you knew she was*
> *pregnant. She would be pleased you kept*
> *her secret safely. She had a little daughter,*
> *I don't know her name.*
> *I think the corals were her good-bye*
> *present to you, even if you didn't know she*
> *was going. I'm glad you have them.*
> *Jenny*

Michael's letter is the hardest. I know him so well and yet so little—it's like writing to a stranger. I try out sentences in my head as I pace the kitchen, but they look artificial on the page. There is so much to say that I can't find the words and I end up writing almost nothing.

> *Dear Michael,*
> *I'm leaving now and I'm not sure when*
> *I'll be back.*
> *Bertie will be happier here. Can you*
> *let him out and feed him before you go?*
> *There's half a tin in the fridge. Mary will*
> *take him in until I get back. I'll phone her;*
> *she'll come and fetch him.*
> *I need to be with my family. I know you'll*
> *understand.*
> *Jenny*

I leave Michael's envelope propped against the coffee jar on the table and address the others to the Bristol house, even Nikita's. I can't remember her address. No stamps, but I can stop somewhere.

Michael's fingers are curved loosely on the duvet cover. When I slip my hand inside his, his grip tightens but his eyes stay closed. I ask him in a whisper where Yoska's parents have been taken, so I'll know where to start from. He sleepily murmurs the name, then his hand relaxes again and his breathing becomes deep and regular.

Newtown. A market town on the banks of the River Severn in Powys, Mid Wales. The tourist website gives me the postal code and I put it into the GPS. I must drive slowly; I haven't slept. It's been four hours since Michael woke me and the time has fallen away, vanished. The shock is echoing in my head; I'm still waiting for the pain.

I let the car roll down the little slope into the road quietly and start the engine out of earshot of the cottage.

THE FOLDED DORSET landscape flattens into Somerset. I drive past Bristol, just a sign on the motorway that disappears behind me. I stop in a garage in Newport, the letters skidding off the dashboard to the floor. I phone Mary briefly; without asking questions she agrees immediately to look after Bertie. Then I phone Ted. When he answers, I hear the radio in the background. I picture him at the window in the bedroom, tightening the knot of his tie, planning his day.

I warn him it's bad news and I hear him turn off the radio and sit down. Then I tell him what happened. In the silence that follows I hear myself say she had been part of a different family. She had given birth to a daughter. She hadn't been raped or maimed, she'd been loved. He starts crying and I try to talk to him some more. I tell him I am going to post him a letter, but there is silence. After a while he puts the phone down.

I buy a cup of coffee, but it tastes bitter and I tip it

on the ground and start off again. The roads are filling with cars and trucks. I drive faster. Michael said they had been biding their time; they might be packing up to go now.

At Cardiff I turn off and take the road to Pontypridd and Merthyr Tydfil. The Black Mountains. It starts to rain, and I drive carefully as the road dips and curls around the Brecon Beacons. Theo must have brought her somewhere here; her eyes were so alive in his photos. We came here once too, just Naomi and I. She would have been nine, maybe ten. Her blonde pigtails pushed under a pink woollen hat, her legs in waterproof pants climbing up the brown slopes, ahead of me, always. She stood on high ridges, too high; leaning into the wind. I couldn't look.

I get to Newtown at midday and find a small pub on the road with parking space. The journey so far has taken four hours. It's warm inside the pub and the smell of stale beer and old dog is overwhelming. Music is playing from the jukebox by the wall, and a few men sitting near the window are reading newspapers and drinking. An old collie lies under the table, eyeing me sleepily. The woman, drying glasses behind the bar, rolls her eyes when I ask if there is a Travelers' camp nearby but stays silent.

Behind me, male voices chip in. The gentle singsong lilt at odds with their speech.

"There's been a camp near Llanidloes for months."

They are watching me, talking around ends of cigarettes, eyes narrowed against the smoke. I thought smoking had been banned in pubs, but I keep quiet.

"They've been nicking stuff. Coming into town causing trouble."

"The police don't do anything."

"Gypos. Did you see that in the papers about the drugs?"

"Pikeys."

I leave quickly without saying good-bye.

LLANIDLOES IS A pretty place with an old timbered market hall. In a Budgens at the crossroads a man in a brown apron is stacking shelves with jars of peanut butter. He straightens and looks down at me.

"You don't want to go there," he says. When I persist, he shrugs, takes my map, and rests it against the empty shelf.

"It's beyond Bwlch y sarnau," he says, pointing with an orange-stained finger. "Take the B4518 out of town. When you see the mailbox by the gray bungalow on your right, take the next left and then left again. It's in a dip. You'll see a stony track leading into their field. There's dogs, mind."

He wants to say something else. Perhaps he wants to tell me there was trouble last night. The police got involved. High time, he might say. He watches me closely as I leave.

I am on a twisting downhill road when a Toyota Land Cruiser comes toward me. I back into a gateway. It's followed by a car pulling a horse trailer. I wait as it moves slowly by. As I inch out, a minibus comes by, so I back in again. It passes, children at the window staring. Bags and packages and suitcases press against the glass; it's then that I realize that some of the Travelers are moving out, as Michael had said that they would, at least the ones who haven't been taken into custody.

If I drive on farther I can turn in the track the man in

the shop told me about. I can catch up with them if I'm quick. Around the corner the track and a field come into sight. There's a group of trailers toward the edge of the field, near some trees a hundred yards away from where I park. Most of the trailers are behind a striped tape attached to poles, which sections off that part of the site. In the middistance, toward the back of the field, there are about ten policemen and men in yellow oilskins, bent over in a line, digging.

There is a trailer in front of the tape, and a man is fixing its towing hook to the back of a muddy Land Rover. This must be the last family the police are allowing to leave. The rain has stopped, and a dark-haired little boy of about six, with a thumb in his mouth, leans against the trailer in a patch of sun, watching the man at work. When I get out of the car and push the gate open, the movement snags the child's attention, though the police in the distance don't notice; if they did, they would probably stop me. The boy turns to stare and the man beside him straightens. His face, edged with gray stubble and reddened with effort, appears older than his body. Sixty? Seventy? He looks at me briefly, nods, then bends again to his task. In a moment he calls something I can't catch. A middle-aged woman comes stiffly down the steps of the trailer; she is dressed in black, with a black scarf tied around her long dark hair. She carries a large canvas bag over one shoulder and takes the free hand of the little boy. Without glancing at me, she opens the door of the Land Rover. The little boy is ushered in ahead of her. As she is stepping in after him, she turns her head toward the open door of the trailer.

"Carys," she calls, singing the word in her Welsh accent.

I look around the site. Besides the trailers, there are pale squares in the green grass where other vans must have stood. There are no dogs on chains; several garbage bags tied neatly lean together in a heap. There is a patch of deeply charred grass in the middle. One of the policemen in the distance calls something and waves me back. I step back outside the gate.

"Carys," the woman calls again, then ducks out of sight into the Land Rover.

The trailer door is pushed wider open and a young woman comes out. As I glance at her, I stop breathing and hold the gate tightly. She has shaved her head so it seems small. The stubble has been dyed red, which matches her long skirt. Her skin is very pale. A tattoo wraps around her neck, and from here it looks like leaves. She is carrying a little girl of about six months in her arms and the child has red hair too; I can see her bright curls from here. The child has been wrapped in a red-and-yellow-striped blanket and it looks as if she is asleep. At the bottom of the steps the young woman half turns so she is facing the gate, the baby held across her like a shield.

The fingers holding the carrier are long, though from here it's impossible to tell if there are still freckles, like grains of Demerara sugar, reaching to the second knuckle. It's too far to see the little mole beneath her left eyebrow. Her gaze meets mine; her eyes are calm, though there are red marks underneath them as though she has been crying. We look at each other. I will think about this forever, but there are things in her glance that I will never know how to name. Recognition. Yes. Vengeance, shuttered. She made Maria vengeful when Tony died. Was that a warning? Something else, something softer . . . Sorrow or forgiveness? She is there. That's all. She is there. The world disappears around her. The lies they told the police fall away. I don't cry or laugh or even smile. There isn't room. There isn't time.

"Carys. We're leaving."

I start running toward her then, but my feet slip in the wet mud by the gate. As I fall clumsily on my side she turns away and the baby's soft face is squashed tightly against her thin neck. She bends into the car, with the child, vanishing from sight.

I get to my feet, coated in mud, and stumble into a run. By now the car has started and the wheels are spinning. It jumps forward, engine roaring. I keep running toward it and for a moment it seems I'll reach it in time, but it's moving faster all the time, speeding toward the gate. If I run in front it will surely stop. As I change direction it comes so close that the bumper brushes my leg, and despite myself I swerve. The side of her face, half hidden by the child, is so near that if the window was open I could reach out and touch her. Then, suddenly, she lifts her hand to the glass, her fingers spread wide. In that fragment of time I see the clear red lifeline on her palm, curving like a line on a map. Then the car has gone by; it doesn't stop as it turns onto the road but it accelerates up the hill and quickly goes out of sight.

FIFTEEN MONTHS LATER

Carys. It's a Welsh name. I looked it up. It means "love."

ACKNOWLEDGMENTS

I would like to thank my agents, Eve White, Jack Ramm, and Rebecca Winfield.

Many thanks to the team at Penguin UK, especially Samantha Humphreys, Maxine Hitchcock, Celine Kelly, Beatrix McIntyre, Joe Yule, Clare Parkinson, and Elizabeth Smith.

Thank you to the team at William Morrow, including my editor, Rachel Kahan, also Kim Lewis, Lorie Young, and Mumtaz Mustafa.

My gratitude to my tutors, including Patricia Ferguson, Chris Waking, Tessa Hadley, Mimi Thebo, and Tricia Wastvedt.

Thanks to my writing group: Tanya Atapattu, Hadiza Isma El-Rufai, Victoria Finlay, Emma Geen, Susan Jordan, Sophie McGovern, Peter Reason, Mimi Thebo, and Vanessa Vaughan.

I am grateful to police constable Nick Shaw for the police details and for his help with the manuscript and to my sister, Katie Shemilt, for her photographic skills.

My family made all the difference. Martha's encouragement was the starting point. Henry and Tommy were generous with their technical skills. Steve, Mary, and Johny were the essential backup team.

To my father and mother, whom I miss every day, thank you.

HARPER
LARGE PRINT

**Introducing a Clearer
Perspective on Larger Print**

With a 14-point type size for comfort reading
and published exclusively in paperback format,
Harper Large Print is light to carry and easy to read.

SEEING IS BELIEVING!

For a full listing of titles, please visit our website:
www.hc.com

*This ad has been set in the
14-point font for comfortable reading.

BECAUSE THERE ARE TIMES
WHEN BIGGER IS BETTER